Quick and Dead

Brand of Justice
Book 3

Lisa Phillips

Copyright © 2023 by Lisa Phillips

All rights reserved.

No part of this book may be reproduced in any form or by any electronic or mechanical means, including information storage and retrieval systems, without written permission from the author, except for the use of brief quotations in a book review.

eBook ISBN: 979-8-88552-156-7

Paperback ISBN: 979-8-88552-157-4

Large Print Hardback ISBN: 979-8-88552-158-1

Published by Two Dogs Publishing, LLC. Idaho, USA

Cover Design by Sasha Almazan and Gene Mollica, GS Cover Design Studio, LLC

Edited by Christy Callahan, Professional Publishing Services

Chapter One

Kenna pulled into a space outside the Hatchet County Courthouse. She shoved the gear lever of her camper van into Park and glanced at her dog. "Stay here."

Cabot hopped up onto the passenger seat and pressed her nose to the gap at the top of the window to sniff the morning New Mexico air.

Kenna grabbed the manila envelope from the dash. "This won't take long." She slid out and looked at the pink line along Cabot's side. The crisscross scars on her back left leg that still didn't work quite right since the car accident.

Visible. Invisible.

It didn't matter if the wound had healed, or if the scars never would. Life seemed to go on anyway.

Kenna clicked the locks and strode across the pitted concrete parking lot. A car passed, low slung and pumping hip-hop. She slowed while it moved by, glancing over at what passed for Main Street in this one stoplight town, and picked up her pace for the front doors. Her boots clipped the sidewalk as she stepped onto it, pushed the door open, and headed for the security guy stood beside a scanner.

Kenna lifted her hand. "Just this envelope."

White shirt, courthouse patches. Gray pants and shined black shoes. "ID?"

She tugged out her Utah driver's license because she didn't have a private investigator card for the state of New Mexico and handed it over. "The Sanchez trial started already, right?"

His name badge read Matthews. Two brown eyebrows rose above a face lined with nearly fifty years of life. "Room three." He motioned to the scanner.

"Busy day?" The room echoed with emptiness.

"It's definitely Monday." He reached for the hot cup next to the scanner. "Two cases this morning. Yours and a guy down the hall facing twenty to life for multiple murders. I'm gonna wander down and listen in."

Kenna walked through the metal detector, grabbed her envelope from the end of the scanner belt, and headed for the hall. She could text Stairns later and inform him that he was right about the baton not being picked up by a metal detector. Then he'd take ten minutes to explain his business plan for 3D printing undetectable weapons.

Considering they'd both been federal agents in their previous careers, maybe that wasn't exactly done. They'd been in the business of trying to stop people who skirted rules and regulations. But in this line of work she needed whatever she could get her hands on to protect herself, no matter what.

If she didn't have a way to defend her life, she would lose it.

Game over.

The doors to courtroom three were closed. Kenna shoved them open, not a huge fan of showmanship when she preferred to fly under the radar. Maybe she'd been watching way too much *Psych* during the dark evenings of the winter months. Shawn Spencer had started to rub off on her.

A half dozen people turned.

More sat between her and the partition that separated the gallery from the area where the case would play out. A cop, a few people she pegged as family members. A reporter—maybe two. The prosecutor sat beside the left side table past the partition like he knew the case was practically over. On the right, the defendant's lawyer stood behind their table. Hair askew. Tie already tugged down.

Kenna strode down the aisle. Wood wainscoting covered the bottom half of the walls, matching the veneer of the witness stand and the judge's raised dais in the center. A matronly woman sat to the right side, tapping on a keyboard. Peach sweater, gray slacks. Fresh manicure and glasses perched on her perm. A county sheriff's deputy stood in front of a door to the right, eyeing the clock. Trace of donut powder on his cheek.

"What's this?" The prosecutor sat up straight and glanced between her and the judge. "Your Honor, the last thing we need is an interruption."

The defendant covered her mouth with both hands. Dark hair hung down both sides of her face, eclipsed by those huge dark brown eyes. Rachel Sanchez wore a department store black pants suit and white shirt.

Kenna headed for the lawyer. "I found it."

Parker Jones, forties and divorced, wearing a brown suit with a waistcoat that may or may not be the reason for the divorce, snatched the envelope and whirled around. "Your Honor, can we approach?"

The judge, an older African American woman, had her gavel raised. "Most interesting thing that's happened all month."

Kenna turned to leave. Job done.

The judge called out, "I'm guessing 'we' means you, too."

She turned back.

The judge motioned with the gavel. "All three of you." She glanced at the prosecutor and slid on tortoiseshell spectacles. "Assuming you want to hear this."

"Yes, Your Honor. I do." The prosecutor buttoned his suit jacket and approached.

Kenna pushed open the gate in the partition and caught the defendant's gaze. Too far gone for hope, but plenty of fear resided there. The shadow of loss in her eyes squeezed the broken pieces of heart that remained in Kenna's chest.

She headed for the bench and ended up between the two lawyers just as Jones handed the judge the envelope.

"And what is this?" The older woman looked more excited than anything else. Her gold desk nameplate read Judge Amira Williams. She flipped up the flap of the envelope and slid out the papers Kenna had found.

A rhetorical question.

The prosecutor twisted around and stared down at Kenna, a feat considering she wasn't more than an inch shorter than him. "Who are you?"

Kenna took in as much as she could without shifting her gaze. "A neutral third party."

She'd met a lot of people in her life. Few told the truth, nothing held back. This man wasn't one of those. Something in his gray eyes reminded her of men she'd interviewed— serving life with no parole—or killers she'd captured. An instinct that had given him the thrust he'd needed to become the prosecutor in a tiny New Mexico border town.

His smile spread wide, and his entire face changed. "I doubt it's going to help Ms. Sanchez."

Rachel Sanchez whimpered.

Kenna glanced over her shoulder.

"And what, pray tell, is all this?" Judge Williams was a mystery. She'd also gained a position of power in this county.

She glanced above the rims of her glasses to glare daggers at the prosecution.

Kenna tried to decipher that expression. It looked a lot like a disappointed boss to a subordinate, with a whole lot of, *You're giving me no choice.*

Coming into the middle of an ongoing situation often put Kenna at a disadvantage. And most cases she worked didn't have this many people with pulses. But case after case trying to find a person most likely deceased wore on her.

Her mind went to the young woman's photo on her fridge. *She's not dead.*

Kenna had been trying to find a missing person of her own, a mission she'd taken on alone, for two months now. All she'd found was a link to Hatchet, New Mexico, and even that was flimsy at best. She was going to have to mull over how all this played out later.

Maybe while she took her dog for a walk.

Jones cleared his throat. "If I may, Your Honor, that is evidence that will prove my client was in Albuquerque with girlfriends at a restaurant the night of the hit-and-run. In fact"—he pointed at the time stamp on the corner of the photo Kenna had printed herself—"you can see she was there at the precise moment it happened, which proves she couldn't have been the one driving her car." He lowered his voice, "And she's been telling the truth this entire time." Jones pulled a handkerchief from his pocket and dabbed at the sweat beading on his forehead.

Kenna left the judge to her assessment of the evidence and looked again at the prosecutor. "What did you say your name was?"

"I didn't." His flat gray gaze studied her for a second, then he lifted his hand. "Davis Burnum."

She shook with him and found he was one of those guys who squeezed so hard pain shot through her hand, and she half expected to hear a bone crack. She bit down on her back teeth to keep from letting him know his handshake bordered on a physical attack.

"Did he break your hand?"

She glanced at Jones. "Does he do that a lot?"

Instead of answering, the defendant's lawyer said, "I'll admit I was surprised you managed to get it."

"Whoever buried the truth about this woman's whereabouts at the time of that hit-and-run is likely surprised also and I'm sorry a young man got hurt, but Rachel Sanchez definitely didn't do it." As a rule, Kenna shouldn't get emotionally invested in cases. It was a bad idea when there was so much pain and evil in the world. Of course, what was a good idea usually had nothing to do with her feelings.

She could swear up and down that she wouldn't get involved.

Then she'd find herself climbing through the window of a garage at three in the morning looking for a laptop with surveillance footage on it, before she drove for three and a half hours to a nowhere town to deliver evidence to a court hearing.

Jones said, "Any problems?"

"He wasn't there. Mail was being held, half his closet was empty. I'm guessing he went on a trip."

"Interesting." Jones rocked back and forth on his shiny shoes. "That the only witness with evidence that could exonerate my client is conveniently absent during the trial. Almost like someone *wants* Mrs. Sanchez to go down for attempted vehicular manslaughter."

Kenna glanced back at the courtroom, every person there staring with rapt attention at the drama unfolding in front of the bench. No one sat close to Rachel Sanchez. She sat alone.

"I'll explain later," Jones said.

Kenna looked at the prosecutor first and caught him eyeing her boots. Then her jeans. Her long-sleeved T-shirt. She turned back to Jones while the judge continued reading. "Another invoice, or the same one?"

As far as she was concerned, she'd done the job she had been hired to do in finding the buried evidence to exonerate Rachel Sanchez. If there was more to do here in Hatchet, New Mexico, it would cost his firm more than he owed right now.

Jones smirked. He knew how business worked. But underneath she spotted the edge of something more. Enough to make her wonder what was going on beyond a young woman being railroaded into a prison sentence she didn't deserve.

"Your Honor," Burnum began, "would you like to take a recess?"

She lifted her attention from the paper. "Would you like to tell me how your office overlooked the fact the defendant was nowhere near highway nine at the time the victim was struck by her car? The one she swore was being worked on by a local garage while she went out of town for the weekend with friends?"

Burnum cleared his throat.

"I don't need a recess. I need an explanation." She removed the tortoiseshell spectacles and let them hang from a cord around her neck.

Burnum glared daggers at Kenna. As though his failure was her fault.

"I'll go sit." She thumbed over her shoulder. "Leave you to it."

Kenna headed for the gallery, her stomach tight the whole time. The last thing she wanted was to be dragged back into their deliberation.

Rachel watched her. Kenna sat in the row behind the defendant, since there was no one else on that side they'd be far enough no one would hear a whispered conversation.

Mrs. Sanchez leaned toward the rail separating the gallery from the court. "Who are you?"

"Is that really the question you want to ask right now?"

"I'd like to know who is trying to destroy me, sure. I'd like to know why my husband was murdered and no one cared. But a kid in town gets clipped on his bike and breaks his arm, and I'm going to prison for it?" She held herself straight. Rachel Sanchez had weathered a lot, and so far she hadn't been knocked down. Or she put up a good front and no one saw the way this ate at her on the inside.

Kenna held out her hand. "I'm a private investigator. Kenna Banbury."

Rachel squeezed Kenna's fingers.

"I'm just here to present the evidence that proves you're not guilty."

Rachel's lips puffed out with a sharp exhale. "As if that will matter."

Kenna caught the edge of tears in her eyes. "It should."

Rachel's dark brown eyes, rimmed with gold, met hers. "Yes, it should. But this is the real world."

"You think someone is trying to destroy you?"

"I never should have agreed to move here." She shook her head. "Matteo was so excited to move back to his hometown when the position opened. A state trooper, here where he grew up."

"You said he was murdered?"

Rachel ran a knuckle under the corner of her eye. Kenna

would've said she was in her thirties, but stress had aged her. She was probably closer to midtwenties.

The judge smacked her gavel on the round wood block. "Take your seats."

Burnum the prosecutor, and Jones the lawyer returned to their seats. Jones reached over and squeezed Rachel's shoulder. Kenna studied the line of the way Burnum sat, trying to figure out what it was that seemed off about the guy. Considering he'd failed to do his job here, and was about to be made a fool of, that could account for his demeanor.

The judge lifted her chin and addressed the room, a gleam in her eyes indicating she enjoyed this very much. "It is the decision of this courtroom that the prosecution has failed to prove Rachel Sanchez as guilty beyond a reasonable doubt. Therefore, I declare the defendant not guilty, and cleared of all charges." She slammed the gavel down.

Jones stood up with a whoop. Rachel gasped aloud and lifted out of her seat.

Kenna sat back in her chair and watched as the prosecutor closed his files, stuffed them in his briefcase, and clipped it shut. He swept through the gate and through the gallery and out the door before anyone could speak to him. A young woman with her cell phone out scurried after him. His assistant, or a local reporter.

The judge gathered her things. Her robe whirled behind her, the officer held the door by her desk open, and she disappeared out of the room.

A thud in the hall preceded the main doors opening. Both doors swung wide so fast they hit the bench behind the door. Kenna twisted in her seat to see an inmate—light blue jumpsuit and white canvas shoes—charge in, his hands still cuffed. Holding a gun.

The state officer who'd let the judge out drew his weapon from the front of the room, calling out, "Stop!"

The inmate fired at him, squeezing off a second round before the guy fell to the floor.

Blood smeared down the wall.

Chapter Two

The inmate turned and slammed the door shut, then wedged a chair under it. "Nobody move!"

Kenna scanned, counting how many people were in here. She didn't get up. The time to draw attention to herself wasn't yet.

The court transcriber matron hurried to the door in the far corner on her side. Jones started to yell. Kenna leaned forward, grabbed his arm and Rachel's, and yanked them both down. Hard.

Another gunshot cracked off in the room. The matron stumbled and hit the ground.

Rachel whimpered. Her legs folded under her, and she huddled behind the gallery partition. Jones did the same, but said, "What do we do?"

Kenna said, "Stay down."

Across the courtroom a family huddled together. The victim's relatives? She counted eight live people, including the inmate, and two dead—or in need of help.

Kenna twisted in the chair and looked at the inmate. "Are you done shooting for a moment?"

"I said, 'No one move!'" As if that justified taking two lives.

She raised both hands so he could see her open palms. "I'm not moving. And neither is anyone else. We're all going to listen to you." She kept her voice steady.

"Good!" He motioned to her with the gun, as though he was thinking about using it again. Or wanted her to believe he would.

Whether he had nine shots left, or she had miscalculated, she didn't want him using any of them. That would be the goal, even if life usually fell short.

He took a step toward her. Looked around. Glassy eyes, sweat on his hairline. Early twenties, a tattoo on the side of his neck. This was a three-strike guy staring down the barrel of a long stretch. No second chances. No way out. No options.

Kenna presented less of a threat still seated than she would if she stood—or raised her voice. "What's your name?" she asked, keeping that same tone. She had a number of questions, but that was a good place to start. There were several ways this could go. If she kept his focus on her and everyone else stayed out of it, no heroics, she might be able to talk this guy down. She'd been trained to diffuse a situation but hadn't used those skills in a while.

"What does it matter what my name is?" He shifted on those canvas shoes.

"Because you need a plan?"

"That's right!" He waved the gun around, checking the doors. Checking no one had moved. "I got a plan! The plan is no one moves!"

Jones shifted. Kenna moved far enough she got his attention and waved him down.

The inmate slammed the gun down on his head. "Stay down!"

Rachel screamed. Someone in the room started to cry.

Kenna stood up, hands raised, and moved into the aisle right in front of him.

"Think you're some kind of hero?" He gave her a flash of gritted teeth, but she didn't see much before that gun was back in her face.

"I'm not a hero." Kenna took a steady breath, trying to keep her heart rate from getting out of control. "But you should know I have injuries to my forearms so I can't keep my hands up much longer."

"You think I'm gonna believe that?"

She used the fingers of her right hand to tug down her left sleeve far enough that he could see the top of her forearm.

The inmate muttered a curse.

"My other arm looks the same. So if I have to put down my hands, it's just because my arms hurt, okay?"

"Fine." He kept moving, waving the gun around.

"Can I go look at the people over there?" The ones he'd shot. "We need to know if they're alive, so we can figure out what to do next."

"I know what to do!"

She took a half step toward the partition gate between the gallery and the court.

The prosecutor had rushed out, as had the judge. Then this happened? The inmate couldn't have known who would be in here and who wouldn't unless he'd prepared a plan.

"So what's the goal here?" She swung one leg over the gate and paused for a moment in a sitting position, her legs either side. Another attempt at looking unassuming. Hands in her lap. Voice soft. Not afraid, just cautious.

"I'm not going back to jail. *That's* the goal."

Someone whimpered. Behind her, Kenna could hear Rachel whisper to Jones but couldn't make out the words. She kept the guy's attention on her. "I need to see if they're dead or alive."

"And get the cop's gun?"

"I don't need to get that close." She swung her second leg over and stood.

He pushed through the gate, and she stepped slowly to where the cop lay. His chest unmoving. Blood pooled on the floor under him. One shot had hit his vest, but the other caught his neck. He'd have been dead seconds after he hit the floor. That much blood, that spot on his neck. There was nothing anyone could've done.

Kenna sighed.

"He deserved it. They all do."

"So this is about revenge?"

"Are we making friends? Are you gonna sympathize with me until I lay down the gun and turn myself in to be shackled and dragged off?"

"No," Kenna said. "I'm gonna go over there and see if that woman is alive or if she's dead. And if she's alive, then I'm going to try and help her."

"So you're some kind of good Samaritan?"

Kenna stepped over to the other side of the dais slow and steady.

He moved with her.

The woman's feet were visible, unmoving like the dead cop. As she got closer, Kenna could see the woman's broken inhale. "She's alive. That's good." She stepped over the woman so he'd be able to see her and she didn't have to put her back to him. "That's really good."

"Who cares?" He snarled the words, but the initial adrenaline was waning, and reality had begun to settle in. "It's done. We're all locked in here and they're going to have to get me an SUV and a plane if they want me to let y'all go instead of just kill you."

"That's good." Kenna wanted to roll the woman and find out where she was hit but kept her attention on the inmate for a second. "The more people you keep alive the better."

Blood had dampened her shoulder, on the sweater over the outside of her bicep.

Kenna figured it would hurt whichever way she did this, so she just reached over the prone body, got the woman's hip and shoulder, and pulled toward herself.

A split second into the roll, the woman launched up. Hands flailing. Screaming as blood ran down her face.

An elbow slammed into Kenna's temple. She tumbled back onto the floor.

The gun went off.

Kenna clapped her hands over her ears, her head pounding.

The woman kept screaming.

His arm lowered, a bullet hole in the ceiling.

Kenna pushed a breath out through clenched teeth then said, "Stop screaming!"

The woman whimpered.

His scowl split into a smile, and he barked out a laugh. "You yelled at her." He chuckled. "That was pretty funny."

Kenna looked at the woman. "Did you get shot?"

Her eyes rolled back in her head. Kenna barely caught her before her upper body tipped back. She managed to get one hand under the woman's head before it hit the floor. She slid her hand out and sighed.

"Guess she's okay." He rounded the witness stand and plunked himself into the judge's chair. "Where's that mallet thing? I wanna hit this. You're all guilty!"

"And when the local police kick the door in and shoot you where you sit?"

He tipped his head back and laughed. "You don't know this town if you think you're gonna get rescued."

"So no one's out in the hall now, gearing up to take you out?"

His lips curled. "Most hilarious thing I've heard." He pointed the gun at her. "Stay right there. No funny business, or you'll end up dead like that cop over there."

Kenna looked past the gun to his eyes.

This young man had little to lose and the nerve to take more lives. He didn't have a plan, unlike what he'd said.

She got off the floor and decided to lean on the edge of the unconscious woman's table. A catalogue of the weapons she had on her didn't yield anything she could draw before he'd shoot her. Not the baton in her right boot, or the tiny pepper spray on her necklace. Though, that would be what she'd go for first if it came down to it.

Her head pounded from that elbow to the temple. She touched the spot and winced.

"Yeah, that don't look too good. You should get it checked out." He lifted a foot onto the desktop, stacking the other on top while he leaned back in the chair and chuckled. "You come here often?"

Kenna looked across the room at the people huddled, whispering.

"I asked you a question." He called her a foul name.

"There's no need to be unpleasant. I'm just concerned about the other people in here." Kenna clasped her hands in front of her. "After all, you don't know if someone has a heart condition, or if they're pregnant."

"Why would I care? If I'm supposed to keep people alive,

they should just do what they're told and I won't kill them. Got it?" He turned his head to the room and yelled, "Got it?"

Someone murmured, "Yes." Another person whimpered.

Rachel said, "No one is doing anything. Why can't you just leave us alone?"

"Get up." He lowered his feet to the ground. "I said, 'Get up!'" Another foul name.

Kenna needed his attention back on her. "We can figure this out between us. You don't need to bother these folks."

"Yeah? You gonna get me what I need?"

"You said the police won't respond. So how are you going to get an SUV and a plane?"

"I guess someone will have to make this federal. Get a bunch of special agents down here to meet my demands."

"And if I can make that happen?"

He grinned. "Like I believe that? No. We wait it out. Make them come to us." He sucked in a breath. "Y'all hear that? *No one* is leaving! So get comfortable!"

She let calm settle once more. "I'm Kenna. You have a name?"

"I go by March. Because I give the orders. Got it?"

Kenna nodded. "Nice to meet you, March."

"This where you try to make friends. Talk me down?" March settled back into the seat, both feet stacked on the desktop. "What are you, some kind of cop? That how you got feds on the line?"

"I'm not a cop. I'm a private investigator, but I was an FBI agent a few years ago."

"You get fired?"

Kenna shrugged. "Kind of."

He laughed again. "Now there's a story I wanna hear."

"If we have time. But how about you tell me why you

needed to do this?" Kenna looked around. "You could've taken your own courtroom hostage. Why come in here?"

"More people. No one cared about me, they all wanted to see the woman who wanted to kill a kid go down for it." He peered over the table at Rachel. "That who you are? The kid killer?"

"He broke his arm. And I didn't do it."

"You know everyone says they're not guilty, right?" March shook his head. "Doesn't matter."

"It actually does in this case." Kenna got his attention back on her. "That's why I'm here. I was hired by Mrs. Sanchez's lawyer to prove she was nowhere near that highway on the night a reckless driver struck that child."

"That right?"

Kenna nodded. "How about you? I might be able to help your case."

"Can you make a bar full of people forget they saw me pop Harlem and his girl?"

"Probably not."

"Too bad. I don't need you." March motioned with the gun. "Guess that means you're expendable."

"No one is expendable. Not even you." Kenna took a measured breath. "Every life is valuable."

"You should meet some of the guys I know. You'd change your mind."

"I'm sorry you don't know good people." She could see the best she'd ever met if she closed her eyes. But that led to daydreams which ended with a church in Northern California exploding. She'd hit the ground hard, knocked out. The same thing she'd seen every time she closed her eyes for the last two months.

A church full of people, most of them with badges.

All the evidence they'd gathered on a powerful organization who played God with innocent lives.

Kenna flicked her wrist over so the face of her watch illuminated with the time—and her notifications. "If we're going to be here long, I should call someone to let my dog out of my van. It's in the parking lot. Otherwise she'll make a mess in there."

"You think I care about your dog?" March got up and gave a side glance at the clock.

Kenna bit the inside of her lip.

He clambered down and moved across the courtroom, a wave at her with the gun. "Stay where I can see you."

Kenna lifted both hands.

Arm outstretched, March pointed the gun down at Rachel. "Get up. Like I said before. You don't listen?"

Kenna lifted her foot where he couldn't see and drew out the baton with two fingers.

March grabbed Rachel by the hair and dragged her to her feet.

Kenna moved toward them.

Jones grabbed March by the leg and pulled his body in. He bit the inmate. Rachel grabbed March's wrist.

Kenna saw the bad idea play out to where they'd all end up dead in the next thirty seconds. But she was close enough.

March kicked at Jones. He shoved Rachel away.

Rachel fell to the floor. "I won't let them kill me!"

March swung the gun around.

Kenna slammed the baton on his forearm, and he dropped the gun. She whipped it up in the opposite direction, spinning her hips as she moved to get as much force as she could. It clipped his chin and flicked it back. Before he could recover, Kenna hit his throat.

March fell to the floor, choking.

Rachel swiped the gun off the floor to point it, hand shaking, at March.

The courtroom door crashed open, wood splintering. A uniformed cop was first in. He saw the woman holding a gun on a man, and intention washed over his face. Finger to the trigger.

"No!" Kenna slammed into Rachel, and they both hit the floor.

The judge's chair erupted into a cloud of foam.

Chapter Three

Two months ago

Kenna held the leash. They'd walked nearly three miles, the last leg of a convoluted journey that got her into Salt Lake City under the radar of whoever was watching.

She watched the street for half an hour until she was satisfied no one had the place under surveillance.

"Come on."

Cabot stood from the spot behind a trash can where she'd been lying. Thankfully there wasn't snow on the ground, or she wouldn't have had Cabot lay down longer than a few minutes. Even with the doggy coat keeping her warm.

Kenna sent a text.

She ran a gloved hand around the dog's head to scratch her chin. Cabot pressed her head against Kenna's leg as they walked and she scratched, and they made their way to the house. Kenna pushed open the gate on the sidewalk when the front door opened.

Ryson stuck his head out. "Good timing. I just got off shift." He opened the door wide so she and Cabot could step in. "What's with the burner phone?"

"I can explain." She reached for the leash but paused. "Valentina and Luci?"

"Tina is feeding Luci dinner."

"Okay." Kenna unclipped the leash.

"Is that my friend I hear?" Valentina's voice drifted in from the kitchen. "Or my husband's former colleague?"

Kenna grinned at Ryson, who smiled back. "That's the same person." She peeled off her coat, and Ryson stuck it on the hook. She trailed into the kitchen after her dog. "Merry Christmas."

The whole place was aglow, the open kitchen and living area in the same state of disarray as it had been the last time she was here—like two people and a baby lived here, and they both had jobs. Kenna only kept her van tidy because if she didn't, there was nowhere to sit.

"Merry Christmas to you, too." Valentina had their baby on her lap, holding a bottle while Luci sucked down milk like a champ. "How come I don't have the secret phone number?"

Kenna leaned down and kissed the baby's forehead. "Hi, Luci."

"If you wanna distract me from the fact you're not going to answer the question, you'll have to take over feeding her."

Kenna looked behind the smile and saw that new mom tiredness but wrapped up in that was a deep joy. Things were good. "Hand her over."

"Is your dog going to sit on my couch all night?"

Kenna grinned. Valentina gently shifted the baby to Kenna's arms. That soft warmth in her arms settled something in Kenna she didn't like to think about much. What life might have been if things had gone differently. "Merry Christmas to me."

Kenna kept moving, holding the baby and the bottle, even though the walk from the van and being out in the cold had left her stiff and tired. She headed toward the fireplace and stood with her back to it so it warmed up her legs. "I know you've been on their radar."

"I've had people following me." Valentina hugged herself. "I called the station, but the person turned off the street behind me, so I stopped."

Kenna glanced at Ryson. "And you?"

He nodded. "Same. And feeling like we're being watched."

Ryson sat on the arm of the couch at the far end. He tugged his wife down to sit on his lap and wrapped his arms around her, his chin on her shoulder.

Kenna didn't need anything else. "It's good to see you guys. Despite the"—she didn't want to say it—"threat. It's still good to be here, so long as it's safe." If something happened to Luci, she would never forgive herself.

Ryson's jaw flexed. "You're going to let them send you running scared?"

"If it keeps you safe?" Kenna stared at him. "You know."

He nodded.

She'd stayed away before. She would do it again for their protection.

Valentina whispered, "You need to tell her, Javier." Kenna had been friends with Ryson for years, but hearing his first name still felt unfamiliar. She'd never called him anything other than his last name. Though, he only ever called her Special Agent Banbury to try and be funny.

"Tell me what?" She set the empty bottle on the coffee

table and picked up a cloth, which she laid on her shoulder before she shifted Luci and patted her back.

"Dinner is almost ready." Ryson shifted Valentina off his lap and stood. He squeezed her hand before heading for the kitchen.

Valentina came over to Kenna. "Jax can't make it. He was sent on an undercover thing."

Kenna looked down at the baby. "Okay, that's fine."

"I guess you'll have to settle for us," Ryson called from the kitchen.

Valentina grinned at Kenna, who called back to him, "I am hungry. I guess you can feed me." She reached back with one hand and slid an envelope from her back pocket. She handed it to Valentina and whispered, "Merry Christmas."

Valentina slipped the envelope into her back pocket because she knew it was for later, so they could open it together. Kenna didn't need to be here to see their reactions to a college fund set up in Luci's name.

Two pans clanked together.

Valentina grinned. "Let me help you, Javi."

Kenna watched them in the kitchen, soaking up this slice of family. People who didn't think it was weird that she spent most of her time alone or with Cabot. They didn't care she traveled all over and only called occasionally. They just cared about her.

She held the baby to her chest and soaked that in, too. The sound of Christmas. Lights. Family. Warmth and care for each other.

Before she headed back to her normal life. Quiet and cold —until she made it to a state with a warmer climate.

Ryson barked, "Kenna, get over here and sit at the table."

She snuggled the baby. "I'm busy."

Chapter Four

Present day

Kenna took the last sip of coffee from the paper cup. A terrible brew that tasted like it had been filtered through an old boot inside a vending machine. Better than letting them see how much her hands shook.

A woman being set up.

Kenna shook her head. "First the case gets dismissed, and then moments later, an inmate happens to run in and take us all hostage?"

The uniformed officer stood over her. A young guy, maybe twenty-three.

"March grabbed the gun and got up. The officer shot him in the shoulder."

"Captain Marling." The young officer nodded to the side, motioning to the uniformed man talking to an older guy in a suit. Awe appeared on the guy's face as he looked at his superior.

Kenna stared at the inside of the empty cup, trying to work it all out. She hardly cared if this young officer had never fired his weapon in the line of duty, or if he hero-worshiped his superior. Rachel Sanchez had been determined to protect her life by killing a guy before he could kill her, because she believed someone intended on taking her life.

The question was whether that threat was real.

Kenna glanced around. "Are the other people from the courtroom okay?"

"Sure."

"So where are they?"

"The ambulance has been back and forth several times to the medical center down the street."

Rachel hadn't been injured. At least, not more than the bruises Kenna had also received. "Where is Mrs. Sanchez? Or her lawyer?"

He glanced around. "I'm not sure." An ambulance had taken Parker Jones to the hospital. The officer had to know that.

Kenna got up, making like it was just to throw the empty paper cup in the garbage. She'd seen someone lead Rachel down the hall, the courthouse security guard. Her head pounded. She hadn't been able to catch every detail in the confusion after March had been subdued with that shot. They'd been yelled at to stay where they were. Separated. The injured were treated. Someone called for the coroner, doing it right in Kenna's face like she hadn't been standing there.

Rachel hadn't been in the hall with the rest of the witnesses.

At the edge of her vision, far down the hall, Kenna spotted the door to holding. Where prisoners were placed until they were walked out for their trials. The officer followed her, but Kenna picked up her pace. At the last second she sidestepped and pulled the door open. Wind whipped down the hall.

At the far end, a line of people headed out an open door as Rachel stood by.

"Stop!" Kenna ran down the hall.

"Ma'am!" An armed state police officer held up a hand. "You can't be down here."

Kenna paid him no attention. She ran right up to him and pointed at Rachel. "That woman isn't going anywhere. Her case was dismissed, and the charges dropped. Someone made a terrible mistake." She stared at him.

A second later, his composure cracked, and the stubbled chin moved. "What are you talking about?"

"The hostage situation?" Rhetorical question. "We—"

"Ma'am." The officer grasped Kenna's elbow.

She whirled around. "Did you just put your hands on me?"

He reeled back and lifted both hands. "I didn't mean—"

Kenna moved. She worked her way along the line, past two people to where Rachel was being herded out the door. "Come with me."

Rachel stepped out of line, and they turned back to the officer.

"What's going on?" The guy outside noticed the disruption.

The officer in the hallway called back to his colleague, "Get the others in the van!"

Kenna stood in front of Rachel. "Take the cuffs off this woman. Call her lawyer. Call Judge Williams in here."

The young officer said, "The judge left for the day, what with everything that happened."

Kenna turned to him. "The *judge* wasn't even in the room.

She left before it happened. Right after she declared this woman innocent and dismissed the charges against her."

Rachel whimpered, leaning her arm against Kenna.

"I'll repeat myself until it sinks in. *Her case was dismissed.*" Kenna looked at the state guy. "Why are you transporting a free woman back to prison?"

"Her name was on the list."

"Then you have bad paperwork, and I want to see it." Kenna lifted her chin. "You wanna get sued for a human rights violation that costs your career, and your department has to pay her millions for emotional damage? Or you want to call the judge and confirm what I'm saying? It's up to you."

The officer frowned. "She was released?"

"The prosecution failed to prove she was guilty. I was in there when Judge Williams said she was free to go." Kenna shifted, keeping Rachel behind her. She didn't ask them to take her cuffs off yet.

"Who are you?" the state cop asked.

"A neutral third party who doesn't like when people get railroaded just because someone else has more power and they want to throw it around and destroy people's lives."

"That's quite a mission."

"Today, my mission is you guys," Kenna said. "And this entire courthouse. And an innocent woman about to be put back in the system because you guys screwed up." She folded her arms. "I expect this to be fixed immediately."

The young officer said, "I'll go find the judge."

"I've gotta get to my van." The state officer headed for the door.

"Take your cuffs with you." Kenna glanced at his retreating back. The officer was young but still shouldn't have left them. He probably figured the transport officer would stay until it was resolved.

Instead, he turned and uncuffed Rachel Sanchez, then headed to the door. The second it closed behind him, Rachel whipped around. "Thank you."

"We're not out of here yet." Kenna headed for the door to the interior hall. "Stick with me."

"You don't need to worry about that." She followed right behind Kenna, out into the hall where the suited man and the captain who'd shot March watched them break off their conversation.

Both men strode toward them.

The suited man eyed Rachel, then Kenna. "What's going on?"

"Apart from the wrongful imprisonment of an innocent woman?" She wasn't sure the civil rights violation would hold much weight as a threat with these guys, so she stuck to the scenario playing out. "Your officer is confirming with the judge that Mrs. Sanchez is in fact free to go."

The captain looked at the suited man.

Mayor, or chief of police.

He could be the local bank manager for all Kenna knew—or cared. She wasn't getting caught up in a town again. Last time she'd lost someone she would've liked to get to know and been right in the middle of a cascade of events that left devastation in their wake.

Kenna turned away, dismissing them entirely. And intentionally. She smiled at Rachel as though everything was perfectly normal. "Let's go and wait in the lobby. There's no reason to remain here."

Rachel shot her a nervous glance. When they were out of earshot of anyone else, she whispered, "This might actually work."

"How did they get you nearly on a prison transport?" Kenna slowed in the lobby and turned to Rachel, her back to the door so she could watch both of the hallways and everyone in here. She looked beaten down, out of hope. Despite the win in the courtroom, this was a woman who knew she held no power if someone else wanted to take it from her.

And she hadn't even noticed Kenna's question.

"Look at me, Rachel." They were about the same age, though Rachel might be a few years younger. When she lifted her gaze, Kenna said, "You don't know me, but this is what I do."

Hope mixed with a whole lot of doubt in Rachel's expression. This woman had been drifting alone for a while now—maybe even since her husband's death. Something Kenna wanted to know more about.

"I'm not leaving your side until you're somewhere safe. I don't care if that's two miles north of the Canadian border. It's what I do." She held out her hand.

It took a second, but Rachel laid her hand in Kenna's.

She held on. "I'm not leaving you. And that's a promise you can count on."

Questions swirled in Rachel's eyes.

"We can talk on the drive up to Canada."

Rachel's lips twitched, a fraction of a smile.

"Just hang on. Don't let them win."

Rachel nodded.

The officer jogged in from the opposite hall, into the lobby where his superior and the suited man approached. Maybe he was the mayor and the police chief.

Kenna didn't want to care, or she'd look into him to find out what kind of man he was, and how he exerted that leadership over this town. If the way they'd treated Rachel was any indication, Kenna wasn't going to like what she found.

"The judge left already," the officer said.

Kenna's stomach tied in a knot.

"But I found her aide, and she had the paperwork. The case was dismissed. Mrs. Sanchez is free to go."

"Great." Kenna shifted, guiding Rachel toward the door. "We've given our statements as to what happened. There's no reason to waste our time any further."

"Hold up now." The captain started toward them. "We need to speak with Mrs. Sanchez. In case there's any connection between her and the inmate who decided to shoot up *her* courtroom."

Rachel let out a tiny whimper behind her.

Kenna held up a hand. "Any questions you might have for Mrs. Sanchez can be directed to her through her lawyer. She's currently unavailable for a statement and refuses to submit to questioning until her lawyer can be present."

"He's in the hospital," the young officer said.

Kenna glanced at him. Since she'd been there when Parker Jones was pistol-whipped and when EMTs walked him out, she did already know that. "When he's better, you can call him and make an appointment."

"Giving his client time to leave town?" the captain asked.

"As a free citizen, Mrs. Sanchez is at liberty to go wherever she pleases. Including leaving this courtroom." Kenna pulled the door open. "Let's go, Rachel."

"I didn't catch your name."

She glanced back at the captain. "I know."

It wasn't much of a comeback considering she'd given the officer her name along with her statement. They would run her information and realize who she was. The question after that would be what they planned to do next.

Or if she would even still be in Hatchet, New Mexico.

Rachel walked to the edge of the sidewalk where traffic passed in both directions.

Kenna laid a hand between Rachel's shoulder blades. "See that van in the parking lot?"

She found it.

"That's where we're going. Via the crosswalk." Kenna led her to the button. Traffic slowed for them, and she scanned the street. The parking lot. Glanced back at the courthouse where people on the sidewalk noticed them.

"Are you a bodyguard?" Rachel asked. "You told him you're a private investigator."

"Today I'm whatever you need. That's how it works. Investigation. Protection. Doesn't matter what it is, I can do it. The goal is to fix your problem, whatever it is."

Rachel glanced at her. "You won't want to."

"Your lawyer took it on, didn't he? Jones must've thought he could win the case."

"I thought he would throw the whole thing. Secure my conviction." Rachel strode from the sidewalk on the far side of the street onto the parking lot.

Cabot sat in the front seat of Kenna's van, watching. Dog breath steamed up the window.

"He hired me," Kenna said. "That says something."

"And you came here just to help?"

"It pays the bills." Kenna tugged her keys from her pocket and clicked the locks. "You're not allergic to dogs, right?"

"Um, no." Rachel looked at the courthouse.

Kenna opened the door. "Cabot, stay." She held the door and motioned for Rachel. "Hop in. Let's go."

Rachel climbed into the van. Kenna walked around to check the car, hooked onto the tow hitch behind the van. Satisfied everything was secure, and the van didn't look like it had been messed with—no obvious impending flat tires that would stall their progress on the freeway. No one lurking or watching them.

Despite the green light to head out of here, she didn't wonder if Rachel had some kind of delusion.

It was possible, until Kenna could unequivocally rule it out. Until then she would work as though everything Rachel said was true.

"The case was dismissed, and now they have no reason to hold you," Kenna began. Then a thought occurred to her. "Are you hungry? I like to eat chips while I drive."

Rachel let out a tiny burst of laughter.

Cabot hopped off the chair, wound past Kenna, who slid into the front seat, and sat to be petted by their new friend.

Kenna smiled. "Take a seat. We're moving out."

Rachel swiped her face clear of the tears that had fallen. "Where are we going?" She came over and slid into the chair.

"I drive. You talk. Or sleep. Or eat all my chips," Kenna said. "Cabot needs some grass to pee on, but I've got nowhere else to be."

"Is this a good time to ask if you want recommendations for an out of the way place to bury me in?"

"Is this a good time to pull out my gun and keep it handy but out of *your* reach?"

Rachel buckled her seatbelt and covered her face with her hands. She groaned. "I can't believe I'm not in jail right now. I thought for sure it wasn't going to matter that I didn't hit that boy."

Kenna put the van in drive and headed for the street, turning toward the freeway. "Wanna head for Canada?"

"I need to check on my mother."

"Load up the address." She pointed to the dash screen, where Rachel could enter the information. "We'll find a park real quick, and go there first."

"You're really helping me?"

Kenna held the wheel with both hands and glanced over. "Looks like it."

"Just like that?"

"Do you need help?"

Rachel nodded.

"Then why would I leave without doing what I can?"

Rachel's eyes gleamed with tears.

Kenna couldn't look long enough to see if she cried but heard a sniff. "Tissues in the console."

Rachel blew her nose well. "I'll make breakfast at my mom's house. Bacon. And hashbrowns."

"Sounds good." She figured this woman had been held in prison until her trial. Given how much she'd been railroaded, that made sense. But why was she the target of police suspicion? And whose head would roll first when Kenna dug up the truth.

"While I eat I'll tell you my whole story." Rachel sighed. "After that, I'm packing up my mom and everything I have and getting out of this state. As far away from here as possible."

Kenna watched the mirrors, half expecting a police car to start shadowing them, looking for any infraction. A reason to pull them over. They'd tried to convict Rachel of a hit-and-run she didn't do. Then in the confusion, someone had ordered her taken back to prison.

This was either simply about Rachel, or it was something much bigger.

Kenna intended to find out which.

Chapter Five

"I need everything you can find on Rachel Sanchez and her husband." Kenna held the phone close to her mouth, her thumb long holding on the bottom of the screen to record a voice message.

"As well as everything you can get on March—that's what he said his name was—an inmate from the courthouse this morning. Security said it was a double homicide case. He's the one who took the courthouse hostage this morning. Shot in the shoulder. He was escorted to the hospital." She let go of the button.

Cabot sniffed around the bottom of a state park trashcan, her business finished.

"Let's go, dog."

Cabot put some bounce into her turn, then trotted over. Moving as though her back leg didn't even bother her. Later she would be limping—if Kenna allowed her too much exercise. Right now it was difficult to tell she still suffered from the car accident they'd both been in. If it wasn't for the scars, it might be impossible to tell.

"You don't like to let people know how you're really feeling." Kenna reached down and patted the dog's side. "Maybe it's a family trait."

Her phone started to vibrate in her hand, not making any noise. The screen said *Stairs*.

Kenna sent the call straight to voicemail. He'd barely had time to listen to her voice message.

Her former boss, the man responsible for cutting her loose from the FBI, currently considered himself her coworker. She was thinking it was more like he was her research assistant. And only informally.

The text came through a couple of seconds later.

> You can't ignore me forever.

Kenna figured he knew as well as she did that wasn't true.

She pulled open the door to the van. Cabot hopped in first, tail wagging as she looked for their guest. Rachel exited the tiny bathroom, drying her hands with a paper towel. It looked like she had washed her face as well.

"Ready to go?"

The other woman nodded, headed for the passenger seat, and entered her mother's address into the GPS. Cabot accepted a treat a from Kenna, then went to lie down in the bedroom area at the back of the van on the floor between the twin beds.

Kenna followed the directions for a couple more miles from the state park, across town to the neighborhood. "Have you always lived with her?" Rachel had explained that the woman was actually her mother-in-law.

The young woman shook her head. She seemed more nervous of Kenna than Kenna would have been of her. Whether or not Cabot gave her any indication there was a problem she was unaware of. If the dog wasn't on edge, then

Kenna tried not to be either. But that left Rachel Sanchez, curled in on herself sitting in the passenger seat.

Better than being in prison.

Rachel swiped back some of her dark hair. "We got married three years ago and lived in an apartment in Albuquerque. Mrs. Sanchez has always lived here. When she got sick, he looked for a transfer. He was so excited to find an open position in his hometown."

Kenna navigated the pitted streets, then turned onto a residential road lined with cars on both sides because none of the houses had driveways.

Rachel pointed. "It's the third house down there."

Kenna took the next corner before she found a spot big enough for her van, still pulling the car behind. If she were to stay in this town much longer, she would need to find a campsite or RV park.

With Cabot behind her, Kenna slid a holstered pistol onto the back of her belt. She flipped the tail of her jacket over it, and they backtracked to the house.

Rachel's steps faltered on the crabgrass that made up the lawn. "The front door is open."

"Hang back." Kenna waved her to the sidewalk and slid the gun from the holster.

"I'm not going to let you leave me out here by myself."

"And if the threat in there is worse than it is out here?" She stared down the fear on the other woman's face, comprehending precisely what that felt like.

"Whatever it is, we're supposed to do it together. Right?" Rachel lifted her chin.

"That is right." The truth was, Kenna didn't feel great about leaving Rachel by herself. Something with this situation gave her an uneasy sensation.

Not that anyone was watching them. It was more like the

slow creep of mist across the grass of a plain in the early morning.

There was something about this town. And considering the last place she'd engaged with turned out to be under the thumb of an elite group, she wasn't all that excited to get her hands dirty. Even though she was on the case, investigating as best she could by herself, it was different when she had to look people in the eye and know they were at risk.

The whole point of what Kenna was doing was to minimize the risk to everyone else. After all, and entire team of state police, the California Bureau of Investigation, and federal agents had been killed by these people. Kenna had been seconds away from dying in that explosion, as had Stairns. There was no way she would watch anyone else die.

Or hand over evidence only to see it destroyed.

Thankfully she'd had enough on her hard drive she had somewhere to start. That, and the anonymous source who seemed intent on feeding her leads.

The first lead, though Kenna didn't know how it tied together, approached the open front door right behind her.

The square adobe house had a white front door flanked by empty flowerpots. A man's boots lay beside a cat litter box on the square slab of concrete that made up the porch.

Kenna took a look at the open door, just a couple of inches gap between it and the frame. "Someone kicked it in." Cabot stuck her nose in the hole and sniffed, but gave no alert aside from the possibility of scents to investigate. "See how it's splintered?"

She pushed the door open, moving a rock with it. Placed there to keep the door closed as much as possible? Someone who didn't have the ability to fix the door but wanted it held shut.

Cabot hopped over the rock and trotted down the hallway. Kenna followed, her gun angled down toward the floor, aware of Rachel behind her.

"Mama?" Rachel called out.

Kenna winced.

The response came from the direction Cabot had gone. "Rachel? Is that you?"

When the kitchen came into view, Kenna stopped.

A stout woman in a night dress, a robe over it, stood wide-eyed in front of the sink facing them. One hand on her front, stubby fingers spread out. She had a dark-blue bruise around one eye, a scar on her temple, and a cane in her hand. Beside her sat an oxygen tank, connected by a tube that ran up and across her upper lip.

"Cabot, leave it."

The dog moved on from the oxygen tank as Rachel rushed across the room and hugged the old woman.

Kenna cleared the rest of the house, making sure no one else was there while the two women cried a little, smiled at each other, and shared a moment to themselves. She then secured the front door with the rock again, so no light was visible between the frame and the door.

Cabot lay on the floor in front of a threadbare recliner. Beside the chair was an equally tattered couch. A colorful handwoven quilt hung on the wall. Another wall held a painting of a horse completed by someone better at appreciating horses than they were at painting. Which meant it was likely sentimental. Art done by a family member.

"Come. Sit down." Rachel helped the older woman into a wicker chair at the dining table. "Kenna?"

Kenna turned in her spot where she had the most advantage of the entry points.

"Sit down with us." Rachel paused. "Actually, sit with Mrs. Sanchez while I go and take a quick shower. Is that okay?" She directed the question to the older woman, the sheen of grief and happiness in her eyes.

"Yes, dear." The older woman nodded. "I'm sure you'd like to change."

"While I do, you can tell Kenna what happened to you. Since you refuse to tell me..." Rachel trailed out.

Kenna spied a kettle on the stove. "Tea, or something else?"

"Yes, tea." The older woman certainly sounded stronger than she appeared—someone who'd been underestimated enough times.

"Mrs. Sanchez, my name is Kenna Banbury. I'm a private investigator, and Rachel's lawyer asked me to locate the evidence that proved she was nowhere near town at the time of the hit-and-run. She was cleared of all charges."

The older woman's jaw flexed as she visibly struggled to contain her emotions. "I thought for certain I would hear one day that she'd been killed in prison. Just like how they came to tell me that Matteo was dead." She swallowed.

Kenna set a mug of tea in front of her and took a chair. "Were you assaulted?"

"They broke into my home two weeks ago and pushed me around." Her hands shook as she lifted the mug. "And for what?"

"What did the police say about it?"

"Now why would I go and do a fool thing like call them?" She took a sip of tea. "They'd only tell me it was a couple of teenagers playing a prank, and the parents don't want it turned into something."

Kenna studied the older woman over her own mug of tea. "I would very much like to turn it into something."

The older woman's lips spread into a smile. "As satisfying as that sounds, I'm not worried about myself." The brief moment of humor slipped away, and grief, coupled with fear, crept back into her expression like that morning mist.

"You think something is going to happen to Rachel?" Kenna asked. She had seemed to think March might have been there purposely to kill her.

"She wants to leave town as soon as we can pack up."

"I can certainly understand if the two of you decide to do that. No one should be held hostage somewhere they don't want to be."

The older woman set her tea down on the linoleum surface, a cigarette burn beside Kenna's mug. The ceiling did have that yellow tint of a resident smoker. But the smell had dissipated, as though illness had forced Mrs. Sanchez to quit in favor of a longer life. "I've never lived anywhere else."

"Rachel told me that Matteo was excited when a position opened in his hometown," Kenna said, wanting to direct the conversation.

"Then he was killed by drug dealers from out of town. They're led by a young man who lives here, but they didn't belong in Hatchet. And the police told me they couldn't find enough evidence to prove these people killed my son." The old woman sighed out a breath that rattled. "They didn't even arrest him. He would follow me at the grocery store. Everyone knew he killed my boy, and then they caught him with two girls from the church choir. They were half dead. The chief had to cuff him then."

"At least he's locked up where he can't hurt anyone else," Kenna said.

Mrs. Sanchez shook her head. "That's not justice. But I won't waste my life wishing for things I'll never have. Not when I know how it feels when it's good."

Kenna stared at her mug, the tea half gone.

"I know who you are. And I know you understand the depth of loss."

Kenna's eyes burned. She blinked away the sting. "The time I had everything I ever wanted are moments I will always treasure."

"Even if we get to experience pure happiness for a moment, it won't last. People let you down. Your children cheat on their spouse. They get themselves killed." Hardness crossed the older woman's face. "It doesn't matter where we go. Nothing is going to change."

Rachel appeared in the doorway in fresh clothes, her hair wet. "We need to be where it's safer. I need to know you aren't alone anymore, unprotected. Just in case something happens to me."

Kenna twisted in her chair.

Before she could ask more questions, Rachel continued, "We're leaving as soon as we can pack up the car."

"You'll have to get my things." Mrs. Sanchez lifted her tea.

"Fine." Rachel twirled around and headed back down the hall.

Kenna went after her and found Rachel in a small bedroom. She lifted a duffel from the closet and set it on the bed, tugging items from inside, which she discarded on the comforter. Until she got to a sweater.

Rachel pressed the sweater to her face. Her body shook with a sob.

Kenna turned to leave her to her grief for a moment.

"I miss him so much."

Kenna twisted back. "The world keeps turning. You keep moving because the alternative is that you just stop." She had done both in the years since Bradley's death. Maybe it had worked, and perhaps what some folks said about time healing things was true. Or the brain had a way of moving painful memories to the background where eventually they would simply fade away.

Rachel went to the closet and tugged out two handfuls of clothes, half the hangers falling on the floor as she turned to the duffel and stuffed the shirts inside. "He thought he could save the world, and they killed him before he could prove the town is corrupt."

"Did he leave anything behind that I can take to look at?" If there was a case here, Kenna could look into it. Or at least pass the information the FBI office in Albuquerque. Well, not her. Stairns had been an assistant Special Agent in Charge, so his name on an email with attachments would hold far more weight than hers.

Rachel shook her head. "I didn't even do anything, and they were going to destroy my life. It never even occurred to me to take up the cause, but it didn't ever matter to them." She took down a shoebox from a shelf in the closet, flipped the lid onto the bed and pulled out a cell phone, which she powered on while she added items from drawers into the duffel.

"If something's going on, then the people who are breaking the law need to be held accountable."

"Great." Rachel folded her arms. "But since I just skated out from under whatever they had planned because of you, I can tell you it's not going to be me that goes up against them. I couldn't hold my own with everything I tried. Now I have nothing but an old lady who needs me to be here for her. So long as here happens to be nowhere near Hatchet." She picked up the phone, swiping the screen before she handed it to Kenna.

The video was already playing.

Kenna stared at the screen and felt her brows pulled together. "This looks like body cam footage."

On the video a man cleared his throat, then closed the

door to a patrol car. Red and blue flashing lights illuminated trees on either side of a dark highway. The blue Camry that had pulled over in front of the patrol car appeared to have a single occupant.

The officer strode to the driver's side.

A gun appeared in the window, light flashed from the muzzle, and audio cracked. The view swept upward to only stars in the night sky.

The officer gasped and shifted, blurring the view from the body camera.

Boots slammed against the asphalt, a half dozen steps. The dark figure leaned over the officer. *That face.* "Should have kept your nose out of our business."

The man disappeared. The officer groaned again, coughing. A wet sound that made Kenna think of blood between lips. Those moments before light extinguished from a person's eyes.

Tires squealed and an engine revved as the car sped away off the screen.

In the corner was a capital C written in a medieval Old English font that looked like scrollwork she had seen before, on a video on the screen of a laptop.

She handed the phone back to Rachel.

"Keep it. I never want to watch that again." Tears tracked down her face. "I'm done with this town, and whoever did that."

"You don't know who they are?" Kenna swallowed against the lump in her throat.

This woman had a video of her husband. She could hear him, and she discarded it because the pain was too great. It didn't show Matteo's face, so Kenna figured she would feel the same. And she had a couple of videos of Bradley she was never going to delete. An ultrasound picture. Those photos she wanted to look at, she had kept tucked away all this time. Rachel needed to take those memories with her.

"I have nothing to give that can possibly help you," Rachel replied. "And with any luck, I'll never see this place again."

Kenna slid the phone into her back pocket.

"You're going after them, aren't you?"

"I have someone who will be extremely interested in this video."

"Your funeral." Rachel zipped the duffel. "Literally."

"We'll see."

Chapter Six

Kenna lifted the plastic cover on the side of her van and connected the water. A dog barked across the RV park, and she glanced over at a top-of-the-line full-size RV. Through the open window she could see the inside was decked out in chrome accents. The woman at the table had huge blond curly hair and a pink western-style shirt with jeweled snaps and black edging on the pockets and seams.

She wanted to watch that video again and would in a moment. Just to make sure she wasn't inferring something. That what she'd seen was really what was there.

Kenna hooked up the sewer line for her van, removed her gloves, and tossed them in the trashcan two spaces down. Neither of which were occupied. In fact, the RV park was mostly empty—just a maze of pitted concrete driveways. In between, a strip of gravel with a picnic table and a couple of decorative boulders broke up the monotony of the ground.

Cabot caught up with her on her way back to the van, only a slight limp in her stride. Much better than the few times Kenna had to carry the dog on her shoulders because she had overexerted herself. They had probably looked ridiculous heading back to Kenna's van like a shepherd hauling a wayward sheep, but it wasn't like Kenna could carry her dog in her arms. She was working on holding a gun for more than a minute or two without it shaking.

"You know that wasn't the pee area, right?" She petted Cabot's shoulder.

In the middle of the next row of RV spaces, the owners had set up a fenced off dog area. Cabot tended to be a little more free-range about doing her business, but that was a battle Kenna intended to fight another time.

Kenna washed her hands at the kitchen sink, refilled Cabot's water dish, and set it outside next to the step she put on the rug outside the door.

If she ended up here for more than a few days, Kenna would set up the awning that provided shade for her front door and the picnic table she could use.

She scrambled an egg and rolled it up in a tortilla with some cheese. Made coffee in her French press. Turned the laptop on and checked her phone notifications. She called back Stairs since he had left her a message, opting for a video call so she could prop the phone against the backsplash and have her hands free.

The older man's gray face appeared on the screen. "Took you long enough. You checked into that RV park like an hour ago."

"Do I want to know how you know that?"

"Considering the circumstances, I decided to do a little due diligence keeping tabs on you."

"What about Rachel Sanchez and her mother?"

Stairs glanced to one side. "Location sharing has them on the twenty-five, heading north toward Albuquerque."

"She isn't wasting time putting distance between her and Hatchet. Not that I blame her." Kenna had promised to keep tabs on them but decided to stick around town rather than follow them away from it.

It wasn't any wonder Stairns was keeping tabs on her. Kenna had asked Rachel to share her location from her phone so they could monitor her progress. The other woman had also agreed to texting every time they stopped somewhere so Kenna would know they were okay.

Stairns would say they'd been cut from the same cloth. He wasn't so wrong about that, but Kenna wasn't going to admit she felt the same. At least not to him.

"I gave her a call," Stairns said. "Rachel and her mother-in-law will come here on their way north. They won't be here until late tonight, but I want to fully debrief them in person about what's going on in Hatchet. I can also load them up with supplies, new phones, and a clean car. Make sure they get somewhere safe."

Kenna set her plate in the sink and then sat back down. Cabot lay on the floor between the twin beds at the back of the van. Kenna walked back there, only a few paces out of Stairns' view, and crouched. "Up?" She pointed at the twin bed.

Cabot got her feet under her and stood. Kenna bent her knees and lifted the dog onto the bed, where Cabot lay down with a groan.

Kenna went back to her call. "What else is going on?"

"After I get Rachel and Mrs. Sanchez squared away, Elizabeth and I are going to a marriage retreat in Denver for the weekend." Stairns paused a beat. "Maybe I want you to interrupt me with an emergency, but I also think it'll be good for us."

"I've never been married, so I wouldn't know." She picked up her coffee mug and leaned back in the chair, facing the phone. She put her feet on the seat of the chair behind the driver's seat.

"You got close enough with Bradley."

She had to admit, if only to herself, it was getting easier to hear his name spoken aloud. "Some people would write me off because we got pregnant without getting married first."

She'd landed on a radio station a few days ago with a fire-and-brimstone pastor preaching on just that subject. Kenna was now unworthy of salvation because she had fallen short and should be walking around in a cloud of shame. Maybe that was the point.

Stairns made a face she couldn't exactly decipher. "How do you feel about it?"

Sounded like his wife, the counselor, was rubbing off on him. Kenna shrugged—or tried to. "I think he's dead, and I don't need my choices reduced to a moral absolute. Being with Bradley. What we shared and the life we created together—even if it wasn't 'right' and even if I lost both of them—was the best thing I ever had. I won't apologize for it. It wasn't perfect, but it was mine." At the end of the day, she figured that how she felt about it, and whether she had done wrong or not, was up to her to figure out on her own.

"You know what I've realized?" Stairns said. "There are truths and untruths, and there is right and wrong, but when our hearts get involved, things get messy. It's not always easy to make a judgment."

"Good thing I don't have to worry about my heart getting involved anymore."

"Right."

Kenna left that comment alone. It didn't matter if he believed her or not. "Your message said you had an update for me." She should tell him about the guy in the video, the man who'd killed Matteo Sanchez, but she wanted to be sure first.

Stairns nodded. "About four months ago Matteo Sanchez sent an email to his boss's boss about rampant corruption in Hatchet."

"He was going to blow the whistle?" Kenna lowered her mug. "Did they open an investigation?"

"Looks like it never went anywhere."

Outside the van, the woman with the pink shirt and Dolly Parton hair walked a tiny dog on a pink leash along the asphalt between the rows of RV spaces. She didn't hide the fact she was interested in Kenna's van. Until she looked at the open blinds and caught Kenna watching her. Then she whipped around straight and called to her dog as she set off walking again. The dog dropped some business in the gravel and then scurried after her.

"So whatever Matteo was worried about, it got buried." Which was what Kenna had been worried about. "This isn't just Hatchet. It goes all the way to the state level." And since she had seen that video, the body cam footage of Matteo's death she knew exactly how far this thing connected.

It was no coincidence that Kenna had been directed to come to this town considering the same organization was at work here.

"He kept the whole email pretty vague," Stairns said. "The town had issues, and whatever was going on, it was widespread."

"At least Judge Williams didn't kowtow to them. But in the face of the evidence, maybe she had no choice." Kenna could speak to her in the next few days. Find out if she'd been pressured or was part of this.

"The lawyer did a good thing calling you." Stairns glanced aside again.

She took another sip of coffee.

"So who told you Rachel Sanchez was being railroaded?"

Stairns lifted a pen, ready to make another note in his notebook.

That meant she had to tread carefully. "I'm getting information from an anonymous source. Like those texts in Bishopsville that the tactical team was coming when we were in that storage unit? Remember?"

"I thought you never figured out who that was."

"I didn't." Kenna shook her head. "But I've had a couple of other info dumps on the blog—one of which was Rachel's case. The connection to her husband's murder wasn't part of it." Possibly because anything related to Matteo's death had either been destroyed or would be too difficult to go after, and meanwhile Rachel had been facing sentencing. "So I showed up and helped her before it was too late."

Now she had the body cam footage of Matteo's death the situation had changed, and she knew for sure the organization was at work in Hatchet.

She opened her browser on the laptop. An idea formed as she pulled up the webpage for Utah True Crime. Kenna hadn't been posting on the site, though it did get occasional traffic. So far all the activity happened in the drafts area.

Like the post about Rachel Sanchez, fully written up with links and images. As if it were a real article. Never posted.

It could have been an entirely benign blog post. Someone with access to her admin end of the website thought it would make a good post. Maybe they didn't even know the original owner of the site was dead, and they contributed on occasion.

Eric Wilson had been killed in a house fire months ago, no matter that her mind played tricks on her and she thought she'd seen him since then, which was impossible.

"So who sent you those texts in the storage unit?" Stairns asked.

Kenna shrugged. "I have no idea." She didn't glance aside at the photo on the fridge. A high school age blonde, missing.

Was she the person who now communicated with Kenna via the website back end? Like people who communicated through draft emails on the same email account, leaving messages for each other in that folder without ever sending anything. It was a great way to talk with no electronic record.

Kenna uploaded a link to the local Hatchet news article that explained how a state police officer had been tragically killed while working one night. No one knew how Matteo Sanchez had been shot, and the investigating officers had no suspects. At the end of the article was a note about how Matteo's body cam from that night had been damaged, leaving the authorities with no footage.

At the end of the article she added a couple of questions, as though leading to a discussion on the site. *What got this man killed? Is the town of Hatchet engaged in a cover-up?*

She saved the blog as a draft and logged out of the website. Maybe she should upload the body cam video to go with it.

Stairns said, "Do you want me to dig into who is accessing the blog site? I can find someone freelance that's able to get us an IP address for the person leaving the information."

Kenna figured that life after the FBI, working freelance, had led Stairns to resurrect some old contacts. He was probably building an entire team of people he could lean on to solve cases.

But the last thing she needed was more people going after the organization that had held the town of Bishopsville in a choke hold.

A group of people who had killed every cop and agent assigned to the case.

"I don't want you to dig." Kenna cleared her throat. "I want to see where it goes."

"These people could be leading you astray or into a trap."
"I'll be careful."

She had seen a man leave the church ahead of them, seconds before the building exploded. A man she believed had been the one to set the charges and to destroy the whole place—along with everything and everyone inside.

Kenna and Stairs had been tossed across the parking lot by the force of the explosion. Neither of them could picture his face well enough to give a sketch artist what they needed to create a composite.

Kenna looked over at the refrigerator, where she had magneted the photo she had of Maizie Smith. Printed out from an incoming high school student transfer form. Kenna didn't even know if that was her real first name.

But the girl was part of this somehow.

And Kenna was going to find her.

"Anything more on that girl?" she asked.

Stairs remained quiet for a beat. "Thomas did me a favor. He age-regressed the image you sent me. Then he ran it through missing persons with a few different versions. Toddler age, elementary school. Early teens. He will let me know if he gets a hit, and we can figure out her real name."

She didn't know how he'd persuaded an FBI lab tech to help, but also wasn't about to complain.

"And in the meantime?" Kenna squeezed her eyes shut. "It's time to get to work in Hatchet."

"What's first on the list?"

She plugged Rachel's phone into her computer and started to copy over the video. "I need to go talk to the lawyer. See what he has to say about all this."

Chapter Seven

Parker Jones' law office was located at the far end of Main Street, which made up the bulk of the town. Kenna drove past two-story store fronts that had probably housed a similar business in each unit for the last century and a half, the business names were Spanish for most of that.

Surrounded by desert, the town seemed to have sprung up from the sand. Maybe a stagecoach stop from the Old West days where horses had to be rested instead of cars that were simply refueled or charged.

Cabot had been asleep when she left, so Kenna had armed the security system. Her van had a typical household security setup of internal and external cameras, which would alert her phone if there was any motion inside or directly outside it.

She pulled her car into a space outside the law office, third in a row of five storefronts with a log cabin façade. The front door jingled a bell above it as she entered. The high ceiling gave an expansive feel to the office, though it was only a waiting area and four chairs in front of a reception desk occupied by a woman with arched eyebrows and horn-rimmed eyeglasses. The rest of the interior was split by a hallway to provide a room on either side.

Above her glasses, the receptionist eyed Kenna with a disapproving scowl most people only gave her when her dog trailed in after her, wet and tracking mud. "Can I help you?" The woman wore a purple silk blouse that accentuated her shoulder bones and elbows. The rest of her disappeared between angles. But there was something resembling Parker Jones in her features. His mother, maybe.

"I'm looking for Mr. Jones." Assuming he'd been released from the hospital. "I'd like to speak with him about Rachel Sanchez."

The receptionist lifted a gold pen. "He didn't get in yet."

The clock on the wall indicated it was just after nine twenty in the morning. "Are you expecting him soon?"

"He'll be here when he arrives." Before Kenna could comment on the logic of that statement, the woman said, "You're that private investigator." She indicated the gold pen. "He didn't need any help."

"And yet he hired me." But she didn't think that was the point here. Or at least it wasn't the one this woman was trying to make. Kenna figured if she was a small-town lawyer, then she likely wouldn't have been amenable to interference either.

Considering everything she'd learned so far, it was entirely possible Parker Jones had been leaned on to not fight the case so hard. And that was what she wanted to talk to him about. Regardless of the way it had gone, she needed more information about the Sanchezes and whoever that C belonged to in the video of his death.

Someone had to know.

"Rachel Sanchez was innocent," Kenna added. No one

could argue with the judge's ruling. "If I hadn't brought that evidence, she would've gone to prison."

The receptionist squinted at her.

"I'd like to know where to find him."

"You're going to track him down like some kind of bounty hunter?" She scoffed.

"You know...that's something I've never done. Sounds like fun, though." Kind of like how if she didn't have a dog right now, she would have traded the car for a motorcycle months ago. "What if you were to give me his address. Then I could swing by his house just to make sure he's all right. Unless it's perfectly normal for Mr. Jones to not show up for work a day after an important case."

The guy had been hit over the head. He'd spent the afternoon in the hospital but was released later that day according to the information Stairs had managed to obtain by going on the lawyer's social media accounts.

Parker Jones had been all about gaining sympathy for his ordeal—until he posted he was being released. He mentioned nothing about Rachel Sanchez and the fact he had won the case. Nothing about Kenna's help. Nothing about the inmate who had held them hostage until the police burst in and tried to kill Rachel.

The pointy woman eyed her. Then she dragged over a pad of sticky notes and wrote on the top one. She tore it off and held it out. "I was just about to go over there and check on him, but I also have a lot of work to do here."

Kenna took the note. "Of course. I'll leave you to it." She turned to the door and glanced down at the note to see an address a couple of streets over. It would probably take the woman ten minutes to make sure Jones was all right, but she wanted to stay here?

"If something happened to him, it's probably because you interfered in the case."

Kenna pulled the door open and glanced back. "Why would something have happened to him?"

The pointy woman blinked. "It's a figure of speech."

Kenna headed for her car, where she put the address into her phone. Phone in the bracket on the dash that held it. Probably that woman hadn't been his mother if she didn't care enough to go to Parker's house to check on him when he didn't show up for work.

Then again, some people's parents might be in it for the money only. They might scam the business owner on the side, taking a little for themselves.

She pulled up out front of the house, pocketed her keys, and headed for the front door. The fact she didn't have a private investigator license for the state of New Mexico didn't make much of a difference if no one opened the door and invited her in.

Kenna tried to avoid breaking and entering. But in a town where she was possibly being observed, and where innocent people were put on trial for crimes they hadn't committed, it was probably better to try and fly under the radar—or at least not offer up ammunition that could be used against her.

Kenna knocked for a while. She wandered to the front window and stood in the planter to peer through the glass, between the drapes.

From what she could see inside, it didn't look like anyone had destroyed anything.

She didn't see anyone around but didn't risk entering the backyard just to take a look. Instead, she slid out her phone and called the law office.

"Parker Jones, Esquire, Candace speaking."

"It's the private investigator. You can call me Kenna."

Before Candace could respond, she said quickly, "I don't see anything at Parker's house. I'm wondering if—"

Candace cut her off. "Is his car in the driveway?"

"No, it isn't." Kenna frowned, walking back to her car at the curb. Across the street, a mail truck made its way toward her. "Do you know if he went somewhere yesterday after he was released from the hospital?"

"The same place he goes every night."

A bar? Kenna didn't want to sound judgmental. It could be a meeting of Alcoholics Anonymous for all she knew.

"It's on the highway, at the edge of town." She gave Kenna the cross streets. "There's a motel next door he goes to when he can't drive home. Probably didn't wake up yet."

"Would you like me to try and find him, make sure he's all right?"

"Doesn't matter if you do. It's not like he's going to listen when you tell him he needs help."

Kenna slid into her driver's seat. "So why do you keep working for him?"

"I pay my mortgage and make sure his rent is current." Candace sighed. "He's not a bad guy, and he's a better lawyer. He just has some problems."

"We all do." Maybe she needed to hear that he wasn't the only one.

Candace huffed, and the line clicked. She had hung up.

Kenna drove over and headed for the motel first since the bar was closed. She twisted the loose handle and stepped into a stuffy office. Candy hung from plastic hooks on the wall above shelves of chips and cookie packages, sunscreen, and spray bottles of glass cleaner. A freezer logoed with the brand in bright colors held ice cream Kenna spied through the glass lid.

"Help you?" The dark-skinned man behind the counter

sat on a stool beside a twenty-year-old computer. Glasses hung from a string around his neck over a Hawaiian shirt.

"Yeah, I'm looking for some information." She had a couple of folded twenty-dollar bills in her pocket just in case, but she first found the lawyer's photo from his website. She showed the guy the screen of her phone. "You know this man?"

His brows raised, and he didn't put his glasses on. "You expect me to hand out personal information?"

"I'm concerned for his safety."

"We've had no trouble, so I'm sure he's fine...*Officer*?"

Kenna shook her head. "Do I look like a cop?"

"I steer clear of the ones in this town. Though, occasionally we get staties in here. You undercover?"

"I don't have a badge." Anymore. "I just want to make sure my friend is okay."

He eased the glasses on his nose and squinted at the screen. "Ah."

"I heard he stays here if he had too many and can't drive home."

"No one usually checks on him the next day."

"Yesterday was a rough one." She had no idea if he, or anyone in town, had heard about the hostage situation at the courthouse. Maybe this was the one place news didn't travel. Because if you talked, there were consequences. "And he was injured. He could be having a medical emergency."

He shrugged. "I wouldn't know anything about that. We aren't friends. He's a guest."

"Which room?"

"I'm not giving you a key if that's what you're asking."

Kenna leaned her belt buckle against the counter. "Could you call his room and see if he's all right? That would be enough for me to know he's okay."

"Can't get him on his mobile phone?"

"He isn't answering."

The guy picked up the desk phone and dialed three numbers. He held the phone to his ear and listened. "Same with the phone in his room. Maybe he's sleeping and has earplugs in. A lot of people do that, you know."

She could peer between the curtains like she had at Parker's house. Then again, that might prove equally as fruitful.

"I'd like a key so I can let myself into his room and check he's all right." Kenna lifted her chin. "If he has earplugs in, he won't wake up if I knock on the door."

"He some kind of important person? I thought he was just a lawyer." The man squinted. "Maybe he has the information you want, and you'll beat it out of him."

Kenna studied the guy for a moment. "I can do it somewhere else, so I don't leave a mess on your carpet."

He tipped his head back and laughed. Kenna figured she'd made the right call and grinned.

She held up both her hands, palms facing him. "I really do just want to see if he's all right."

When she lowered her hands, he eyed her forearms. After the heat in Parker's law office, she'd rolled her sleeves up.

People reacted in their own ways to her scars. Kenna had given up trying to hide them from people she would never see again. Anyone with a browser could look her up and find out exactly what happened to her.

A shadow crossed his eyes, and she knew he had experienced an injury. Wherever life had taken him before he landed here, she could see in the way he shifted on the stool that he understood. She didn't need to connect with him that way.

"I only need the key card and a couple of minutes."

There was just something about the situation she couldn't

let go of. A man with a successful law practice hadn't shown up for work the day after a major case? It had to be suspicious, especially when it hadn't turned out the way the powers that be determined. Every avenue they'd tried yesterday had been foiled—by Kenna, mostly.

She needed to know if Jones was okay. Then she would know how much she should worry about her own safety.

With so many dead already when that church exploded, she didn't doubt more would lose their lives before she finally uncovered who had been behind it all.

Kenna would rather no one else died, but life didn't guarantee that. Not even if she followed all the rules people imposed on others and lived like a saint.

He clicked the mouse on his computer, then inserted a key card into a card reader. A second later it beeped and he removed the card, holding it out. "Room eighteen. I don't want no blood on my carpet."

"Not what I'm here for." She trailed to the door and outside, striding toward the row of motel rooms. Twin lights ran on the underside of the balcony above, providing an extra bit of light on this overcast day as she headed for the eighth door, almost at the far end. Painted dark green. Curtains slightly parted in the window.

Kenna paused. A bloody handprint on the glass on the inside gave her enough information.

She drew her weapon from the holster at the small of her back and used the key card.

Kenna twisted the handle and pushed the door open enough she could see inside without entering.

Quiet greeted her. The TV flashed images, the sound muted.

Parker Jones lay on the bed, blood across his chest that had nothing to do with the injury he'd sustained at the courthouse. He wore only underwear, his clothes discarded on the floor in rumpled heaps beside his shoes and socks.

After a second more of assessment, Kenna holstered the gun and flipped the back of her shirt over it.

Whoever had done this was long gone.

Chapter Eight

Between the time she called 911 to report the murder and the arrival of two marked police cars, Kenna had also called Candace and taken pictures of as much as she could see from the doorway without stepping a foot into the room.

She leaned back against the wall beside the open door as two men climbed out of their cars. The younger officer from the courthouse—the one who had run off to find the judge and make sure Rachel Sanchez was cleared—and the older captain.

"Kenna Banbury." The younger officer glanced at his superior and approached her, looking like he wanted to shake her hand. "We had a meeting about you this morning. The retired fed who takes down serial killers."

"Unfortunately for you." The captain sidled up to the two of them and stopped. "This isn't the work of a serial killer. We don't get that much excitement here in Hatchet."

The officer looked down at her hands. "You aren't wearing gloves." He glanced at his captain. "We should get her some gloves."

"I'm not investigating this murder." Kenna lifted her empty hands. "But I didn't catch your names."

The officer's expression brightened his pale face. "I'm Ethan Valette. This is Captain Marling."

"Right." Kenna nodded. "I remember that now." She gave the officer a polite smile. "It's nice to meet you, Ethan."

This kid was way over his head. If something was going on in Hatchet, he had no idea. And when it all came out, he would likely end up in the middle of a whole lot of nasty business.

She almost felt sorry for him.

"I'll get my evidence collection kit." Valette jogged to the trunk of his car.

Marling glanced at her from peering inside the room. "I don't know why he's moving so fast. The guy is dead."

She just stared at him.

"You feds never used gallows humor as a fallback in the middle of a gruesome situation?"

Kenna shrugged one shoulder.

"Did you go inside?" He stared down at her. She tried to take his measure, but this wasn't a man who would let slip what he really felt or thought in front of a junior officer or a woman he didn't know. Someone who might ruin everything he'd built. "Did you touch anything?"

"I've been out here the entire time."

Valette moved between them into the room. "Oh, geez." He dumped the duffel bag and blew out a breath.

"Don't leave your spit on anything," Marling said. "That's DNA evidence."

"You probably have to ship your evidence to Albuquerque." Kenna bent one leg and rested the bottom of her boot against the wall. "It takes what...six weeks to get test results? I figure you'll have solved it by then."

Marling said, "Evidence can confirm the suspect's identity. Otherwise we're just going on a hunch, which is lazy policing."

Valette called from inside the room, "Looks like he was stabbed at least seven times."

Kenna had counted eight when she zoomed in on her photo, but Valette was closer. She winced.

"You know what that feels like, don't you?" Marling motioned with his chin at her forearms. "Maybe enough you might have developed a thing for using a blade on other people."

"Are you insinuating I'm the one who killed this man?" She hadn't even stepped foot inside the room. "Considering how much blood he has on him, I'd be covered in it. If I was the one who'd killed him." She'd rather have quipped back at him about lazy policing, but he was testing her. Seeing how she would react to being pushed a little. Would she lose her cool? Could she be easily intimidated when someone brought up her trauma? He needed to find out.

His eyes flashed. "Sure of yourself, aren't you?"

"While you think you can get enough evidence to make a judgment in a couple of minutes."

Marling said, "Don't worry. I'll wait for the test results to come back."

Meanwhile, his colleague was in the hotel room doing all the work.

Kenna's phone buzzed in her pocket. It was a notification for movement outside her van. She tapped to pull up the live feed from her camera and spotted the woman in the pink shirt with the tiny dog on a leash—currently drinking from Cabot's outside water dish—peering into her passenger-side window.

Kenna saw movement in the tiny view she had of the window.

The woman jerked back and nearly tripped over the leash behind her legs. Kenna chuckled as the woman hurried away from the van where Cabot had suddenly appeared and startled her. Next time she left, she would put up the inside privacy screens. And a No Trespassing sign.

"You're watching a funny internet video at a murder scene?" Marling brushed past her into the room. "Guess you were a fed."

"Of course," Kenna called in after him. "Everything you've heard about feds is obviously true."

There wasn't so much animosity between federal agents and local police these days. Most cops had learned that it was better to cooperate with each other when you all had the same goal. Turf wars didn't help anyone.

She was surprised he chose the former federal agent angle instead of the fact she was a private investigator, not even licensed in this state.

Kenna watched them move around the room. She would rather have gone in and looked around. She would try to find a phone, or some other indication of what Parker Jones had been doing before he came in here—and after he entered room eighteen, prior to his death. Who he had been with, possibly.

That way she might be a step closer already to figuring out who took his life. Or why.

But if she'd gone in, she would have smudges of blood on the bottom of her shoes. Or anything else they might have used in order to pin this murder on her.

She glanced toward the office in time to see the front desk guy step out and close the door behind him. He headed over, slippers on his feet. Those glasses still hanging down at his chest.

When he was close enough to hear, she said, "I found him."

His brows drew together.

Kenna pointed over his shoulder. "You have cameras on the doors?"

He glanced back, then winced. "Just for show. They aren't plugged in. Just the battery for the LED at night so it looks like they're running."

She had already spotted the bar across the street. "You think Shelley's has an angle of your place that might show us something?"

Captain Marling stepped out of the hotel room, clipping her shoulder as he moved. "Ms. Banbury, you aren't working this case. You're barely a witness. Just the person who called it in and who is now hanging around interfering."

And if she pushed it, he would slap her in cuffs for hindering a police investigation. Given the look in his eyes, he wouldn't hesitate to take whatever she offered him as bait and use it to jam her up.

It would be easy enough to assume he was part of it. But like he'd said, that would be a lazy conclusion when she had no evidence. Maybe he was just a cop with a bad attitude.

The front desk guy leaned around her and looked in the room. "Merciful heavens." He reared back, turned around, and threw up on the hood of the captain's police car.

Kenna winced.

Marling spewed out an expletive and shoved the guy away from his car. "Get out of here." He shook his head at the mess.

Kenna left him to his problem and watched the younger cop for a moment. Valette seemed proficient enough, laying down evidence markers and taking pictures with the camera he held, letting it hang around his neck. He used tweezers to pick up something miniscule, dropped it in a beaker, and screwed on a lid.

"Do you have a medical examiner coming over to take care of Mr. Jones?" Kenna glanced at Marling, figuring the captain would have made some kind of arrangement.

"He'll be here after we do our thing." He rocked back on his heels. "It's standard procedure."

He thought she was going to challenge him? "Good," Kenna said.

"In fact, most of this is a formality. After all, we know who killed Parker."

Kenna blinked. "Already?"

From inside the room the Valette said, "The truth is, we've been keeping an eye on the lawyer because we were expecting this."

"Did you have anyone keeping an eye on him last night?" Kenna glanced between the two cops.

Marling frowned. "Get too close, and you infringe on the man's freedoms. We said we kept an eye out, not that we were babysitting him every second of every day."

"But you had enough reason to believe his life was in danger?" No one else had mentioned it. Rachel had been the one who thought she was supposed to be dead. Enough she left town with her mother in the early hours of the morning.

"Yeah," Valette said. "His name is Peter Conklin. He did ten years in prison for murder. Released two weeks ago."

Kenna glanced at Marling. "Did you have your eye on him, too?"

The corner of his mouth curled up. "Rather than asking me questions, how about you tell me how you came to be here. Why were you the one who found Jones?"

"Maybe because I was looking for him." Kenna stuck her

hands in her pockets. "He didn't show up for work this morning, and Candace was worried."

"So you just drove over here and found him?"

Kenna reiterated her steps, but not because she wanted to explain her every movement.

"What was the nature of your relationship?"

She frowned, as though she didn't understand a question she had asked witnesses many times. "You mean how we met in person for the first time yesterday in the courtroom, when I handed him the evidence that exonerated Rachel Sanchez?"

"Right." Marling nodded. "Where is she at this morning?"

Kenna shrugged. "Last I saw her was at her house. Since you all didn't incorrectly put her back in prison because of some kind of clerical error."

She wanted to add how it would have made his department look bad, which would reflect poorly on him. But now might not be the time to rub it in his face. Instead, she pulled out her phone and sent a text to Stairs asking for information for the man they'd mentioned. Someone who had done time for murder and was now back in town. Easy enough to pin a crime on him.

She continued, "What makes you guys think Conklin is the one who killed Mr. Jones?"

Marling said, "He vowed to get revenge after Jones screwed up his case the first time. He ended up getting the full ten years, and he's never forgotten it. The guy screamed up and down the courthouse that he wouldn't let Jones get away with his ineptitude."

Kenna lifted her brows. "Really? He said that. Wow. I guess he should have sought better counsel."

"Exactly."

"Captain!" Valette called from inside the room. "I found his phone."

Marling moved first, so he didn't notice that she almost followed him. She realized what she'd done on instinct and stayed outside. They spoke in low tones to each other in a way she couldn't hear. Though she did see them use Jones' thumb to unlock the phone.

A car squealed into the parking lot. The long Crown Victoria bumped the curb of a planter and parked haphazardly between two spaces, corner to corner at an angle across both. When the driver door opened, Kenna realized it was Candace.

The older woman's face was pale as she hurried over on pointy heels. "Where is he!" She screeched the words as she ran toward the hotel room. The curb caught under her shoe.

Kenna reached out with both hands and caught Candace before she fell. The added weight of another person on her forearms shot pain toward Kenna's elbows. She gritted her teeth while Candace righted her footing. "Don't go in there."

Marling stepped out. "She's right. You aren't going to go in there, Candace." He even closed the door behind him, leaving his colleague in there alone.

Candace batted her fists on his chest. "Let me in there." She cried around the words. "I need to see him."

Marling grasped her elbows. "You're going to stay out here."

"Let me see my baby."

Kenna winced. "That isn't a good idea right now."

Later, she would be called in to identify him. By then the medical examiner would have cleaned him up so that Candace didn't have to face what Parker had been through. Right now she would only see the horror of what he had suffered and that was the way she would remember him. The last thing she saw every night when she closed her eyes.

"You need to trust me on this and stay out here," Kenna said.

Marling moved toward the clean vehicle and partly walked, partly dragged the woman with him. "Come over here and have a seat, okay? You didn't need to come here."

Candace blinked watery eyes and spoke around gritted teeth. "I didn't need to sleep with you, either. It didn't do me any good now, did it? You didn't keep him safe, and you promised."

Marling stiffened. "You make it sound like I coerced you. We both know that's not what happened."

"Parker is dead." She shoved him away.

A thud sounded behind the hotel room door.

Kenna glanced at the closed door to room 18, next to the blood-stained window. Valette must've been having an issue with something in there, but it wasn't her jurisdiction to figure out what the problem was. Instead, she wondered how a man on his back on the bed dead from his injuries had managed to make it across the room to plant a bloody handprint on the window.

The killer should have wiped it off. No way could Jones have made that print, and the person who murdered him didn't realize. Jones wouldn't have pressed his hand against the window and then climbed all the way back on the bed himself—the killer must have laid him there. That, or the handprint belonged to the killer.

Whoever they were, they would have been covered in blood doing that.

She needed to know what time Jones had been murdered.

Marling said something low to Candace, then turned back to the door. He grabbed the handle and pushed, but the door didn't move. He knocked on the door. "Valette. Open this up."

He pushed against the handle, shut the door with his shoulder, and got nowhere. "Officer Valette!"

Kenna moved around him and looked in the window. She could barely see his legs, but from what she could see he was convulsing. "He's lying behind the door. You need to call for an ambulance."

Marling grabbed the radio on his belt.

Kenna retrieved a glass breaker from her car, strode back, and punched at the window.

The pane shattered inward and across the room.

Chapter Nine

"Two-six requesting ambulance. Officer injured." Marling paused.

Kenna kicked out glass at the bottom of the window. "Looks like a drug overdose."

"That's insane."

She shot the captain a look. "Maybe. You have naloxone in your car?"

His radio crackled. The ambulance was on its way.

Candace wrung her hands together. "What did they say?"

"It'll be a few minutes." Kenna glanced at Marling. "Naloxone?"

He sprinted toward his car.

Kenna swung her leg over the window ledge and hopped in. Her boots crunched glass, and she crouched beside Valette, in the throes of a seizure. She laid a hand gently on his chest.

"Do something!" Candace shouted.

Marling shifted her out of the way and climbed in. "Stay there. Watch for the ambulance and tell them where we are." He rushed over, the tiny nasal spray in one hand, and gave it to her.

Kenna removed the cap, inserted the end in Valette's nostril, and administered the dose.

"What happened?" Marling asked.

She shook her head. "He touched something? Or sniffed something, not knowing what it was?"

The seizure eased. Valette stirred and started to wake.

She patted his chest. "Listen to me, Ethan. Stay right where you are. No moving." She gave the order, then kept patting his shirt buttons. "Take it easy."

Kenna got up and walked over the glass again, looking for whatever might have affected the young man. The victim's keys and wallet sat beside the TV. Kenna spied something on the floor between the dresser and the table under the mirror. She shifted the chair out of the way and crouched. "I need tweezers. Or gloves."

"I got it." Marling crouched beside her and tugged the tiny baggie from the underside of the dresser. "He...what? Took a sniff and dropped it?"

Kenna frowned at the door. "And tried to get to the door, but fell when the effects hit him?"

"The ambulance is pulling in!" Candace began. Her last words were drowned out by the approaching siren.

Kenna said, "Can you drag him out of the way of the door?" She crossed to open it.

Valette lay on the floor, blinking at the ceiling. His skin pale. Marling tugged him closer to the bed so she could get the door open.

Two EMTs strode in, and the first one blanched at the sight of the victim lying on the bed. "The call said, 'Officer down.'"

Kenna moved out of everyone's way, which put her over by the dresser. She took a look at the far side of the bed because she hadn't been able to see there from her spot by the door before. Nothing on the carpet. His clothes lay scattered over the floor, suggesting they'd been discarded in motion.

She checked the bathroom but didn't see anything on the counter or in the sink. Nothing in the bath except a couple tiny bottles of generic shampoo and body wash. A couple of white towels were still folded on the rail.

The tiny trash can between the toilet and the cabinet that housed the sink had a tissue with a lipstick smudge on it.

"A woman was here." She strode out of the bathroom. "Evidence in the trash needs collecting, though I doubt we'll get DNA from lipstick." She wouldn't rule it out, but Marling should find the killer through investigation before the test results came back. Then he could confirm what he'd discovered.

"Right." Marling stood as the EMTs lifted Valette on a backboard and walked out the door with him. "Like I said, we already know who did this. Conklin has had a grudge since Jones lost his case."

"Is he aware the police intend to treat him with prejudice?"

Marling lifted his chin. "This is an active crime scene. You need to leave me to my job."

"While I go somewhere else and do mine?"

"If you had a PI license in this state, maybe. Though, the Hatchet police department could hire you as a consultant. Have you bring in Peter Conklin." He folded his arms. "Careful though. You might have to use extreme force."

"And why's that?"

"This is a different kind of place than you're used to." He paused. "Things happen here you might not like."

"Is that so."

Marling shrugged one shoulder. "Guess you're gonna find out. Not for nothin' though, you might want to be careful. If I find you operating as a PI here in town, I can arrest you for interfering in a police investigation and hindering prosecution."

"Unless I let you hire me to do your job?"

"We're down a man," he said. "No thanks to you."

And she was as useful as a rookie? "Because you were in a lover's quarrel with the victim's mother and didn't have your partner's back."

Kenna strode out, tapping her fingers against the side of her leg. She should take a moment to speak to Candace, but the look on her face… She'd lost her son.

Kenna's stomach roiled.

She knew what that felt like. She knew intimately just how deep the loss of a child cut. So she climbed in her car and drove to the RV park, where she pulled in the spot with her van so the two vehicles were nose to nose.

Two spaces away, the pink-shirted Dolly Parton hair lady sat at the picnic table by her chrome RV. The little dog sat in her lap while the woman tapped her nails on the keyboard of a laptop. Also pink. Kenna would've thought dyeing the dog's blond fur pink would round out the color scheme nicely.

The woman watched Kenna without even bothering to hide it.

If she had to live by this woman for a while, she might has well make things pleasant. They weren't going to be friends, but Kenna didn't always keep to herself. She could talk to someone. Spend time with them.

The last person she'd done that with had been a small-town sheriff who'd died a horrible death in a fire days after telling her he knew her father. But that didn't mean anything bad would happen to this woman if they did become acquainted.

Just being polite didn't mean anything would happen. It also didn't mean Kenna would care about her.

Kenna stared right back and lifted a hand to wave. "Good morning."

Statistically, this woman's life now had greater odds of ending tragically.

"It sure is." The woman lifted a tall glass of what looked like iced tea. Probably sweet. Maybe that was a stereotype. Kenna wasn't sure.

She disarmed the cameras and unlocked the door to the van. Everyone she cared about was far from here. Nothing would happen to them. It wouldn't make sense for them to be targets, bargaining chips used by a powerful organization.

"You shouldn't leave your dog alone for so long. It's not good for them." Her accent sounded like molasses, rich and thick.

Is that why you were peering in my window? Kenna didn't answer her. She pushed the door wide. "Cabot." She scanned the interior as the dog padded along the linoleum floor of the van toward her and stopped at the door. Kenna shifted to hold the door open with her hip and rubbed Cabot's chin with both hands. "Hi, dog."

The animal across the way started to yap.

Kenna grinned at Cabot. "How was your nap?"

Cabot leaned back and stretched, then shook her body. She let out a whine.

"Walk?"

Cabot turned her head to sniff the leash hanging from the hook inside the door.

"Good idea. Let's stretch those legs."

Kenna should do a workout of her own, but her workout buddy hadn't called since before Christmas. During her visit to Salt Lake City, Ryson and Valentina had spilled that he was undercover. She figured he'd call when he was done with that if he wanted to talk to her. But the fact Stairs had told her before the holidays that he was investigating the church bombing—Kenna's case—meant the whole silence didn't sit well.

Where was Jax?

Regardless, she didn't need an FBI special agent to keep her in shape. Things were going fine without Jax waking her up in the morning with a video call so she could contort her body into different positions, which he probably only did to amuse himself.

Whatever he was working on, he was surely fine.

If he became a more significant part of her life, then she'd only have to worry about him as well. How would that be better? Ryson and Valentina, and their baby, could already be targets because of Kenna. She'd ensured no one knew of her visit to their house for Christmas but continuing to connect with them only put them on the radar of anyone watching Kenna.

The last thing she wanted was for them to get hurt because of her. It was bad enough that she needed Stairs on occasion to make her life easier. He wanted to be her research assistant—or whatever he called himself. Stairs had been in California with her when that church exploded, killing so many cops and feds. He was on a mission to uncover the identity of everyone tied to the organization that used that scrollwork C on their website.

She still had no idea what it was.

In Bishopsville they'd been videoing captive young women. A steady supply of victims giving them media they could sell over and over on the dark web.

The video Rachel had shown her featured her husband's body cam footage. Now on her laptop, Kenna needed to take a screen clip of the killer's face and find out who he was.

And who had paid him to blow up a church full of first responders.

Did they also film deaths? It could be that whoever had killed Parker Jones had taken a video of the murder, but that was a reach. Nothing about the scene indicated a camera had been used—unless it was on Jones' phone and shared from there, or the killer used their cell. Or a second person had been there.

She could ask Marling about the phone later.

Cabot hopped down the step with only a slight hitch. Kenna locked up and held the leash with one hand. As they walked, she thumbed in the address Stairns had sent for Peter Conklin. He lived with his mother about a mile from the RV park. She could at least give the guy a heads-up that the police had their eye on him—something he probably already knew.

Plenty of people might've had reason to kill Parker Jones.

It didn't necessarily have to be the one person Marling thought it was. He'd been way too quick to jump to that conclusion, especially when it was clear a woman had been in the room. It was at least worth talking to her before they decided she didn't have anything relevant to offer.

Someone had to have seen Jones in the bar last night, or whoever he'd been with. She could swing by there and ask the bartender who'd been working about the murder victim. See if that generated a lead Marling could follow.

If it had been a hit, someone had done the work to make it look like a tryst gone wrong.

A food truck had been parked in front of the local church, a white building with a tall steeple. The line at the truck was primarily families, or moms with little kids who pointed at Cabot. Kenna wandered by on the opposite side of the street, spying a couple of nuns handing out jackets and sweaters to people. A few bicycles leaned against the back of a pickup. Inside the truck, a priest handed boxes out the open window. Food maybe. Or other supplies.

Kenna found the neighborhood Peter Conklin had listed as his residence when he got out of prison. Where he lived with his mother. According to the map on the wooden sign, 16B was two rows over and four trailers down.

She found Conklin outside, holding a two-by-four. He wore jeans and what looked like second-hand boots—or he'd owned them since before he went to prison. The guy was young enough he had to have been a teen tried as an adult when he was locked up.

It looked like he was repairing the front porch. An open can of soda sat on an overturned ten-gallon bucket beside a portable stereo playing a country radio station. He had sawdust on his T-shirt and a prison tattoo on the outside of his left arm.

Conklin set the wood down and looked at Cabot first. Dark-blond hair shaved close to his head, and a beard on the lower half of his face. "What happened to you, puppy?"

"Car accident."

He eyed her, and she spotted those ten years in prison in his immaculate ability to let absolutely nothing show in his expression. The guy was blank. Cold eyes. Flat mouth. "Looks like she's doing all right now."

Kenna nodded.

"You new here?"

"Just passing through town."

"And you happened to come into this trailer park, straight to my place?"

"I was looking for you."

His expression flickered, but still gave away nothing.

"Any chance you were over by Shelley's bar last night?"

He took a sip of the soda. "No alcohol. It's a condition of my parole. Same as associating with known felons or owning a weapon of any kind. I'm still waiting for an answer on how they feel about steak knives."

"Good idea, asking."

His brows shifted. "Who got stabbed?"

"Funny you should ask."

Peter Conklin took two long strides closer to her. Cabot moved to lean against Kenna's leg, fast enough Kenna rocked a fraction with the impact.

Conklin stopped. "Why are you here?"

"Maybe you have nothing to worry about, because you weren't anywhere near it."

"I wasn't."

"Then they can hardly pin it on you." She eyed the front door. "Unless there's a bundle of bloody clothes in your trailer. Or the murder weapon."

He lifted his chin. "And if I did kill whoever it is that's dead?"

"You'd probably know the name of the victim."

"I figure they'd argue that wouldn't stop me." He took another swig of the soda.

Rachel Sanchez had been convinced she was in danger. Almost convicted of a crime she didn't commit. "You want the real killer to get away with murder? You're locked up again, and they can turn around and take another innocent life."

"I forget...I'm supposed to care about other people?"

Kenna bit the inside of her lip. "Generally speaking, it's a sign you're not a sociopath."

He shrugged a shoulder. "Maybe you should go inside my trailer. See if I didn't kill my mother, too. Of course, I'd have to get rid of you as well. Since you figured it out." A tiny glint of humor flashed in his eyes.

Kenna scoffed. "Marling sent me here on a wild goose chase, didn't he?" This had to have been a setup. A way to get her out from under his feet while he did...what? "Did you even do ten years for murder?"

Stairs would have told her if the information didn't check out. So she knew before he nodded. "Got out a couple of weeks ago." He lifted the soda. "Hey, maybe you could go check with my parole officer, make sure I'm legit. While you're there, get me a pass to go visit my sister." The first sign of life entered his expression. "She's in medical school in Albuquerque. Full ride."

"Do you want to see her graduate?" She paused. "Or do you want to get railroaded back into prison?"

His jaw flexed. "I do what's necessary."

Chapter Ten

"Parker Jones was found this morning, stabbed to death in a motel room," Kenna told Conklin. She then watched his face, observing his reaction to this news.

Cabot leaned against her leg, offering her solidarity where she would have otherwise chosen to be alone. She might be determined not to allow anyone she knew to be killed because of her. The organization would eventually discover she hadn't given up trying to find them. Kenna was the only one who would protect Cabot. Something that gave her a low-grade constant worry in the pit of her stomach.

If anything happened to her dog, heads would absolutely roll.

A muscle on Conklin's jaw flexed, just a tiny movement.

"Like I said, do you want to be railroaded back into prison?" she asked. This guy might have been sent down just the way someone had tried with Rachel Sanchez. Then again, he also might have committed the crime he was convicted of. Until she looked at the case, there was no way to know other than simply taking his word for it. Most people's word meant nothing these days.

"I didn't kill Jones."

And yet Marling had been convinced he was the exact person to speak with. "And the fact he lost your case and got you sent to prison?"

"I'm supposed to want revenge for that?" Conklin shook his head. "I'm just trying to live my life."

Kenna had been lied to during an interview more times than she'd heard the truth. As far she could tell, the truth was what she could prove. She settled on saying, "For your sake, I hope so."

She left him to his porch repairs and headed out with Cabot, walking back the way they had come but on the opposite side of the street. Her mind spun with the mystery of who might have killed Parker Jones.

Most likely, Captain Marling had simply wanted her out of the way of his duties as a police officer in this town. So he'd fed her a line about a possible suspect and insisted that person was the killer. Even going so far as to insinuate they could hire her to find him for them. More likely, it had been nothing but a ploy to get her out of their way.

With one of their officers now in the hospital, she figured they genuinely might need her help. But one lawyer's murder wasn't what she was here in town for. She only needed information on Rachel Sanchez and her husband—so she could figure out why his body cam footage had been online, with that same symbol in the corner. And find the identity of the man who killed Matteo Sanchez—and a church full of people in California.

As far as Kenna knew, the only people in town connected with that elite organization were Rachel and her deceased husband.

It might not have anything to do with anyone else here.

Or this entire town could be entangled with whoever

these people were. Like the town in Northern California she'd been at just a few months ago. A place held in the grip of powerful people who would do anything to continue making money. Keeping people under their thumb, victimizing them, and leaving brokenness behind.

The food truck she had passed on the way to Conklin's house had worked through its line. Now only the priest hung around in front of the vehicle, wiping down the table with a wet washcloth. She spotted one of the nuns inside the food truck and figured that was where the others were as well.

The priest straightened as she approached.

Kenna lifted her chin.

"Good afternoon." He gave her a polite smile, the dark skin of his face wrinkling beside his eyes. "I believe there is a dog biscuit in the truck if your friend would like one."

Cabot wasn't hiding her limp as well as she usually did.

Kenna figured she might have walked too fast from Conklin's house, so deep in thought. "I think she'd like that."

"And an empanada for you?" The priest's eyes glinted.

"Sure. Thanks."

"Have a seat. I'll be right back."

Kenna blinked, then headed for the picnic table. Cabot lay down beside her. She'd been so deep in thought, not looking for connection. But here it was, at a time when she was purposely avoiding getting to know people, or letting them in. She should probably pick up Cabot and keep going. Not put a target on yet another person.

The priest headed back over, flour on the sleeves of his gray shirt. "I make these myself. Beef and potato."

Kenna took the empanada, and the priest crouched in front of Cabot. He held out the dog biscuit, then stood when Cabot eagerly accepted it. The dog crunched the biscuit into pieces on the ground in front of her and dug in.

"She was injured recently?"

Kenna swallowed the first bite of warm pastry. "In a car accident. The third passenger didn't survive." Because the person who had run them off the road killed him and left her and Cabot for dead.

The priest settled on the opposite side of the picnic table. He interlaced his fingers in front of him on the table. "The things we go through affect all of us in different ways." He glanced down at Cabot. "She doesn't seem wary of strangers or cars. A lot of people can suffer emotional or mental aftereffects of something like that."

Kenna nodded. "Are you from Hatchet?"

He shook his head. "We travel around, serving those who need it. Here and up north on the reservation. Providing food and clothing to those with lack." His voice held a trace of an accent that made her wonder if he often spoke a language other than English. "We are based across the border."

Kenna frowned over her empanada. "You live in Mexico, and you come to America to serve people in need?"

"Poverty doesn't abide by national boundaries." He shrugged one shoulder. "The needy are everywhere."

"That's certainly been my experience as well."

"In Mexico, we know who and what we are. America seems to want to look the other way when it's more comfortable to forget there are people living in its borders whose houses have no electricity. People that struggle to provide for their families even when times are good." He shrugged a shoulder. "Often they are the happiest people you will meet. Because they know how to be content." He motioned to Cabot, resting on the ground.

Kenna smiled. "She's a happy dog. It helps."

The priest eyed her as though she had said something significant. But then he asked, "Are you new in Hatchet?"

"I live in my camper van. I travel all over for work." She did occasionally meet people who knew who she was. More so lately, considering the catastrophe in Bishopsville had made national news. More than a dozen police officers and federal agents had been killed. She would have said murdered if the FBI hadn't deemed it an accident. A gas leak, according to the report.

Kenna didn't believe one word of it. She thought that someone in the FBI had caved to a deadly organization and failed to investigate, declaring a gas leak the cause. The evidence had been destroyed along with all those lives. Everyone seemed to think the case was closed.

Except her.

"Have you ever been to my country?"

Kenna nodded. "Once, years ago, I spent some time in Mexico City with my dad." She smiled. "I remember how warm it was. The hotel had a pool, and I drank a lot of soda. Because my dad told me the café took American dollars."

The priest chuckled. "You should visit us again."

"Yes, I should." Kenna crumpled the wrapper the empanada had been in. "That was excellent. Thank you for lunch."

"It helps," he said. "An empty stomach is like an ache in the soul."

"There is something comforting about being satisfied."

"Food, and friendships. These are the things that keep away the darkness. Because they allow a little bit of light into our lives."

Kenna glanced down at Cabot. "Yes, they do."

"A reflection of the true light."

Sitting in the daylight with her dog and a welcoming face who had given her a gift meant she could almost believe there was no darkness. And yet, it lived in the corners of her life the way it always had. For a while, she had been swallowed up by it. The things she'd been through in the last few months allowed her to press away the worst of her experiences, move them back to where they should be—almost out of reach.

"But the fear always remains unless we do the work to cast it from our lives."

"With food?" She meant the question as a way to lighten the conversation, but it hung in the air between them.

"There are few things that cast out fear." He reached a hand to pat the cross on a chain around his neck. "You either welcome the darkness, or you walk in the light and let it fill you. The way I try to do with more meals, coats in the winter, and the Bible to a weary soul."

"And you think that's what I am? A weary soul?"

"I'll let you in on a little secret." His eyes wrinkled again. "We are all weary souls. Like the desert, desperately in need of rain. We forget, we get busy, or we try to believe we are capable of strengthening ourselves. Or finding peace or hope on our own. Eventually we learn that we cannot do these things alone."

"Unfortunately, alone is all I have." Kenna shifted and stood. "But it's okay. It's actually for the best." She wasn't about to explain to him that lives were in danger. She would end up the subject of his prayers, and then who knew what would happen.

Kenna needed the situation within her control as much as was possible.

"Thank you for the meal." She clicked her tongue, and Cabot came with her.

They walked more slowly to the campsite while Kenna's head spun with everything. She needed to focus on the investigation at hand, and whatever was going on in Hatchet. What she didn't need was to be distracted by existential thoughts from a priest who made admittedly fantastic empanadas, but also insisted on immediately taking their conversation somewhere deep.

That was his job. But Kenna needed things to be lighter, or she would wind up with her emotions tangled up in this town. It happened in the last place she was in, and she lost Sheriff Joe Don Hunter just days later. The guy who had known her dad. Now she'd never know what he would have told her about her father and their friendship.

What he might have known about her mother.

She'd started to open up—or at least think about it—and then he was burned horrifically in a fire and lost that fight for his life. All she had left were a case file that made no sense, and questions that would never be answered. Something she wasn't prepared to allow to happen with this case.

The priest might insist on connection, and figuring out how to eliminate fear. Kenna had lived with the fear for so long she wasn't sure she could get rid of it. Let alone if she wanted to. It had fueled her, and given her the strength to face down the darkness knowing she could do that in spite of it.

The fear had been there so long. What would it even feel like to lose it?

Kenna and Cabot entered the RV park. They passed a family riding bikes in the other direction, a dad with a toddler seat on the back of his bicycle. The mom behind them. Behind her were two boys and a smaller girl, the bigger boy behind her keeping an eye out. Each of them waved to her. The little girl said hi to the doggy. A slice of life with no fear—at least on the surface.

She wasn't sure she wanted to go as far as to wish for a family. Even in the distant future.

She'd had a shot and lost it. Did people even get second chances like that?

There was a case to solve. It wasn't like Kenna had a whole lot of time to sit around and think about it. Usually she moved on and got to work on the next case. That left less time for her mind to spin around and drag her down into the past and everything she'd been through. Or wish for a way to accept the truth the preachers on the radio spoke about.

To grasp that peace.

Kenna walked far enough she could see her van now. The shiny RV next door, and empty space between them, had the shades pulled over the front windows. The tiny dog belonging to the blonde who lived there ran around outside, racing in the grass where it turned and yapped at something. A ball skittered into view. The dog pounced.

The blonde looked over as Kenna approached her van. She set a hand on the hip of her skinny jeans. "There is a note for y'all under your wiper."

Kenna glanced over her shoulder. Sure enough a folded paper had been tucked on her windshield, the corner flapping in the breeze. She needed to check her notifications on the cameras to find out if she'd missed something, but also didn't need this woman seeing her do so.

Kenna retrieved the note and glanced at the woman. "Thanks."

The yappy dog ripped the rubber ball in two.

"Did you see who left it?"

The woman shook her head. "Nah, it was there when I brought Tilly out to potty this morning." Her Southern drawl gave Kenna the impression of several Southern states, but the outfit was pure Nashville. Though, given the hair to toe impression, maybe this woman was just a fan of country music. She gasped and pranced over the grass in her silver sandals. "Tilly, you're a bad girl." She crouched and took the ball while the dog growled. "No. Give it to me."

The dog spat rubber on the grass.

Cabot walked to the end of the leash. Kenna unclipped it and let her dog inside.

"Hon, your dog is antisocial."

Or she's a good judge of character. That had been true more than once before. "She's just tired."

Silver sandals clacked over the drive between them toward Kenna. The woman stuck her hand out. "Dixie Cabrera."

She shook the hand. "Kenna Banbury."

"Yeah, hon. I know." Dixie giggled. A few years older than Kenna, and at least four inches shorter. A powerhouse packed in a pint-size package. "So what does the note say?"

Kenna blinked. "It was nice to meet you."

"Come on, darlin'. I'm curious."

Kenna pulled the door open.

"Sue me for being interested. You're practically a celebrity."

Kenna turned back. "No, I'm—"

The other woman was far too close. Kenna's instinct had her stumbling back. Dixie ripped the note from her fingers.

Kenna planted her foot and stepped toward the woman. She tried to grab it, but Dixie spun. "One late in. One to eight in. One and eight in." She looked at Kenna. "What does that mean?"

"Is there more?" Kenna gritted her teeth.

"The corner of the note has a smudge. Looks like blood."

Kenna snatched the note and looked for herself.

One late in. One to eight in. One and eight in. Who is next?

Chapter Eleven

"It is blood, right?"

Kenna looked up from the note. "I think so. You didn't see who put it there?"

Dixie shook her head, but the halo of hair didn't move out of place. Kenna needed to get inside and check her phone notifications for the security system. Then she would know definitively if anyone had been snooping around her van. Leaving notes on her windshield.

"Who are you, Dixie Cabrera?" Kenna frowned. "Is that your given name?"

The other woman's eyes glinted. "You didn't run my license plate yet?"

"Assume I didn't."

"Who was late?" Dixie motioned to the paper.

Kenna looked down at the words and read again. *One to eight.* One and eight was eighteen, the motel room number. And eight might be the number of times Parker Jones had been stabbed. She needed to make sure Dixie wasn't the one who had killed him. "Where were you last night?"

Dixie cocked her hip. "What time?"

It was entirely possible Kenna had video footage of her leaving her RV at some point. Though, probably not. Considering she didn't actively take video of other people without their knowledge—given everything she'd seen, that was a point of honor now.

Kenna said, "How about eight last night to eight this morning for starters."

"You ain't a cop," Dixie said. "And even if you was, I still wouldn't submit to questioning."

"And you're not some hillbilly on vacation." Why had Dixie Cabrera come to this place right now? It seemed entirely too coincidental she was next to Kenna in the RV park. "Come here often?"

Dixie laughed. "You wouldn't believe me if I told you what I was. And that's the whole point. But I'm not here for work, so don't worry." She motioned with a flick of her fingers to the note. "Let me know if you need help with that." Dixie turned and walked away toward her shiny RV. "Tilly," she called out to her dog, "get your tushie over here."

The yappy dog spat out another chunk of rubber ball and scurried after her.

Kenna turned to the door of her van and headed inside. She kept it a little warmer than outside, but not by much. Rather than be so warm, she was peeling off her outer layers. Kenna preferred to wrap up in a blanket—usually one her father had used as a winter quilt.

For her entire childhood they had been on the road. Living a nomadic lifestyle, while he took contracts for cold cases and murders no one could solve. Her father, famous investigator Malcolm Banbury, kept journals of the cases he had worked. Then while Kenna attended two years of high school—the longest they had ever lived in one place up until that point—he turned those journals into bestselling fictionalized accounts of his life as an investigator. The books had then been turned into movies, further embellishing the stories for entertainment.

A killer had never approached her dad's trailer—their home. Let alone left a note on the windshield.

Kenna grabbed a plastic storage bag and slipped the note inside, sealing up the top. Not exactly an evidence bag, and she was preventing this note from being admissible in court. But there was absolutely no way she was going to turn it over to the police.

At least not the police in Hatchet.

Cabot sat in the hallway, her front legs straight and her nose in the air. Tail wagging side to side on the floor so that her whole body swayed with the movement.

Kenna chuckled at the normalcy of it. "I'll get you some dinner."

She pulled out her phone and took a picture of the note, then sent it to Stairs. It wouldn't take him long to call her back, and in the meantime she opened a can of wet dog food and mixed it with the dry stuff Cabot liked. She set the bowl down in front of her dog.

Cabot didn't move, her tail still wagging side to side.

Kenna straightened. She waited a second, then said, "Yes."

Cabot dove for the food and dug in. Kenna patted the side of her neck and said, "Good dog," just as the phone started to ring.

She propped the phone up against the backsplash and swiped to answer the incoming video call. The organization Kenna was investigating already knew of her association with Stairs. The app he used to call her was untraceable, which made it difficult to track their communication. But it wouldn't be impossible.

His gruff face filled the screen. "Explain to me what that is." He lifted a blue mug and took a sip.

"A guy was killed last night. Stabbed eight times in room eighteen of the local motel."

"And who was late?"

Kenna got a can of sparkling water from the fridge and came back. "Me? The note has blood on it, so maybe he left it after he killed Jones."

"You know for sure it was a man?"

She shrugged. "Maybe the blonde across the way held him down and murdered him. Though, she would probably have drawn hearts over the i's on the note."

"She's a bounty hunter."

Kenna choked on the sip of the water. "Dixie Cabrera?" She wiped her bottom lip on the back of her hand. "She's a *what* now?"

Stairns grinned. "I got a look at her social media accounts. I can see how you might be fooled."

"I don't think she's harmless. So you don't need to worry about that."

"Good. Given a couple of the people she's brought in, she's not the kind of woman you want to underestimate." He took another sip from his blue mug. "Then again, neither are you."

Cabot finished licking at the empty bowl and headed for the bedroom.

Kenna looked at the note. The last thing she would have pegged Dixie Cabrera as would be a bounty hunter. Then again, some folks likely would never guess that Kenna was the kind of woman who hunted serial killers. "It's the last question I'm most worried about."

He nodded. "Update on everything else?"

In years past, that would have meant she should now give

him an update on all of her work. Back in the days when she was a special agent for the FBI, and he had been her assistant Special Agent in Charge. These days with him working for her, it meant he would give her the information he had for her. Not that she paid him any money to do it. This was his retirement hobby, and his wife still worked her very successful therapy practice online.

Kenna said, "Go ahead."

"Rachel and Mrs. Sanchez showed up this afternoon. They rested for a while, had something to eat, and then I took them to the airport. They're on a plane, free and clear."

At some point, when they knew without doubt the communication was secure, he might tell her where Rachel and her mother-in-law had gone to escape Hatchet. Then again, Kenna didn't need to know their precise location even after they got where they were going.

"Thanks." She nodded. "I appreciate your help with that."

"I owe you more, and you know it."

Kenna didn't want to get into their history, and how much he felt like he should pay her back for what he'd done. "What else?"

"The town of Hatchet, New Mexico, is all legit on paper. Taxes, law enforcement. All the social services and city council. Health and Human Services. All of it is aboveboard in case anyone should happen on the idea of checking."

Up until that last part, Kenna had been convinced. "But..."

"Exactly." Stairns cleared his throat. "It's too clean."

"Given human nature, and the way anybody with power has the tendency to be corrupt, or at least just selfish, you're actually telling me not one single person in this town takes an extra dollar for themselves? No one has ever received a bad review for not doing precisely what they said they would?"

He shook his head. "Apparently it's the most perfect town in the world."

"If that was true, they would have no crime," Kenna said.

"I'm surprised they didn't clean it up before you got there."

"Then it's a good job I showed up first."

"Yes, it is." Stairns saluted her with his blue mug. "Next up is Peter Conklin, who you asked me to check into."

"Let me guess. Everything was absolutely perfect with his conviction." She expected him to say it was a little too perfect.

"I took a look at the court case and read all the transcripts and the police statements. There are definitely some discrepancies in what was noted down. His lawyer could easily have cast doubt on the police report, and everything that prosecution brought against him."

"Was it the same prosecutor who pushed for charges against Rachel Sanchez?" Kenna asked.

Stairns glanced to the side, and she heard the click of keyboard keys. "Looks like...yes. Davis Burnum."

"The same two guys go head-to-head in yet another case, and the defendant might be innocent in both cases? What does that tell you about Conklin's case?"

"I'm guessing you spoke with him," Stairns said. "Does this mean you think he didn't do it?"

"I have no idea." Kenna tapped her thumb against the counter. A bird landed on the table outside, between her and the next RV spot. She didn't care what Dixie Cabrera the bounty hunter was doing right now—or why she was here. There were far bigger things to deal with.

If she'd been here to capture Kenna, paid by the organization Kenna was trying to uncover, it was doubtful she'd have introduced herself.

Stairns said, "I could see if I can get into contact with some of his cellmates. Find out if he talked at all while he was in there."

"Sounds good." But the chance was they wouldn't get the necessary information in time to prevent something bad from happening again. "The note says, 'Who will be next?'"

"Just make sure it's not you."

She glanced over at her former boss, seeing the earnestness in his eyes did more to repair the fracture between them than using the internet to find information for her ever would. He had been there when the church exploded, full of cops and feds and all the evidence. The two of them had hit the ground side by side.

She could still hear the screams of one of the victims trapped, on fire. Half concussed and on the far side of the building, there hadn't been anything she could do. By the time the fire department showed up and gained access, all the victims were dead.

"I need to send you something. A video. It's got to be secure."

Stairns frowned. "Log in like I showed you. Upload the file."

Kenna used the VPN he'd set up and transferred the video straight from the phone to the server they shared. Then she got up and poured coffee while he watched it.

Only moments later, he grunted. "That guy."

Kenna sat again. "The one I saw leave the church before it exploded."

"The same guy who killed Matteo Sanchez." Stairns frowned. "And he works for these people. The letter was probably added afterword when the video was uploaded for whoever needed proof that Officer Sanchez was dead."

"I need to find him." But she also had a killer here in Hatchet to find—because the alternative was to leave the murder investigation to the police. And who would trust them with anything?

"I'll get in contact with someone who might be able to find this online, figure out what websites they are using."

"Be careful," she said.

"You're the one out there, unprotected."

Kenna rolled her eyes and ended the call. He might be right, but it wasn't as though she hadn't proven she could defend herself. That would be the case, up until the day she faced someone and wasn't able to protect herself. That would be the end of her story. What happened between now and then consisted of putting one foot in front of the other. Because what else could she do?

As much as she might be interested to think on what the priest had said. Letting in the light, with friendship. Contentment and satisfaction. All she could think was that those things would wind up slowing her down. She'd lose her edge if she didn't have to fight every second of living.

Instead of peace, what she needed was information. If she could solve Parker Jones' murder, it would lead her to the person who had written that note, someone who needed to be stopped before they hurt anyone else.

As simple as that.

She pulled up the Utah True Crime website and checked where she'd left the draft detailing Rachel's case, and the sham investigation. The draft was gone.

What did that mean?

She started a new draft and wrote one thing.

> The person who blew up the church also killed Matteo Sanchez.

She saved the draft and closed her computer, then found the number for the local police department. When the call connected, she asked to speak to Captain Marling.

"Who should I say is calling?"

Kenna smiled to herself. "Dixie Cabrera."

"One moment."

Kenna turned and leaned against the counter while the call connected.

Marling came on, already talking. "I told you earlier I have nothing for you."

"Is this a romance thing, like with Candace Jones?" Kenna asked.

Silence filled the line. Then, "You."

"For the record, that was payback for sending me on a wild goose chase to Peter Conklin's house."

"Did you really think we were going to work together?"

Kenna said, "I don't do partnerships."

"What do you want?" Marling asked.

She heard a note in his voice. "I'd like to know who the last person was to talk to Parker Jones. After all, I'm good for some more legwork if you want me to go ask more questions around town."

"Now's not a good time."

"It's a good time for the Hatchet Police Department to provide Parker Jones' next of kin with answers as to what happened to him." He had to know it was important to keep working. To fight for the truth. Unless they'd gotten to him.

Marling sighed. "I just found out Officer Valette died. He couldn't fight the respiratory damage from the drug. He coded in the ambulance, they revived him. But the doctors said the machines were all that was keeping him alive."

Kenna bit her lip. "So he was next."

The note indicated someone else would die. She had no idea who they intended, and maybe the killer didn't plan for the cop to be a casualty. But he was. The loss of that life meant something to Kenna even if it meant nothing to the killer.

"Gotta go." She ended the call and hung her head, picturing the young cop in her mind.

Someone help me!

The scream came, shrill enough Kenna winced even now just at the memory of that female agent from the California Bureau of Investigation. Dying.

Please!

She lay down on her bed and squeezed her eyes shut as too many disparate memories flooded her mind.

Chapter Twelve

Six years ago

"Please."

Kenna lifted her head from the cold tile of the bank floor to see the woman who'd spoken. Twenty or so people were surrounded by three masked gunmen. She saw the one farthest away, over by the door, and amended her thought. Two guys. One woman.

"I'm gonna be late for work," she muttered.

The gunman brought his gun up and smacked a hostage on the head.

Kenna winced, and an older lady cried out, a mixture of sympathy and the fear it would happen to her as well.

"No one moves!" He swung the gun around in a wide arc. "You move, you get shot!"

Two minutes, and they'd made some decent progress. One of the gunmen had dragged the bank manager into the back. The other two were on crowd control, though the guy didn't rely on the woman to do much more than stand by the door and periodically check the street—on the lookout for approaching cops.

Kenna was done pretending to be just another helpless victim. She shifted and sat up, her legs tucked in. Knees up made it look like she'd curled in trying to protect herself. In reality, she could stand in a second, drawing her weapon as she rose.

This was taking too long.

As she moved, another person did the same. He had dark features, a little older than her. Built in a stocky way, like a football player but maybe five eight. Though, that was a guess since they were both sitting. He eyed the gunmen—and woman—in the same assessing way she clocked him, and Kenna knew what that meant.

The guy was a cop.

His dark gaze came to her. Slight nod.

Okay, then.

Kenna wasn't going to wait for police to respond. Or wait for someone to get shot.

The cop shifted.

She eyed him, trying to find a gun on his person. She'd left hers in the car and didn't even have a backup weapon.

That won't happen again.

She'd been so consumed with thoughts about her new partner, Bradley Pacer. The governor's son of all things. He didn't seem like he was super uptight, throwing around that political connection, but he was definitely too good-looking for his own good.

The cop's expression shifted to a question.

She figured all that irritation over Bradley was displayed on her face. Kenna shook her head.

He moved his hand, catching her attention before she

could look away. She gave him a second and read the message in his hand signals.

She'd done some interagency training with local PD, but she'd never met this guy, who wanted her to distract the gunman so he could take him down. Then she was supposed to go for the second masked figure by the door. Because he considered the woman a lesser threat?

Kenna studied their assailants.

"I said, 'Don't move!'" The guy spun, thankfully moving too fast scanning the hostages on the floor to focus on one person. "We get what we came for, and we leave."

But people in here were getting antsy—not just the ones with guns.

"Let's go with that money!"

Kenna needed a plan to resolve this without an innocent being hurt. She inhaled as loudly as possible and pretended she was hyperventilating. "I can't be late for work." She glanced at the clock, like the fact it was 8:47 was significant. "My boss will kill me. I need to call him."

"One minute!" the assailant in the vault called back.

The woman in there with him screamed.

Kenna gritted her teeth. They'd already been told to put their cell phones on the floor in the center of the room, where the gunman kicked them all at the front doors. If anyone came in fast, they'd either make a ruckus or fall. "I have to call him. I'll get fired."

His attention came to her. Behind him, the female drew close. Away from the front doors. Entirely too interested in his interaction with Kenna.

"He gets real mad." She gasped. "You don't know."

The guy stood over her, a hood up and mask over his face. She could see the top half, enough to clock him easily as Caucasian. Flat blue eyes with no life in them. Pupils contracted to pinpricks. "Unless you want to get shot, you shut your mou—"

A heavy figure slammed into him. Kenna scrambled up as they hit the floor. The female had come close enough Kenna only had to take two steps, and she was on the woman.

Gun first. Then the assailant.

She hammered her arm down on the woman's forearm as it came around. The assailant screamed and dropped the gun. Kenna grabbed the arm, stepped between the woman's feet, and slammed her to the ground. She flipped the woman to her front and glanced back to check how the cop was doing.

He called out, "Third guy."

Right. They had another to take care of.

Before she could reply to him, the third gunman pushed the teller out of the hallway from the vault.

Kenna twisted back around and grabbed the gun the woman had been holding. She swung it over and took a split-second inhale. "FBI! Gun down—"

Intention registered on his face.

Kenna took aim and squeezed the trigger. The man fell back in a spray of blood. The teller screamed.

The front doors to the bank slammed open, and a team of police officers ran in. Kenna sat back on her heels, the gun loose in her grip.

Someone yelled, "Put it down!"

The guy said, "She's good."

"She's not one of us."

Kenna set the gun on the ground. "I'm FBI."

She got nudged aside so they could slap cuffs on the subdued pair. The guy who'd helped her came over, his hand out. She clasped his wrist, and he helped her up. "Thanks."

"Excuse me. Out of my way." A suited man with a fresh

cut on his blond hair wove between SWAT officers through the door. "Kenna? You okay?"

"I'm good, Special Agent Pacer." She realized she still held the cop's wrist and let go.

Bradley flicked his head back, got the hair off his forehead, and looked around. "What happened?"

"A bank robbery happened, Special Agent Pacer."

The cop's lips twitched.

She held her hand out. "Kenna Banbury." He already knew she was an FBI Special Agent by now.

"Sergeant Javier Ryson." His handshake was firm, and brief. "Thanks for your help. Pretty sure you saved my life and that teller's, Special Agent Banbury."

"She did?" Bradley looked at her. "You did?"

"Pretty sure it was a team effort," she said. "And it's Kenna."

"Ryson. Nice to meet you." He shifted and drew out a phone. "Gotta take this."

Kenna nodded.

He turned away. "Hey, honey." He paused. "Yeah, babe. I'm good." He did something at the bank counter, then returned to hand her a business card with his info.

"Thanks."

"I'll let you know if I need a wingman for the next bank robbery."

Kenna grinned. "You do that."

Chapter Thirteen

present day

Kenna pushed away the blankets and sat up, sweat on her hairline. Not the worst dream she'd ever had, but a strange one, to be sure. And it looked like she'd slept all afternoon and then all night in one go. Cabot lay on the floor by the tiny bathroom. The dog had her eyes open, watching Kenna.

"I'm fine." She patted the dog's head on the way past her.

The dream made her want to call Ryson and Valentina. Check in and make sure they were all right, even though she had seen them a few weeks ago at Christmas. Even though doing so could put them on the radar of some dangerous people.

She glanced over at the kitchen, where she could see the file. A thick stack of pages that included the FBI's final report. *Gas leak.* She'd included a photograph of each of the victims who died in that "accident."

She wrote a note at the top.

> ID the suspect and work up a complete profile.

If she'd talked to Jax at Christmas, she would have asked him to look quietly into the agent who ran that investigation. She knew he was following up, but he needed to find out how and when the agent had been contacted and leaned on to close the case like it was nothing. As opposed to what it was—a coverup.

Maybe it was better that she hadn't had the chance, because she could've been putting him in danger as well.

Kenna got the coffee going and checked her phone. A call from a private number and a voicemail. Nothing from the Hatchet Police Department about Valette, Jones, or anything else. Nothing from Stairs.

She waited for the pot to start its trickle and played the voicemail. She drank a glass of water while the coffee brewed. Otherwise she wouldn't drink water at all. She'd just down a whole pot of coffee in one morning while she worked the case —or any case.

Kenna lifted the glass to her lips.

"It's me," the voicemail began.

She choked on the first sip. *Jax*. Not that she believed thinking about him had drawn him to contact her, but she'd felt like he was far away a second ago. Now he was close.

"Listen, I'm sorry I've been absent the past few months. This case got hairy, but it's settling down and it should be done soon." He paused. "Maybe after the reports are all filed, I can take a couple days off. Come see you...wherever you are. If you want."

The message ended.

Kenna played it again and felt the words hydrate her soul

like the water hydrated the rest of her. Not that she thought her broken heart would ever heal. But she could use friendship, especially with people she trusted the way she trusted the Rysons—and Jax. None of them had betrayed her the way Stairs did. She would always hold back with him, no matter how long they worked together.

Jax had been there for her. They had separate lives, but she had come to rely on his friendship before he went dark on this undercover thing.

With the life she lived, close friendships weren't people she spent time with daily. Even if, for a while there, she and Jax had spoken every day. They were people she sought out and connected with over the years.

Cabot nudged her leg.

Kenna grabbed a sweater, took the dog outside for a minute, and fed her. She fried herself an egg and reheated potatoes from a couple of days ago. Her toaster had quit before Christmas, and she hadn't bothered to replace it. She made do with what she had. Inviting in new things—or new people—just opened her up for more hurt. Even if it was only a toaster.

What was the point?

An hour later Kenna drove her car across town and strode into the county courthouse. A couple of days ago she'd done the same thing, but left her van with the car hooked up in the parking lot. This time she had no dog and no van—just her car. She left her weapon behind and brought what wouldn't set off a metal detector. Basic personal protection didn't go out the window just because a place had security.

It hadn't helped when that guy, March, burst into the courtroom and took them all hostage.

She headed for the security guard.

He said, "Appointment?"

She shook her head. "I'm looking for the prosecutor, Davis Burnum."

"He's in. Not sure how available though. Check with his assistant."

"Thanks." Kenna tossed her keys and phone into a bin and removed her shoes. "Any word on that kid, the inmate—March, I think his name is—who took a courtroom hostage. Do you know if he lived?"

The guard's gaze lifted. "Not sure. Either he's still in hospital, or they transferred him back to the prison already."

If the inmate had died, this guy hadn't heard about it. She could ask Marling next. Or she could follow up on the note and the murder investigation and see what came of that.

Either way, Hatchet was going to get a taste of Kenna Banbury.

Whether they were under the thumb of a powerful organization or not, someone would answer for whatever was going on here. The killer had drawn her into this by leaving that note on her van. Whoever it was, they wanted her to play. It would be a game. A way to toy with her.

How she responded was up to her.

"Have a good one," she said.

The security guard nodded and turned to the person behind her, an older guy with Native American heritage.

Kenna followed the signs to the second-floor offices and headed the direction it told her Davis Burnum worked. His assistant had the phone to her ear. Dark hair, and glasses perched on her nose. She looked to be approaching fifty and the name plate on her desk read "Laney Wallace."

She eyed Kenna and spoke into the phone. "I can send it

now for the judge. Thank you." She hung up, and her brows rose as she scanned Kenna. "Can I help you?"

"I'd like a moment with Mr. Burnum. I'm Kenna Banbury."

"Ah." She pushed her chair back. "He mentioned you might come by."

"I don't know how he could have known that, since we spoke only once and I wasn't asked to come here." She'd figured showing up might throw him off guard and he'd say something he hadn't intended to. That looked like it might not be the case.

Laney opened the door to his office but didn't enter. "That private investigator is here."

Hmm. He didn't like that she messed up his case? She'd chalked it up to the plan being foiled. The fact she'd kept them from wrongly convicting Rachel Sanchez. Maybe it was simply that he'd believed she was guilty and Kenna had proved otherwise. Possibly even made him look like a fool.

"Come in." His voice echoed to her.

Kenna moved past Laney into the room.

"Coffee, please, Laney."

Kenna glanced from him back to the assistant. "None for me, thanks."

"Have a seat." Davis Burnum sat behind his desk, waving a hand at the two chairs in front of it. The office was small, but someone had spent money on the furnishings. An air-conditioning unit in the window ran on low, and the edges of the open curtains fluttered. "What can I do for you, Ms. Banbury?"

"So you've looked into me, since the case was dismissed." She leaned back in the chair. "You've done your homework on who I am." The police department had. The lawyer was dead. Likely everyone was on edge.

"I assume you're here on a case, is that right?"

"Sure, that would be the case against Rachel Sanchez. An innocent woman your office put on trial." She needed him on the defensive.

"That was unfortunate business, but we got it sorted out."

"Waste of everyone's time, and county resources." She paused. "How much does it cost to hold a trial?"

He stared at her a moment. Then his head snapped back, and he burst out laughing. His entire face changed. "How much does it cost?" He kept laughing. "That's a good one." Burnum shoved his chair back and stood. "Sure you don't want that coffee?"

The door opened.

Burnum met his assistant with her tray and took it.

"I brought an extra mug, just in case." Her cheeks pinked.

"Thank you, Laney."

The assistant watched him walk back to the desk where he set the tray, then shut the door.

Kenna turned back in time to see him pour the milk. He first lifted the tiny pitcher high, so the stream of milk stretched up at least seven inches, then set it down with a flourish. "Here." He held out the mug to her.

Kenna figured the chance he was trying to poison her was low. "Fine. Thanks."

"I make my own vanilla sugar. Real vanilla beans."

She paused before taking a sip.

"Try it."

Kenna sipped. "Wow. That is good. Just a touch of sweetness."

Burnum settled on the edge of his desk in front of her. He drank from his mug.

"What do you know about Matteo Sanchez?" she asked.

"Who's that?"

She wasn't entirely surprised, even if he was feigning confusion. "New Mexico State Police. He was killed on duty, the assailant never found. The case hasn't just gone unsolved. It's been completely buried."

"And after Rachel Sanchez, you believe the police in this town make it a habit of subverting the law for their own aims?"

"You tell me."

Burnum eyed her. He was nice-looking, but she got the impression he allowed his looks to play in his favor.

She wasn't looking to make a connection here, or anywhere else, regardless of this guy's intentions. It could be he only wanted to cover up the truth, and being charming was his intention. Or it was completely harmless.

Burnum said, "Do you think there's a police department in this country that doesn't have at least some level of corruption in it?"

"Yes. I think there is one. Hopefully more." Kenna needed to believe that. Otherwise, what was the point, if everything was already past hope? That meant evil had already won. "You either welcome the darkness or walk in the light and let it fill you."

"Is that a quote or something?" He shifted, and his arms flexed in the sleeves of his crisp white shirt.

"Just something someone said to me recently." Kenna didn't want to talk about it with this guy. Not before she figured out for herself how she felt about it. "I don't know what it means yet."

"Sounds weird." He let out a breathy chuckle. "I prefer to deal in reality. Guilt or innocence."

"And who gets to decide that?"

"Maybe you should've gone to talk to the judge instead of

me." A look flashed across his expression. As though she might've considered him less than. He didn't like that.

"I didn't. I came here first." She would visit the judge next.

"To interview me, like a suspect?"

"I figured you know what's going on in this town better than most." But did he call the shots, or was he a guy who had to follow orders whether he liked it or not? "Seems to me like more than one person might've been railroaded. Like Matteo Sanchez."

"You said his killer was never found?"

"A state police officer killed on duty. Where is his body cam footage? How is it that state police haven't ID'd the guy?"

"I can look into that."

She wouldn't hold her breath waiting for a result. Not when she had a killer who'd left her a note possibly the start of more to come. She had plenty to do—and she figured she could find the guy faster anyway. She had his photo. "Any ideas who might have wanted to kill Parker Jones?"

"If the police have any leads, I'm unaware of it. They usually only loop me in when the case is built, and the suspect is in custody."

She nodded, honestly surprised he hadn't tried to pass the murder off as the work of Peter Conklin like Marling had done. But she was beginning to be more certain that it'd only been a way to get her out of the investigation. Send her on a domestic goose chase to a guy who had nothing to do with it so he could work the case without her interference.

As if she wanted to work a murder when the police in this town should be perfectly capable of doing so. Kenna didn't need to subvert them. Unless it pertained to *her* case. Though, since officially she didn't have a job here in town, she didn't really have a case. Yet. The Rachel Sanchez job was done.

Kenna probably wouldn't get paid now that the lawyer who hired her had been murdered.

"Of course." Kenna nodded, switching tactics. She sniffed. "I saw him, you know? In his underwear on the bed, blood everywhere." She glanced at the shelves under the window, a couple of books artfully displayed with a tiny pot that looked indigenous in its design.

"As many bodies as you've seen, it still hits you?"

"How could it not?" She shook her head. "A life ended violently." She could elaborate, see if he'd react to graphic description of the murder, but she wasn't trying to break him. "The person who did that needs to be held accountable."

"The person who did it is a disturbed individual."

"Then I'm in the right place. Because catching people like that is what I do."

He broke their stare down, set his cup on the tray. Rounded the desk. "I should get back to work."

"Of course. I didn't come here to monopolize your time."

"Perhaps you should question the police here next." He settled in his high-backed leather chair. "See if they have answers as to why that officer's death was never investigated."

"And find out who the last person to speak with Parker Jones was." That meant a visit to the bar, probably tonight when it opened. "I appreciate your time."

He picked up a gold pen.

A good-looking guy with a position. He used his God-given genetics to make inroads where his work did not. Add that to his career choice, and he made for a charismatic package.

"If there is corruption in this town, would you want to know about it?"

"Might not be as simple as that." He held his pen over the page in front of him, and she couldn't help thinking of the note. It was too late to finagle a way to take a look at his handwriting. She should've thought of that.

Her phone started to ring in her pocket.

He continued, "Life isn't often black-and-white. Where would the fun in that be?" He grinned. The charming prosecutor had returned. "If you want to meet up for a drink later, just call my assistant. We can continue to go over the case."

Kenna simply nodded, then headed out. Past Laney, who was on the phone again. She gave the other woman a wave and got a frown in reply.

She took the stairs instead of the elevator, opting to go for a side exit rather than the front door. On the way down the concrete steps, she tugged out her phone. She had a missed call from an unknown number.

Kenna held the phone to her side, checked both ways out in the alley, and headed for the street. It rang again in her hand.

"Kenna Banbury."

"Who is next?"

Her steps faltered. The voice had been augmented by computer, so that it sounded neither male nor female, or even human. Kenna stopped right where she was, about to cross the street. She backed up and had to sidestep for an older couple. "Who is this?"

"A young mother with poor judgment. Or an old mother with poor judgment. Who will be next?" The caller paused. "You decide."

The line went dead.

Kenna stared at the street, then up at the windows of city hall behind her. A truck blew past and whipped her hair. Someone walked by, on the phone.

Kenna listened to them for a second, then dismissed it.

A mother.

She didn't know about the poor judgment part, but the only mother she'd heard mentioned recently was Peter Conklin's.

Kenna jogged to her car and headed for his house, tapping her finger on the steering wheel as she drove. No way to trace the call or figure out who the voice belonged to. She didn't have those kinds of resources, and there wasn't time to resurrect them.

She pulled up outside the trailer. No sign of Conklin. But that didn't necessarily mean he was up to something.

Kenna drew her gun and approached the front door. The killer could be inside. Or she might have chosen wrong and he wasn't here at all, but was across town.

Ending a life.

Nausea roiled in her stomach. She made a fist and rapped on the door hard, like she used to in the days when she'd served warrants as an FBI agent. "Open up!"

This was life or death.

Chapter Fourteen

The door opened on its own, as if it hadn't been quite latched. "Mrs. Conklin! Peter! Anyone here?"

The lighting inside the trailer was dimmer than outside. A person accustomed to keeping curtains closed to block out the heat of the sun in those long hot months. Outside was bright but not hot. Kenna didn't smell anything that would indicate a deceased person inside.

She glanced around, noting the van parked on one side of the trailer she hadn't seen before. Looked like top of the line. Someone was here.

Kenna stepped inside.

"Honey, I ain't never been Mrs. Conklin a day in my life." The voice moved through the room as she spoke, pushing what looked like a brand-new wheelchair. Cigarette between two fingers. Stringy hair, and an oversized theme park T-shirt.

"Excuse me." Kenna said it like an apology. "I was under the impression something bad might've happened to you." She looked around. "Is your son here?"

"What's it to—oh, I know who you are." She pointed with the cigarette. "The nosy PI."

"Right." She didn't offer her hand to shake, but said, "I'm Kenna. What's your name?"

"Deb."

"It's nice to meet you."

"'Cause I'm alive?" Deb lifted her bushy salt-and-pepper brows. "Sorry to disappoint you."

"Being alive isn't a bad thing."

"Depends on your perspective." She shrugged one shoulder.

"Is your son here?"

"Haven't seen him today," Deb said. "Is that all you want?"

"Have you seen anyone hanging around today, maybe lurking outside your windows?" She might have scared the caller off by coming straight here. Kenna hoped she had, but wishful thinking had never sat well with her when faced with reality.

She dealt in cold, hard facts.

Life or death. Truth or a lie.

"If I did, you think I'm gonna call the police?" Deb took a drag from her cigarette.

"Did you?"

She snorted, blowing out a mouthful of smoke.

"The police in town haven't done you many favors, I'm guessing."

"I do all right, no thanks to them." Deb looked around. Maybe she didn't like others' opinions of her situation, and she was used to having to turn the other cheek.

From what Kenna could see, the TV was new. The recliner wasn't faded or frayed like the carpet—and the dingy kitchen counters that looked to be 1970s linoleum. The refrigerator was probably original to the trailer. Parts of Deb's life had received a serious upgrade, and parts were still original, including her health.

Not everything could be upgraded.

"You're just like every other person with a gun, or a badge," Deb said. "No different than the rest."

Kenna slid her pistol into the holster on her belt and flicked her shirt over it.

"Stay away from my son."

"That's not what this is," Kenna said. "I'm interested in what's happening in this town, that's all."

Deb chuckled, a crackly laugh that originated deep in her lungs. "Last person that came around was a reporter looking into Peter's case. Found some inconsistencies, or some such. Decided there was a story in it somewhere."

"What was the reporter's name?"

Deb's lips twitched. "Ryan Bartlett."

She didn't bother to ask where she could find him. It seemed like no one in this town told the whole truth if they could help it. She wasn't going to trust *anyone's* word. But she did have a question. "Do you think Peter is the kind of man who might've stabbed his lawyer to death and let him bleed out in a hotel room?"

Deb paled.

It was probably a little much, but Kenna needed a reaction, not the brush-off. She might've effectively been taking the power back that she'd lost when whoever that was called to taunt her, and it wasn't Deb's fault she got caught up in it.

Kenna sighed. "I'm—"

Deb cut off what would've been an apology. "You have no idea the kind of man my son is."

"I'm thinking no one does. Except you." Maybe not even her. After all, Conklin had been in prison for ten years.

Outside on the street, police sirens blared.

"You should go chase them," Deb said. "See if anything good is happenin'."

More than one car passed.

"Go on." Deb motioned with the cigarette, now barely a stub. "Get."

Kenna didn't bother thanking her for her time. "Lock your doors. Do you have a gun?"

"I'll be gettin' it now. So no more barging in. You won't like how we treat strangers 'round here."

Kenna closed the front door behind her and headed for her car at a jog. An ambulance passed as she climbed in, so she followed at a legal speed, keeping an eye on the vehicle ahead of her.

All the while, thoughts spun through her head.

She should call Stairs, but she was already driving, and making a phone call could mean she lost sight of that ambulance.

Her watch did the same function, but she'd have to navigate the menu there as well. In the end all she would be doing was reiterating her thoughts.

And why take up his time with that, when she could leave him to whatever research assistant tasks he was doing today? She didn't need to rely on him just to process what she was thinking about this case, even if he didn't mind.

The ambulance turned ahead of her.

Kenna followed, heading onto a residential street with houses slightly bigger than the street before. Spaced farther apart.

The ambulance pulled over behind two police cars blocking the road, their lights still flashing. It could be a traffic accident, but Kenna's gut wasn't so sure. Like the question of how someone left a note on her van windshield without the cameras picking it up.

They couldn't have known there was a blind spot between the headlights, though it could be surmised if a person studied the camera placement and knew anything about how they worked that it would be possible to avoid them by the hood. She only wanted to know if someone was sneaking around, coming to her door. She didn't need to know who was at the front.

Or, she hadn't. Until now.

Kenna slid the holster off her belt and stuffed it in the glove box, then headed for Marling and a couple of uniformed officers entering the house.

The EMTs hung out on the curb with a yellow backboard and their gear.

Marling stuck his head out the door and said to the first responders, "Too late." He spotted her, and she noticed dark circles around his eyes. "Get in here."

Two police officers stepped outside. "It's clear."

"No one comes in unless I admit them. And call the ME." Marling took a breath and yelled, "Kenna!"

She didn't move. "Yes?"

Marling made a face. "Could you come here, please?"

Kenna passed the EMTs and headed up the front walk. She reached the front door but didn't go inside. "What's going on here?"

He shifted his mouth, but she didn't care much if he didn't like that he had to contend with her.

There had been no need for the EMTs. "Who is it?" Kenna motioned into the house.

Marling stepped back to admit her. "Judge Williams."

Kenna's stomach clenched. She stayed where she was on the front step. "Was she a mother?"

Marling frowned. "She has a son. He lives in Atlanta."

"A mother who makes poor judgments."

"What was that?"

Kenna shook her head. "It's nothing you can use to give you a lead. It's nothing that will help you prevent a future crime."

"But it's also not...nothing?"

She moved to go inside.

He held out a hand to stop her. "You should tell me what it is anyway. Since it's pertinent to this case."

Kenna folded her arms. "I got a call on my phone from a restricted number. They used a voice modulator of some kind."

"And said that thing about mothers?"

"A young one, or an older one. Both made poor judgments." Kenna swallowed. "It was a taunt, because I couldn't possibly know which one would be 'next.'"

Marling tugged on her shoulder and shut the front door. "You need to be careful what you say, and who you say it to. Got it?"

"Is that a threat?" She wanted to find the judge's body but had to get past this gatekeeper first. "Because I would be very careful about making threats to me."

"As if I'm the problem you need to deal with. I've got my own thing going on, okay? What do I care if the killer wants your attention? I'll be busy solving the case."

"Pinning it on someone who didn't do it?" Kenna paused. "Does anyone in town actually believe what the people in charge tell them?"

His jaw flexed.

"So who were they talking about...a young mother who makes poor judgments?"

"How am I supposed to know?" He lifted a hand, then lowered it back to its side. "I've got a murder scene to process."

"What happened to her?" She moved to look.

Marling moved with her. "Hold up."

"You need help. And I want to find out who is doing this, so I stop being taunted."

"Does that mean you're signing on as a consultant for the Hatchet PD?"

She wanted to say, *No way. Not ever.* "What did your chief say when you floated the idea?"

"You don't want to know. But it amounted to, 'Not on your life.'"

"There you go." She shrugged, then leaned around the entryway wall in case she could see the body from here.

"So I guess you're my newest confidential informant."

Kenna snorted and turned back to him. "You don't want to know what I charge for that."

"No, I figure I don't. You'll be extorting me whether I like it or not."

Kenna's snort morphed into a full smile. "Finally, he gets it."

She needed to figure out who killed Jones and now the judge. Then she would be putting a stop to those calls. The last thing she needed was more bodies on her conscience. It was why she did what she did, but lately that seemed to have gone out the window.

Instead of taking cases no one wanted and finding people no one could find.

Kenna seemed to have been dragged into investigations she had a stake in and had no choice about whether or not to work it.

"I don't want people to die," she said. "But I'm also not part of this."

"Seems like you should find the killer. Tell him that."

"Might be a her."

Marling snorted. "Don't get all women's lib on me. It's usually a man."

As if that was the point here. "The 90s called, they have a job offer for a cop like you." Kenna rolled her eyes. "Can I see the body?"

"This way." He turned. "You get a minute, and you can leave unless of course my CI happens to provide relevant information for this case." He stopped at a door in the back hall and waved her in.

Kenna didn't want him behind her where she couldn't see what he was up to. It wasn't about trust, but the fact she couldn't protect herself from what she couldn't see coming. "You first."

He frowned but entered the room and stepped to the side. After she came in, he said, "Stabbed in her bed, just like Jones."

Kenna assessed the scene, starting with the walls and moving her gaze in. Or she would miss something in the wider room because she was too focused on the body itself. "Came in through the sliding door?" She waved at it, closed but unlocked by the look of the latch.

"Could be." He glanced at it then back at her.

Jewelry on the dresser. Clothes hung up in the closet because there were none on the carpet or the armchair in the corner, and there were none on the floor beside the wicker basket in the corner that was likely a dirty clothes hamper. No shoes. No dust.

The judge still wore her pajamas, light-blue silk. There were tears in the shirt where the killer had plunged the knife in.

"He knelt over her," Kenna said.

Marling tugged a pair of gloves from his pocket and pulled

them on. He moved to the patio door and slid it open an inch. "Because...?"

"Two indentations on either side of her hips." Kenna walked over to the opposite side of the bed, away from the patio. Judge Williams had on a fitness tracker, probably for sleep tracking if she'd been wearing it overnight. "Flip her hand over."

He came around and turned the judge's hand. "Watch is broken."

"Tap the button on the side."

The watch flashed on, and the time displayed on the screen even though it was cracked. Marling read, "Five sixteen."

"She was killed early this morning. Hours before I got that phone call." Kenna backed up and turned for the door. It wasn't a foolproof lead, but it was something. "He called me, knowing she was already dead."

"I'll have the officers canvas. One of the judge's neighbors might have doorbell footage of the killer leaving or entering around that time," Marling said. "Good eye on the watch."

She didn't bother correcting him that it was a fitness tracker. "So we could have another victim somewhere. Assuming the taunt about young and old was real."

"I guess you should figure it out, considering I've got work to do here." She'd processed scenes before. He'd be here for hours working this, making sure all the evidence was correctly collected so there was as little chance as possible this would be thrown out of court on a technicality.

Kenna nodded. "Let me know if you find anything else that might be a lead."

"Where are you going?"

"To find the second victim." She headed down the hall to the front door. "If there is one."

"How can you possibly know who it is?" His boots pounded the floor behind her.

"I know she's not here. So it raises the chance I find her if I'm *not* here." Kenna didn't have much more than that, but she had some places to start. She wanted to be out in the daylight. Under the sun.

Marling's mouth shifted, and a look crossed his face.

He'd been withholding information. "What haven't you told me?"

"Okay, fine." He leaned over and pushed the door shut.

"I'm leaving." Kenna wasn't obligated to stick around. In fact, it was better if she wasn't at a crime scene.

"In a sec." He sighed. "Jones' phone had a number on it. A woman, a hooker. I was planning on finding her today. We think she was the last person to talk to him before he got killed."

Kenna shifted her weight, ready to go. "Does she have kids?"

Chapter Fifteen

Two steps from the woman's front door, Kenna heard, "Who are you?"

She spun and found a teen boy behind her. Running shoes, workout shorts, and a T-shirt, over which he wore a light-gray hoodie. He had a backpack slung over his shoulder. Hair fell over his forehead, partially covering his eyes.

Kenna said, "You live here?"

"What's it to ya?"

Some kids had street smarts, and some lived in a safety bubble. This kid had seen more than most people would in a lifetime.

"I'm Kenna Banbury. I'm a private investigator. I believe your mom might be in danger." She didn't want him to see something traumatic, but she needed to get in there. "Do you have a key?"

He studied her for a second, then brushed past her. "It's not locked."

"Whoa." She didn't touch him but held her hand up in front of him. "This could be bad. Can I go in first?"

"You think she's dead?" His fingers curled around the door handle.

"It's possible." Two people already were.

He shoved the door open and stepped in. "Mo-o-m!" His voice cracked for a second, like a little kid's. The boy he'd been years ago who didn't know the worst the world could show him. "Mom!"

Kenna unholstered her gun, just in case, then held it low so it could stay out of sight.

The kid went one way, so she went the other. Through the living area to the kitchen, where she saw a foot first. She rushed to the woman's side. Pajamas. Blood. A choppy inhale that rattled like blood in the lungs.

Kenna crouched and saw her chest move. "Justine?" She rolled the woman to her back and tugged the nightdress down to cover the woman. "Kid! In here!" She heard his running shoes thunder down the hall. "Get some towels, and washcloths. Anything."

He stopped in the doorway and blanched.

Kenna stood and got in front of his face. "What's your name?"

"A-Austin." He swallowed.

"Towels. Washcloths, Austin. She's alive. This is good." Kenna squeezed his shoulder. "Now go."

He turned and raced down the hall.

Kenna pulled out her phone and called 911, asking for an ambulance at her location.

Austin landed on his knees on the other side of his mom. "This isn't like normal."

She set the phone aside and grabbed what he held in his hands, wondering what he meant by that but having no time to ask. Two towels and two washcloths. She grabbed his hand, put a washcloth in it, and pressed it to the front of his mom's thigh, where a long slice bled in a steady stream. "Put pressure on. Like, press hard. Okay?"

He nodded.

Kenna took a towel and wiped Justine's clavicle. "Okay, let's see what we've got." The wound kept bleeding. She pressed a washcloth to it and used her other hand to feel for Justine's pulse at her neck.

Faint, but steady.

"You're hanging in there." She spoke to the woman but checked elsewhere for cuts and other defensive wounds. *You didn't let him kill you. You faced the monster and fought back.*

Kenna turned her wrist. Justine had a tattoo on the inside of her forearm. The letter C, written in a medieval font. Kenna's stomach tightened.

"What happened to her?"

Kenna blinked and looked away from the tattoo to the distraught teen boy.

"You know." Austin's implication was clear.

"A guy was murdered a couple of days ago. A lawyer."

"Everyone knows about Parker Jones."

But did this kid know his mom was possibly the last person to see him alive—except for his killer. "Did you hear about Judge Williams? It happened this morning?"

He shook his head.

"I think whoever killed her also tried to kill your mom," Kenna said. "But I can't be certain they also killed Parker Jones."

He pressed his lips together.

"Austin, look at her arms." Kenna lifted Justine's hand. "These are defensive wounds. She fought him, she fought for her life. And she won."

Austin gave her a short nod. The barest of acknowledgements.

"Paramedics!"

"Back here!" Kenna called out.

The two who'd been at the judge's house strode in with their stuff, and a backboard.

"She's bleeding pretty badly. Pulse is low, but steady." Kenna shifted when the EMT took the washcloth. She levered back on her heels and stood. "Austin, come with me. Let them see to your mom."

He hesitated.

Kenna put her hand on his shoulder and guided him back. "They'll take care of her." The EMTs were already bandaging the wounds and getting her ready for transport.

"What do I do?" Austin asked.

"Pack her a bag with a change of clothes," Kenna replied. "Anything she might want while she's in the hospital. Okay? I'll drive you there."

He trailed away down the hall, on a mission now. The paramedics lifted Justine on the backboard and headed for the front door.

Ten minutes later, she unlocked her car and Austin tossed the duffel on the back seat. They climbed in, and he told her what the medical center was called. Kenna put it in her GPS.

"You really came over to try and save her?" he asked.

Kenna turned onto the main road and glanced over for a second. "I'm glad she's alive. I'm so glad." She blew out a breath, acknowledging the relief she felt. The surprise. The gratitude. It meant something to her that this time the victim had survived. But that didn't matter since Kenna had nothing to do with it. Justine had fought and saved herself.

"Me, too." He tugged at the hem of his shorts. "Lot of

people in town wouldn't care. They'd probably be glad she was dead."

"But she's your mom."

He nodded.

There were questions Kenna could ask, but that would amount to an interrogation. Or at least asking questions that would help her case. She figured the kid didn't need that. "It was good you came home from school early. You helped, and that might've saved her life."

"You'd have saved her. You didn't need me."

"But she needed you." Kenna glanced over.

She pulled into the medical center parking lot and found the ambulance on one side. She parked by the front doors and they headed in. "They aren't going to let me see her. You're family, though."

His mouth shifted.

Kenna stopped in the middle of the lobby. "What is it?"

"They'll call CPS and remove me from the home 'cause she can't take care of me."

She turned to him, her back to the front desk. "Have they done it before?"

He nodded, that same short movement from before.

"There might not be much I can do about it, but I'll absolutely try." Kenna squeezed his shoulder. "How old are you?"

"Sixteen."

"Good. That's good. You're old enough we might be able to argue you're capable of taking care of yourself for a few days while she's here."

"You think they'll listen to you?"

"I think it's worth a try."

He stared at her. "Okay."

She didn't ask what kind of situation he was put in previously when he'd been removed from his mom's house. She couldn't make any assumptions about his home life or the state of foster care in this town. The same way she couldn't assume the killer's identity or motives until she could prove it with evidence that dispelled doubt.

He went to the desk, and she checked her phone—and sent Stairns a message with an update—before he came back. "She's been admitted. They want that paperwork you had me get, so I need to do that. We can wait, and they'll call us when she's awake."

Kenna nodded. "Okay."

"You're just gonna stick around."

"I don't have anywhere else I need to be right now." She pulled up the cameras and showed him. "If my dog is okay, I'm free to be here."

His face lit. "Is it a he or she?"

"She. Her name is Cabot." She pronounced it the French way, *Cab-oh*. "It means mutt."

Austin grinned. "It's bussin'."

Kenna smiled. "Let's figure out that paperwork so we're ready when your mom is awake."

He'd want to see her, and Kenna had plenty of questions for his mom. Like the reason behind why she had that letter tattooed on her. A letter that, as far as Kenna could tell, stood for a secret organization that victimized people for money. Because they could.

Austin focused on the pen and his clipboard.

Kenna's phone rang. She recognized the number on the screen and winced but answered it. "Captain Marling, how nice to speak to you."

Austin looked over, recognizing who she was talking to.

Kenna made a face that set his worries at ease and continued, "Because yours was dead and mine is alive?"

"I wasn't going to put it that way, but that's your prerogative," Marling said.

"I thought you were busy processing the scene." She'd left him at the judge's house.

"And now I've got another one to do. Thanks to you."

"Not unless you get the homeowner's permission to enter the residence." She wasn't going to let cops with an agenda walk around in Justine's house, looking at whatever they wanted. "And since Ms. Greene is in the hospital, you can send someone here to ask her son for that permission."

Austin made a face and whispered, "That's why you had me lock up the house?"

Kenna mouthed the word, *Exactly*. "They'll let you know if you have permission to collect evidence from their house, Captain."

"So it's gonna be like this?"

"That's your prerogative." She repeated his words back to him. "Listen, I've gotta go. Things to do." She ended the call.

"Did you just hang up on a cop?"

Kenna shrugged one shoulder. "I didn't lie. I do have things to do."

"You're leaving?"

"Nope." Kenna leaned back in the chair and crossed one leg over the other.

Austin finished up the paperwork, and a staff member came over to tell him that his mom had been treated and was awake.

Kenna stood up, shoulder to shoulder with the teen. "Is she being admitted?"

"The doctor is about done treating her injuries. We're also giving her medicine to ensure she doesn't get an infection, but she's resting."

Kenna squeezed Austin's shoulder.

The staffer said, "She's a little drowsy, but you can go sit with her."

Austin turned to her. "Come with me?"

Kenna nodded. They followed the staffer, were directed to a nurse, and then led down a side hallway of treatment rooms. His mom lay in the hospital bed, her eyes closed. Gown and blankets. Bandages on her arm, and her collar above the gown. Dark circles around her eyes.

She shifted and blinked her eyes open, probably hearing their approach.

Austin moved to the side of the bed while Kenna hung back at the door. "Hey." He lifted his mom's hand gently. "Mom?"

A smile drifted over her face. "They gave me something for the pain." She blinked, her expression glassy. "I'm a little foggy, but it should wear off soon. I'm not staying here." Her legs moved restlessly under the covers. Some of the words got lost, but Kenna heard, "Can't stay."

Austin glanced at Kenna.

She nodded. "We'll get her home as soon as she can go. I'm not going to let anything happen to her."

Kenna would also clean up a bit at the house. What was important was that Justine was alive. Austin didn't need to be traumatized any more than he already was for the sake of some tiny thing.

Marling was just going to have to figure this out based on the scenes at the motel and the judge's house. Kenna would make sure justice was done regardless of whether the police officially worked Justine's attack as a case. In a small town like Hatchet, with two murders, Justine's attack would likely end up being a low priority.

But not for Kenna.

Finding someone still alive rejuvenated Kenna, gave her

energy and not a little bit of hope. Enough she took a moment for herself to watch Austin pull up a chair and sit beside his mom, just so she could fully absorb what had happened versus the reality of what could have so easily been the outcome.

A killer had targeted Justine, and there was no way it was coincidental. She knew something—and given that tattoo, she could be connected in more ways than just being the last one to see Parker Jones.

Yes, this was about saving a life. It was also about Justine potentially being a material witness to more than one crime. Even though she might be the last person to have seen Parker Jones alive, it would always be more about life than information.

Movement in the hall caught her attention. Kenna glanced in that direction and saw an officer talking to the nurse. She pointed at Kenna—or more likely Justine's room.

Kenna ducked inside and shut the door. "There's a police officer on his way down the hall. He'll want to question your mom and get your statement."

"They can't do that," Austin said. "She's hopped up. Not thinking straight."

"Most cops might think that was a good thing. She'll have less chance to lie."

Justine blinked, trying to focus on Kenna. "I can lie."

Kenna said, "Did you see the person who attacked you?"

Justine blinked and glanced at the wall away from where Austin sat. "I just wanted better for my boy. This is what I got."

Austin started to talk.

Kenna halted him with her hand and moved closer to Justine. A secret organization, the emblem tattooed on her wrist like a brand. She touched Justine's shoulder. "You wanted out?"

Tears filled the woman's eyes.

Someone knocked on the door.

Kenna called out, "One second," hoping the cop would think it was Justine and wait a moment. She turned back to Justine. "Do you still want out?"

"They'll kill me." Justine inhaled a choppy breath. "I won't be able to fight him off next time."

"Did you hurt him?"

"I got my knife, so it was a fair fight."

Kenna frowned. If the killer backtracked and stashed that knife at the judge's house, it could prove to be a serious problem for Justine. She would be framed for that murder because she'd had the audacity to be strong and stand up for herself.

The judge hadn't been given the chance.

"Justine." Kenna spoke slowly. "Did you kill Judge Williams?"

Justine gasped.

Austin was about to object when Kenna told him, "She didn't, but I had to check." She looked back at Justine. "Did you kill Parker Jones?"

There were two others Kenna needed to ask about. First, Matteo Sanchez. Just on the off chance Justine knew something about his death. Then there was the reporter, Ryan Bartlett, that Conklin's mom had mentioned.

Justine made a face.

Austin said, "Mom?"

Tears leaked from Justine's eyes, and she mumbled something that didn't make sense.

He looked at Kenna. "Did she..."

When he didn't finish, Kenna straightened. "We don't

know for sure. She needs to be more lucid before anyone asks her questions." She moved to the door and opened it. Sure enough a cop stood in the hall. "Ms. Greene isn't able to answer questions right now. She's in pain and on medication. You'll have to come back."

"Unfortunately, that's not possible." The cop tugged the cuffs from his belt. "Ms. Greene is under arrest for the murder of Judge Williams."

Chapter Sixteen

Kenna paced up and down the sidewalk out in front of the medical center for twenty minutes before the sleek black rental pulled in. The guy who climbed out wore a perfectly tailored suit. Gold watch, gold ring. Freshly cut hair, darker than it should be at his age. Probably got regular manicures and pedicures and had his shoes shined because he wasn't the kind of guy who did it himself.

He was perfect. She'd all but done a web search for *most cutthroat lawyer in Albuquerque*.

"Ms. Banbury?"

She shook his hand. "Thank you for coming, Mr. Southampton, I appreciate it."

"I'll appreciate your payment of my bill for coming two hundred miles at a moment's notice to the armpit of New Mexico."

Yep, perfect. "No doubt you charged me double."

He grinned, flashing freshly white teeth. "Gotta pay off this watch somehow." He flicked his wrist and looked at the time. "I'm glad I made it in a timely manner. There was quite the hubbub at the airport."

Kenna headed for the lobby doors, frowning. The small local airport shouldn't have been busy at this time of day.

"How about you catch me up on what's happened since you called and offered me this unique opportunity?"

She held the door open, and he entered ahead of her. The vetting process to ensure this lawyer wasn't going to do anything but fight tooth and nail for the client wasn't as comprehensive as she'd hoped, but everything she'd found said this guy never backed down and he was immune to outside pressure. She'd made it more than worthwhile for him to take on Justine as a client.

"Something is up in this town." Kenna stabbed the button for the elevator, then told him quickly about Rachel Sanchez. She left out her follow-up thought, namely that Justine might be the target here because their original scapegoat was gone now. "People get railroaded. Crime is overlooked. It's like an oil spill, slowly creeping through everything. Now the whole town is covered and stuck in the mess."

"All I care about is Justine Greene, not the town."

Kenna nodded, and they stepped onto the elevator. "Good. Leave the town to me."

More than ever, she was determined to figure it out. Justine had wanted out, and they did this to her. That was what she'd said. She'd tried to get free like Rachel. Now she was even more stuck—and it could cost her freedom. Her life.

The fact it hit close to home for Kenna wasn't lost on her.

For all she knew, Justine had killed the judge. Kenna couldn't prove otherwise. However, everything in her refused to believe Justine had murdered either Parker or the judge. It didn't matter what the police said.

"She didn't do this."

Carl said, "Can you prove that?"

"I will if necessary." It might delay her other investigations, but if it saved a woman from life in prison, then it would be worth it. "Your firm could hire me as a private investigator."

He tipped his head back and laughed. "And you'll charge me double?"

"That's the price of business." While they chuckled together, her heart squeezed in her chest. She would never be okay after facing the fear and pain in people like Justine and Rachel. Kids were the worst. She would always do everything she could to stand up for people whose power had been taken away.

The lost or forgotten.

She kept seeing Rachel in her mind, those big dark eyes in the courtroom. Then March, when he'd held that gun on them. Just another cog in the wheel—someone pressured or trapped. Under duress.

She should visit him. See if she could get more information about why he'd gone after their courtroom that day. The last she heard he was still alive and being treated for the gunshot wound Marling had inflicted on him. March might be able to give her information.

They stepped off the elevator, and she saw several uniformed officers in the hall. "The taller one is the captain."

Carl nodded.

Marling broke off from the other officers and came toward her.

Kenna said, "I'm surprised you haven't carted her off to prison yet."

Marling frowned at Carl instead of responding.

Before he could, the high-priced lawyer said, "Carl Southampton. Ms. Greene is my client, and no one is to speak with her without me present."

"Captain Marling, Hatchet PD." He glared at Kenna. "This your doing?"

"Securing Ms. Greene the legal representation she's entitled to?" Kenna folded her arms.

Marling snorted. "Figures."

"What evidence do you have that Justine even did this?" Kenna said. "Last we spoke, you were processing the crime scene at the judge's house." She'd love to know if they found actual evidence.

"She killed both of them. The judge and Jones."

Kenna ignored the fact that sounded like a country song. "Yeah." She scoffed. "Because there's no other reason she would have wounds and be covered in blood? Except maybe if she was a *victim*."

Carl said, "It's up to your department to find the evidence to prove my client committed that double homicide you suspect her of being responsible for. So I'll leave you to that and speak with her."

"Room three." Kenna waved at the door. He headed away from them, and she turned to Marling. "This is a joke. Please tell me you realize that?"

"I have no idea what you mean."

"I wouldn't trust the justice system in this town if I had no other choice. It's a farce." Kenna didn't need to get sucked up in other people's fight. But when she hadn't found the man who blew up that church, what else was she supposed to do? She needed these women to be free—and the rest of this town. "Whatever is going on here, I'm going to figure it out."

"Nothing is going on." He shook his head. "It's just the way things are in this town."

"So you regularly put people on trial for things they didn't do?"

"Rachel Sanchez was the...unfortunate victim of some clerical errors."

"Are you kidding me?"

The door to Justine's room flew open, and Austin strode out. "Is this guy for real?"

Kenna turned to Marling. "If you'll excuse us..."

She walked with the teen out of sight. "Carl will make sure your mom doesn't get railroaded by the police into anything. He's going to make sure she's fairly represented and that the truth comes out."

Kenna needed to talk to Justine when she was lucid and able to answer questions. She'd even let Carl know. But it had nothing to do with her defense. Except if Carl would be able to use the questions and Justine's answers to paint a picture that would aid in her case.

She was a victim.

Carl would have to be able to defend that stance, though. Considering the fact that the victim was a county judge, it was unlikely another county judge would be able to keep from being swayed by their emotion—or the fear they might be next.

"You know for sure he's legit?"

"He has no ties to this town, no agenda with your mom other than doing what he's being paid to do. And he's very, very good at it."

Austin shifted. "We can't pay him. We don't have—"

"I took care of it." When he started to argue, she waved a hand. "Don't worry about that. Just keep your mom focused on the fact this won't stick. She'll be released because she didn't do this."

The kid blew out a breath.

Kenna's phone rang. "Before I get this, is there anything else you need?"

He shook his head.

"Go be there for your mom. Let me worry about everything else." She slid out her phone and saw a local number on the screen. Not private like the last time.

Her stomach flipped over, but she hadn't eaten since breakfast. Was it the killer again, taunting her with crimes he'd already committed? As though he gave her time to stop them.

Kenna sucked in a breath through her nose and answered. "Kenna Banbury."

"Uh, yeah..." The voice belonged to a woman, not a recording or computer-augmented voice. "Peter is missing."

Peter Conklin's mother had called her. "Deb?"

"Who else would it be?"

"When was the last time you saw him?" Kenna turned away as she spoke, moving off from the group of police officers at the door to Justine's room.

Deb stayed silent.

"How long?"

"Couple of days."

Kenna frowned. "I saw him a couple of days ago." She told Deb when, and the circumstances.

"He finished the porch, then went to get food. I ain't seen him since."

"Any idea where he was going?"

"He isn't still at the burger place after two days."

Kenna sighed. "I need somewhere to start."

Deb named the chain restaurant.

"I'm gonna save your number." Kenna glanced back at the cops, then headed for the elevator. "Text me the make and model of his car, and the license plate if you have it on a paper."

"Okay."

"I'll call you when I know something." Kenna pocketed her phone.

She leaned against the elevator wall for a moment. She'd done what she could to help Rachel. Now it was Justine—who would be okay with her lawyer doing his thing. Kenna still needed to talk to her, but Justine had to be lucid for that.

She drove across town to her van to let out Cabot and check on things. When she opened the door, Cabot leaned back in a stretch, then shook all over.

"Come." Kenna stepped back and grabbed the leash but didn't clip it on Cabot's collar. She walked with the dog to the pee area, and they got that taken care of. Cabot sniffed around while Kenna tried to figure out where Conklin could've gone.

Right now nothing good was going to come of a guy going missing.

Though, if he was here, he'd probably have been arrested for murder before they pinned it on Justine—or tried to.

Meanwhile the killer did that augmented voice on the phone to Kenna. And who was responsible for that? Someone who already knew they'd both been targeted. Or the judge was dead, and he—or she—had been on their way to Justine's.

Kenna didn't have nearly enough information to figure this out.

"Hey, y'all."

"Dixie, hey." Kenna watched Tilly scamper to the dog area and go straight for Cabot. Her dog stood still and sniffed while the tiny thing tried to incite her into playtime.

"Hopefully you're having better luck in this town than I am." Dixie set a hand on her hip, over her purple western shirt. She barely came up to Kenna's shoulder.

Marling had answered the phone, thinking it was Dixie calling and said something about refusing to help. Or officer information. Kenna couldn't remember his precise wording. "Trouble in Hatchet?"

"Hatchet *is* the trouble." Dixie sighed. "Did you know this town has zero contracts for bounty hunters?"

"So no one has skipped bail recently?"

"No one *gets* bail. Though, that might change now the judge got herself murdered."

"Second one in a few days."

"Yeah, no one's caught onto the fact you were there in that courtroom? The person in this situation who doesn't fit?" Dixie lifted her brows. "That'd be you. So excuse me, but if the prosecutor—boy, he's a cutie—gets popped next, I'm gonna be puttin' some distance between you and I."

Kenna watched Cabot do a little jump, then lie down while Tilly clambered over her. "You think *I* killed them?"

"Given that note? No. But everyone else should be entertaining the idea you *might've*. Or they're idiots."

"Is this one of those 'everyone's capable of murder if they're pushed to it' things?"

"Nah." Dixie waved a hand with pink-tipped nails. "But you and I aren't everyone, are we?"

Did she think they were in the same category? Kenna didn't know Dixie well enough to make that judgment. "Don't you break a nail every time you take down a skip?"

"'Course," Dixie said. "That's why I've got my manicurist on speed dial." She blew out a breath. "One time I had to fly her to Miami, the situation was so bad."

Kenna blinked.

"You've never had someone make a house call?"

"My research assistant showed up on the last case, but I think he was just bored." She distinctly recalled Stairs saying, *This is fun.* "I should head out, anyway."

"Whatcha workin' on?"

"Guy I met the other day? He went missing. Out of prison two weeks. Captain Marling said he was good for Parker Jones' murder. I think he just wanted me on a wild goose chase." Kenna shrugged. "His mom said she hasn't seen him since."

"Maybe he broke parole." Dixie shuddered. "I think I'd split town the first chance I got if I had to come back to the place I got accused of a murder I didn't do." She picked her way across the grass and swooped up Tilly. Cabot licked her on the face. "Aren't you a sweet thing."

Kenna clicked her tongue for her dog. Cabot wandered over and leaned against Kenna's leg.

"Great," Dixie said. "Let's go find this guy."

She frowned. "I don't need help, and I haven't had a partner in years."

Dixie shrugged, already walking away. Her shoes clacked the asphalt. "I'm available to help. And if I get bored..." She glanced over her shoulder and made a face, shaking her head. "Ask my momma. But it ain't good."

Kenna looked down at Cabot. "I'm gonna need moral support for sure."

They trailed back to the van while Dixie headed back into her RV.

Kenna could've left quickly then but wanted to check the blog first. She powered up her laptop and let the page load while she grabbed a granola bar and downed a bottle of water, then refilled it at the sink to take with her.

A new post loaded.

Dixie reappeared in the door frame, standing on the step stool outside. "Who's that? He's cute."

Kenna ignored her and sank into the seat closest to the counter. She scrolled down the web page, and read the draft.

Cabot had lain down in the bedroom, so apparently she didn't think there was a threat here.

"I don't have my readers. Tell me what it says."

Kenna sucked in a breath. "FBI Assistant Special Agent in Charge Oliver Jaxton—"

"The cutie?"

"Yes." Kenna kept reading. "—has been placed at the top of every hit list there is. His name is all over the dark web, along with an offer of a million dollars for finding him. There's a number to call."

"They'll be crawling out of the woodwork," Dixie said. "Why's he the target?"

The food in her stomach soured. "He's protecting a high-profile target. That's who they're after."

"And they'll pay a million to get him back?" Dixie whistled. "Your friend is in *trouble*."

Chapter Seventeen

Kenna gripped the phone against her ear. "His life could be at stake."

"I'll call the FBI," Stairns said. "Like I said. Don't worry about Jax. You know he can take care of himself."

"Do I?"

Stairns paused. "What does that mean?"

"We ask for backup. We work in teams. We go together."

"*We?*"

"The FBI." Kenna sighed. "You know what I mean."

"How do you know he's alone?" Stairns asked. "And you don't think Jax can hold his own?"

"I want to believe he can." Kenna bent forward and sucked in a few breaths, one hand on her knee. Cabot came over and sniffed at her hand. She gave her dog a quick scratch and straightened. *I want to believe that so badly.* Tears pricked her eyes.

She was practically having a panic attack.

Kenna spun to see where Dixie had gone. The woman was in her RV, and apparently "quickly changing" meant she needed more than fifteen minutes. "I have to go."

"You're on the Conklin thing?"

She'd explained to him about Deb's call. "Until I hear otherwise."

"Sounds like that town needs you to stick there, figure out what's going on."

Kenna pressed her lips shut. *Would I let the town burn and go help Jax?* There had to be a reason she was reacting this dramatically, though it seemed like half a woman's life was spent trying to figure out if there were extenuating circumstances for the fact you were overly mad, or sad, or reactive. Or on the edge of panic about the fact her friend might be in very real danger.

She and Jax were friends. That was all.

She didn't need to leave an entire town to whatever was happening here and go off half-cocked to save a guy she'd met once and stayed friends with long distance.

"Kenna, does that town need you?" Stairns sighed.

She squeezed her eyes shut. "Yes."

"I'll find out what Jax is working on and who he's protecting. Okay?"

The word *protecting* stuck in her mind. Rachel. Then Justine. That was what had her on edge.

Their situations brought up in her all kinds of triggered emotions she'd moved on from. Everything that happened to her lay dormant under the surface...until something poked at it and the feelings leaked out.

Ugh.

She turned and looked at the trees. The scenery. It was what she did on the road when the memories crept close. Or first thing in the morning when she took Cabot out, after a particularly nasty nightmare.

Trapped. Powerless. Watching Bradley die.

She'd run for her life out of that house…and in a way, she'd been running since.

There was nothing in Kenna that wanted to settle. Not unless she was looking at the scenery around her—creation. There was something peaceful there she didn't find anywhere else. That elusive calm she couldn't seem to grasp elsewhere in her life.

"Find out what the case is," she said. "Who's the suspect? Where is he?"

"You have to accept that might be impossible. It could be a high-level clearance case."

Kenna gritted her teeth. "Find out, or you're fired." She hung up the phone.

"That your assistant?"

Kenna spun around to see Dixie walking over, or rather tromping on black motorcycle boots with buckles on the sides. "Yes."

The rest of her looked much the same, though to be fair she had toned it down a smidge. There was a denim jacket over the western shirt, and she'd tied the top half of her hair back. "I should get me one of them. A minion I can give tasks to."

"If they can deliver." Kenna locked up her van and clicked a button on her car fob. "Tilly is staying here?"

"What's that saying? I work hard so my dog can have a better life?"

Kenna opened the back door, and Cabot jumped in. She frowned at Dixie, but the other woman slid into the passenger seat already and left Kenna staring over the top of the car at that same family she'd walked past the other day.

Simple people. Honest folk just spending time together.

She slid into the front seat and set off, toward the fast-food place Peter's mom said he headed to before he disappeared.

Kenna sighed.

Dixie had her attention on her phone. "That about your friend, or something else?"

"I've seen enough dead bodies in the last few days. I hope Peter isn't gone as well."

The cases she'd worked over the holidays and through January had her finding a couple of missing people. Nothing that helped her with her own missing person—the teen girl on her fridge. It didn't net her a lead as to who the organization were, or the identity of the man who blew up that church.

Now she had a killer in Hatchet to find.

"Who sent you that information on...what was it? A blog?"

Kenna nodded. "It was a blog." But she wasn't going to hand the ins and outs of it all to someone she barely knew and trusted less. "What I'm trying to figure out is why now?" She tapped the steering wheel with her index finger. "Everything else has related to this case. It could be he just ran into trouble and needs help."

"So he asked you like that?" Doubt rang in Dixie's voice.

"Not him. Someone else." Kenna shook her head. "But what if it's connected?"

It would be a stretch. A coincidence—something she didn't usually believe in. Could Jax's undercover case really be connected to her investigation into this organization? That would be a serious twist of fate.

Either that, or he had purposely looked into what was going on after that church exploded.

Kenna frowned.

"I don't like that look," Dixie said.

"He wouldn't have told me if he was looking into it. I all but let him know it would all be under the radar. Nothing traceable." It hadn't been worth the risk.

"So he gets interested, he sticks his nose in, and now he's on a hit list."

Kenna groaned. "I bet that's exactly what happened."

"So now your friend is in danger, and you have no idea where to find him." Again, a tone rang in Dixie's voice.

Kenna didn't know what it meant, but she knew she didn't want to talk about Jax anymore. Not with a stranger. "What brought you to town?"

"A family thing. It's complicated."

"Family stuff usually is."

Dixie let out a breathy laugh. "Ain't that the truth. But if I'm gonna stay here, then I need a job."

"A contract?"

Dixie nodded. "But there's nothin' in this town. Bail gets set, and people go to jail or they're found dead."

Kenna glanced over. "Stabbed?" Maybe it was a thing in this town.

It wasn't efficient. It was messy, up close and personal. A person had to have a serious grudge—or be really angry—to stab someone repeatedly.

Dixie said, "Who knows."

"How did you even get into bounty hunting?"

"Because women can't be bounty hunters?"

"Did I say that?"

Dixie shifted in her seat. "Fine. I'm used to having to lash out first, or I look weak." She let out a breath. "My daddy was a biker. He was the one who enforced club rules."

"That's a rough life."

"One night. I was about twelve. I snuck out of my house in the compound because there was this boy...he showed up with some guys from Mississippi. I heard something from the barn, and the lights were on in there. I saw them tuning this guy up, and I gasped. They all turned to me, and I scrambled back. Knocked something over. They made me get a hammer and finish it."

Kenna winced.

"Like you said. Rough life."

"But you got out?"

"It wasn't like escape. Life goes on." Dixie shrugged. "People die, or they betray each other. There's a rift, and you go your separate ways. Now I live alone like you do. Doing what I need to do to survive."

"Like helping me find a missing guy?" Kenna wasn't sure Dixie was built to be altruistic, but maybe that wasn't fair to her.

Dixie shrugged. "Even I don't like being alone all the time. I figure that's why we have dogs, but sometimes I need a person to talk to."

Kenna chuckled. "I live alone—with Cabot—and it seems like there are too many people in my life." She pulled into the parking lot of the fast-food restaurant. "We're looking for a white pickup." She scanned the spaces. "There."

Kenna drove down the row to a truck parked in the corner. Because Peter wanted to park out of sight, or not bothered by anyone so he left his vehicle on the edge of the lot? Maybe the fact he was just a few weeks out of jail left him antsy, and he was still adjusting to the freedom he had.

Dixie read the license plate.

"That's what his mom sent over." Kenna pulled in a couple of spaces away, then told Cabot to stay as she and Dixie climbed out.

"Does she like fries?" the other woman said. "Tilly goes crazy when I dip a fry in a strawberry milkshake and give it to her."

Kenna chuckled. "Nope. It has to crunch. If it doesn't

crunch, then don't bother giving it to her—unless it's bacon." Bacon was good no matter what.

Dixie peered in the bed of the pickup. "Some tools. Surprised they haven't been stolen yet, left out like that."

Kenna tried the passenger door handle and found it open. "The vehicle isn't locked."

Dixie pulled on the other side. They peered in opposite doors. "Nothing in the footwell." She flipped the seat forward to look in the scant space behind it. "Ice scraper. Winter jacket. One glove."

Kenna said, "Check the glove box."

There was nothing but receipts for gas in the door pocket. A reflection on the steering wheel caught her attention. Kenna leaned in. Just a dark spot. She turned on the flashlight on her phone, just to get some extra illumination. Even though the sun beamed down from high in the clear sky, the temperature hung just below sixty-five.

"Blood."

Dixie looked up. "Where?"

"Steering wheel. Like he slammed his face down on it." Or someone did it for him.

She stepped back and looked at the chair. And then they hauled him out? Shut the door, so it didn't look like anything was amiss?

It would take time to get a look at the camera footage. What was the likelihood the restaurant would cooperate and show two private citizens their security video? Kenna had mixed results when she tried that in states where she held a valid private investigator license—which was most states in the Western US.

Dixie shut her door and came around. "So he was grabbed?"

Kenna scanned the parking lot. "If someone stuffed him in a vehicle, he could be anywhere."

"He could be dead in the ground in Mexico by now. For all we know."

"Or he made it look like something happened, and he split town."

"You're crafty." Dixie grinned. "I like it."

Kenna said nothing.

"So he does the prep. Figures he'll tell mom he's going out for food. Then he makes it look like something nefarious happened and makes a run for it. Skips out on parole and probation and all that and starts a new life somewhere."

Kenna had to admit, "If I lived here, I would probably do the same."

Dixie chuckled. "Ain't that the truth."

"But I'm not sure it makes the most sense."

"Things should be the most likely story, and that's what happened?" Dixie tipped her head to the side, and her hair moved with it. "Is that how it normally goes down for you?"

"No." Kenna folded her arms. "Unfortunately."

Dixie cackled a laugh and slapped her on the shoulder. "Didn't think so, darlin'. But we can keep dreamin'."

Kenna sighed. "Too many people would be looking for him if they thought he was missing."

"Or it's perfect." Dixie shrugged. "Police in this town don't care about him. Not enough to try and save his life, on account of that being effort on their part."

"In the middle of two homicide investigations." Since they figured they had their suspect in custody, maybe they weren't working that hard.

"And they probably figure he's dead already. So why bother going out of their way to find a dead guy they don't like all that much?"

"Because it's their job," Kenna said.

Dixie snorted. "They've been doing an *exemplary* job from what I can tell." Again, that same tone crept into her voice.

Kenna's phone rang. "It's Conklin's mom." Who *wasn't* Mrs. Conklin, which would make it harder but not impossible to corroborate Peter's story about a sister. "Hello?"

"Peter just called me." Deb gasped. "He's hurt. He needs help, so you've got to help him."

Kenna started for her car, Dixie moving with her. "Did he say where he is?" She got the car started as Deb described a building across town. "I'm gonna need an address."

"Go to Union Street. The old post office is at the end. Turn right, and it's along there. The red sign in front of a gray building."

"Okay, I'll call back if I need help finding it." Kenna clipped her phone in the holder on the dash on the left side of her steering wheel. "Did he say where in the building he is?"

"Some kind of storage room." Deb gasped. "He sounded hurt."

"Okay, I'll find him." Kenna hung up and drove.

How many times had she told a family member, next of kin, or the nearest and dearest of someone who was missing, that she would find their loved one? More than she could count. Usually she delivered—and she strove to do so as much as was within her power. The rest of the time, circumstances remained out of her control.

With Jax, she wasn't willing to leave it to someone else. He was in danger, and the FBI had safeguards. Surely they would protect him—if this was a sanctioned operation and he wasn't off the map doing his own thing.

Lord, I...

Kenna didn't even know what to say. She was in no position to ask for favors. Not that she had complete enmity with God. More like a grudging distance, necessary because anything else meant she would have to face what was in her. Maybe she wasn't ready to do that.

Not that she knew when she would be.

But the words that the priest had spoken stayed with her, about letting in the light to combat the darkness.

She'd tried ignoring it. Pretending it wasn't there. Moving on, living free of the past.

It could be it was time for a different tactic.

Kenna found the building Deb had described. "I think this is it." The place was rundown, like a defunct business, and no one had bothered to clean up. "Let's go."

She let Cabot out of the back seat.

Dixie pulled a gun from the small of her back. "I'll find a door around back."

"It'll be faster if we move together." Kenna didn't trust the woman enough to let her out of her sight, and certainly didn't want to risk getting shot by her. "There." She motioned to a side door.

Dixie kicked it open with her heavy boot and went inside, gun first. She moved like she knew what she was doing. Cabot trotted alongside them as they wound through hallways and rooms. They came on the main warehouse—a huge room lined with machines and long tables. Whatever was made here, it hadn't been done for years judging from the thick layer of dust.

"She said a storage room."

Dixie scanned. "Over there?"

"Let's go." Kenna took the left aisle, while Dixie went right. They both moved swiftly to the rooms at the far end. Cabot sniffed under a door. Kenna twisted the handle, and her dog entered. She gave it a second, just to make sure she wasn't about to get killed. Then she kicked the door open to cover Cabot. "Got him."

Dixie approached the door behind her.

Kenna stepped in and headed for Peter Conklin, who sat on the floor in the corner with his knees up and her dog licking his face. "Your mom called."

He shifted, maybe a slight laugh. Then he groaned. "Thanks." Blood coated his lips. One eye was swollen almost completely shut. His hands had been bound, but now all that remained were the abrasions where the ties had cut into his skin.

"We should get you to a hospital."

"I've got a better idea," Dixie said from behind her.

Kenna knelt and glanced back over her shoulder.

Dixie held her gun pointed at Peter.

"What are you doing?"

She looked at Kenna. "My daddy? I'm the one who killed him."

Chapter Eighteen

Kenna lifted both hands. "Dix—"

"Don't bother trying to talk me down." Dixie held the gun steady, but her tone wasn't. That note had crept back in.

Kenna eyed her, then looked at Peter. "Whatever it is, we can figure it out."

"What it *is*," Dixie said, "is this guy starts talking and he doesn't die." She took a step toward Peter, but still had Kenna easily in her line of sight.

"Okay." Kenna holstered her gun. "No one needs to shoot anyone. We can figure this out."

The fact Dixie didn't shoot Peter the first second without saying anything meant there was something to figure out.

She took a step toward Peter and crouched. All he'd said so far was one word, *thanks*. She crouched and pressed two fingers to his carotid.

"I'm not dead." He flickered his eyes open. The one not swollen shut zeroed in on Dixie. "And I'd like to stay that way."

Cabot trotted back into the room, caught the scents in the air, and went on alert.

Kenna clicked her tongue, ordinarily enough to get her dog's attention. To Dixie she said, "He needs a hospital. Not a gun in his face."

Peter shifted. "No hospitals."

Kenna pulled out her pocketknife and cut the tape on his wrists, just in case it might save his life. "You also need two EMTs, because we can't carry you out of here."

"I'll walk." He pushed his upper half off the wall and leaned forward in his seated position.

She couldn't help him stand. Kenna didn't have enough strength in her arms to lift him let alone hold him up all the way to the car.

"Neither of you gets it." Dixie shifted her stance, the adrenaline rush making her antsy. "He's not getting out of here!" She yelled the words.

Cabot barked, the hair on the back of her neck raised.

"I will shoot you if that dog comes at me."

"No, you won't," Kenna said. "She's seen me get shot before. Neither of us wants a repeat of that."

Dixie frowned. She said nothing.

Kenna slid her back down the wall and sat beside Peter. She could get to the weapon in her boot, but less easily to her gun, sat like this. It put her at a disadvantage. She was banking on Dixie not wanting to kill him, though. "What do you want, Dix?"

"Don't call me that." She huffed. "That's what my *friends* call me."

"I'm hurt." Kenna watched the look in Dixie's eyes and her body language. She sounded tough enough, and she was holding a gun on them. But it was like she'd said before. She was who she needed to be in order to survive.

Dixie turned her attention to Peter. "You screwed him over, and now you're gonna tell me why."

Kenna looked at Peter's hands, and the abrasions on his wrists. She listened to his breathing and caught the pained snag at the end of each inhale. Broken ribs. He'd been used as a punching bag.

Dixie needed him to believe she was prepared to take his life if necessary. Otherwise he would never tell her what she wanted to know.

Peter took that same kind of breath and grunted. He really needed to get out of there, so he could be treated.

"Who are you talking about, Dixie?" Kenna asked. Not demanding, more like coaxing Dixie to tell the story while keeping her tone friendly. Sounding combative wasn't going to help anyone.

"Peter fingered March for those murders so he could get out early." Dixie motioned to him with the gun. "All so March would end up back in prison. Like he can't get to you from there?" She laughed. "Guess again, *traitor*."

Kenna twisted to look at Peter. "Did you rat him out?"

Peter had gone to prison for a crime he might not have committed. On the other hand, March had been on trial for double homicide. He'd taken over that courtroom after Rachel was pronounced innocent, and Kenna had no idea if it had been for that exact reason. It could have been a coincidence, but...

Yeah.

Cabot barked again.

Dixie shifted. "Get that dog away from me, or I'll—"

"Don't finish that. Cabot." Kenna leaned forward in her seat. "Come here—"

She felt movement behind her back and realized Peter was going for her gun. She twisted and grabbed his wrist and squeezed as hard as she could. With her other hand she reached for her pepper spray necklace. "Don't."

Hardness settled over his features. "You're gonna let her point that gun?"

"Did you get yourself into this mess?" She paused. "And I'm supposed to fix it for you?"

He moved his hand from behind her to back in front.

Kenna kept her attention on him, shifted a little so he couldn't reach her gun. "Dixie, who is March to you?"

"He's my brother."

Cabot moved closer to Kenna, but with her back to Kenna so she would be ready at any moment to...Kenna wasn't sure. She hadn't taught Cabot any protection tactics. After all, she was a pet, not a working dog. Kenna didn't want a work partner when she could have a friend and companion.

Conklin spoke. "Shoot her."

Kenna shook her head. "I'm not going to do that. So start talking."

He groaned, pain and frustration all rolled into one sound. "You were supposed to be here to help me."

"Talk!" Dixie yelled.

"Okay." Peter held up his hands. "I didn't do it to get him in trouble." He sighed. "We were cell mates a few years back. I knew what he was going to do, so I figured tell someone and maybe keep him from doing something dumb. I wasn't out yet, so there was nothing I could do. I told Parker, my lawyer." Peter blew out another breath. "Only he called the cops instead. Said he was legally obligated to report a crime."

Kenna frowned. To Dixie she said, "What's your plan here?"

For all she knew, Dixie was the one who had killed Parker Jones and Judge Williams—and tried to kill Justine.

The other woman's arm lowered a hair. "He's back inside because of you."

"No," Peter said, "he's there because he killed his girl and her new boyfriend. The cops did nothing, even though they were warned ahead of time. They waited until *after*, then swept in like they were going to clean up the mess."

Dixie's shoulders slumped.

"Put the gun away. Let's help this guy we came here to help." Kenna waited a moment. When nothing happened she said, "I know you want to help your brother. This isn't how."

"*You* help him." Dixie shifted her feet, to keep blood from pooling in her feet and making her light-headed. "The way you help everyone."

"Put the gun away."

Dixie sighed. She lowered the gun and tucked it in the holster under her jacket below her shoulder. "You're gonna help him. He needs you."

Kenna shifted to face Peter. "Dixie, he killed two people in front of me."

"I'm telling you he had no choice. So figure out why he would do that."

"Or you'll shoot me?"

Dixie rolled her eyes. "I wasn't gonna shoot you." She took a step.

Cabot lifted her belly from the floor and growled, her body leaned toward the other woman.

"Call that dog off."

"Why?" Kenna asked. "She's such a good judge of character."

Peter barked a laugh, coughed, and groaned. "Can I get out of here?"

Kenna and Dixie both helped lift him to his feet. Cabot

stood watch as they started walking toward the car. Kenna made sure no one was within reach of her weapon and figured Dixie did the same. "Were you serious about that no hospital thing, Peter?"

The guy grunted, probably from the effort of moving with all his injuries. "I don't want anyone to find me."

Kenna pulled the back door open. Cabot jumped in before she could say anything. Peter ducked his head and sort of fell onto the seat. He shifted enough to lie down, though how he figured he'd manage that with a dog back there she didn't know.

Dixie spoke over the roof, on the passenger side. "I was telling the truth. I saw him when they returned him from the hospital to jail yesterday, even though there's no way he's healthy enough to be back in gen pop." She shook her head, a sheen of tears in her eyes. "He had to go in that courtroom. They wanted Rachel taken care of."

"Why didn't he tell someone?"

"He told me."

Kenna got in, and they pulled out. "Where to?" she asked Conklin. "Your mom's house?"

"They'll find me there."

"Whoever took you?" Kenna wondered if they'd let him go on purpose, for a deeper reason. "We can make sure you're safe."

"Then take me somewhere safe."

Dixie glanced over. "The RVs? I've got medical supplies." She twisted in her seat and made a face at whatever was happening in the back.

Kenna couldn't see that low in her rearview. She wasn't ready to acknowledge what she was about to do. "Did March tell you who coerced him into taking that courtroom hostage?"

They might have told him to kill a couple of bystanders to make it look good, and they might not. It would've covered the target being Rachel, but he hadn't killed her.

Had it been an act of rebellion?

He still didn't need to have killed those two people, no matter what was going on.

Dixie shook her head. "He didn't know who."

"Peter," Kenna called to the back. "Who did this to you?"

"I never saw their faces."

Kenna bit the inside of her lip. "What did they want?"

"For me to agree to confess to the murders of Parker Jones and Judge Williams."

"They have a suspect in custody." Kenna pulled up to a stop sign and frowned. "Since you got yourself tuned up. They found someone else."

"Maybe 'cause I escaped yesterday." Peter paused. "Maybe they're covering for the real killer. History is repeating itself, and I'm the poor sucker caught in the middle."

She could hear the pain in his voice, but she needed more from him. "Do you want to not be the sucker anymore?"

"Can't do that in Hatchet. Gotta break parole. Run."

Kenna needed a plan. She glanced at Dixie for a second. "Would March testify to what's happening in Hatchet?"

"If we can get him protection. He needs a deal though."

He killed two people. And it sounded like that number might be four—if not more. Kenna sighed. "March isn't going to walk. But we can get him out from under their thumb. Or at least try."

"So you're gonna save this town?" Peter called out from the back.

Kenna let go of the bite on her lip. "We'll need to record your statement on video." If she posted it on the Utah True

Crime site, it could go viral before anyone could pull it back or erase all record of it. Kenna could send copies to trusted government officials. Even people she never wanted to speak with again.

Just in case things turned bad.

"You're gonna help him, and everyone?" Dixie made a face in Peter's direction. "Seriously?"

"Isn't that what you wanted me to do?"

"You think I care about everyone?" Dixie scoffed. "I only care about March. Why would you try to save him?" She thumbed toward the back.

Kenna pulled up at the stop light and turned to look at the back seat. Peter lay with her dog half on top of him, rubbing her belly and letting her lick the healthy side of his face. "That's why."

"Because she's a good judge of character."

Kenna set off again with a sigh. She should let Dixie out to walk the rest of the way back to the RV park. Instead, she dialed her phone and held it to her ear, not caring if it was illegal or not. There was little traffic and slow speeds.

Austin picked up on the second ring. "Kenna?"

"Yep. How are things there? Cops still hanging around?" Mostly she wanted to know if the cops were still there, or if they were out in Hatchet on the war path, trying to find Peter.

"The lawyer still won't let the cops in. He's barring the door."

"Good. It's his job to make sure she gets a fair shake, and that involves not letting this farce continue." There was a lot of that going around this week. Kenna didn't have much sympathy for March, but her empathy for everyone else targeted in this was off the charts right now. She needed a dose of reality. The kind that reinforced the fact people weren't all good or all bad. Like Dixie, there was more below the surface.

"The cops want her moved to the jail but he won't allow it, and the doctor said she shouldn't be there." Austin paused. "They're yelling about court orders. He's yelling about suing."

Kenna said, "When there's a lull in the yelling, can you put Southampton on the phone?"

"Sure. Wait a minute."

She pictured the lawyer in her mind while she pulled into the RV park. Exasperated. Looking forward to the invoice he was going to send her—the one that might threaten her inheritance if it was big enough. All her dad's royalties that she now got for those overblown stories he'd insisted were accurate.

She'd had a shot to find out that truth, the things she hadn't gleaned from living with him, but Joe Don Hunter had perished.

Kenna swallowed against the lump in her throat.

The lawyer came on. "Yes?"

"Hey, Carl. It's Kenna." She didn't pause long enough for him to object to her use of his first name. "Are you available for another client? Maybe two. I'm working on it."

He let out a long sigh. "You're going to have me sleeping here for a few days aren't you? It had better not be longer."

Kenna winced. "I'm not sure I can recommend a good motel."

After a moment, he spoke in a low voice. "Who's the client?"

"First is an incarcerated gentleman. Goes by March." She spotted Dixie shift in surprise, likely that she didn't lead with Peter.

"Send me the information."

"I'll contact the FBI in Albuquerque also. He'll need

protection worked into the deal. He's got information to offer."

"What kind?"

"Coercion. Corruption." Kenna paused. "Probably more."

On the other end of the line, she heard a rustle, then he said, "Sounds like a fun weekend, Honeybear. I would love to."

Chapter Nineteen

Kenna pulled into the RV park, the phone still to her ear. "Cops?"

If they were hanging around the hospital room where Justine was cuffed to the bed, they might be trying to listen in to Carl Southampton's phone call. Trying to get information they didn't have.

Carl said, "Yes, darling. Catch you later."

"Anything else?" Kenna rolled her eyes.

"Bye, dear."

She hung up, chuckling. Knowing he'd been saying all that so she'd be aware the call was being overheard. She needed to call Stairs but wasn't about to do that when these two would be listening. Peter might be in the back snuggling with Cabot—and what on earth was that about? And Dixie sat in the passenger seat pretending like she might've pulled the trigger if she was pushed to it. But Kenna didn't trust either of them.

She was doing this for Rachel. For Justine.

In a way it was for Conklin, as well. Later on she could interview Justine and get a statement. She needed to, considering that tattoo of the C she had, and the fact she would have unique knowledge of this organization. Justine's ability to provide Kenna with information was on a knife's edge and would depend on the cops and the lawyer Kenna was paying for. But right now she had Conklin and the statement he could give her would shed at least some light on what was going on in Hatchet.

"You got me a lawyer?" he asked. "Did I hear that right?"

"And March?" Dixie shifted in her seat and looked at Kenna.

"Let's get inside. I don't like being out in the open." But her van was small. "What about your RV?"

"I've got a first aid kit in there. I'll grab it and bring it to your van." Dixie pushed the door open.

That wasn't what Kenna meant.

Her phone notifications buzzed in her pocket as they entered the van, and she got Conklin in the front passenger seat, the chair turned to the interior. He put his feet on the seat of the chair behind it—between him and the door. Cabot walked back to her bed to lie down.

"I'm going to record your statement on my laptop." Kenna stared at Conklin. "I need you to tell me everything."

He closed his good eye. "I can do that."

The door swung open again, and Dixie climbed in with a bulky medical bag. "Huh. It's pretty tight in here."

"Usually there aren't so many people." Kenna stood facing them, between the refrigerator and the sink. "You left your gun behind, right?"

Dixie flipped open the side of her jacket. "Of course not."

"You don't need that in here."

"Are you putting yours away?"

Kenna folded her arms, which shot twinges of pain up her forearms. Those old injuries had been aggravated by lifting

Conklin and helping him to the car. She'd need a couple of days before the pain went away. Hopefully there would be no more heavy lifting anytime soon.

The cuts to her forearms had severed the tendons, and surgery had repaired the damage. It was a shame there wasn't the same kind of treatment for hearts and minds. Broken spirits couldn't be fixed except by time—and maybe the light that priest had mentioned.

If she knew for sure. Had already figured it out—she'd be in a better position than this by now.

Kenna turned on her laptop. She sent Stairs a text, alerting him to the fact she intended to video call him and record it so he could hear Conklin's whole statement and corroborate. His reply indicated he was good to go.

Dixie looked Conklin up and down. "You'll have to take off your clothes."

Kenna frowned.

"What?" Dixie looked between them. "He could have internal bleeding."

He leaned forward and started to remove his jacket.

Kenna moved and gave him a hand, then said, "T-shirt?"

He nodded.

Kenna tugged it up and helped him pull it off. He had a number of scars, including one across his abdomen. It had been roughly stitched by the prison doctor.

Dixie laid a hand on his chest. "Take a breath."

"You're a doctor now?" He shot her a look.

"Just do it."

He inhaled and then groaned at the top. Kenna got two bags of frozen vegetables from the freezer compartment.

"Broken rib?" Dixie said.

"Who cares?" He shrugged a shoulder.

Kenna handed him both bags. "Face, ribs. Need any pain

meds?" She had over the counter stuff, but if he wanted something stronger he'd have to look elsewhere.

She connected the video call with Stairs, keeping him muted and out of sight when she turned the laptop to Conklin and Dixie. She sent a text to let him know she didn't want these two to be aware of him, just in case they needed to be protected.

"Let's get your statement." Kenna stayed behind the laptop but checked Conklin's face was visible on the screen.

Dixie dabbed at the blood seeping from a cut on his arm.

Kenna continued, "If you could state your name and date of birth for the recording?"

"Peter Conklin." He rattled off a series of numbers. "Do you need my social security number?"

"I mean, it wouldn't hurt. But for now, that's good." Kenna met the gleam in his eye with a slight smile. "Let's start from the beginning, okay?" She leaned her hip against the counter, facing the two of them. "Tell me about the crime you were convicted of."

He closed his good eye, and grief washed over his face. "He was my best friend. We were more than that. We were brothers."

"What was his name?"

"Billie Walton." His voice cracked. "My dad used to..." He cleared his throat. "Billie left his window open. I'd climb in and sleep in his room. One night I couldn't get up that high. His dad found me in the planter in the morning, passed out. Billie's mom was a nurse."

"What about the night he was killed?"

Dixie touched his ribs, gooping on a kind of gel. He sucked in a sharp breath, and she said, "Don't be a baby." A look passed between them. Evidently all the animosity of Dixie holding that gun on him was dissipating fast.

"How did your friend die?" Kenna asked.

Conklin turned his head to her, anger and fear in his gaze. "We were out at the mill after dark."

"How old were you?"

"Fourteen. Billie just had his birthday. His mom made him a football cake, like the whole field with the goals and everything. The two of us were little figurines on the top—playing against a bunch of army men." He sniffed. "Us against the world. Or just my dad, the general."

Kenna had only had her dad, and she'd never had that kind of adversarial relationship with a person who was supposed to care for her the way a parent should. There was a fear in Conklin's eyes she would never understand even though she knew fear to her soul in a way most never would.

Everyone's journey was different. She could empathize—and doing so got her in deep with this case where Rachel and Justine were concerned. But that was a road she would, hopefully, never have to walk. Hers had enough potholes and sheer drop-offs.

"Billie and I were out at the old mill. Not far from where you guys found me. We were..." Dixie taped a square of gauze over an abrasion on Conklin's shoulder, and he glanced at her, then continued, "drinking. We would line up the empty bottles and shoot them with slingshots and these tiny pebbles we got from the planters in my neighborhood." His expression shuttered, and his throat bobbed. "I went around the back of the building cause I had to pee. When I came back..."

"Is there any way Billie might have"—Kenna cleared her throat—"done it to himself?"

Conklin shook his head, fire in his open eye. He held the frozen peas over the other. "No way. We were gonna join the marines together. Get out of Hatchet and never come back."

Kenna nodded. They'd been family, in a way Conklin's

biological relatives never would be to him. "Did you see anyone else around?"

"That didn't matter to the cops when I told them."

Dixie sat back, listening now but also holding the frozen corn against Conklin's ribs.

"I was...finishing up behind the building. I saw a shadow and ducked behind the stairs that led to the second floor. I don't think he was looking for me, though." Conklin paused a second. "I've had ten years to think about it. He wasn't looking for me. I think he was just there to kill Billie so I didn't have him anymore."

"Do you have any idea who he was?"

Conklin shook his head.

"For the recording."

"I didn't see his face." He sighed. "I don't know who sent him either." His gaze drifted to the side, and Kenna decided that might not be true.

"Anyone in your life who resented your relationship?"

"Aside from everyone?" he said. "Our friendship was everything I had."

Escaping an abusive father, Kenna wasn't surprised. A relationship like that would've been Conklin's safe haven. She wanted to ask if his father might have done it, but that would amount to speculation. She could end up leading him to a conclusion that was false, simply because it was the easiest connection.

Any investigation had to be based on facts, not assumptions. Or the quickest answer available.

She certainly wouldn't have pegged Dixie as having anything to do with March. The guy who had shot up a courtroom and killed two people might have been under duress, but he was also past the point of no return on being able to save himself from the consequences of his actions. He'd willfully killed those two people.

Conklin, on the other hand, might still be able to turn his life around.

Kenna said, "Tell me what happened after you saw the man and hid."

"I waited until he left. He walked out of sight, and then I heard a car engine." He sniffed.

Dixie had taped his nose, but it probably hurt like crazy. Definitely broken. Kenna could see in his expression that he wasn't happy. A lot of people would lash out in pain, but she hoped he'd be able to let the frustration of being hurt out some other way.

He continued, "I went back to Billie, and he was just...laying there. Blood everywhere. I laid down with him." Tears welled in his good eye. "I didn't care about the blood. I wanted to be where he was." He looked to the side in an attempt to hide the strength of his feelings. "When the cops showed up, they tried to move me off him. I grabbed the knife and went after them."

"So they arrested you," Kenna said.

His prints would've been on the murder weapon. A teen boy, covered in blood. Given the abuse he seemed to have insinuated came from his father, he might've been a loner—even only just out of embarrassment and not wanting anyone to know.

He nodded. "Pinned it on me, like I'd have killed him."

Kenna's phone buzzed. She saw Stairs' name on the screen and a message asking her to call. She closed the lid of her laptop. "I need to make a call."

"You need to rest." Dixie stood, her attention on Conklin. "Look, I'm sorry about holding a gun on you earlier. March and I? We're a little like you and Billie."

Conklin glanced at her.

"Except I lost him to prison." Dixie sighed. "I wasn't going to shoot you. Let me give you a spot to lay down, make it up to you."

"Okay."

The two of them hobbled out of Kenna's van and over to Dixie's, rounding the front to get to the door on the far side. Kenna dialed Stairns' number while she watched the lights come on and saw Dixie through the window, helping Conklin to the back.

"Wow."

Kenna huffed in response to Stairns' greeting. "Right."

"That was a lot, but I'm not sure it amounts to duress. More like lazy policing."

"Seems to be the name of the game in Hatchet." Kenna cleared away the wrappers from Dixie's medical attention and dropped them into the trash bin in the cupboard. Doing a rote task left her mind free to process everything. "His statement might not be enough to get his original conviction overturned, but it could open the door to asking questions."

"Not when the evidence certainly points to him," Stairns said. "Unless there's any way to find the man he saw and get the guy to confess."

"I'm more interested in now. Not sure I've got the time to right a ten-year-old wrong." Plus, Conklin hadn't seemed so passionate about righting that wrong. He'd never made a scene about his innocence, seeming more resigned to what'd happened than anything else. She could understand not wanting to get caught up in another murder rap now that he was free.

Then there was Dixie, and her connection to all this.

"Things are getting more and more complicated the

longer I stick around." Kenna sank onto the end of her bed. "Anything new about Jax?"

"No one knows much about what he's up to."

"But it's a sanctioned case?"

"Far as my friend can see. He's not AWOL. He is undercover," Stairs said. "He and another agent are transporting a high-profile witness back to Salt Lake City. From Mexico."

Kenna frowned. "Who?"

"No idea, but we don't think that's a coincidence he's near to you, right?"

"Is he? Near me?" She hadn't heard that. "He could be in San Diego for all I know. Or on a flight to Canada."

"Word is, he's coming up from Mexico. Using a small local airport in New Mexico to take the guy to Utah."

"And he was likely looking into the case I'm working. The church explosion." Kenna bit her lip.

"Still? It's been months."

"What else could he be doing? Now you're saying that out of anywhere he could be, Jax is in the same state I am?" Kenna sucked in a sharp breath. "And there's a hit out on him. So I need to know exactly where he is—or where he's headed. And I need to know *now*."

Kenna hung up on Stairs. She immediately dialed the last number Jax had called from.

It went straight to voicemail.

As soon as the beep sounded, she said, "I don't know if you're aware of this. I hope you are. There's a hit out on you. People are after you, so watch your back."

Kenna hung up and flopped back on the bed.

Multiple cases here, and a friend in danger. What was she supposed to do?

She'd been taught to break things down into smaller tasks.

Like text Austin to check in, make sure he was all right for the night. Safe.

Make a note to look more into Dixie, her brother, and Conklin. Something wasn't right there. He should be at a hospital getting treatment, regardless of the repercussions. Safety wouldn't matter if he had a blood clot and lost his life. The guy had lost his friend, but it didn't quite feel right to her. Maybe it was the fact he'd spent ten years in prison.

She wasn't sure he was hiding something. But there was more to the story.

Kenna rolled over and stared at Cabot. If anything happened to her, she would probably react a lot like Conklin had finding his friend. She could understand that part. All those feelings in her wanted to rise to the surface, but that would only lead to a bad dream.

She got up and made tea instead.

It was that, or call Stairns back and apologize for being abrupt, and yelling. And being a terrible coworker—or boss—or whatever she was to him. Kenna tapped her foot while the electric kettle boiled. Jax needed to call her back, or she would put this town in her rearview and go look for him. Not that she had any idea where to look.

She groaned, but only because she was alone so no one could see or hear her except her sleeping dog.

Leaving would only lead to a fruitless search. If she stuck around Hatchet, she'd be able to help. Maybe even make a real difference for the people who lived here, under duress. Railroaded.

Her phone rang.

She checked the screen and had to tamp down the disappointment. All Jax had to do was let her know things were fine. The way he had the other day. But it wasn't him.

"Kenna Banbury."

"Our game was so fun. I thought we might play another." The voice was the same, augmented by computer.

"It wasn't fun for me." Everything in her went cold. She gripped the phone. "Though, whoever you're going to kill, you already did it. Right?"

That was how it had happened with Parker Jones, and the judge. Justine had fought him and survived—or so Kenna presumed. It was entirely possible no one in Hatchet was telling the truth, and she'd landed right in the middle.

He—or she—had said nothing.

Kenna sighed. "It's late, and I'm tired. What do you want?"

"Your fear."

"You think you're the worst I've ever faced?" Kenna said. "How about you try me, instead of targeting other people?" She didn't want a showdown, but that was better than someone else in town dead.

"Try this..." The caller paused. "Should I kill the sister, or the brother?"

The line went dead. Kenna lowered the phone.

She took a couple of deep breaths, giving herself a second to acknowledge the fact she couldn't rush anywhere if she didn't know who to save.

Two people were going to die tonight, but unlike last time, she knew of a sister and brother. And one of them was close enough Kenna could check on her right now.

She slid her shoes back on and grabbed her gun.

The second she pushed the door open, Kenna heard the scream.

Chapter Twenty

A gunshot echoed across the RV park. From inside Dixie's RV.

Kenna ran for the front of Dixie's home and stopped at the left front bumper of the rig so she didn't run right into a life-threatening situation. The door was open and a man ran away, limping, toward the trees. She braced her feet and lifted her gun.

Aimed.

A light turned on in the trailer beyond Dixie's. Tilly barked from the RV door. Kenna blinked, and he disappeared into the dark.

She gritted her teeth and headed for the front door. Tilly kept up that yapping. "Girl, you need to shush." She stepped up to the edge of the door. "Dixie?"

"Yeah." The response was pained.

"Don't shoot, it's just me." Kenna lowered her gun and left the door open. Tilly might run off, though. So she shooed the dog into the bathroom even though she didn't like it. "Stay, Tilly."

Kenna winced, making her way along the plush carpet to

the bedroom, decorated with a whole lot of padding and satin. Dixie wasn't on the bed. Just rumpled sheets and blood.

The other woman lay on the floor, a pained expression on her face and a gun in her hand.

"Can I have that?" Kenna stayed out of the line of fire but came close enough to take the gun from her. "You're injured?"

Blood already pooled on the carpet below her.

"We need a tourniquet. You got a scarf?" Kenna stowed her own gun in the back of her belt.

"Second drawer."

Kenna found what she needed, crouched, and tied it around Dixie's upper leg. "I need to make a call, and then you need to tell me what happened."

The 911 call was first. As soon as she hung up, Kenna called Marling.

He answered with his last name, sounding groggy.

"Time to wake up, Captain."

"Ms. Banbury?"

She leaned against the end of the bed with her shoulder, still kneeling in front of Dixie. "Whatever prison or holding facility he's in, you need to contact the person in charge. There's a hit out on March." She lowered the phone and asked Dixie, "What's his given name?"

"Simon Marchane."

"But you're Cabrera?"

Dixie nodded. "My mom didn't want us connected to him."

"The ambulance will be here in minutes. Hang on." Kenna got back on the phone.

Before she could speak, Marling said, "What's going on?"

"Peter Conklin is the one behind the murders." She didn't say, *You were right.* And neither did she plan on doing it. "Simon Marchane, aka March, is next on the hit list."

"And you know this how?"

"Make the call and get him protection and then come find me. I'll tell you." Kenna paused. "I'll be at the hospital." She hung up, already hearing sirens in the RV park. She went to the front of the RV, put the keys in the ignition and flashed the lights over and over until the ambulance parked in front.

She went back to Dixie. "You realize you're in slot eighteen, right?"

"What does that mean?" Her voice slurred, her face pale.

"He has a thing for numbers." Kenna heard commotion outside. "Let's get you on the bed. The EMTs will need room."

She lifted. Dixie pushed on her good leg, and Kenna got her on the bed. "What happened?"

Dixie slumped, her head on Kenna's shoulder. "One second he's being..." She cleared her throat. "Then there's a knife. He would've stabbed me in the stomach if I didn't kick him. Caught it in the leg though. Ugh. He went for Tilly. I got my gun and shot at him."

The EMTs called out, "Anyone here?"

"In the back!" Kenna turned back to Dixie. "Did he make a phone call?"

"Guess he didn't think I'd have a gun under the pillow." Dixie pushed out a breath. "As if I'm going to let him kill my dog."

An EMT, an older Hispanic guy, crouched. "Let's wrap this, and then you're seeing a doctor."

Kenna nodded. "Dix, the call."

The EMT put a huge square of gauze on the cut.

Dixie winched. "He took a shower right before. I thought he was talking to someone, but he said he wasn't. That he didn't have a phone."

"Okay." Kenna nodded.

The EMT wrapped gauze around Dixie's leg while Tilly yapped in the bathroom. His partner, a woman in her fifties, stood in the hall because there wasn't enough room to get back here.

Kenna patted Dixie's arm. "I'll be at the hospital after I lock up, okay?"

Dixie lay back on the bed, and Kenna got out of the way of the EMTs.

The female EMT held up a hand. "You need to stick around and give the police a statement, ma'am."

Kenna said, "Captain Marling already knows where to find me."

She locked up her van, grabbed a jacket and shoes, and left Cabot sleeping. Tilly needed a bit longer to calm down, but Kenna got her to lie in her bed and then locked up the RV with the bedroom shut in case the police wanted to collect evidence.

She stepped out of the RV and locked up before anything else happened.

The neighbor trailer's light had gone out. No one walked around outside. Kenna didn't see anyone in the sparse street lighting, and the long shadows. Dixie had space eighteen.

There was no way Conklin could've known that. And given his connection to March, she certainly hadn't been targeted randomly. Kenna watched the paths and spaces where someone could lurk and made her way to her car. She armed the security cameras, which she'd adjusted to account for the windshield blind spot. Conklin might leave her another note.

She knew who he was.

Their game was over. Marling could find him and arrest him. Kenna had better things to worry about than a twisted guy only interested in playing mind games with her.

Kenna drove to the hospital. She'd believed Conklin's story about his friend. Even now, she wasn't sure she thought he'd been lying about that. It didn't make sense, but not much in Hatchet did so that was no surprise. He might have killed Billie and made up the story about another person—and there might be real reasons why his prints had been on the knife. He could have lain down with his friend after, out of some twisted sense of remorse.

If the parents wanted justice, that was one thing. But Conklin had already served ten years for that crime. He'd be going back to prison for a lot longer when he was caught this time.

Kenna found a space in the hospital parking lot. She turned off the car and gave herself a moment with her forehead on the steering wheel while the engine ticked as it cooled.

Where is Jax?

If he had looked into the church explosion and caught wind of what she'd stumbled into, she had no doubt he'd start quietly asking around. Now he was who knew where, bringing a guy home. Some kind of high-profile target, a protected witness.

Someone who could speak out against the organization?

Kenna wanted to know who it was almost as much as she wanted to know where he was. She blew out a breath and lifted her head. "Should've put a GPS tracker on that guy."

She headed into the hospital, chuckling to herself about what he'd have said if he found out she bugged him so she could find him. But what did he expect? People cared about him and they weren't supposed to do something that would give them an edge on finding him if he ever went missing.

If he were kidnapped.

Trapped somewhere, hurt and unable to get out. Powerless.

"Uh, ma'am?" The receptionist frowned. "Are you okay?"

Kenna blew out a breath and nodded. She didn't bother trying to smile. "Dixie Cabrera. She was just brought into the ER?"

"Are you a family member?"

"No, but you could get her a message. Tell her I'm waiting out here when she's stitched up."

The guy frowned. He'd unbuttoned the top of his shirt at some point and loosened his tie a fraction. Now he hen pecked at the keyboard. "How do you spell—"

"Never mind. I'll come back in a bit." Kenna headed for the elevator so she could check on Justine. Most hospitals, to be fair, were pretty good about security. You had to visit during visiting hours. Badged entry. Alarmed doors. But on the higher floors, things weren't so strict.

Kenna ducked into an alcove when the nurse passed and snuck down to Justine's room.

The officer sat in a chair beside the door, chin to his chest and snoring softly.

Kenna turned the door handle as slowly as she could, then heard a nurse approach. She whipped the door open and ducked in, closing it quietly behind her.

Austin lifted his head from the cot beside the bed—really just a chair that converted into the hardest bed known to mankind. Kenna waved him back down. "It's just me."

Justine had been uncuffed. The TV was on, flickering light across the wall behind the bed. The sound muted, she had subtitles on so she could watch the cop show while her son slept.

Kenna moved to the opposite side of the bed and sat close

so she could whisper from the chair next to Justine. "How are you feeling?"

Her lips pressed into a flat line for a second. Her attention shifted to Kenna. "Like I nearly died."

"But you didn't. That's what counts."

Justine said, "What's going on?"

Kenna wasn't sure she should tell her that he'd tried to kill someone else tonight. Instead, she said, "Can I ask you some questions?"

Justine blinked in a way that seemed like a nod.

"Did you see the guy who tried to kill you?"

Justine inhaled, then grimaced.

"It doesn't matter what you told the police. Or if what you tell me is different. They'll never hear it from me." Kenna pulled out her phone and got a photo of Peter Conklin. "Is this him?"

Justine's jaw flexed. "I fought him off."

Enough he'd looked like he did when Kenna found him? "How much damage did you do?"

"I can hold my own. He got mad. I hit the knife out of his hand, and he ran. I think something spooked him, or he'd have finished the job."

It was possible he had been caught after that, then beaten more. "Why do you think you're a target?"

Justine gave a tiny shrug.

"I need to ask you more about a few things." When she nodded, Kenna said, "Did you know Parker Jones?"

Justine swallowed. "We were...together."

"Why would he be killed?" She'd mentioned wanting to get out, and this attack had been a clear signal she wouldn't ever be released. "Because he was helping you?"

Justine nodded.

"It's okay to want to be free." Kenna squeezed her hand. "You should be free."

"I never will be. Not anymore."

"I'm going to prove to you that's not true. If you'll let me." It was what Kenna wanted to do for the missing girl, whose photo she pulled up on her phone next. "Have you ever seen her?"

The person Kenna believed was the one behind the blog drafts.

"Maizie."

Kenna's heart squeezed in her chest. "Do you know where I can find her?"

"I don't know where they keep her."

"Where was the last place you saw her?"

Justine frowned. "Vegas, but that was a year ago. I was flown up there for a special job."

"Thank you." Kenna smiled. "That's more information than I've had about her yet." She hadn't even been sure Maizie—the name used on a high school intake form—was her real name. "I'm trying to find her."

"Some people don't want to be found."

"I think she's been communicating with me. Giving me information."

Justine's eyes flashed, reflected in the TV light. Suddenly bright. But it looked a lot like angry fear. "She'll be dead before you find her."

Kenna didn't accept that. "I have to try."

Justine looked away.

"I need to show you one more picture. Then I'll leave you to rest."

"At least I'm not in prison. Thanks to your lawyer."

"Good," Kenna said. "You shouldn't be there if you don't deserve to be."

"Maybe I do. I'm not a victim," Justine said. "I won't be a victim."

She would need that strength to get out of her situation. "I'd like to sit down with you more. Ask you about these people who have you under their thumb. Get you protection and a new life, where they can never find you."

"I already tried that."

Kenna needed a way to persuade her to trust, but if Justine was too scared she never would.

"Show me the photo and go."

She found the image of the man who'd killed Matteo Sanchez and showed Justine. "He killed a state police officer."

"Ward Gaulding." Justine took in a choppy breath. "Stay away from him."

"I've heard that name before, but it wasn't him." It was the name on the lease at the house where she found the evidence proving Rachel Sanchez couldn't have hid a child with her car.

"Then don't believe me. Get yourself killed." Justine paused. "Everyone is after him. Word is, he's flipped, and he's talking to the feds. He's going to do what I tried to do, but the police have no idea who he really is."

"He's turning state's witness?"

"Everyone is gunning for him. They won't let him get to testify. And everyone in their way will get mowed down along with him."

Kenna stood. "I know you're scared, Justine. But if you love your son—if you want out of this life so the two of you can be free—you need to face that fear head-on and move anyway because it'll be worth it." She gave Justine's hand a gentle squeeze. "I can get you out of here safe. I did it with Rachel Sanchez. I can do it for you, too."

Austin had her number. Kenna left them to their rest and

snuck back out to the stairwell, fighting the fatigue. Physically drained from the day, and emotionally drained from that conversation. The man who had killed Matteo Sanchez was the same man who had blown up that church.

And he might be the person Jax was transporting under federal protection.

A man who could blow this whole case wide open.

In the quiet of the concrete landing, she checked her phone. Marling had sent a text.

> Can't come to the hospital. Dispatched to the airport. Something is going down.

Kenna stared at the screen. "Jax."

Chapter Twenty One

The house turned out to be a cute adobe tucked back in the same neighborhood Judge Williams had lived in. Someone's pool house, now accessible through a gate and available for rent on one of those short-term rental sites.

Kenna hammered her fist on the door until it opened.

Carl Southampton blinked at her, dressed in silk pajamas and slippers that he got from who knew where. "Ms. Banbury?" He managed a disapproving look even rubbing crusties from his eyes.

"Tell me about the airport."

He frowned.

"You said things at the airport were crazy. What did you mean?"

Her mind felt like it was misfiring, trying to put all the pieces together. She didn't want to believe half of what she'd concluded, and the rest of it...she had no idea. Yet. Which was why she'd come here, to the only impartial person she could think of for information.

Dixie had been admitted to the hospital overnight, considering how late it was. They wouldn't have let her go until the morning doctor came on shift and checked her out. The message relayed back to Kenna was that she'd been told she might as well get some rest.

Kenna would've rather seen Dixie with her own eyes. She'd have been able to get a read on how the other woman was doing with everything.

She wouldn't refer to Dixie as a friend. At least, not yet. Dixie was far too unpredictable for that. And in the middle of a situation like this, there was zero way Kenna should let down her guard, even if she thought it might turn out fine.

Carl turned back from the door. "You may as well come in. I need a glass of water."

Kenna shut the front door and followed to a kitchenette. "This place is cute."

He swallowed and lowered the glass. "I'm making do." He set the glass down. "The airport?"

She nodded.

"I landed in the company jet. There were four times the security officers as I would expect. All my ID was checked, and I got waylaid for twenty minutes with questions."

"Like an interrogation?"

"Exactly like that," Carl said. "Who was I with? What was I doing there? Am I certain I wasn't working for the FBI?" He snorted. "As if I'd do a fool thing like make a bargain with them."

That old loyalty flared up in her. "What've you got against the FBI?"

Carl's shaped eyebrow rose.

"Habit." And too much empathy.

In the two years since she left the FBI, she'd moved on from that betrayal enough she was starting to remember the good they did. The force for justice they were. Her story was, and had to be, an anomaly. Not a sign that the Bureau had a systemic problem. At least, the problem wasn't that what happened to her would ever happen to anyone else.

She lifted her hands. "They wanted to know if you're helping with a case, then?"

Carl shrugged a shoulder.

"So they're waiting for someone. Did it seem like they were doing that so they could help when the FBI people did show up?"

"Huh. Now that you mention it, there was a vibe. They were definitely hunting."

"And the FBI is the target?"

"That would make sense why there were also a lot of gang member types hanging around. Those cash-payments, no-questions-asked kinds of people who are probably"—he made a face—"undocumented."

Kenna didn't have time to address that issue. "What do you mean a lot?"

"Groups of them, twos or threes. When we left they were camped at every exit." He frowned. "What's going on?"

"I'm figuring something out."

Jax was in danger. He was working. Could it actually be that he was coming through Hatchet and the tiny regional airport here to get a high-profile witness transported home? She squeezed the bridge of her nose.

Marling—and how many of his colleagues—had been sent there.

To protect Jax, or to kill him and his witness?

"I have to go." Kenna strode to the door.

Carl said nothing as she let herself out. She sent Marling a text.

> What's going down at the airport?

His reply came quickly.

> Dunno yet. Govt plane just landed. We got put on crowd control with state police.

Kenna jogged to her car, drove to the RV park, and disconnected the van. It wasn't a great plan. In fact, the idea she came up with on the way there wasn't more than a long shot. But what else could she do? If Jax was on his way to the airport, she needed a way to head him off. Get him to detour before he even got there, because once he did there wasn't anything she could do to help him. Not against that many people.

She disconnected everything, hooked her car onto the back of the van, and pulled out. Cabot sniffed her pant leg and then laid her head in Kenna's lap as she drove.

Kenna gave her a scratch on her head. "Go lay down."

She hit the freeway and drove toward the airport. It was twenty miles, but a couple of exits before, she found an overpass that would work. Kenna pulled off the freeway onto a quiet rural road and parked just past a ranch gate.

Spray paint she hadn't used yet to patch up the wood jewelry box she bought at a flea market years ago—and probably never would. She strode to the middle of the bridge over the freeway and contorted herself through the bars far enough she could spray the side.

Is he even going to see this?

She didn't often talk to God. But on the road alone, before Cabot more than recently, she'd had Him with her. That was something Kenna had always known. Even though she didn't have everything figured out about faith, and what people used it for. Or how they wielded it against others. What she had was enough in her she could acknowledge He was there.

This is all I've got. Maybe it'll be enough.

She sprayed one word on the side of the bridge and then jogged back to her vehicles. She left the van and unhooked the car again, grateful she'd figured out how to do it reasonably quickly. This way she could get to the airport just in case there was anything she could do to help Jax.

Kenna left the reservation information for the campsite, along with the page of directions on how to get there folded behind the steering wheel against the dash dials.

She tucked the keys under the seat and shut the door. From inside the van, she grabbed the lockbox with her extra weapons, and a day's worth of dog food just in case. Someone could steal the van, and anything she didn't take with her, and she might lose it all. But she could also be saving Jax's life.

"Come on."

Cabot quit sniffing the brush on the fence line and ran over. Kenna let her in the back and drove to the airport. She passed the main entrance and took the next exit, looking for a side gate. She pulled past it, to the side of the street, and called Marling.

"I told you I was busy."

"I'm here to help," Kenna said. "Where are you at?"

Marling stayed quiet for a moment. "I'll get you on the list."

"Great. I'm pulling around to the gate now." She did a U-turn on the street and pulled up to the security panel, just a speaker and button on a pole out of the ground.

"I see you on the cameras."

The gate started to lift.

"Drive to warehouse B," he said. "It's the white one."

"Copy that." Kenna kept a smile in her voice, as though she was excited to be here. Ready to help. Not itching to check her van cameras every second. Maybe refresh it just in case the notification was delayed.

Fighting the urge to actually pray for real.

Surrendering to that would end in a cascade that would mean she either realized she'd failed completely at trying to be someone with a God-relationship. Or it would work, and then she'd realize she was one of those people. When that happened, everything would change—because it was supposed to.

She didn't know which she preferred. It was easier to ignore the issue and just do her thing. Live her life the way she wanted.

Marling strode out of the warehouse.

Kenna parked alongside it so he had to round the corner. No one else was around. She let Cabot out and said, "Come on," so the dog didn't go too far. "I need you to tell me what's going on here."

Marling met her at the side of the building. "You didn't figure it out yet."

Kenna grabbed the two sides of his jacket and shoved him against the warehouse. "Don't give me that smarmy, know-it-all attitude. Give me real answers."

"Or you'll continue to assault a police captain?"

She let go of him but didn't step back. "Didn't hit your arrest quota for the quarter? I know a guy you can bring in. Getting him off the streets would be far better than worrying about me. Peter Conklin nearly killed a woman tonight."

An expression she didn't expect washed over his face.

"Start talking."

"Because you haven't figured it out yet?" He glared. "Don't take your anger out on me just because you can't seem to do your job."

She didn't know what to say to that. He wasn't going to be privy to the fact she wasn't just scared for Jax. She was *terri-*

fied. "People are dying. What are you doing about it? Because arresting Justine Greene, that was a joke."

"I have to admit. I wasn't expecting the high-priced lawyer. That was a nice move." He lifted a foot and bent his knee, relaxing against the exterior of the building.

"And what have you been doing?" She motioned to the front of the warehouse, but this was about more than just tonight's activity.

"What I can." He spoke through gritted teeth. "Why do you think you're here?"

"I'm here because I was directed to help Rachel Sanchez. Something you caused. And you had nothing to do with the solution." Kenna folded her arms. "So tell me, Captain Marling, why do you persist in arresting people who haven't done anything wrong?"

"It's the price of business in Hatchet." His expression darkened. "And we all have to pay it."

Kenna pulled out her phone and found the picture of the man who killed Matteo Sanchez. "What does it have to do with this guy?"

Marling's gaze slid to the phone. His reaction was a resigned shake of his head.

She lowered the phone. "Who is he?"

"Ward." Marling sighed. "He's one of the lost ones." He winced. "It wasn't supposed to be me telling you all this."

"But you thought I should figure it out?" Kenna shook her head. "Because it's convenient. Because I'm new in town, and I haven't been corrupted by whatever is going on. What—" Something occurred to her. "You sent me straight to Peter Conklin after the first murder."

"But you haven't caught him."

"I had him earlier." She stuck a finger in his face. "I *had* him. But because you didn't tell me what's going on, he nearly killed a woman. Now he's missing again. And who's going to round him up?"

"Guess you'd better get to work."

Kenna wanted to scream at him. "I have my own problems. You think I should clean up your mess so you don't have to do it?"

He grabbed her elbow and dragged her along the building, away from the front. Cabot barked. Marling let go of her arm. "I can't do it. That's what you don't understand."

She swung around to face him. "Why not?"

"Because I can't." He sighed. "But I also know things can't continue. This isn't what I signed on for."

"Justine wanted out." Kenna folded her arms. "I'm guessing they sent Conklin to take care of her. Austin would've come home and found his mom sliced up. Blood everywhere. The person who was supposed to be there for him, dead in the only home he's lived in. Everything in his life that means safety...gone. What do you think that does to a kid?"

Marling's eyes flared. "I know exactly what that does."

"And you were going to send Rachel Sanchez to prison for a crime she didn't commit."

"Her husband asked too many questions."

"So I should expect someone to shoot me? Since I'm planning on doing the exact same thing."

Marling leaned toward her. "Good."

Kenna let out a frustrated sound. "But you aren't going to help."

"I'm not going to repeat myself either."

"Tell me what happened to Ryan Bartlett?"

He flinched. "That was three years ago. He showed up asking around about Conklin's original case. I guess he was Billie's cousin, and he was interested. He went to the jail and interviewed Conklin, and I don't know where he went after that. No one ever saw him again. State police—Sanchez, actually—showed up. His family wanted to know where Bartlett had gone, since he was missing."

"Which started the chain reaction, and now Sanchez is dead, too. Because this guy killed him." She showed him her phone again. "People caught up in this want out. Killers walk free. Innocent people go to jail. And you're okay with it?"

"Of course not!" Marling's face reddened. Even under the yellow streetlight, she could see it. "Why do you think I've been trying to push you to figure it out?"

"Who has everyone in this town under their thumb?"

"If I tell you that, I lose everything. I get killed, and my family gets nothing. That's why I'm doing what I can."

"Using me as your ticket out," Kenna said. "And if I left you to deal with your mess on your own?" She had a friend who needed her help right now.

"People will die."

"Both ways." Someone would lose if she did what he wanted, and someone would lose if she didn't. All for the sake of taking down a dangerous organization—which wasn't even guaranteed. But the trade-off of Jax versus more than one innocent person wasn't a choice she was comfortable with.

Whichever way she decided, a price would be paid, which was why Kenna had been determined to do this alone. So people she cared about didn't lose everything.

So she didn't have to watch anyone else die.

Kenna's phone buzzed in her hand. She looked at the screen and choked on a gasp. She yelled, "Cabot!" already running to her car.

They jumped in, leaving Marling standing there.

Kenna had to go help a friend.

Chapter Twenty Two

Kenna forced herself to brake, driving through the RV park. It was late, and likely no one would be about, but drawing attention to herself and risking hitting someone wouldn't help. She needed to move below the radar. Incognito.

Her van had been parked back in the spot where she'd been staying the past week almost. Longer than it seemed, and yet not given everything that had happened.

Cabot stood up on the seat in the back.

Kenna opened the rear door, and she hopped out. "You were in the back with him."

She frowned as Cabot took care of some business on the dirt beside the front bumper of her van. Kenna winced. She'd have to reorient it a little in order to hook everything back up. The parking job was enough to get a seasoned RVer to stop and question if she knew what she was doing.

"Are you done?"

Cabot trotted back over.

"Turns out you're a terrible judge of character." They got to the front door of the van, Kenna still trying to make it appear to anyone who might be watching that everything was normal. "Or you're just like any other female charmed by a pretty face."

Kenna opened the door and let Cabot go first.

Just in case.

She stepped in and heard a grunt. Jax had landed on his behind in the hallway that ran from front to back of the van.

Cabot stood in front of him, licking his face.

"Okay, okay." Jax hissed. "Ouch. All right, get off me, girl." He gently pushed the dog away from him, but she hopped over his knee and went to the back.

A man lay on Cabot's bed.

Kenna locked the door from the inside. "She won't like that."

Jax lifted those golden-brown eyes to her, somehow not in the slightest bit diminished by the fact he was sitting on the floor. Jeans, too short for his tall runner's frame. An Arizona college hoodie two sizes too big. Gun in his hand.

"You look like you've been through a couple of rounds." Not as beaten as Peter had been, but there was an abrasion on his temple and a bruise on his high cheekbone.

Kenna held out a hand. He clasped her wrist and stood, though in deference to her forearm injuries, he didn't drag any weight from her. She barely had to tug, and he rose to his feet like a guy who taught community yoga classes three times a week.

He didn't let go but came toward her.

Kenna took a step back. "What *on earth* is going on?" She looked around him, trying to see the man on Cabot's bed. Her dog stared at the guy but didn't go near him.

Jax set the gun on the kitchen counter. He listed slightly to the side.

"Whoa." Kenna caught him—at least, as much as she

could. "Why don't you sit?" She got her shoulder under his and moved with him two steps. He chose the seat by the door, with a view of Cabot's bed. "That's her bed, you know."

"You want him in yours?"

"Fair point." Kenna stared down at him, watching while he closed his eyes and leaned his head back for a while. "How long have you been moving?"

"Days? A week, maybe."

"What do you need?"

"I already raided your medicine cabinet." His lips curled up at the corners. "I enjoyed your array of over-the-counter pain medicine, none of which is the good stuff." He'd told her months ago, shortly after they first met, that he'd been injured in high school and fell into opioid addiction when he was prescribed pain medication.

"Tea?"

"Sugar and milk, please."

Kenna glanced at the guy on Cabot's bed. Her dog leaned against the side of her bed. Kenna moved down there. "Leg hurts?"

The guy was Hispanic, dressed in dirty clothes and covered in grime—even his hair. He was less banged up than Jax, as far as she could see. But given what she knew of her friend and the kind of FBI special agent he was, that didn't surprise her.

He didn't move. Fast asleep, maybe.

Not exactly peaceful rest, but not the troubled slumber of a man who'd blown up a church full of cops that she'd have been satisfied to see.

Cabot whined.

Kenna crouched and lifted her onto the bed. Thankfully it wasn't much higher than Cabot's shoulder. She'd have had trouble lifting seventy pounds any farther. "I'm not tucking you in." She filled the kettle and made Jax a sandwich. "Is he asleep?"

"We're both exhausted."

"You're still going to tell the story before you fall asleep as well," Kenna said. "Do I need to worry he's going to wake up and try to kill me?"

"So far he's cooperated. It's why we're here, because he wants to make a deal."

"After he killed all those cops in that church? He thinks anyone will give him a deal after that?" Kenna frowned. "I'm not sure even I care what he has to offer."

Those golden-brown eyes implored her. "It's big."

"I saw him leave the church before it exploded." Seconds before, and he'd walked out like it was any other day. Seconds later everyone was killed.

"*You* left the church before it exploded."

So it could be argued she might also have committed mass murder? "And I have less credibility than this guy?" On paper she was a retired FBI agent. The story in the media was far more extensive than that. And added to that would be little snippets people caught hold of and believed as truth whether or not they were.

"I have to try."

Kenna said, "Why?"

"Because all this is happening." Jax took the tea she handed him. "That's how I know. *Because* they're fighting back so hard." His brow crinkled. "Why did you pull me off going to the airport? There's a plane there waiting."

"Along with an army of thugs and anyone else waiting to capture you and him." She thumbed over her shoulder. "Ready to collect the million dollars for bringing him in."

"There's a hit?"

Kenna nodded.

Jax blew out a long breath. "That explains it."

"One minute, then tell me what happened." She rolled up the front window shades and pulled forward, then back again, and reparked the van. "I'll hook up the water and the sewer and get the power off the battery in a bit so you can take a shower."

He nodded. "We have some clothes. Not much money. No phone." Relief washed over his face. "I couldn't believe it when I saw *RYSON* sprayed on that overpass. Nearly rolled the car, trying to get on the off-ramp. This is a nice rig."

Kenna settled into the chair across from him. "It fits Cabot and me." She thought through what she'd heard from Stairs. "Word was, you were travelling north with a high-value target, bringing him in. And you had a partner with you."

"Special agent out of Reno." Jax shook his head. "A reward makes sense, 'cause he pulled a gun on us crossing the border. I'm pretty sure he was going to leave me in the desert for the crows. Collect the money for himself."

"You don't think the agent might've been in on it from the beginning? Working for these people?"

Jax stared at her, looking like he needed sleep more than talking.

"I really want to know how you got caught up in all this. I know you need to rest, but if I know what I'm dealing with, I can make a plan while you sleep." Then she'd maybe have a handle on what all was going on here.

She'd taken Peter's statement on her computer and could do the same with Ward. But how was she to know it wouldn't turn out the same. Less than an hour after telling her his sob story, he'd tried to murder Dixie. Tilly was probably feral by now, alone in that bathroom.

So many people in town's lives had changed since she showed up. And most of them not for the better—yet.

Kenna continued, "You were looking into the church explosion after it happened?"

"I knew there was something there." He made a face. "A gas leak? That never made sense to me."

"You didn't tell me."

"It wasn't exactly sanctioned," he said. "I figured if I could get something, it'd help you."

"How did you know I was still looking into it?"

One of his brows lifted.

"Fine."

"You were pulling away." He paused. "I knew it was because you were worried more people would get hurt, so I gave you your space."

"And went undercover instead?"

He shrugged one shoulder. "I had our tech team—Thomas heads up the whole department now—look into the cases you worked in Bishopsville. The missing girls. There was a rumor going around about videos being uploaded, so they scoured sites on the dark web they have on their radar looking for something connected."

"And?"

"We found two different victims. The videos had a logo in the corner we tagged, indexed, and ran as a search. A letter C but in a medieval kind of script."

Kenna nodded. "There's a woman here in town with that letter tattooed on her wrist."

Jax winced. "We need to know what she knows."

"What led you to Mexico, and this guy?" He'd found the man responsible for what the FBI officially labeled a gas leak.

"The videos all led back to the same server. The site they were uploaded from is based in the US, but the server is in Mexico. So we paid a visit. The guy I was partnered with and I."

"Some stranger?" she asked.

"I knew him at Quantico. Thought I could trust him." Jax shook his head.

"Is he dead?"

Jax nodded. "I had no choice. He would've killed both of us."

"I can tell Stairns. He can report it, get someone out there to bring the body back." She paused. "How did you get from the server to the guy who blew up the church?"

His gaze drifted to the back. "He approached us. We made contact with the company where the server was hosted, trying to find out who is behind it. Maybe trace the money. Got word from some locals that a transaction was going down, and there he was."

"How did you know it wasn't a trap?"

"We let it play out. Ward broke off and came to us, said he wanted to make a full statement." Jax shifted in the chair and groaned. "He'd confess to everything in exchange for a deal. But I've got to get him back to the office."

Kenna still couldn't believe he'd landed himself in Hatchet. "Who told you to use this airport?"

He frowned.

"They had to have planned for you to come this way."

"Because it's where you are?"

"No," she said. "Because this whole town is involved with whoever is behind that letter C."

Jax pointed at the witness. "He can tell us. He told me he'll give the FBI everything. Even if that means prison and protective custody, it's better than what he's facing if they catch up to him."

"Assuming I'm not going to turn him over to them in exchange for a million dollars." Or shoot him herself for what he did to all those people. Though, she tried not to commit murder if she could help it. "We have to get out of here first." Kenna ran her hands down her face.

"Are you going to give him up for money?"

She lifted her head toward him. "Of course not."

The corner of his mouth curled up in a soft way, his expression full of warmth. "You saved my life."

"That was the idea of painting that overhang." Kenna pointed toward the bedroom end of the van. "Him, I don't care about."

Jax laid a hand on the strings of the hoodie over his chest. "You care about me?"

"I happened to be in town. Close enough you didn't drive right into a trap."

"Because God put you in my path."

Kenna didn't know about that, so much as it being an entirely more evident reason. "Because you stuck your nose in something that's bigger than you thought it was and wound up on the run. In trouble. How's that gonna look on your personnel file, Mr. Assistant Special Agent in Charge?"

"You think I was gonna let you face this by yourself?"

Kenna sipped her tea so she didn't have to look at that steady gaze.

"Stairs told me about Hunter."

She didn't want to talk about that. "He's gone. What is there to say?"

"He knew your father. I'm sure it brought up a lot of grief over missed opportunity."

Sheriff Joe Don Hunter of Bishopsville California had been her father's friend, and she would have that at least. She had the papers and files she collected from his safe, and the personal effects from his car. His office and house had both burned. If there was even something to inherit from that, she wasn't convinced she was his nearest and dearest given they'd met days before he was killed.

Kenna had the picture he'd given her. The one of Joe Don and her dad, and a few others—including her mom—as young people. She'd shelved looking into personal stories until after this organization was unveiled. People were dying. She wasn't going to ignore it when she could right that wrong.

The personal stuff would be there when she was done making sure these people didn't hurt anyone else.

"You were there." He cleared his throat. "I talked to Stairs. You both left the church seconds before it blew. You could have died along with the rest of the people in there."

She didn't want to hear that note in his voice. She knew exactly how that ended up under his skin, the idea he might've lost someone he knew. It was how it happened with her. A sense of responsibility. Grief, even though she'd barely met those people.

There because of her.

In the line of fire.

Gone.

"It wasn't your fault."

Kenna squeezed her eyes shut. "I told them to get out. I screamed at them and pulled the fire alarm. Nothing happened."

"You did what you could."

"It wasn't enough. They all died." She gasped, and tears filled her eyes. "All the evidence in one place. All the witnesses, and suspects. All those cops investigating. What did they think was going to happen?"

"They didn't know, but we do." He paused. "That's why you pulled away, right?"

"Whole lot of good it did. You're here, aren't you."

The corner of his mouth curled up again.

"Stop it." People were dead. She didn't need him and all his Jax-ness filling up the van. "We need to focus." She motioned to the back again. "You're gonna have to protect me on protecting his sorry behind. He killed a lot of people. And he murdered a New Mexico state police officer in cold blood."

The amusement dissipated. "I know."

"And he thinks he's gonna get sympathy? Or a deal?" Kenna wasn't an agent, so she didn't have a say. Jax was the ASAC. But running with this as a case would only put a target on his back more than there already was.

"This is bigger than that."

Kenna shook her head. "What is going on?"

Chapter Twenty Three

Kenna sucked in a breath and sat up. "Tilly." She shoved at the blanket over her.

Two men stood between the sink and the refrigerator.

"Your dog already went out." Ward Gaulding's voice held a trace of an accent but not much.

"Her name is *Cab-oh*." Jax pronounced it correctly. "Who's Tilly?"

She shook off the sleep, looking out a gap between the blinds and the window. "Neighbor dog. Stay here."

Cabot squeezed between the two men and followed her out the door. She closed it behind her and realized too late they were cooking her bacon. Hopefully they'd make her a sandwich without her having to ask.

Dixie's RV had a light on inside. Kenna wasn't sure she'd left one on, but so much had happened since her neighbor was nearly stabbed to death. This was the part of a case that always got overwhelming, where there seemed to be too many things going on she didn't know where to start fixing them.

Peter. Justine. She needed to call Peter's mom and make sure she was safe. Check in with Carl Southampton. Ask

Captain Marling what happened at the airport, and what everyone there was doing now—after the target never showed up.

She didn't even know if Marling was on the side of wanting to protect Jax and his witness, or if he'd been there like everyone else. For the money.

Tilly stood at the open door and barked through the screen.

"It's just me," Kenna called out. "Dixie?"

Cabot sniffed around their table. Tilly barked a couple more times.

Dixie limped into view, one hand on the counter. "Tilly, shush." The dog didn't back down but did get quiet. "You gonna clean up the mess she made in the bathroom?"

"Sorry about that," Kenna said. "Everything else all right?"

"Will be when this town is in my rearview. I'm thinking Miami."

Kenna pulled the screen open and stepped in, staying by the door so she could keep an eye on Cabot. Tilly pounced on her sock and started a war with one of Kenna's toes—until she gently shook off the dog. "You're leaving?"

Dixie put a container in the cupboard and clicked the door shut. "I'm done here." She took two mugs from the dishwasher and put them away as well. "March wanted Peter dead. I was going to get him to confess on tape, so he'd get arrested again and not get out of jail. What March did when Peter got back to jail is up to him. Not my business."

"Is March all right?" The call had said the sister or the brother. "I thought he might've been a target, though I'm not sure how Peter would've gotten to him in jail."

Dixie made a *pfft* sound with her mouth.

"I don't know what that means."

"Doesn't matter." Dixie shrugged one shoulder. Her thigh had been bandaged to half as big again as the other one. She'd probably be in shorts until it healed, so Miami was probably a good choice. "I'm not getting suckered into March's drama anymore."

"So he's all right?"

"I guess. I mean, as far as I know." Dixie shook her head, her hair moving with it as though it had no choice. "He's been leaving messages." She sighed, then limped to one of the recliners and sat. Tilly scurried up a tiny set of carpeted stairs to sit on the other, and Dixie leaned over to give her a scratch. "I thought someone was controlling Peter, and March was the victim. Like Peter needed help or something, and that would solve March's problem."

"And now?"

"Now I think Peter is the one calling the shots."

"In Hatchet?"

Dixie shrugged. "Maybe in the prison, too. He talks like it."

"The shot caller." Kenna turned to check on Cabot, now lying on the ground outside the door where Dixie had a rug before but now she didn't. "So you're just leaving?"

"Nothing makes sense here, and I'm not getting in the middle of it."

"If he's in charge, why did he get bound and beaten?"

"To better sell his sob story," Dixie said.

Kenna glanced at her.

The other woman shrugged. "It's possible."

Kenna sighed. "Seems elaborate."

But then, she'd seen people go to all lengths to sell their stories. As long as she'd been investigating crimes, and solving mysteries, it seemed like she should be past being surprised about what people were capable of. Instead, she was continually having to roll with the punches and comprehend what someone had done to get what they wanted.

"Still," Kenna said, "we have to find him before he hurts anyone else."

Dixie scrunched up her nose. "Get that police captain to help. I'm leaving soon as I unhook. You can clean up the mess here."

With two men and a situation in her van? Kenna clenched down on her molars.

"You'd never walk away, right?"

"If I thought someone might get killed because I did nothing?" Kenna was willing to admit that yes, she would never walk away. How Dixie would be able to sleep at night knowing she had someone's blood on her hands, for all intents and purposes, Kenna didn't know. She couldn't do it. "A murderer is loose."

"Only because I didn't let him kill me."

"Did you hit him when you fired your gun?"

Dixie muttered a curse word. "He ran."

Kenna said, "I need to eat breakfast."

"Aren't you worried about your friend? Maybe focus on that and leave Hatchet to consume itself like one of those sea creatures that just eats away at itself."

Kenna frowned. "And the innocent people who get swallowed up in the process?"

"No such thing. They all know something," Dixie said. "I saw it when I was around town. Furtive looks. Too much cash. Flashy stuff. It's like the whole town is on the take."

Kenna started to speak.

Dixie cut her off. "Whatever. I don't care. You should go eat." It sounded very much like a brush-off. A whole lot like, *Nice to see you, now leave.*

"See you around." Kenna waved.

Dixie said nothing.

The screen door snapped back into place, and Cabot got up to follow Kenna back to her van.

Two steps from the door, a police car turned onto the blacktop that ran through the RV site. Kenna let Cabot in but stayed outside. "Cops here. Sit tight."

She heard a low, "Copy that," and let go of the door.

The day had barely started, and things were already piling on her.

Kenna took a second to look at the sky, stretching above her. A pale-blue expanse, with whisps of white cloud. Nature and man joining to make one picture. Not harmony, or even coexisting. Just reality. The way good and evil lived side by side.

She'd tried for years to fight the fact it seemed like evil overwhelmed the good in the world every day. In a lot of ways, it did. Christians believed God was ultimately in control. Accepting that seemed like a placebo. She might be fooled into feeling better, but it didn't change the underlying disease —which they called sin.

The marked police car pulled up at the end of her rented spot, leaving no question of who he was here to see. Thankfully the blinds were secured on the front windows of her van all the way around.

Captain Marling climbed out of his car.

Kenna glanced at Dixie's RV, then went to meet him by the front of his car. The farther he was from her van, the better. "What happened after I left the airport?"

"That's what I wanted to talk to you about." He slowed to a stop in front of her. "Why'd you rush off so fast?"

"I thought someone was breaking into my van."

He glanced at it but didn't mention the fact it looked like she was ready to pull out any second. The water and sewer hookups on the far side weren't visible from here. Maybe he wouldn't notice. He looked back at her. "Did you call it in?"

"Turned out it was nothing." She motioned toward Dixie's vehicle. "Unlike what happened to Ms. Cabrera." Did he know she was March's sister?

"I need to talk to her about that, but it's been a busy morning, so I may not get time to do it until later."

"Why not right now? Isn't that why you're here?"

He shook his head. "Too much to do."

"Peter Conklin attempted to murder someone last night, and you're gonna do nothing? After nearly arresting Justine Greene for it, you're going to completely ignore the fact crime is occurring in this town. Serious crime." Kenna took a breath. "Did you check on his mom?"

Marling winced. "She wasn't there."

"Like she didn't answer the door, or like you walked through the trailer and she was gone. Bag gone. Half her clothes gone?"

"Car and her. Clothes and all that was still there, including a pink toothbrush in the bathroom."

"Then check back later," Kenna said. "You need to make sure she's still alive."

Marling sighed.

Before he could argue, or give her some other garbage excuse that would have nothing to do with the truth, she said, "What happened at the airport?"

He shrugged. "No show. About four this morning people started to give up and leave. Or hunker down. All that adrenaline hits you hard, and then you just crash."

"Really." Kenna made a face. "That's too bad they didn't show, though. Coulda got you that million dollars."

"You think that was why I was there?"

"You said the feds were there. They showed up in a plane. Are they still there?"

"Far as I know." Marling broke off and went to his passenger seat. He pulled out a file box, heavy given the way he adjusted it in his arms. "This is for you." He walked to the van door.

Everything in Kenna tensed as she followed him. Her face twisted into a grimace. She had to stop him from going inside. "Marling, I don't have time for your crap. This isn't a yard sale trade, and I have nothing you want anyway." She worked hard to keep irritation and nothing else in her tone.

He dumped the file box by her door and straightened with a groan. "You're gonna take it in."

She clenched down on her back teeth. *Unlikely.* Given how heavy he'd made it seem. "Just slide it in the door. I don't have counter space anyway." She said the words louder than they needed to be and opened the door so he'd have to stand to the left side, unable to see anyone who might be hiding over with her dog. And if he heard any movement, maybe he'd attribute that to Cabot. "Right by the door is fine. Then I can tip it out when I realize all you're doing is giving me trash."

He slid the box in, taking her little entryway mat with it. "You can act however you want, but that doesn't change the truth."

Kenna shifted in a way that forced him to back up and shut the door. "And what truth is that?"

"Life isn't nearly as black-and-white as you think. People aren't all good, or all evil. They're more than that. Complex, and baffling."

"Working on your psychology thesis?" Maybe she'd concluded doubling down on being irritated was a way to get him to leave faster, or maybe she was just mad.

Marling sighed, the way men did. Usually at women.

"Maybe you should get back to work."

"For the record," he said, "Justine Greene has been cleared of all suspicion of being involved."

"That'd be good, considering she's one of Peter Conklin's victims." Kenna folded her arms.

"I thought you figured that was just a wild goose chase I sent you on?"

"I'll admit," she said, "I did think that at first. Now I have no idea what to think except that you routinely ignore evidence. Arrest innocent people. Ignore the fact there are dangerous criminals walking the streets and go after a payday because you care more about money than justice."

Marling smirked. "Guess you've figured it all out, then."

The other explanation meant he'd sent her to Conklin knowing full well he was the exact person who'd killed Parker. And he couldn't do anything about it? Like maybe...arrest the guy? "Who ties your hands?"

"It's not that."

"So what is it?"

"Hatchet is...just Hatchet. It's the way things are here."

"Letting murderers walk free and arresting innocent people?"

"Sure. So innocent." Marling shifted his stance. "That's why you captured Conklin and didn't for one second believe he might not be guilty."

Kenna waved toward his car. "I'm sure you've got a lot of things to do."

Marling smirked again and strolled to his car. She watched him walk away, then hauled open the door to the van.

Jax stood near the door. "Your sandwich is cold."

Kenna turned around and walked out again, then rounded the van and hooked everything up. When she got back inside, she said, "If you want to take a shower, it's connected."

Jax studied her, unmoving. "Ward, you wanna shower?"

"Sure." He stood behind Jax.

The fact her friend would put his back to a dangerous man said a lot. But then, she'd interviewed Peter and bought into the story that he didn't kill his friend. She still wasn't sure he had, but he'd certainly killed a lot of other people. Maybe the death of his friend had been a trigger.

His beginning.

Or a life forced on him when his friend was killed, causing a psychotic break he couldn't control. On the outside he seemed affable, maybe even charming. He'd certainly fooled Dixie, which was likely why she was leaving.

Kenna usually only cared about who committed the crime, not usually the reason behind it. Yet her mind seemed to be stuck on the question of why Billie had been killed.

Ward shut himself in the bathroom.

Jax said, "You okay?"

Kenna stared at him.

His expression softened. "How can I help?"

She crouched and flipped the lid on the box. Full of police case files. Kenna grabbed out the one at the front of the stack and opened it. "William 'Billie' Walton." She looked up at Jax. "Make a pot of coffee. This might take a while."

"Why, what are we doing?"

Kenna handed him the file. "We're going to solve a murder."

Chapter Twenty Four

"Kind of small in here." Jax bent and sat in the front passenger seat, which she'd rotated to face inward.

"You're gonna critique the accommodations?"

He held up both hands. He'd plunked the file box on the chair in front of him, while she still had Billie's murder file now opened on the counter by the sink. The smell of coffee permeated the van, and Cabot lay snoring on Kenna's bed.

Her back cramped between her shoulder blades from spending the night in the driver's seat, but Jax might be right. "It wasn't built for three people and a dog."

"Thanks for helping us."

Kenna sighed. "I need to figure out what's going on here, not get tangled up with your case."

"Because you don't want to help a murderer."

"Too late. I already did." On two counts as far as she could see. First, she'd believed Conklin and taken his statement. Now she had a mass murderer in her shower. "What does he say about the church bombing?"

Jax nodded, his face softening. "He was forced to set the charges. He was army. They threatened his family."

"So he just bows to threats? I don't know many army guys who would roll over at the first sign of pressure." She leaned her hip against the counter.

"They sent me pictures. Videos."

She spun around.

Ward stood in the hall, his hair wet and wearing clean clothes. "They had my wife. My daughter."

Kenna's stomach clenched. "Did you get them back?"

"They're safe now. Thanks to Jax."

She glanced at her friend, who gave her a tiny nod. "Good." She looked at Ward. "That's good."

Ward said nothing.

What was there to say, when he'd killed people for the lives of his family. It was noble. And very, very wrong at the same time. She could argue he should've called the police—or the feds—before it happened. But she also knew this organization, even if only a little. They weren't the kind of people she wanted to tangle with.

It was a lot like what was happening in Hatchet.

People like Rachel were railroaded. Good folks like Matteo Sanchez, and that reporter who'd gone missing, suffered while those with power were able to do whatever they wanted.

And what had Marling said? It was just *how it was* here.

Kenna didn't buy it, even if the culture of this town had been ingrained in people over the years.

She took the file and sank into a seat, heavy with the weight of what this organization was responsible for. Another town had been sucked into it, maybe for years now. Marling might be part of the problem, but giving her this box of files might also be his way of trying to change things. Without putting himself at risk. Not actually standing up against the tide. Just giving her a way to do it—while she took all the risk.

It would never be right what Ward had done, but she could also be glad his family was safe.

She stared at Jax. Not a chore, given he was kind of easy on the eyes. Attractiveness wasn't any measure of a person. People looked how they looked, but—

His head cocked to the side. "You're staring."

"I slept in a chair. I'm tired." She had scarfed down a cold bacon sandwich and two cups of coffee, but that didn't seem to matter. Which was a crying shame given the mystical properties of bacon.

They needed to focus.

Kenna said, "Have you contacted whoever you need to check in with?"

Jax shook his head. "No phone. You have a way to make a secure call?"

She tugged out her phone from her back pocket and made a call on speaker.

"Sending me someone else?" Stairs' voice sounded rough.

"How was the retreat?"

Jax's lips curled up. Because she and Stairs greeted each other with questions instead of an actual greeting?

"Never mind that, anyway." Kenna paused. "I need you to pass a message to Ryson. Get him to visit the FBI office in Salt Lake City. Deliver a note from…a mutual friend. And he needs to do it ASAP." Jax mouthed the name of an agent she'd worked with briefly a few years ago. Kenna passed the name along and continued, "Our mutual friend has a package to deliver, but transportation seems to be an issue."

"You can't provide that?" Stairs said.

Did she want to give Jax her house? Let him take it with him and get Ward to Utah? Kenna frowned. "Possibly."

She hadn't even thought about it probably because it was

her house. Maybe her car, though. But that left her driving around town in her van and having to hook it up every time she came back to this spot.

An engine revved outside. She crossed the van and pulled aside the window blind just a fraction. Enough to see Dixie's RV turn out of her space.

Jax shook his head and whispered, "I'm not taking your car. Too much road for something to happen."

"Our friend wants a plane," she said. "Maybe a helicopter."

"Too loud." At the same time Stairs said that, Jax mouthed, *Too loud*.

Kenna shook her head. "An out-of-the-way ranch with an airstrip and a private plane." She knew of someone she could borrow one of those from if the FBI couldn't get their plane from the airport to a private spot. But would Carl Southampton help her even more than he already had? "I need to make a call. See if I can get some help."

"Driving seems simpler," Stairs said.

Jax shook his head.

"No go," Kenna said to the phone. "Not a fan of long open highways."

It would take the better part of a day to make that trip. Maybe longer. While a plane got them there in a matter of hours.

Since it meant she didn't have to give up one of her sets of wheels that was fine. Though, she could give Jax her van again. Let him use it to get to whatever airport he would fly out of. She could pick it up later.

And they'd go their separate ways again.

Kenna wanted to roll her eyes. Her emotions were all over the place, seeing him here and having help for a moment on her case. It was tempting to forget she had one of her own to work. Jax couldn't stop what he was doing to help her find Peter Conklin. She needed to do it on her own, the way she normally worked cases.

Just because he was here didn't mean everything had to go out the window.

She should probably get him on that plane as soon as possible, or she'd get even more used to having him around. Pitching in.

She did not need a partner.

Case in point: This van was entirely too full of people right now. It was making her want to walk around outside and get some air.

"I'll call Ryson," Stairs said.

"Find out if the plane is still here. We might need it."

"If not, I'll get working on another. I met a guy at the marriage thing."

Kenna frowned. The line went dead.

"He met a guy with a plane at a marriage retreat?"

She shrugged. "It's Stairs. If anyone can network and find contacts to help him in the kind of emergency where you suddenly need to use someone's private plane at a marriage retreat, it's him."

Jax shook his head. "I guess we're parked here for a while."

"I just want to say thank you." Ward looked from him to Kenna. "For letting me throw you guys for a loop. You didn't have to believe me."

You didn't have to kill all those people. But in his heart, he'd been convinced he did.

Kenna might want to argue he'd chosen wrong, or not done everything he could have to save as many lives as he could, but there was nothing she could do to change the past.

"My family is safe," Ward said. "That means I'll do whatever it takes to bring these people down. I'll make a statement, I'll testify. I'll go to prison for what I did, but I'll do it right."

"You know who is behind it?"

"A few names," Ward said. "And what they're planning."

Jax leaned forward on his chair. "I really need to know what that is, Ward."

"There's time." Ward motioned to the files. "You two have work to do, and I need to lie down. Get some more rest." He trundled to the back of the van and lay down on Cabot's bed. The dog opened her eyes and shifted to put her head on her paws.

But considering she'd cozied up to Peter Conklin, Kenna wasn't about to trust Cabot's judgment right now. Her radar was off.

She turned to Jax. "What do you think?"

"Something is going down." He sat back in the chair, stretching out his legs between the two middle seats. "He needs to tell me what, but he keeps putting it off."

"Because it's a bargaining chip."

Jax nodded. "He'll play it when it's best for him."

"I hope it's best for people whose lives are on the line." She winced. "Too many are dead."

She'd seen so much blood the last few days. Every time she closed her eyes she heard the screams from that church.

"He's thinking about his family, not the people he killed."

"Maybe he should think about *their* families." She shot him a look, but the frustration collapsed, and she slumped back in the chair. "This whole thing is a mess."

"So let's figure it out."

"What have you got so far?" Kenna leaned over to look at the case he was reading. "That murder happened while Peter Conklin was in prison. Ten years for the murder of this kid." She showed him the file she had.

"Okay." Jax frowned and picked up the next file, opened it. "Same timeframe?"

"Yes." Kenna put aside her file, groaning. She flicked through the files. "These all happened while he was incarcerated." She found files for Parker Jones and Judge Williams in the back. "For the most part."

"Same MO?" he asked.

They worked through the files, cataloguing manner of death and the weapon used.

"He likes to carve people up," he added.

Kenna thought back to Parker Jones' murder. "Not in a way that's methodical. It was fast, and full of anger. He must've knelt over the victim and stabbed him eight times with as much strength as he could, because those wounds were deep."

Jax frowned. "But it wasn't efficient."

"It was determined." She thought for a second. "He enjoyed it."

"Great."

She told him about the phone calls. "He wants the game. The rush of getting away with it, knowing he has that power over whoever he chooses."

Did he kill as ordered as well? There had been some strategy to the murders. But there was Dixie, too. Maybe a crime of opportunity—or an attempt at one.

"But you said he was incarcerated at the time."

Kenna nodded. "Ten years for the first murder." She tacked on, "But not necessarily his first kill. We'd have to talk to the warden. Find out what's going on."

"He can't have committed all these crimes if he was in prison."

"That's the thing about this town," she said. "I wouldn't put it past them. Anything, no matter how crazy it sounds."

Jax flipped a page. Kenna looked through the file she was reading, the report Marling wrote about the Parker Jones scene. Valette's death—a suspected drug overdose.

The young officer's death seemed to have gone unnoticed, and maybe that wasn't surprising to anyone living in Hatchet.

"I've got a witness statement." Jax angled so she could see. "Who redacts portions of a witness statement?"

She frowned.

"Think we can get ahold of the original?"

Like with Rachel Sanchez? Kenna had found the evidence to exonerate her in the crawl space of a house. Ward Gaulding's home, in fact.

"What is it?" he asked.

"Maybe we should ask him." She pointed to the far end of the van. "He killed a guy just up the highway. A cop."

Jax's jaw flexed.

"Maybe I don't care what he has to say."

"It's big. I know it." He gave her a look. One that very clearly communicated, *Trust me.* And the bit that stalled her out was the fact she did.

Most of their relationship had been on the phone, only minimal face-to-face and much of that was investigating murders. How much did she really know about Oliver Jaxton? He'd been relegated to Utah. Then promoted pretty fast. He was young.

"Now you're gonna doubt me?" he said.

"It isn't personal."

"You really believe that?" He sighed. "If I could go outside, I'd go take a run. Burn off some of this tension. But I can't, so you're going to have to deal."

"Maybe I'll run. Cabot needs a walk." Kenna started to rise from the chair.

Jax laid a hand on her forearm, barely any pressure. "Or we could talk it through."

"I prefer quiet." Still, she let him tug her back to her chair. Kenna leaned her head back and closed her eyes, trying to gather some semblance of peace.

There was none to be had in the middle of a situation like this.

Everything had converged like two high-speed trains. She'd seen a crash years ago, in the French countryside. Supposedly idyllic, it had been shattered when she saw two TGV engines hit each other at full speed. Her dad dragged her out of the car to help pull survivors from the wreckage, but there hadn't been many.

As much as she didn't want to relive that, it was easy to see the correlation. She'd come here to satisfy the need to help Rachel Sanchez on the off chance it would help her identify who was part of the organization that controlled Ward Gaulding. She'd been given a way to get answers, but not by any means she'd attained on her own.

Instead, it was down to Jax and his investigation.

She turned to him. "Who told you to come this way north, and use the airport by Hatchet?"

He shrugged. "No one argued, but it was my suggestion."

"It wasn't because you were convinced it made the most sense."

"It did." He shrugged, a frown on his face. "Because we were right across the border, not far from here." It might have been the most logical route, but the bad guys also knew that to be true.

"You need a way to get free and clear. No attention. No notice. No roadblocks." Kenna's phone buzzed with a text. She reached over and tilted it so she could see the screen. "It's Marling. The cop who dropped off these."

"What's he say?"

"He got a call in. Someone found Peter Conklin's mom, dead in her car." Kenna held her stomach tight long enough she could say, "She killed herself."

Chapter Twenty Five

Marling hadn't replied to Kenna's text all day. She could only assume no response to her question of whether he was out looking for Peter Conklin was because he was busy. Or because he was actually *out looking for Peter Conklin*.

At least, she could hope.

Now the sun had dropped behind the mountains on the horizon and the sky had turned to an orange abraded with lines of clouds parallel to the horizon. Cabot sniffed along the line of bushes around the dog area at the RV park. Kenna held the leash in her hand until her girl came back over, done for the time being.

The RV park had settled in early, like a quiet night in the country where even the insects quieted. Kenna didn't tug her phone out to check it again. She needed all her awareness on the situation, or she might miss something important before it was too late to avoid it.

Some people might call it paranoia, but in her experience it could save her life.

She'd known before it happened that the church would

explode. She'd begged and pleaded with the cops inside. Tried to explain why it was a bad move to pile everyone in the same place, along with the witnesses and all the evidence. No one listened. The organization had struck. People died, and the FBI labeled it a gas explosion.

Kenna was listening now.

And thinking through everything, processing the way she needed to do in order to allow her mind time to put the pieces of a puzzle together. Especially when it was this complex.

Each murder committed during the time Conklin had been incarcerated fit the same modus operandi as Parker Jones and the judge. Not conclusive proof he'd committed those crimes, but enough for her to wonder who had potentially allowed him to what...leave the prison? It was a great alibi. And it couldn't have gone unnoticed.

The alternative was that nearly everyone in town knew exactly what was going on and no one said anything. A conspiracy that wide was baffling. Someone had died every few months of the ten years he'd been in. Had they really let him out to commit murder and then brought him back to the prison? And why allow him to leave for good two weeks ago?

The entire system here in Hatchet, the local jail and at the state prison, needed to be gone through by state and federal authorities to figure out what was going on.

She needed to talk to the prosecutor. Maybe March as well—assuming he was willing to both testify and speak the whole truth and nothing but the truth.

She could threaten to teach him what *so help me God* meant, but who in town would cave to Kenna? She'd faced down March in that court. What could she do, take away his freedom?

Kenna sighed aloud.

Jax had jumped willfully into the middle of this investigation with no thought to the cost he might have to pay. Like Ward Gaulding, saving his family but costing other families so much more.

No one is all good or all evil.

Be that as it may, she wasn't going to warm to a guy who did something like that. Nor would she condemn him for not allowing his family to die. Kenna planned on not incorporating the guy into her circle, no matter how much time she spent with him over the next few days. She didn't need to hear more of his sob story—nor did she want to think on who his victims had been.

It might sound cold, but she had to keep that distance in order to survive.

Cabot stopped. She lifted her head and stared at the trailer where the RV park owner lived. Kenna watched to see what had caught her dog's attention.

A cat rounded the side of the trailer, walking past the white latticed wood between the floor of the trailer and the ground.

"Come on, Cabot. Let's go."

She jumped toward Kenna, then set off in a trot toward her. The dog walked beside her back to the van, that same disquiet in the air.

Kenna scanned before she closed the door.

"What is it?" Jax asked.

She shook her head, not sure how to explain it.

"Something in the air." Ward Gaulding stood leaning against the sink, drinking from a mug. His body language rang with a kind of bone-deep fatigue she understood well. The weight of grief and regret.

"Seems like it." She didn't want to feel that way. "I should go back out when it's fully dark. See if I can see Conklin. Maybe he's lurking. Watching."

"If you think that's a good idea." Jax's words had a discordant tone, a lot like the feeling she got when she'd been outside. But she didn't think it was that. He'd been cooped up, but she was able to walk around outside. The guy was athletic. He worked out every day, and he'd been unable to do more than stretch.

"You could do some pushups." Kenna motioned to the floor. "This is where I am when you call to torture me."

A spark of amusement lit in his eyes. "Yoga is good for you."

"So is not getting shot. So then you don't need to work your muscles, so there's no *need* to do yoga."

He grinned around the frustration and exhaustion on his face.

"You guys banter like my wife and I."

Kenna glanced at Ward. "We should all focus."

"Good idea," Jax said. "I'll show you what I found, and Ward can tell you what he has."

Kenna sat back in her chair. "You've been working while I was out."

"I showed Ward the files, and he knows this guy." Jax handed her a copy of Peter Conklin's birth certificate. He pointed to the name listed under "Father" then ran his finger across the mouse pad of her laptop. "This guy, Peter Alan Conklin. I put him in the FBI database."

"You logged in from my IP address?"

"I noticed you had Thomas' proprietary firewall program. The one he wrote for sale through the private sector."

Kenna said nothing.

"So I used that and connected remotely to the FBI's server. It'll let them know I'm online—since I used my username and password—but it's also a way to check in. Without checking in. No one will get my location."

Kenna knew that to be true, but it didn't mean she had to be a fan. A risk was a risk regardless. "What did you find?"

"Peter Alan Conklin, aka Allen Conklin, aka Doug Partassus—"

"How many IDs does he have?"

"Seven that I can tell, and a moniker, 'The General,'" Jax said. "He's on an FBI watch list. He's named as the leader of a motorcycle club in the sixties and seventies."

"And now?"

He continued, "I have no idea how he ended up down here. That was in South Dakota, but it was also fifty, or sixty years ago."

"Before Conklin junior came along," she pointed out.

Ward kept drinking from his mug.

Kenna asked, "What did he do to get on a watch list?"

Jax read from the screen. "His rap sheet starts with assault, aggravated assault, and assault with a deadly weapon. Domestic abuse calls. He's suspected of stabbing a guy in a bar in Reno. Weapons sales in Colorado. A bombing in Arizona in the midseventies."

"Sounds like a stand-up guy."

"One of his earlier wives went missing. Lots of interviews and not much evidence," Jax said. "At some point he must've landed in New Mexico and met Conklin's mom."

"Deb. She said she was never Mrs. Conklin," Kenna said. "That might've been a choice that saved her life." She checked her phone again.

No calls.

Kenna needed to contact Stairs. Find out what was taking so long getting them a ranch or farm to land a plane at so Jax and his witness could get out of here. Then she had a murderer to hunt.

She restarted her phone just in case there was a problem that explained why she wasn't getting any texts or calls.

Ward spoke then. "They called the kid PJ, even though his dad's name was Albert."

Kenna turned. "You're from Hatchet."

"I spent enough time here. Thought I got out."

She nearly jumped out of her chair. Jax reached out a hand and stayed her.

Ward continued, "He was messed up from the beginning, and dad was in and out. Mom did what she could. The kid was the boogey man. PJ would come after you if you didn't do what they said. For years. These days he'd have been pegged as most likely to become a school shooter. But it was so much worse than that."

Kenna waited, a sinking feeling tugging her lower in her chair.

"Started with squirrels. Rodents. Kids all over town would find them cut up. Pinned open. Then the neighbor's cat." Ward swallowed. "Everyone knew he'd be one of those psychopaths. Then Billie moved in next door. They became best friends. The Lord only knows why. But PJ loved Billie with a love..." He shook his head. "It was obsessive. His dad didn't like it. Stormed into a football game one Friday night and dragged PJ off the field. No one said a thing. We could hear him beating the kid behind the snack shack. Billie ran home crying."

"You think the dad killed Billie?" Jax said.

"Don't know who killed him." Ward sniffed. "But I can tell you where I buried him."

Kenna bit her lip. "How did he die?"

"Coulda been a heart attack for all I know, wrapped up in a rug in the trunk of a car. I got a call, and the voice told me to take the car and get rid of the body. They didn't care how. Just that no one ever found him."

She sat forward in her chair. "Hang on. This voice on the call, can you describe it?"

"It's been years." Ward shrugged. "Like a computer, I guess. Why do you ask?"

They were both looking at her now. "I ran across a similar thing." She didn't know if Conklin had been behind it. *This town.* She wanted to roll her eyes again. "Anything else about him or the dad?"

When Ward started to shake his head, Jax said, "The original murder. This Billie kid, his friend. Peter Jr. was convicted?"

Ward nodded. "He was fifteen. Didn't put up a fight. Far as I remember, he didn't say anything the whole trial. The judge found him guilty and shipped him off to the adult prison."

Kenna blinked. "At fifteen?"

"He was six two and two fifty even back then." Ward shrugged. "I guess he was tried as an adult."

"Wow." Jax scrolled on the mouse pad. "This whole thing is messed up."

"I can't even believe I'm contemplating that they let him out to commit murder," Kenna said. "But nothing else makes much sense. Only did they let him kill whoever he wanted, or did someone do this so they could turn him into a weapon? I mean, it's crazy, but what if Billie was killed to trigger something in Conklin? Like causing a psychotic break on purpose."

"Risky." Jax winced. "You wouldn't know what the result would be."

"And then you try and reason with him? Get him to work for you?" Kenna remembered something. "Conklin mentioned a sister. Something about wanting to go and see her graduate from medical school."

Jax tapped on the computer.

Kenna got up and walked in the small space as much as she could. She tugged back the edge of the blind over the window by her bed. Someone was outside walking around, though with the light in here and the dark outside, she couldn't see who it was. Or what they were doing.

She gave Cabot a scratch. The dog rolled to her back and stuck her two front paws in the air. Kenna used both hands and rubbed the sides of the dog's ribs. She'd filled out since Kenna found her in Salt Lake City, tied up outside a restaurant, left there for hours in chilly weather.

No one had ever claimed her.

"Got it," Jax said.

She went back and found Ward in the chair behind the driver's seat. If she sat in the rotated driver's seat, she'd be knee to knee with him. Kenna stayed by the sink, occupying the spot where he'd been. "What did you find?"

"Peter Conklin never had a sister as far as I can see. But do you know who did?"

"I'm gonna take a wild guess," Kenna said. "And say Billie had a sister."

"Bingo." Jax nodded. "Currently a medical student in Phoenix."

"As if anyone would let a parolee leave the state." Kenna shook her head. "Plus, he's a murderer and a psycho. If I had him on a leash, it would be short." She thought about the ligature marks on his wrists. "They tried to reason with him. Or at least contain him. He got away or was left, and he managed to call his mom, who called me. Or he coerced her into sending us."

"And now we can't ask her."

Kenna nodded, with no words to reply to Jax's statement. Another life ended. Not by Conklin's hand, at least not directly. But she figured he was responsible anyway for the fact Deb had taken her own life.

A noise outside drew her attention.

She flinched. "The cameras. They didn't go off." She lifted her phone from the counter and tapped the screen as soon as it lit up. "I restarted it. Now it's back on but frozen. What is going on?"

Someone bumped the side of the van.

Another person shoved the hood down, rocking the whole vehicle.

Cabot got off the bed and barked.

Kenna said, "Shut off all the lights."

They all hit a switch. As soon as it was dark, she grabbed her keys. Just in case. Then she lifted the blinds on the front windshield and the side windows.

Kenna quickly rotated the seat and put the key in. "We're completely surrounded. You guys should find a belt and clip in, or you're liable to be thrown around."

"Guns?" He leaned down to look over her shoulder.

Cabot barked again.

"Shush, girl." Kenna showed Jax how to reorient the passenger seat. "Find a seatbelt, Ward." To Jax, she said, "Just people. A crowd of them."

Standing there, watching the van. Jackets and hoodies with the hoods up so no faces were visible. Her phone wasn't working, and now this? An ambush. And they were cut off from being able to call anyone for help.

Though, in a town like this, where would help come from?

Jax's voice remained steady when he said, "Where are we going to go?"

"We have to get out of the RV park first." She hadn't turned on the engine yet. As soon as she did, would that set off them being jumped? "Then we figure out where to go."

Jax palmed a pistol. "Let's go."

"Okay, but—"

He pointed at the window. "Kenna, drive!"

A guy rushed at them with a sledgehammer.

Chapter Twenty-Six

She turned the key and hit the gas as soon as she could put it in drive, wincing as all the hookups tore out. The van shot forward and the crowd surged. People on all sides, grabbing the handles.

She grasped the wheel and winced again when two guys jumped out of the way.

But the third wasn't so lucky.

Something hit the back of the van. She felt the impact and heard a pound—and glass shattered.

Ward fell to the floor with a thud and a grunt.

Jax said, "Ward, you good?"

Cabot barked.

Kenna spotted two cars up ahead, parked so they were pointing toward each other in the middle of the asphalt road that wound through the RV park. She pressed harder on the gas.

A gunshot cracked the back window.

She ducked, even though the bullet never penetrated. "Cabot! Get down!"

Jax glanced over. "Are you doing what I think you are?"

She didn't look at him, or he'd see the answer on her face. Kenna grabbed for her seatbelt and snapped it in. Two hands back on the wheel. Leaning forward. She bit her lip. "Let's go."

The van slammed into the hoods of both cars, spinning them apart. Impact slowed them for a few seconds.

Jax said, "There's maybe thirty people behind us."

"I'm guessing not even everyone who was at the airport." She gripped the wheel and held steady.

Ward grunted, clambering back onto the seat with an audible exhale, and the seatbelt clicked in.

"Everyone good?" she asked.

Jax didn't move from peering in the side mirror. "We won't be when those cars catch up. You only delayed some of their response."

"Better than nothing."

"That's not—"

"Whatever," she said. "I'll figure something out."

"How about that cop friend of yours?"

Kenna let out a sharp noise. "Right. Some friend." She glanced at Jax then. "Kind of like yours back there, getting us all wrapped up in this. You realize it was a trap, right?"

"I never said you had to sign up for protection detail," Jax said. "Just drop us somewhere. We'll be less noticeable on foot than in a van everyone's seen."

"That's why I'm figuring out somewhere we can go." What did he think she was doing, just driving? Running away with no thought on where they would end up. She couldn't run all the way to Utah like this. They'd have to stop for gas, and what would that get them?

These people were after the million-dollar bounty on Ward Gaulding's head. They would kill Jax and Kenna without a thought, take the witness, and leave behind nothing but carnage. And Jax's mom's broken heart.

She let off the gas a fraction for the corner, but not much. They sailed out the exit and onto the highway. She checked the side mirror and spotted two or three vehicles in pursuit.

Kenna tapped the dash. The speakers rang as her vehicle connected to her phone made the call.

"Marling."

Hopefully the two men in the van with her kept quiet. "I need your help. Actually it doesn't have to be you. But it does need to be police."

"What's going on?"

"I'm in a car chase."

"Who's the target?"

"Me," Kenna said. "They're trying to run me down." He asked her location, and she gave him a mile marker since they were just outside town proper. "I'll be passing the grocery store in a couple of minutes."

"Copy that." He spoke like he was moving fast. "I'll have someone there to intercept in a couple of minutes."

"I'm not stopping." Just so he had that clear. "I just want them off me."

"And I'm not supposed to assume you've got whoever was headed to the airport with you?"

"Doesn't matter. It's none of your business." Kenna hit the button on the dash, ending the call.

"You think that's going to help?" Jax asked.

"It can't make things much worse." Except as soon as she said that she thought maybe it could.

A gunshot slammed into the back of the car. Another hit the side mirror next to her, taking a chunk of the plastic and leaving cracks in the glass.

"How did they know we were in your van?" Ward asked.

"Probably the same way they knew you'd be coming to the airport."

Jax shot her a glance, but she didn't look to see the expression on his face. He had his elbow on the window, the gun still in his hands while a guy leaned out of the window in the car behind them and took potshots.

An agent with the FBI. The supervisor in his office. Now he sat in the passenger seat, unable to do anything to resolve this. Realizing he'd been strung along and directed right into this setup.

"Sorry," she muttered.

He grunted.

"They can't have known you were there." Only Marling had been by, and she didn't think he'd seen inside. That only left... "Dixie."

"What?"

She took another corner, so fast they nearly went up on two wheels. A pair of black-and-white police cars raced toward them, lights and sirens going. The vehicles in pursuit turned the corner after them.

Kenna couldn't have planned it better. The second the cars turned to follow her, the cop cars passed the van and cut them off.

Metal slammed into metal as one of the cop cars rammed another vehicle—whether by accident or on purpose.

She took a turn and then another, trying to evade the others. Get some distance. They weren't far from Carl Southampton's rental house. That might work, but they'd have to ditch the noticeable van somewhere, and she wouldn't be able to return to it for some time—if ever.

"I have an idea," she began.

Jax shot back, "About how this is a trap I walked into?"

She wanted to argue back that it wasn't her doing, but if it was Dixie who'd spread the word there was someone in Kenna's van, then it could be argued this might be her fault. Just a little. There was no reason for Ward, or Jax for that matter, to sell them out. Jax would've changed the plan away from whatever the dead special agent had wanted to do.

"This isn't about that." It was better to be constructive. "Are you good to walk a bit, Ward? We need to ditch the van and circle back around on foot. There's a pool house."

Jax said, "Whose place?"

Kenna watched the mirrors and told him quickly about Justine and the lawyer she'd hired from Albuquerque to fight the charges. "He's still here."

"Okay."

"Just like that?" Kenna glanced over then, just for a second. "Okay?"

"I trust you."

She drove another two streets, then circled around to a busier one at the edge of the neighborhood next to the one where the judge had lived—and died. All the while she tried to figure out why that statement of his birthed a warm feeling in her.

She was probably just out of practice having someone in her space she actually appreciated. Jax's opinion was one she cared about. They talked about their lives, on the phone while they worked out. Or, rather while he told her what moves to do so she could strengthen her muscles after she was shot last year.

Kenna pulled over and parked. "Let's go."

She pulled down the shades and pocketed the keys. Backpack with a couple of non-negotiable essentials in case it was a while before she got her van back. She'd downsized to this vehicle and got a storage unit in St. George, Utah, in Ryson's name with a lot of her dad's old things in it. His journals, his

Bible, and the books he read. She packed a couple of changes of clothes, the cash she had, and a gun. She put extra magazines in the side pocket where most folks would've put their water bottle.

Ward flipped up the hood of his sweatshirt.

Jax pulled on his jacket and did the same with the hood.

She put a beanie over her hair and tucked it inside, then grabbed her overcoat. She flipped up the hood with the fur on the edge and clipped on Cabot's leash. Doors locked. "Let's go."

Jax looked back. "Which way?"

Cabot whined beside her. "Keep going down this street." Kenna leaned down and rubbed her shoulder. "You okay, dog?"

Cabot walked all right, no limp right now. Sometimes that was a factor of the amount of adrenaline pumping through her system. The way Kenna could often use her arms if she absolutely had to, lifting more than she usually could or holding up a weapon for more time than she ordinarily clocked.

"Go right at the next street."

Jax set a fast clip, just below a jog. Anyone watching would notice their speed and the tension they displayed, but there was nothing they could do about that. Just get to safety. Then rest.

"The gate halfway down." Between two houses, tucked back out of sight.

They parted and let her bang on the door. After a few seconds of no answer, Jax made a fist and pounded on the door the way a fed would serving a warrant. But he had no ID on him.

The door swung open.

Jax muscled his way past Carl Southampton, pushing Ward ahead of him. She stepped in after them with Cabot.

"What is this?" He had those silk pajamas on, tugging a robe over his shoulders.

"Sorry we barged in. We needed a safe place to stay."

"And you decided to wake me up, rather than heading to the police station?" He followed after her through to the living room, where Ward and Jax stood around.

She unclipped the leash.

Ward slumped onto the couch. Kenna took off her backpack and tucked away her gun in the holster on the back of her belt. Jax stowed his on his hip.

Kenna said, "If you were in trouble, would you trust the police in this town?"

"No, I would not."

Kenna introduced everyone. Carl didn't react at all to Ward's name, which she figured was a good thing. Jax got a raised eyebrow. "We need to get the two of them to a meeting point with the FBI so Ward can be put in protective custody."

"And you decided to trust a lawyer you've never met before to help you with this?"

"You're on a list."

Carl shook his head. "What list?"

"People who don't roll over. Who aren't likely to cave to outside pressure, and who don't seem to be affiliated with anyone but themselves." Still, she wasn't going to hand him everything. He could still make a move to betray any of them, and she had to be prepared for it.

"Ah, so I'm selfish?"

Kenna didn't know what to say.

Carl started to chuckle. "I'll give you my ex-wife's phone number. You can tell her my being shallow and self-centered turned out to be good for something."

She gave him a slight smile. "Do you have a phone we could use? I left mine in the van in case they're able to trace it and it was the only one we had between us." Never mind that she brought her laptop along, but it couldn't have a connection to anything when it was switched off. Her phone hadn't connected right all day.

Someone had messed with it, and she never got any of her messages.

Carl said, "The moment my cell phone is used, I become part of this. Before that happens you're going to explain to me who this gentlemen is and what is going on."

Kenna sat on the arm of the couch. Cabot had curled up on the floor with her back along the couch. Jax gave the lawyer the quick version, where Ward was only a person of interest who would testify if they could get him into custody.

"He definitely needs to be with the feds." Kenna wasn't sure Ward should be free, even if he had been under duress. But that was for the US Attorney's Office to decide.

"So this isn't another one of your underdog fights."

She shook her head, exhaustion lifting humor closer to the surface than it should be. "How is Justine?"

"The police chief just cleared her of all suspicion."

"That's good," Carl said.

Then Ward spoke. "I'm not proud of anything I've done, but they won't ever let me go. I've got a better shot at bringing them down and having a life if I can get a deal with witness protection."

Carl nodded.

"He might need a lawyer," Kenna pointed out.

"I have enough clients of my own, Ms. Banbury. I don't need any more you send my way."

She shrugged. "Special Agent Jaxton and his witness need a way out of Hatchet. Preferably to an airport or some place they can get picked up."

"One of the houses in this neighborhood has a helipad."

Jax said, "That's perfect."

Kenna didn't like the idea. "It's a little conspicuous. Could be deadly before you even get off the ground."

Her mind flashed with images of them hanging on for dear life while gunmen shot up the chopper. They'd crash to the ground and go up in flames. Not the way she wanted to die.

"Worth a walk over there to see if you can borrow his chopper. Get yourselves to the Albuquerque airport before…" Carl paused, and she got a weird note from his body language. "Who is it that's coming after you?"

"Every bad guy from here to the Mexican border. Felt like half the town of Hatchet was right behind us." She blew out a breath. "You know this town by now. There's no telling who's going to crawl out of the woodwork."

"Unfortunately," Jax said, "there's a hit out on us. A million dollars in exchange for Ward."

Carl snorted. "Is that it? I'd ask for more." He turned slightly and brought a gun up with his left hand. "Put your weapon on the floor."

"I'm not gonna do that." Jax didn't move.

"So you want a cut of the money, is that it?"

Kenna eased her hand toward her gun.

Jax snorted. "I'm not disarming myself. But we can work something out, make this lucrative for everyone."

Ward glanced between them, probably shocked Jax had turned so fast.

Kenna wasn't worried about that. She studied Carl, waiting for his decision. She caught a subtle shift as he tensed to pull the trigger.

She fired her gun. Three shots.

Carl's body jerked. The gun discharged in his hand, and blood sprayed the wall behind him. He fell to the ground.

So did Jax.

"No!" Kenna scrambled over on her hands and knees.

He sat up with a wince, and the guy actually winked. "Told you."

She gasped for air. "What?"

"You do care about me."

Chapter Twenty-Seven

Kenna backed off from Jax and got up. She shot a double-check glance at Ward and headed for the dead lawyer.

"You got that I was just distracting him, right?"

"Of course." She crouched, rummaged in his robe pockets, and found his phone. "Check no one is coming from the house. They might've found the shot."

Her bullets were lodged in Carl's torso. Center mass.

She'd been taught to have a detached view of taking a life, treating it as an if-then scenario. If she believed her life or the life of another person was in imminent danger, she should fire. In that exchange she was authorized to take a life. Treating it dispassionately like this was probably meant to be a coping mechanism.

It didn't work. Right now Kenna was running on adrenaline, her hands shaking enough she dropped the phone.

Jax came over from the window. "No one is outside."

She scooped up the phone and hit the power button. Thumbprint.

Carl's let her in, and she changed the setting to a password she programmed into it. Then she dialed Stairs.

Kenna walked out into the hall.

Jax could watch Ward, and she didn't want to spend more time than necessary in the room with a man she'd just killed. Sure, she could worry about leaving physical evidence behind. She might have to answer questions. But more likely, given the fact this was Hatchet, some innocent person would end up charged with this like it was a premeditated murder.

The call connected, and Stairs said, "Please be Kenna."

"It's me." She slumped against the wall and dipped her head, the phone to her ear.

"I've been calling and texting you all day, trying to get a plan situated."

But she hadn't received any of the messages. "What's going on?"

He spoke with a groan to his tone. "The agents who landed at the airport outside Hatchet yesterday? They're gone now. They believe the whole thing was bad intel, so they took off and went back to Albuquerque."

"We lost our ride?"

"I couldn't contact you. They figured I was lying, causing trouble for them."

Kenna winced. "I need to get Jax and Ward out of town, somewhere safe."

"You, too. They have your photo as well so they know the three of you are together."

"How do you know that?"

"I got an email." He paused. "It was really weird, actually. Untraceable as far as I can tell, and just attached screenshots of a conversation between two people. Your name was used. They have your car license plate, and your van."

"I ditched both of those, and my phone."

"Good." He sounded relieved but was also getting that "boss" tone that meant he was about to start giving orders. "I'm getting on a plane now, headed to Albuquerque. And when I get there, heads are gonna roll, let me tell you. I'll have a plan by the time I land and a team of agents in play as soon as possible to get down there and watch your backs."

And until then? Hatchet could very well turn into a war zone. With a murderer on the loose as well.

Still, he was doing everything in his power to help. She knew it was still based on guilt and feeling like he needed to make amends. But if it proved helpful, she didn't need to complain?

"Thanks, Stairns."

"Gotta go. We're boarded, and they're giving me dirty looks."

"Bye." Kenna hung up. She looked through the phone, scrolling down texts and finding a thread with Justine Greene as the saved contact. The texts looked to be from Austin, given the syntax. Austin and Justine had left town, driving his car and going west toward Tucson. If that was the truth. She would follow up later and make sure they were safe.

In the process she would ask Justine more about Maizie so Kenna could find her. And then, if she needed it, Kenna would get her free of the situation she was in.

His emails were all pretty benign. A lot of store news blasts and messages from his assistant. "Nothing on here about the million dollars, or the organization." She glanced over at Jax, in the doorway between the living room and front door.

"Are you okay?"

"Stairns is on his way. He'll loop in a new team of FBI

agents closest to us and get them down here to escort you where you need to go." Or he could get in a car and drive to Tucson. "Unless you know how to hotwire a car, in which case I have some other workable options."

Her vehicles were out.

"Are you going to come with us?" He took a step toward her.

"Three people instead of just two makes us more noticeable. Besides, there's a murderer on the loose in Hatchet. I need to make sure he's contained." And not the way he'd been for ten years. "Then I'm gonna blow this thing wide open. The prison. The police department. The court system. All of it."

"I could get Ward where he's going and come back and help."

"Don't you have a job to do in Salt Lake City, Mr. Assistant Special Agent in Charge?"

He winced. "Right."

"You've been undercover too long."

"I still remember myself, don't worry." He studied her. "Somehow I saw you, and it all came back."

"You're gonna want to call me *before* you go on a case like this next time. Okay?"

He chuckled but it was short-lived. "We need to deal with the body."

Kenna felt her brows rise. "You know how to do that?"

"I just mean clean up. For the police." He frowned. "What are you talking about?"

She winced. "Nothing." More of that dispassionate thinking. Gallows humor, even though she wasn't laughing, and she hadn't told a joke either. "I'll make sure the state police get my full account of everything that happened."

He nodded. "I'll do the same as soon as I can."

Kenna wanted to talk more to Ward while they figured out their next move. She pushed off the wall, and a shadow darkened the window beside the door. She waved Jax back. "Get out of sight."

A knock on the door.

Cabot came out of the living room.

Jax moved in there, and she heard him whisper to Ward. Now she just had to make sure whoever this was didn't realize she'd killed the occupant minutes ago. Had they heard the gunshot?

She unlocked and opened the door, already smiling. The woman on the doorstep had a robe on, tied tight on her slender waist. Full makeup and curled hair from the day, slippers on her feet.

"Where is Mr. Southampton?"

"In the shower." Kenna smiled. "I can tell him you stopped by. You are..."

"The homeowner." She motioned over her shoulder, then frowned down at Cabot. "You can't have a dog here. It's expressly stated on the lease agreement." She tapped one foot. "I didn't decide to be a short-term renter to have a dog pee all over the carpet."

Kenna wanted to tell her that Cabot was too much of a lady to pee inside a house but didn't want to prolong the conversation. "I'll be leaving soon. Not to worry."

"I didn't agree to late-night visitors." The lady frowned. "I heard fireworks, or something like that. There better not be damage when he leaves."

Three gunshots. Blood all over the carpet. This woman might live in Hatchet, but she wasn't likely to be happy with the aftermath of Carl's stay.

"I'll have Mr. Southampton call you," Kenna said, holding tight to the door and making sure this lady didn't see in the living room. "I'm sure he'll want to apologize for the misunderstanding."

"I don't know what's happening here." She sighed, a pronounced sound. As though she'd become accustomed to having to overdramatize her displays of emotion. Maybe she'd done theater in high school. "First the neighborhood is full of...ruffians. Now a dog." She turned and started to walk away. "What's next? Snow?"

Kenna closed the door and leaned against it, blowing out a long breath. "Why do I feel like we're the criminals?"

"You protected someone you care about," Ward said. "I know what that's like."

Kenna hadn't expected him to be the one to respond.

"We're not the same. He had a gun to Jax's head." Ward had set a bomb to save his family, and she'd saved a federal agent. Her friend. "It's not the same."

"We need a plan."

Despite Jax's words, Ward continued to stare at her. Kenna didn't want to know if he thought he should be able to convince her around to his side of things. Testifying—or planning to—didn't make him a saint.

The fact was, he hadn't ever been a good guy as far as she could tell. No doubt there had been plenty of decisions and opportunities in his life where he could have made a different choice. Just like with everyone, it wasn't a one-and-done crossroads. More like a series of tiny steps that all led to a path the person had decided on themselves.

Not because he'd been forced into it.

Her life hadn't fallen apart in one night. It had been a series of chips falling, one after the other. Sometimes two at a time.

A bunch of choices she'd made that brought her to the place she'd lost everything. Had she made others, it would have been different, or a shade of the same thing. Life could go plenty of directions, all based on a simple choice. Every day since then had been a choice as well.

The choice to get up.

To keep moving.

Live her life.

Fight for justice, and the safety and security of people who needed help.

She was glad she'd landed in Hatchet because it had been about helping Rachel. Then Justine. Ultimately, it was about finding Maizie.

Jax made his own choices and planned to solve the case his own way. Between the two of them, it gave them double the chance to uncover this organization and end them, which made them a good team. Even if she'd have preferred it if he talked to her about it. Though, he'd probably say the same about her.

Ward's dark eyes narrowed. "Looks to me like she's planning on exchanging me for the money herself."

Kenna rolled her eyes. "You think I'd jeopardize Jax like that?"

"You think I'd let you?" Jax grinned.

She grinned back. "Who would wake me up just to torture me with exercise?"

"Who would I call so I can listen to complaining to start my day right?"

Ward shifted to look from Kenna to Jax and back again. "Are you guys sure you're not a thing?"

Kenna started. "We don't...I'm not..."

Jax stiffened. "I don't do long distance." A blank look settled on his face.

They needed to get this train back on the tracks fast. Otherwise her mind would get stuck on what that lack of expression on his face meant. So much of their friendship had been over the phone, or text and email. He was harder to read in person.

Or she'd never thought she had to try so hard to figure out what he was thinking.

Kenna pushed all those thoughts away. "I should check my computer, just to make sure I'm not missing something. Either of you know how to hotwire a fancy car?"

Maybe they could steal from the homeowner she just met, but that could get sticky if she caught them trying to grab her keys. And if she had a gun in her house.

Ward said, "Depends on the car, but older is better."

"Right." Jax folded his arms. "I can go take Cabot for a walk. Stick to the shadows and see what I can find parked on the street."

When the homeowner had said the neighborhood was crawling with—what had she called them? *Ruffians.* Kenna figured that meant she hadn't lost the gang members following them quite as far as she'd wanted. They knew the general area the three of them had fled to, just not what house they were in.

Which meant they could stay here long enough for the FBI to come right to them.

With a dead guy on the floor.

Ward whirled around to him. "And leave me with her? I'll end up with a bullet in me like that guy."

Kenna turned to her backpack and pulled out her laptop. She took it to the kitchen because it was wearing on even her being in the same room as a man she'd killed. Not the first time, or the last. It was what it was. He would have killed Jax. As far as she was concerned, that was unacceptable.

She'd lost the man she'd loved before. These days her tolerance for losing someone she even just vaguely liked was nonexistent. That was why she had to keep the animosity for Ward. The last thing she needed was sympathy for a guy who killed so many.

She sat at a tiny circular dining table with a glass top and uncomfortable wicker chairs. The laptop took its sweet time booting up, but she logged onto the free Wi-Fi using the password on the mantel. Not ideal, but she got on the VPN as fast as she could and masked everything before she opened the admin side of Utah True Crime.

Nothing new.

Kenna typed a short thank-you for the heads-up that Jax was in danger. She'd been able to save his life, and that was because of this person. Whoever they were. She owed them, enough she put at the end of the message that if it was within her power, she would do anything to repay the favor.

If this was Maizie, whoever the person was behind the photo, Kenna wanted her to know that she would help her as much as she was able.

If it wasn't? She had zero clue who it was.

"Anything?"

She turned to Jax and shook her head. "Nothing new."

"You really wanna wait for Stairs to land? I can call the nearest FBI office and get a tactical team down here in a few hours."

"They left us here." The plane at the airport had taken off. "They left *you*."

Jax's expression softened. "Are you going to freak out if I hug you?"

"I thought you were going for a walk to look for cars to steal?"

He chuckled. "I'm going, I'm going."

As they walked together to the door, Kenna told him, "It'll

be light soon. Be careful. There are guys about." Then pulled the door open. "Smells like smoke outside."

A column of black trailed up into the sky.

"Isn't that close to where—" he began.

She gritted her teeth. "They set my van on fire."

Chapter Twenty Eight

Kenna grasped the handle, on her way out the door. Her van. It was on fire. Those guys had torched her home, and she had to—

Jax's arm snaked around her waist. He dragged her back so fast, he lifted her off the ground.

"Get off." She smacked at his arm.

"You can't go out there." He set her down and came close so that she had to take a step back.

Her back hit the wall.

"No running away."

"I'm not running." She wasn't a coward. "I need to put out that fire!"

Jax shook his head.

She could push against his shoulders, try and make him move. But what would that serve except to prove she lacked the strength to move him out of the way. She'd need to duck and get her shoulder into it. Push with her hips.

As satisfying as it would be to get into a slapping match.

Her head swam from breathing too hard and fast. She

needed to get control. He started to speak, but she cut him off. "Don't tell me to calm down."

His expression did that softening thing again. She didn't need pity or care. Whichever it was, she needed strength and resilience not the tendency to soften whenever she said anything. "Focus up, Special Agent Jaxton."

His lips twitched. "That's what I was going to say."

"Yeah, right." Kenna nudged his shoulder. "Why am I up against the wall?"

"We each need someone to stop us from running headlong into danger sometimes."

"Yeah?" The moment the word came out, she regretted it. She needed to tone down the animosity or she would push him away from the semblance of friendship they had. *I don't do long distance.* But was that true, what he'd said?

The closer they were, the more she caught that spark of attraction she'd pretty much ignored since they met. It was easier to be independent than adjust to fit someone else. She liked her solitary life. And why was she even thinking about... whatever this was anyway? Like with gallows humor, her mind seemed to want to focus on something random—and safe because it was *never* gonna happen—instead of the reality of the situation.

Gunmen chased them and it seemed she was more angry at Ward for what he'd done.

Even with her van on fire, she was more worried about Jax and this banter. The sparks she liked to play off as friendship she wasn't going to ever allow to develop into something else. After all, what was the point?

He hadn't quit studying her with that steady gaze of his.

The witness could probably have run out the back door at that moment, and it would have taken her a second to figure out what was happening. Not good. Jax shot her situational awareness to pieces, which was just proof it was for the best that they didn't work together.

Her van was in flames.

Destroyed.

He cleared his throat. "A few years back we were chasing this arms dealer in San Diego who was running guns and smuggling people through the LA port over to Thailand. Except he has this one girl he takes everywhere with him. He's basically obsessed with her. So we try and make contact, get her to testify." He took a breath. "Two days later, we found her in a landfill, carved into pieces."

Kenna winced.

"So we double down then and go after him harder."

She nodded.

"He got a new girl. Spreads it wide he's gonna take her to this out of the way house he's got and 'break her in.' That's how he put it."

Kenna couldn't say anything. There were no words for something like that when it happened so many years ago. It wasn't a cause she could take up now when probably the entire situation was over.

"We found the spot and got ready to breach," he said. "Everyone is in position, and I hear this scream from inside. So I go to kick the door in. An agent I worked with tackled me. Dang near broke my ribs he hit me so hard. He'd seen a trip wire."

"It was a trap."

He nodded. "The whole place was wired to blow as soon as we hit the door."

"Was she in there?"

"Nope." He exhaled. "It was a voice recorder of the dead girl."

"Please tell me you caught him."

"Took months, but we brought him in. He's doing life now. No chance of parole."

"Good."

Jax squeezed her elbow. "If I'd kicked that door in, me and everyone with me that day would be dead. Kind of like if any of us step outside this house—or the yard."

Kenna pressed her lips together.

"I'm sorry about your home."

She wanted to brush it off. Instead, she said nothing.

"I need to call the FBI. Bring the local supervisor up to speed."

She handed him the phone, and he went to the living room. Kenna found Ward in the kitchen, drinking water from a glass. Cabot stood watching him like a quality guard dog. Given she'd had no training, Kenna had no idea what she would do if Ward did something Cabot didn't like.

"What's going on out there?" he asked.

In a nutshell? "They're trying to flush us out and cut us off."

Ward lowered the glass. "Are you going to let them?"

She wasn't even going to respond to that. "This is a tense situation. Let's just get through it."

"Sure. We can all stare at the wall until help comes."

"Or, you could answer some questions." Kenna lifted the lid of her laptop and sat at the tiny dining table. She logged on, brought up a notetaking program, and opened the app she used to record Peter Conklin's statement. She'd videoed him. But nothing about what had happened, or Ward's story, made her want to do the same now.

"It's not the time." Ward stayed over in the kitchen. "I have to get safe before I can tell my story."

Kenna clicked her fingers. Cabot came over and lay down.

"You work for this organization." Kenna needed him to

say something to get information out of him. Then this whole thing wouldn't be a waste of time that left a man dead.

"I did."

Past tense. "Do you have the tattoo?"

After a second where he stared at her, he shifted. "I'm surprised you know about that." Ward set the glass down and rolled up his sleeve. The scrollwork C had been inked on the inside of his forearm.

"What does the letter C stand for?" She'd seen it on videos, on the dark web, and now tattooed on two people.

"Cerberus."

Was he for real? "The dog that guards the underworld?"

Ward shrugged. "I just thought it was a cool name."

Kenna hit the mouse button on her laptop and started recording. "Can I show you something?"

It did double duty, showing her the image on her phone. He came close enough he sat at the table rather than remaining standing. His gaze narrowed on the girl, a picture of the photo that had been on the fridge in Kenna's van.

Probably burned and ashes right now.

"Do you know her?" she asked. "Have you ever seen her?"

"Lot of girls go through the organization, if you know what I mean. What's special about this one?"

"You tell me." If she was the person feeding Kenna info, then she had access to a computer. Which meant she wasn't just any teen caught up in a trafficking business.

"Why do you care about her?" Ward shook his head. "Not much point when there are so many."

Kenna wasn't going to try and articulate why she cared about Maizie—if that was her name. She knew trafficking and crime generally had hundreds, thousands, millions of victims worldwide. What did one matter when she couldn't save them all?

But putting a name with a face and making contact? That changed everything.

Maizie might need her help.

Not just because that could've easily been Kenna if her dad hadn't been the man he was.

If he didn't know where Maizie was now or how to find her, it didn't matter. "I need to ask you about Peter Conklin."

"You think I know all the players in this organization? I thought you wanted to take them all down. This is about some girl and a sicko who slices people up?"

Kenna's mind put Maizie in context with Conklin, and then all she saw was blood. "You'd better hope you know the players if you want a deal from the FBI."

"They won't want any do-gooder law enforcement shutting them down," Ward said. "This is business, and it's widespread. No way you'll get them all."

She was certainly going to try. "So it's systemic. They've got players in government and law enforcement branches—state and federal, right? And what do you know that's such a threat they have a million-dollar ransom out for you?"

"First of all," Ward said, "bagging an FBI agent gives you street cred. So it's not just me. Your boyfriend is in danger as well. But he also has the resources to do this."

"To get you to safety?" She wasn't touching the *boyfriend* thing. That part of her had been dormant for a long time, pretty much since the day Bradley died. Now that she was having feelings for Jax? Didn't mean anything would happen.

Ward nodded.

"So you need him. But that's not why you agreed to testify."

Ward lowered his gaze to the table. "My wife found out what I did, blowing up that church to save her and the kids.

She took them to her sister's place in Cabo San Lucas. She won't talk to me until I make it right."

She wanted to say, *Good*, but didn't.

Regardless of how she felt about others' decisions, they didn't need to carry the weight of her opinion. If he felt regret, that would only make it worse. If he was determined to live free of guilt, piling it on would do nothing.

He continued, "I did the right thing, whether she agrees or not. She's alive. The kids are alive. They weren't tortured and murdered."

"So you believe you did the right thing, blowing up that church and killing all those people?" Kenna couldn't convince him otherwise if that was the case. And what would it achieve? It wasn't going to bring back those people.

Nothing would bring them back. But justice could be served—and not by allowing this guy to skate out from under a sentence for all those murders. He'd intentionally set those charges and walked out knowing the whole place would be destroyed. That the explosion would kill everyone.

"They weren't going to let the California Bureau of Investigation, or the FBI, figure out who they are." Ward paused. "So they forced me to eliminate the threat."

"I tried to warn them." Kenna shook her head. Cabot sat up and laid her chin on Kenna's knee, so Kenna gave her a scratch.

"Because you saw me leave?"

She nodded, still just looking at her dog. "It didn't sit right. Something about the way you moved. We went in the church, and I realized it was all there. The witnesses, the evidence. I tried to tell them it was too risky."

She'd yelled and screamed at them all, trying to get them to listen to what had been so clear to her. But she'd lost a friend days before because of this organization. Lost a shot at connecting with the memory of her father and getting to know a guy who had been friends with him. A man who'd known her mother.

She'd tried to pull the fire alarm in the church. So all the people inside would evacuate and maybe keep their lives. No one had understood her instincts—her belief they were in imminent danger. What seemed so plain for her to see remained a mystery to others.

"That was the idea," Ward said. "Get them all in one place."

"Set charges. Eliminate the threat, then lean on the FBI to declare it a gas leak. A tragic accident." Kenna's eyes burned hot with unshed tears.

Ward stared at her. "Do you have children?"

She swallowed. "No."

"Then you can't possibly understand what it feels like to hold your child in your arms. To know that part of you—part of your heart—is in this tiny human. Or to watch them grow up." His jaw flexed.

Cabot let out a whine.

Jax strode into the kitchen. "That's enough."

Kenna didn't look at him. Whatever was on her face, he would see it all too clearly. He knew about the baby she had lost. And it didn't matter that she'd never have a child of her own. She understood what love meant, however that came. A parent-child relationship. Or friends that were the family of your heart, the way the Rysons were to her. People who adopted children didn't care for them less because they weren't biological relations.

She would do just about anything for the people she called family.

But not what Ward had done.

"We were just talking." Ward sat back in his chair. His

closed off expression didn't tell her anything, and if it had she figured it wasn't anything she wanted to know anyway.

She wasn't interested in excuses or justifications.

Kenna closed the lid of her laptop. "And we're done. I don't need to hear anything else."

She wanted to explain to Jax that this guy probably didn't have enough to offer the feds if he wanted a deal. He might satisfy his wife's issue with what he'd done, but he would end up in jail for it. There was already a hit out on him. Did he think he'd survive prison with a powerful organization out there, believing he'd sold them out—or tried to?

Despite his assertion this was about appeasing his wife, she wanted to know his true motives. Ward was putting his own life on the line by turning himself in instead of trying to escape.

She didn't figure he was about to turn the tables and get the ransom money for Jax. That wasn't going to do enough to buy his freedom any more than anyone else trying to escape. She sincerely hoped Justine and Austin managed it.

Jax sighed. "We're going to wait here a little longer. The FBI is sending a team to us, but we need to sit tight. Then we can get out of here."

Cabot got up and shook out her body in that way dogs did.

Kenna hugged her laptop to her chest. "I'm going to go get some rest."

Chapter Twenty Nine

Kenna fought the pull of sleep. Jax had woken her just before two in the morning for a stint keeping watch. Things had been quiet, except the occasional drive by of a low-slung V-8 pumping music as it rumbled through the neighborhood. Looking for sign of them.

She'd had to take Cabot out to the tiny strip of gravel behind the pool house just so the neighbor didn't see.

After she switched out for Jax at four, she'd slept until now. The clock said it wasn't quite six, but she needed coffee.

Carl had to have stocked the place.

Maybe she shouldn't be drinking the coffee of a man she'd killed.

Kenna sighed. Maybe she couldn't afford to quibble, since these people had destroyed her van. The smoke trail had drifted to almost nothing during the night. No firefighters had responded. The smell of smoldering embers had hung on the night air when she let Cabot out.

She left Cabot stretched out on the other side of the bed and headed down the hall.

Jax was in the armchair by the couch, asleep with his head cocked in a way that wouldn't feel good when he awoke.

"I know that, *mi Cielo*." Ward's voice drifted through from the kitchen.

Kenna slowed her walk.

"I have to do this. It's the only way to get everything straight." Frustration bled into his tone. "I know." He switched to Spanish, and she only caught pieces of it. Like, "I'm sorry," and "I don't have a choice." Then he reverted to English. "I won't be blamed for something I didn't do."

Kenna frowned. She moved out of sight by the doorway into the kitchen.

"This is the only way to fix things."

Jax shifted in his chair. It sounded like he was waking up.

Ward said, "I gotta go." He told her he loved her in Spanish, and the phone clattered down.

Kenna stepped into the doorway. He saw her right away and stiffened. "Blamed for something you didn't do? Really?"

She'd been working on the assumption he'd set the charges and then left the church. He had no other reason to have been in Bishopsville, California, the day that building exploded. This organization he called Cerberus was involved.

His expression darkened. "You don't know what you're talking about, and I'm not giving a statement to anyone but the FBI."

Kenna motioned to Jax. "He's right here."

"What's going on?" He stretched, moving to stand beside her. "What are you guys talking about?"

Kenna folded her arms.

Ward said, "It's nothing."

"Until you convince everyone you didn't blow up that church? That's what you're doing for your wife to appease her disappointment in you? You're going to lie about what happened and make up some story. Get an innocent person convicted of a crime *they* didn't do to get away with it." That was what these people did. "I'd be surprised if it isn't me they try to pin it on."

"Like I said." Ward sneered. "You don't know what you're talking about."

"As long as you tell the truth, it doesn't matter what I believe."

"But you'll treat me with prejudice anyway," Ward fired back.

The phone started to ring on the counter. Jax crossed to it. "Whatever this is, we'll figure it out in a minute."

"Is it Stairns?" she asked.

He shook his head. "The tactical commander says they're five minutes out, so get ready."

"They're here already?"

"They'll be outside in minutes. Get your things." Jax had shifted to agent in charge mode. She didn't blame him with the tension in the house as high as it was.

Kenna stuffed the laptop in her backpack, slipped it on her shoulders, and grabbed Cabot's leash. She strode back to the bedroom where she'd been sleeping. "Cabot, let's go."

The dog hopped off the bed with only a slight give out of her back leg.

"You did it." She patted the dog's side gently. "Let's go, okay?" Kenna clipped the leash on and they headed for the door.

She didn't look at Ward. Kenna had problems of her own, she didn't want to get in the middle of the FBI thing.

Someone at the Bureau might have covered up the murder of so many agents and other cops. If Jax wanted to pursue it as an investigation, that was up to him. He had the authority to do it.

She would come off as bitter and determined to stir up trouble.

As long as the organization didn't try to blame that bombing on her. Otherwise she and Ward Gaulding would have an even bigger problem than they already did. Was he really in this to try and skate out from under the consequences of his actions?

No way would Jax allow that to happen.

"Okay. I go first." Jax grabbed the door, his gun out.

Kenna had hers. And anyone would've thought she'd aimed it at Ward with the scathing look he gave her. Like she planned to shoot him or something.

He looked out first, then proceeded. "I see the armored vehicle."

She led Cabot out, Ward between her and Jax.

Ward said, "Don't shoot me in the back."

Kenna wasn't going to, but an invitation like that? "Don't give me a reason to."

The armored truck drove slowly, easing to a stop just as Jax got to the gate.

"Hey!" The woman who'd knocked on the door yesterday —the homeowner—stood on her back patio.

"Let's go!" Jax held the door.

Agents lined the walk already.

Two armed men launched out the patio door, and the woman was shoved aside. She screeched and fell into the pool.

"Go!" Kenna pushed Ward toward the gate.

Gunshots erupted.

She ducked her head and ran, Cabot by her side to the gate. Through it, into the pocket of safety created by armed FBI agents in full protective gear including helmets. Gunshots continued to ring out as they sprinted for the street.

Two cars pulled onto the same street.

The men behind her opened fire on the gunmen. She heard yelps, and the attacking fire ceased. Someone leaned out the window of one of the cars and started firing. An agent guarding her already had the guy in his sights. He squeezed off a shot on his rifle, and the guy slumped, half hanging out of the car.

The agent said, "Watch your head" as Kenna ducked and climbed into the vehicle, equipped with two rows of benches on either side. The agents piled in, and the driver hit the gas.

Cabot stood in the middle of the floor, between the rows.

Kenna unclipped the leash so she could move around, but also in case they flipped over and were flung around.

Her dog drew the agents' attention as the vehicle sped away. Gunshots hammered the sides of the cars.

Cabot sniffed around, checking out each of the agents. She got to Jax and spent some time sniffing his hands, then licking his palms.

Jax gave her a rubdown on the sides of her face, then turned to Kenna. "Didn't you say she's a good judge of character?" He grinned, probably trying to diffuse some of the tension.

"Sure," Kenna said. "Then a couple of days ago, she was in the back of the car snuggling a murderer." Someone snorted. "Though we didn't know that at the time." Cabot came back over to her. "Like most ladies, she's a sucker for a pretty face."

Jax looked like he wanted to say something to that.

Instead, one of the agents pulled off his glove. "Jaxton?"

He nodded. "Jax. The ASAC in Salt Lake City. Assuming I can make it back there in one piece."

The guy shook his hand. "Special Agent Bodie Torrow."

"Thanks for coming."

"Glad to help." Torrow nodded. "You know why there's a contingent of armed men shooting up this backwater town?"

Kenna said, "I believe it's referred to as the *armpit* of New Mexico."

One of the agents snorted.

"Don't stay too long, you'll get arrested and charged with something you didn't do." She twisted to look at Ward. "Or murdered like this state trooper. I met his widow. Matteo Sanchez was gunned down during a traffic stop." She paused a fraction of a beat. "Or are you going to claim you didn't do that as well?"

"There are forces at work—"

"I saw the video. Sanchez was wearing a body cam. You shot him in cold blood."

Ward turned his head away, not looking at anyone. "I'll make a full statement to the FBI. Not a nobody used-to-be."

Kenna wanted to chuckle, but the sound wouldn't come out. "I hope it will be the truth, not an attempt to skate out from under justice being done for the families of all the cops you've killed. Is that your thing? You like to—"

"Kenna."

She folded her arms, trying to ignore the fact Jax had pretty much reprimanded her. Another one of those situations where one person kept another from going too far. At least the agents in the vehicle now knew who they were dealing with. They wouldn't give Ward Gaulding any chance to escape or pull one over on them in any way.

"Whoa." One of the agents leaned forward to look out the window.

Kenna twisted to see over her shoulder as they passed her van. She hissed out a breath.

"They destroyed it." Jax didn't have to state the obvious.

"You can drop me at the RV park. I'll get my car from there." If they hadn't done the same with that.

"You're leaving?"

The note in Jax's question brought her attention around. "Does the FBI need my help dealing with Ward Gaulding?"

Torrow said, "That would be a no, ma'am."

"I didn't think so." Kenna wasn't going to insert herself into their business. "I've got to go find that murderer I mentioned. He's loose, and the police in Hatchet don't seem too worried about it. But it'd be good if he didn't spend any more time than necessary free on the streets."

Locking him up the last time didn't seem to have kept him behind bars. He'd need to be taken in by the state police, so she'd have to provide them with evidence. Everything they'd need to never let Peter Conklin out again. No matter what.

And that meant exposing corruption in Hatchet.

"My work in this town isn't done," she said.

As much as she might want to go with Jax and see this Gaulding thing through to its end—and find out what he had to say to the FBI and how it would help them uncover the organization—Kenna also had to finish what she'd started here in Hatchet. She had no clothes and no transportation, but somehow she'd work out how to get the evidence to prove what she suspected.

That Hatchet had been poisoned for a long time.

"If you're looking for Conklin," Ward said, "then your work here *is* done. For now."

She twisted to him. "Explain. And try to tell the truth."

"He's not in Hatchet anymore."

When he said nothing else, Kenna asked, "And how do you know that when you've been in Mexico?"

"It's the plan."

"I'm really sick of your half-truths and cryptic statements, and this whole waiting until you're in FBI custody thing," Kenna said. "You're here now. So talk."

"Hold on!" The cry came from the front, the passenger side. "We've got incoming!"

Kenna ignored it when everyone braced. She leaned closer to Ward. "Talk. What is Conklin doing?"

"He's supposed to kill someone with the last name Masonridge in Albuquerque tomorrow." Ward shrugged, like a death was no big deal.

"Like the former president?" Kenna asked. That was the only person she knew with that last name, though the guy had a wife and adult daughter.

"Watch out!" The cry came from the front passenger.

The driver swerved to the right to avoid the incoming projectile. Torrow scooped up Cabot and held her against his chest.

Kenna saw the front end of a blue semi before the impact slammed into the truck hard enough it flipped them sideways through the air.

Chapter Thirty

The truck came to a stop, bent, and twisted by the force of the impact. One of the back doors had folded inward and now pushed into the chest of a special agent. The other door had blown clean off.

Ward Gaulding lay partially on top of Kenna.

Her ears rang, undercut by the sound of her breath rushing in and out. She shifted enough to plant a foot on the side of the vehicle, now flat on the ground, and rolled Ward off her. He settled face up, lifeless eyes staring at the ceiling.

A dull blast drew her attention. Blood now covered the dividing window between the back and the cab where the driver and passenger had been sitting. Another shot, then a volley—an exchange of fire.

Someone roared. Special Agent Torrow shoved his way up from under a pile of his colleagues, gun already lifted. He fired three shots.

Kenna twisted to look out the open back door just in time to see an armed man fall out of sight.

Torrow's gun hand drooped. He pushed out huge exhales, dragging in more air. Blood trailed down from a cut on his temple. He slumped back against the side wall but kept his attention on the door. His gun ready.

Kenna tried to assimilate what'd just happened. A semi-truck had plowed into the FBI tactical vehicle. They'd been on the freeway, which meant help could reach them. But being only just north of Hatchet, she wasn't about to trust local first responders. Not if she had an alternative available.

She blinked away those thoughts and tried to focus.

Secure the scene, which Torrow was doing.

Treat the wounded.

Jax had the phone.

Kenna pushed to a seated position. Pain rolled through her, all the old injuries she had now pummeled like meat that'd been tenderized. She pushed out a breath through gritted teeth and crawled over Ward. Jax lay facing away from her over there, and between them Kenna spotted her dog's rear.

She shoved at the agent lying on Cabot.

The guy moaned. She helped him shift out of the way, so he could sit up. Then she had Torrow bend one knee. She pushed it to lay across his other leg, and he didn't seem to mind.

"Cabot." Kenna ran her hands over her dog's face, then down her body to the scars from the last vehicle accident they were in. Just a few months ago. Tears ran down her face.

Cabot opened her mouth, flashing teeth as she kind of yawned. Her tongue came out and flicked at Kenna's fingers.

"Please tell me you can walk." More tears rolled down Kenna's face. She was probably shouting, with the ringing still in her ears. Blood coated Cabot's leg, but she couldn't tell where it was coming from.

Hopefully no more gunmen would appear at the open doorway while her back was turned. She looked at Torrow and saw he still had that covered. Gunshots fired off outside, but she had no idea what was happening.

Torrow stared at the back in an intent way that told her she didn't ever want to be on his bad side. He had his phone out, held to his ear, and spoke around the blood coating his lips.

Cabot lifted her head. Then she started to get up.

The move gave Kenna enough space to put her knee down closer to Jax and shake his shoulder.

He groaned and rolled over.

The next second he was sitting up. Kenna wobbled in her odd crouch on one knee. Cabot leaned against her side. Jax's hand came up, and they clasped forearms.

"You okay?" she asked.

He held tight to her elbow, and she did the same to him, their arms pressed together. He nodded. "Ward?"

She shook her head.

"Everyone else?"

She figured that was a mixed bag. "We need EMS and backup." As she spoke, she twisted around to face Special Agent Torrow, the ringing dimming like water draining away.

"On its way," Torrow said.

"Cabot, stay." Kenna shifted to the end of the truck. Close enough she could see outside, where two men with rifles lay on the ground dead. She couldn't hear anyone—only traffic headed toward them on the freeway. Others had stopped to a crawl, watching the scene play out.

"Don't do what I think you're gonna do," Jax warned.

She lowered her feet to the ground and scooped up one of the guns. Kenna looped the strap around her neck and one shoulder, because she didn't have the strength to hold the thing up. When no one immediately appeared, she checked the weapon was ready to fire and stood guard. "EMS needs to hurry."

An SUV pulled over behind them, about twenty feet back. Traffic crawled along the fast lane. Men poured from the parked vehicle, more than she could count in the time she had, all carrying rifles or pistols.

She lifted the gun, just in case. "Take cover!"

The last thing she needed was a stray bullet entering the armored vehicle because she'd ducked out of sight, and it missed her.

One guy lifted his gun and aimed at her. Kenna cut him off before he could fire.

Two others started to shoot. She kept her shots contained to a grouping that angled away from traffic. The approaching men weren't so cautious, falling back while firing. Arms swinging wide, shots going everywhere.

One hit a passing car.

Traffic slowed even more.

One of the men jerked and fell, shot by someone else. A guy who'd got out of his truck and shot across the bed at the men.

A guy swung around to aim at him. Kenna took him down.

Once-distant police car lights and sirens got closer. One guy ran off the side of the highway into the desert. The guy by his truck shot the man as he fled. Two raced back to the SUV. Kenna fired at the grill, trying to disable the engine before they could leave.

The police car pulled over behind the SUV. Whoever had arrived killed the driver, who slumped to the ground below the open door. The guy on the other side raced to the back to meet the threat and got the same treatment.

Kenna stayed where she was, except she settled to a seat

on the back of the armored truck. Which was actually the side wall. Her head swam, but she kept the gun aimed.

The officer raced close enough she recognized him. One hand lifted, palm out. In the other he turned the gun so she could see he wasn't about to fire. "You guys okay?"

"Captain Marling." She held the gun. "You here to shoot us for the million dollars, too?"

It occurred to her after she'd said it that any one of the feds in the truck could've turned on them. Or she'd given them a reason to now. Hopefully Torrow wouldn't be the one, and he'd keep any of the others from shooting her in the back.

"Lower the weapon," Torrow told Kenna. "I just helped save your life."

"I had it under control."

The guy from the truck started to come over.

Marling waved him off. "Move your truck, sir. You're blocking the flow of traffic."

Kenna kept the gun up. Torrow said, "I've got this. Check the others."

She rounded the front of the truck. The driver lay dead in his seat, but the passenger had been shot and left on the ground. The source of the return fire moments ago?

The vehicle that had hit them was nowhere to be found. She let out a long breath and kept walking around the FBI vehicle.

Traffic had picked up.

People slowed to a crawl to stare at the carnage. Kenna walked right up to a van going slower than her walking pace. The woman stared so hard at the dead bodies Kenna hit her palm on the woman's window before she startled out of the focus and looked at Kenna.

She waved the woman on. "Get going. Your kids don't wanna see this."

Marling was on his radio, calling in the need for ambulances. Cabot stepped out of the vehicle, followed by Jax, who put a hand on Cabot's shoulder and bent to give the dog a rubdown. As Kenna approached, he straightened. "She seems okay, but it looks like there's a shallow cut on the inside of her back leg."

Kenna waited for him to ask for the rifle, but he didn't. "Ward is dead?"

"And the former president is in danger? You believe that?"

Marling turned back from the agent he was assessing. "What former president?"

Before either of them could answer, Torrow scooted to the door, dragging an agent with him. "I need to stay here. Get my people seen to. If there's a threat, you guys need to eliminate it." He laid his colleague on the ground. "We knew what we were getting into. Masonridge doesn't."

"If you're good, I'll drive." Marling held out his hand, and Torrow shook it.

Kenna didn't let go of her tension the whole time. "You think I'm going to let you take us there? You've been part of the problem all along, and you did nothing to fix it."

"Well, that's not true now, is it?" Marling challenged.

"Because you sent me to Conklin's house, people are dead. More than should be when you're a police captain in this town who is supposed to *stop* stuff like this. And now there's another target?" Kenna's head pounded. "We've got to figure out where the target is, then find and stop Conklin before he's carved up like the others."

All of it had fallen apart—her best efforts to do the right thing and save lives. The small victories remained, like Rachel and Justine and her son. But this could get a whole lot worse before it got better.

She stared him down. "I don't trust you."

Jax shifted to stand beside her, clearly aligning himself with her. Cabot sat on her other side and leaned against her leg.

"Got it all figured out, don't you?" Marling scoffed.

"Jax can drive." Assuming he wasn't injured, of course. Kenna glanced at him. "That good with you?"

He stuck his hand out. "Assistant Special Agent in Charge Oliver Jaxton. Nice to meet you."

"Captain Jacob Marling. Hatchet Police Department." He let go of Jax's hand and looked at her. "Why do you think I gave you that box of files?"

"Maybe so you could help without doing any work or risking yourself in any way." She wanted to know if he had the C tattoo.

"As opposed to having a death wish or risking my family?"

Jax said, "He can drive," and took a step back.

He spoke with Torrow, but that got drowned out by the sound of a medical helicopter. Then a wildlands fire truck pulled up behind Marling's vehicle. Kenna found her backpack in the FBI vehicle and slung it on, handing the rifle to Torrow.

They got out of there before anyone waylaid them to ask more questions, or make statements. If Conklin really was in Albuquerque going after the former president, they'd need to find and warn him. Call the Secret Service and get a number for whoever was guarding him these days. Pass on a warning they should keep Masonridge protected.

Jax got in the front, leaving Kenna and Cabot to occupy the back seat. Marling set off, lights and sirens going so other cars edged out of their way and they could speed past. Even with that, Kenna hoped Conklin didn't get where he was going before then.

For all they knew, the former president's daughter could

already be dead.

Jax got on the phone, explaining to whoever answered who he was. The Albuquerque FBI office, given the way he explained what was happening and what he needed. They'd have to get a photo of Peter Conklin and forward it to an email address. The FBI would put an agent on contacting Masonridge and his people.

When he hung up, Kenna said, "Marling, have you heard anything about the former president being the target?"

"Wouldn't surprise me." Marling paused. "You've gotta understand me, though, Ms. Banbury. I might want things to change, but that doesn't mean it's possible."

"It's possible." She petted Cabot, stretched out with her head on Kenna's lap. The dog seemed okay—at least, as okay as the rest of them. She still wanted her dog checked out. Maybe while they took care of finding Conklin.

"This is like a poison," Marling said. "Not just one corrupt official. *Everyone* in Hatchet gets kickbacks for staying in town. Incentives for keeping their mouths shut. Not enough it draws attention to us, but the benefits are good. We keep businesses alive with the influx of money the organization brings to the town."

Jax looked up from his phone. "Why would they do that?"

"So we can pay the money back to the city in extra taxes not on the books."

"So it's money laundering," Kenna said. "We looked at your town accounts. It came off as too clean."

"We like it that way."

"So you all just woke up one morning and decided to be overrun, and money launder for a dangerous group, no questions asked?"

Marling shook his head. Traffic had resumed normal speeds and spread out from the congestion. He flipped off the siren but kept his lights going. "The town has been this way longer than I've been alive."

"And no one ever dissented?"

"People move away sometimes. Kids go to college and don't come back." Marling shrugged one shoulder, the other hand holding the top of the wheel. "Reporters come to town and disappear. Cops are leaned on. Cases are prosecuted."

"And no one cares that this poison you mentioned is hurting innocent people?"

"They don't have to come to town. No one makes them stay."

"But doing the right thing makes them a target anyway." Kenna blew out a breath and looked out the window for a few seconds at the desert rushing past. "So they're imprisoned or killed."

Jax lowered his phone. She could tell he was finished sending info to the FBI because he settled down in his chair. "Those files in that box indicated Peter Conklin was routinely released from prison to commit murder."

"Pretty good alibi."

Kenna said, "There won't be one for this murder."

"Then I suggest you don't get caught with your prints on the murder weapon," Marling said. "Because the scapegoat is dead." He blew out a breath.

"Ward Gaulding?" Jax said.

Marling nodded. "He was supposed to go down for some murder as well as the church thing, but he hooked up with you for a deal, so you'd be his alibi for what's about to happen. Pretty clever plan if you ask me."

"Why can't you just give me all the information instead of piecemealing it out?" Kenna asked.

"Because if I did that," Marling replied, "you wouldn't do what you're about to do."

Chapter Thirty-One

"What on earth?" Jax stared at his phone as they strode through the lobby of a swanky downtown hotel in Albuquerque. They were here responding to a BOLO the local PD had put out. Someone matching Conklin's description had been seen entering the hotel.

"What is it?" Kenna asked.

The drive had been long enough she'd found a drop-in emergency room for pets and had Cabot admitted for a full workup to be completely sure her dog didn't sustain any injuries during that crash. They'd swung by on their way here, while Jax made more calls.

As they climbed four slender white marble steps with a chrome rail, she ignored the fact a uniformed Captain Marling walked behind them. He might get them in the door faster than Jax when he had no badge or credentials. "They found the former president?"

Jax nodded. "He's at home in Montana. But guess who's here in Albuquerque? Avery Masonridge. She's in town for a summit on poverty taking place on the third floor where the conference center is."

The father wasn't the target. It was his daughter?

Kenna glanced over at him. "And her room number?"

"I'm hoping the PD can get that information." He motioned over his shoulder at Marling with a thumb. "We can find her and talk to her."

Kenna nodded, about to ask for more information, when Marling cut her off. "Once we tell her what the problem is, I'm sure she'll have us stick around to keep her safe."

Jax tipped his head to the corner of the room. "I'll check in with the concierge, see if we can find her or get a message to her."

Kenna stopped where she was and turned to Marling. "You didn't want to get involved before. Now you're all in for protection duty, even though it's not a former president that's the target." She folded her arms, all the aches and pains from that crash flared every time she moved. She'd taken some over the counter meds from her backpack, but her strength wouldn't last long. Hopefully just long enough to find Peter Conklin.

"You guys called the feds," Marling said. "I knew before you hit the freeway that the organization planned that ambush. I came as fast as I can."

"To save us? Or to swoop in after and do what worked best for you?"

He shrugged. "It worked out how it worked out."

"But you heard there were feds coming, so you jumped?" It still didn't make sense to her, and if she was going to be forced to trust him in the next few hours they needed to get some things straight.

"They're involved now. That means eyes on Hatchet, trying to justify why agents died today." Marling paused. "When this all shakes out, I've got to come up smelling like roses, or I end up in prison. Do you know what they do to cops on the inside?"

"I can imagine." So he was saving his own skin. That wasn't a surprise, and it was honestly oddly comforting. She could trust him to make the selfish move.

"You have any idea how it'll look if I save the life of Avery Masonridge?"

Kenna frowned.

"Okay." Jax strode toward them. "There's a team of agents upstairs who are working on locating her now. I've got to check in with them. They have distributed a BOLO for Peter Conklin to all law enforcement and security in and around the hotel. So far no one has seen him."

"But we know for sure he's headed here?" Kenna glanced between the two men. "He could be lying in wait, planning to kill her somewhere else."

"Except we're on to him now," Jax said. "Security around her will tighten."

Marling nodded. "Plus, he doesn't usually wait. I mean, Rachel Sanchez got cut loose, and he killed the lawyer that night. The judge and Justine Greene were soon after."

"And yet you didn't arrest him after the first murder." Kenna had been sent to talk to him. "He was fixing his mom's porch."

"Let's head upstairs." Jax led the way to an escalator that went to the second and third floors so attendants who weren't guests could access the conference rooms.

One of the feds broke off a huddle and walked through the crowd to them. "ASAC Jaxton?"

Jax nodded. "Any sign of Avery Masonridge?"

"We've been told she headed back to her room before she gives a speech after lunch. We have an agent up there waiting for her to get to her room, but she didn't yet. He's in the hall keeping an eye out."

"Then where is she?" Desperation laced Marling's tone, and he frowned, waving one arm around and nearly hitting a lady who walked by them. The anguish of a man who needed a good deed for leverage when the FBI confronted him about his sins.

Kenna spotted a familiar face in the crowd. "Excuse me a minute." She headed for the high top table by the window, where the priest from Hatchet sat with a ceramic cup of something foamy. "Father?"

His face brightened. "My dear."

She sat on the bar stool across from him. "You're here for the summit?"

"I'm a speaker. This morning." His eyes lit. "I think it went well."

"That's great."

He took a sip of his coffee. "I try to help where I can, raising awareness for those who need a voice."

"Do you know Avery Masonridge? She's a speaker also."

"A darling young woman. We had breakfast." He smiled, making some of the lines on his face disappear.

That 'darling young woman' he referred to had caused chaos while her father served as president. She'd driven White House staff and the Secret Service crazy getting up to what would otherwise be normal teenage antics. Except the world had been watching.

"Do you know where she might be now?" Kenna said. "We think she's in danger."

"Oh dear. I can't say I know." He frowned. "She was very nervous before her presentation later. Said something about getting some air. I imagine she'd have gone to the roof. There's a workout track, you know?"

Kenna hopped off the stool. "Thank you. And if you see her anywhere, will you let her know to find the FBI or a security guard immediately?"

He nodded over his coffee cup.

She waved Jax to go with her and ignored Marling, hoping he would stay with the FBI agents so he could win them over before they found out who he really was.

Jax said, "They gave me a master key for the hotel, so we can use the elevator."

"Good, we're going to the roof." She explained what the priest had told her as they rode up in the elevator.

"Friend of yours?" His lips curled up.

"He gave me an empanada." She grinned. "You should make a note of that."

"I should feed you before you get hangry?"

Kenna felt the pull of a smile. "Generally, bacon works. And coffee."

"Well, I already knew about the coffee," he said. "Good thing I'm not a pescatarian."

She shot him a side glance, wanting to continue the banter, but with Peter Conklin still out there, the humor would be short-lived. "This guy is dangerous. He cuts people up, and he enjoys doing it." She stared at the numbers as the elevator rose. "The last person he tried to kill got away. He won't let the same thing happen with this young woman."

"I'd like to know why she's the target of an organization in Hatchet when she's from Florida, and still lives there now as far as I can tell. But we have to find her first."

"Don't underestimate this guy."

Jax squeezed her shoulder. "We'll find him."

The elevator doors opened on the roof. A bar to their left had a decent-size lunch crowd milling around at the high top tables. Between the bar area, the patio on the right, and the tennis courts at the far end of the roof was an oval walking track.

Jax showed her the screen of his phone.

"Seriously?" Avery Masonridge looked nothing like the pink-haired girl who lived in the White House. Even though she was in her late twenties these days, in the photo she had blond curls and wore lip gloss. She looked more like a sorority girl. She could've been the older sister of the girl Kenna was looking for, but this was a detour in the search for Maizie.

Or was she wrong, and Kenna was closer than ever?

She wanted to believe that. "Let's find her."

They strode to the walking track and crossed the four lanes to the middle, where they both scanned the track. Runners. Walkers. Two older white-haired ladies with matching sneakers power walked.

The New Mexico sun beat down, despite the chill in the spring air.

Kenna stretched her back out as she turned, scanning the people for Avery. Tension rolled through her like that old craving to save someone. The impulse she'd carried with her in the years since Bradley's death. All the cases she'd worked. All the people she'd saved. Every one of them could've been her, trapped in that basement. Watching him die.

Were they too late?

Jax approached a walker. "Have you seen this woman?"

The woman shook her head.

He moved to the two white hairs. Kenna went with him. "Hi, ladies." She smiled while Jax showed them the phone. "Have you seen this woman?"

"Avery Masonridge?" One of the ladies waved her hand. "Oh, we love her Instagram account. It's why we came. She's such a hip young gal, we wanted to see her speech about the hungry children. She does such a good job. Reminds me of my younger years. Protesting. Taking a stand for women's rights—back when we didn't have any."

"Has she been up here at all?" Kenna said. "We thought she might be on the track."

"Oh, she left a bit ago." The woman pointed to the stairs. "Headed out. Since some guy was harassing her. Trying to get her number. The poor thing should wear less form-fitting clothes, but I suppose it's trendy now to show your midriff."

The two women looked at each other.

"Thanks." Kenna jogged to the stairs, Jax beside her, and pushed the door open. "How many floors to her room?"

"Three. She's on fourteen."

Had Avery Masonridge made it that far? "Did we manage to inform her there's a threat?"

"She likely gets threats often. She probably knows how to deal with guys getting too friendly, but she's gonna be cautious."

Kenna nodded. "I hope so."

But they both knew this was different. Avery was in real danger.

Their footsteps echoed off the concrete walls as they descended. Nothing on the stairs. They paused at the door, moving into the FBI procedure for moving through a door with a possible threat on the other side. As though they'd worked together before. As though it hadn't been years since she was an agent. It had been ingrained in her.

He looked out. She held the door open, and he went first.

Gun up, he went one way, and she went the other, then together they progressed beside each other down the hall. Around the corner, making their way to Avery's room.

A man sat slumped in the hall, his head dipped so his chin touched his chest.

The closer she got, the more certain Kenna was. "Conklin

is here. He killed the agent." She crouched in front of him and checked for a pulse. "It's faint, but he's bleeding out." She slid the radio from his belt. "This is floor fourteen. Your agent is down. We need EMS and backup ASAP." She took the radio with her and fixed the clip to her belt.

Jax motioned. "Let's go."

They repeated the maneuver to get into the room, Jax going first and Kenna slightly behind him. An expansive suite lay beyond them, all marble floors and gold-plated accents. Sun streamed in from huge windows to hit the wall.

Jax mouthed, *Call out?*

Kenna shook her head. They headed for the end of the entryway wall, where the room opened into a sunken living room bigger than her van and another one if they'd been side by side with each other.

A muffled sound came from a far room.

Kenna and Jax picked up their pace through the living room. They skirted the furniture and headed for the door. It stood ajar, a shaft of light visible on the living room floor.

Someone moved, cutting across it with a shadow.

Kenna slowed as they approached the door.

It whipped open, and her mind registered something headed for her face a split second later. Kenna's whole body tensed, and everything shut down except one thought. She spun, exhaling hard. Coughing out.

Jax hit the floor with a thud and a muffled grunt.

She continued her turn and spotted a man running for the door.

Kenna took enough of a breath to keep from passing out and coughed. She tugged her shirt up to cover her mouth, inhaled two breaths, and crouched by Jax. She then grabbed the radio again. "Suspect is fleeing, last seen leaving Avery Masonridge's room on fourteen."

He had a hefty knot on his forehead, like he'd been pistol-whipped. Or hit with the handle of a knife. His pulse thumped strong under her fingers, but he'd gotten a face full of whatever white powder Peter Conklin had thrown at them as he ran out the door.

"Another agent down. EMS needs naloxone." Kenna got up, leaving the radio on the floor. She needed to go after Conklin but also had to check on Avery. In her wake, she left a trail of footprints in whatever that white powder had been.

A woman had been tied to a vanity chair, rope around her thighs also securing her hands to the chair. Mouth gagged. Her blond hair hung down on either side of her face. One nostril was coated with white powder—the same that had been thrown at her and Jax.

Kenna pressed two fingers to her neck, as she'd done with Jax. Another case for naloxone. And they needed to hurry if they wanted to counteract the effects of the drug.

"FBI!" an agent called out.

She went back to the door. "EMTs?"

"Right behind us."

Kenna said, "And your man?"

"Being treated."

An EMT entered.

She explained what'd happened as fast as possible, barking single words like they were lengthy statements. "Same in there."

"You know how to use this?" The EMT held up a syringe with a button to inject. Same as with epinephrine.

"Yes." She took the one for Avery, even though she'd rather have treated Jax, and ran for the bathroom. The FBI had her lying on the tile floor.

Kenna crouched and administered the dose.

A few seconds later, Avery Masonridge inhaled and

coughed. Her eyes flew open and she started to sit up. The instinct to run as far and as fast as she could was strong in this woman. Avery Masonridge wouldn't freeze, but she probably hated that she always wanted to flee.

"Easy." Kenna held her down with a gentle hand on her shoulder. "You're okay now. He's gone."

Fear blinked back at her.

"I know. But you're fine now." Kenna sat back on her heels. "The suspect?"

"We didn't see him when we got off the elevator."

That meant he'd been down the stairs, or hiding somewhere else within minutes of racing out the door to this room.

"We need to shut this hotel down. Cut off access to the upper floors. Check the cameras on the stairwell. We need a room-by-room search. Every inch of the hotel if that's what it takes." She stared at the agent. "This guy will kill."

"Copy that."

She blinked. "Just like that?"

"Three people nearly died just now. They're alive because of you." He stood, calling out orders as he strode from the bathroom, including a room-by-room search and a shutdown of all elevators.

The woman on the floor curled her fingers around Kenna's forearm.

"What is it?" Kenna lowered the gag so Avery could talk. The woman really did look about ten years younger than she probably was. But today would age her in a way she'd never be able to turn back.

"Who are you?"

Kenna smiled. "I'm the one that's gonna catch that guy."

Chapter Thirty-Two

EMTs lifted the backboard with Avery Masonridge lying on it and headed out of the bedroom. She'd fallen into unconsciousness after that brief exchange of words. A lot of people didn't stop talking after something like this.

Avery had come face-to-face with a killer.

She'd stared the end of her life in the face and confronted the fact it was coming.

Kenna followed them to where a cloud of whatever white powder Peter Conklin threw at them had settled on the carpet. It had seemed like a lot when it was thrown, but it didn't look like much now. A dusting of powder.

She strode right to Jax, sitting on the couch with another EMT on the coffee table in front of him. A giant medical bag open while she listened to his breathing. All Kenna could think was staring at Valette while he pleaded with her. He'd succumbed later to the effects of whatever he'd inhaled. Was Jax going to die?

The female EMT glanced at Kenna, then continued to shine a penlight in his eyes. "You still need to get checked out.

It's not worth messing with an overdose. You could have another reaction without warning."

And Kenna had no naloxone to give him if that happened.

Her stomach clenched. "You're going to the hospital."

Jax eyed Kenna for a second. He told the EMT, "I'll go in." Then to her, he said, "I can get a statement from Avery about what happened while I'm there."

Meanwhile, Kenna was going to find Peter Conklin. Finish this for good. Eliminate the option of anyone else being dead this week. Or this month. Every life was precious, but if it was someone she cared about, then heads would roll.

"I'll let you know when your ride arrives." The EMT packed up and headed back out.

"Did the FBI agent..." Kenna didn't finish the question.

If that guy in the hallway had died, it would be another life taken by Conklin's hands. There was nothing she could do about it if he was already gone. Just focus on catching the killer so she didn't drown in guilt and regret.

She needed to clear away the emotion that drove her to help Rachel, or Justine.

Focus on the hunt instead.

"He was rushed out fast," Jax said. "I'll find out his condition and pass you updates from the hospital." He didn't stand. In fact, with his shoulders slumped like that, she wondered if it would even be a good idea if he tried to.

"I don't have a phone," Kenna reminded him. "How are you gonna update me?"

"We need to get you one."

"Maybe Stairs will be here soon." He should've arrived already. Hadn't he told her he was on his way? When was that? She couldn't remember and had no phone to check when he'd called. Another person in the line of fire. Stepping out to help her, the way Jax had done by going undercover. Maybe he was lying in an alley somewhere.

"Kenna."

She turned back from her pacing. "What?"

"You're making me dizzy." He checked his phone, which technically was Carl Southampton's, not his. "I can try and contact Stairns, but I need his number."

"It's in my phone." Kenna tapped her fingers on the side of her leg. "I hope something didn't happen to him."

He started to talk, but she cut him off.

"You know what? This is *exactly* what I didn't want to happen. I was supposed to do this myself, so no one I cared about got hurt." Jax. Stairns. The Rysons. If Javier, Valentina, and the baby were hurt... Kenna didn't know what she would do.

"Why don't you sit down?" He motioned to the couch beside him.

As if. "I need to find Conklin, not take a break."

But she had to wait for the FBI agent in charge of this investigation to come back and tell her what was happening. If she ran off and went on her own to finish this, then she'd have no idea where to find Conklin. She could get hit by friendly fire with all the law enforcement officers and agents now in the hotel on a manhunt.

She had no jurisdiction here and no license to carry a weapon.

"Nothing happened to Stairns. I'm sure he's fine."

"Then where is he?" She paced away from that concerned look on his face. It was the last thing she needed right now. Emotions just clouded her judgment—the way they did with everyone. The minute she let care affect her reactions or her instincts was the minute she put her life on the line.

Like the realization Conklin had tossed something at them. She'd reacted even before she really understood what was coming at her, all her airways closing. Her body had turned and kind of curled in on itself in reaction to an attack.

She was surprised he hadn't stuck around to kill her and Jax, but who knew what was in his head?

"I tried to keep everyone safe. I *knew* this would happen." Kenna turned back. "Call someone who has Ryson's number, make sure he's fine. Nothing had better have happened to him."

She wasn't even making any sense.

Everything was starting to spin.

Kenna went to lean against the wall and take some long breaths before she lost it. But then, she'd been a little foggy since she woke up after the vehicle crash.

These people didn't want to know what lines she would cross if they hurt people who were her family. Kenna didn't want to know either. She didn't want to confront that part of herself and had done the work to keep it at bay.

Jax got on his phone, tapping the screen. After a few seconds he looked up. "I emailed and asked him to call me."

"Fine." Kenna pushed off the wall and paced some more, though slower than before.

An FBI agent came back in, the one she'd pretty much ordered around. But then he'd been nice to her.

If the organization she was trying to take down found out about that, it would probably put him on their hit list, too. Assuming that didn't happen as a simple factor of his being here today.

Was this guy going to get attacked as well?

Jax said, "This is Special Agent Dean."

Kenna shook his hand. She'd rather it was Torrow, but

she'd take what she could get. Like her dog back, and her house back, and her peace and quiet back. So, basically the reverse of a country song. "What's the latest?"

"Hotel is locked down, all doors and exits. I have agents looking at surveillance so we know if Conklin left or if he's still here." Dean motioned to the bedroom. "I'd like to take another look at that scene."

Kenna headed there first, and he followed right behind her. "She was tied to a chair. I'm assuming that the drugs were a plan to get her to overdose. Make it look like she partied too hard."

"Makes sense." Agent Dean nodded. "With her reputation, anyone might be inclined to assume that's the case. Not that she was forced it and murdered."

Kenna thought again through what she knew of Avery Masonridge. She'd been a teenager in the White House during her dad's two-term presidency. Eight years living with a microscope on her life while she tried to have a normal teenage experience.

She'd rebelled against all of it, pulling pranks. Skipping out from her secret service detail and getting drunk in a DC park, then getting hauled in by the cops—until they realized who she was.

Recreational drugs, more drinking. Six months in rehab.

"Party girl. Daughter of a president," Dean added. Everyone who followed the news knew her history of stints in rehab and disastrous relationships.

Kenna hadn't paid much attention. She'd been at college for a lot of it, then at Quantico. Working as a rookie FBI agent. But practically everyone knew Avery Masonridge. It was easy to chalk it up to poor decisions, no impulse control. Rebellion. Truth was, everyone had a story that included questioning the way they were brought up. Good or bad, it was part of growing to discover life for yourself. Doubt what you were taught. Keep the parts you agreed with, and disregard what you didn't. That was an entirely natural part of becoming an adult.

Kenna had been taught to investigate. To find out all relevant information—and then ask why. She doubted she would ever accept anything at face value. But most people seemed to have already decided who Avery Masonridge was. Even ten years later she was painted with the same brush. "Why does she pose such a threat they need to get rid of her? It doesn't make sense."

"Latest story is she's thinking of running for senator in the next election." Dean shrugged. "Maybe someone doesn't want her to."

That made some kind of sense, even if Kenna felt bad for her over the uphill battle it would be to gain voter's respect. Maybe that was why she'd come here to the poverty summit. "We need to find Peter Conklin. Then we can nail down the reason for everything."

Avery was alive. The next person Conklin set his sights on might not be so fortunate.

"If there is one," he said. "There might not be any good reason she was targeted."

"A guy like the one that did this? It's a strategic, targeted attack. He's a hitman. And a serial killer."

"How well do you know him?" Dean asked. "Is he likely to flee, or go on a rampage? Or head to the hospital to finish the job?"

Kenna frowned. "Jax needs protection, and so does Avery Masonridge. They could both be in danger still if he tries again. Everyone in the hospital needs to be warned they could be in danger as well as everyone in the hotel. Push his photo out to every phone number of every registered guest that's staying here. Tell security and..." She realized they were likely already doing a room-by-room search, as long as people let them into their rooms to look.

Surely no one would protect Peter Conklin. Even under the guise of not having their privacy invaded or their freedoms infringed upon.

"I'm getting updates. They're going floor by floor trying to find him, including that police captain y'all brought with you." Dean paused. "It's only a matter of time before he's located."

Kenna nodded, her mind still spinning over this scene—and ignoring that reference to Marling. She didn't care what he was up to as long as he was helping. "I just don't get why Avery was targeted in this way if she's such a threat. She had a hit out on her, and a professional is dispatched to take care of her like this?" It would've been much easier to kill her quickly. But maybe the point wasn't for her to be murdered.

Dean looked over the scene. "So it's supposed to look like she overdosed. Not that she was murdered."

"We need to catch Peter Conklin, not kill him." She folded her arms. "We need to flip him for the names of everyone involved with this organization."

Except Conklin was enough of a sociopath he'd made a statement trying to make people believe he was the victim. Like her. She'd believed him.

If that video got out on her laptop, it would cause confusion. She still wasn't going to delete it, as it could also be proof of his instability. That way some people had of being so convincing. Dispelling all empathy and believing they had the power of God over other people's lives.

Someone like that had changed her life irrevocably.

She couldn't let Peter Conklin do that to someone else.

Special Agent Dean moved through the room. "The hotel manager is bringing me schematics." He crouched, lifting something with his gloved fingers as he straightened. "But maybe in the meantime you could explain why there's a photo of you and this woman here?"

Kenna strode to him. He pulled the photo back so she wouldn't try to take it. "Let me see."

He held it up for her.

Kenna frowned. Who printed a legit photo these days? She doubted most people younger than twenty-one had ever even seen one.

"Care to explain?"

Kenna stared at it. "Why I'm pictured there, wherever that wall is...I have no idea, standing next to Avery Masonridge?"

"You didn't tell me you know her," Dean said. "Seems like you know almost all the players in this."

"I've never met her in my life. I have no idea why someone would fabricate a photo to make it look like we're friends." Except that now she'd said that aloud, she knew exactly why. "Unless the whole point is to implicate me somehow in her murder, thereby discrediting me when I unveil the organization who gives Peter Conklin orders as deadly criminals who kill anyone that goes after them."

"A guy like him doesn't seem like the type to follow orders."

"I need to look more into his father, and his upbringing. But he was raised in Hatchet." She tried to figure out how to explain it. "It's the culture down there. You keep your mouth shut, you follow orders, and you get kickbacks. If you don't, you go to jail. Conklin seems to be an anomaly though. It's like they all defer to him."

"So we should keep an eye on that Marling guy."

Kenna nodded, moving back into the living area where an EMT she hadn't seen before spoke with Jax. They headed for the door.

"I'll log this as evidence," Dean said. "Which you can explain to the DA later."

Jax glanced back, and she waved him off, expecting him to leave with the EMT even though he wanted to stick around and help. He said something to the EMT and was handed a pen a second later. He walked to her, tapping on the cell phone, then held out his empty hand.

Kenna put hers in it on a reflex, wondering what this was about.

He wrote a phone number on the inside of her forearm. "Find a phone."

Kenna nodded, and he left with the EMT. A second later there was a commotion in the hallway. Kenna ran after them, but it wasn't Jax and the first responder. A man had stepped off the elevator and now stood facing off with an FBI agent.

Stairs looked up at the taller agent. "Son, I was cuffing backwoods crazies before your momma even dreamed of you."

"Another friend of yours?" Dean asked.

Kenna nodded. "Uh, my assistant actually."

Dean called out, "You can let him through, Baker."

Stairs strode over to her, a slight limp evident in his stride.

Now that she could see both sides of his face, she got a full look at the knot on his nose and the black eye. "What happened?"

"Ambush." He stuck his hands in his pockets and shrugged.

"You okay?"

"*Pfft*. Thought they could stop me."

Kenna grinned. "Let's get to work."

"About that." Dean lowered his phone. "Your friend Marling? The agents he was with say he's missing."

Chapter Thirty-Three

"See you down there." Dean shot the words over his shoulder and stepped into the crowded elevator.

To be fair, there likely wasn't room for both her and Stairns with all the giant FBI agents in there with their body armor and tactical belts. But did they offer any of that to Kenna?

No.

Also, the look on Dean's face right before the elevator closed? A little too happy to be able to leave Kenna and her associate behind.

She turned to Stairns. "We should run down the stairs and beat them there."

He snorted. "Twenty years ago I would've taken you up on it."

Kenna leaned against the wall by the door. "What happened?"

"The marriage retreat was good stuff. Glad we did it." He shifted, awkward about talking through these things. "Flight was fine, 'cept the guy in 2A was paying way too much attention to me. Figured I wouldn't clock him for what he really was, I guess."

"They knew you were coming?"

"He followed me off the plane, so I headed for a side hall the custodians use for an exit. They had it covered." He rolled his shoulders, the movement stiff. "He jumped me. Two guys joined in. Few seconds later a van rolled up. Airport security clocked the whole thing since I breached a sensor on the way out that side exit. They pulled up behind the van and stepped in. Guess they figured they had to save my life."

"As if you needed help."

Stairns returned her grin. "I had it handled."

"Did you get checked out by a doctor?"

"Well, see...one of them got in a lucky elbow to my eye. Knocked me out cold. I woke up in the ER. Had to go through the whole rigamarole getting looked at. X-rays. Checked out by the doctor and discharged. Trying to call you the whole time, getting told off for yelling on my phone."

"You're here now."

"The cops were about to show up. Take my statement. Told them who I was, and that I'd come see the detective assigned the case later. Though, I ain't pressing charges so what does it matter? Bigger fish to fry right now."

That was sure enough.

"What about you?" he said. "Go see a doctor after that crash?"

"I'm fine."

"I got an alert more than one agent is dead." Stairns patted her shoulder. "Glad you're all right. What about Cabot?"

"The vet office is supposed to call the phone Jax has and let them know the results of her checkup. They're going to board her until I come get her." Kenna wanted to run her hands down her face, but that would be far too telling. "They burned down my van. I might have a car, but that's it. Everything was in the van."

Still, she felt guilty mourning the loss of a thing. It wasn't like a person she cared for had died. She felt for the agents who'd lost their lives, but her heart didn't like the fact her home and everything in it had been taken away.

"I guess I need to buy a new one."

Stairns was about to say something when the elevator doors opened.

Kenna said, "Let's go."

"How you feel about the van is how you feel. Not for anyone else to say how you're supposed to feel. Or if you should feel bad about something else, not your home being destroyed. Mostly cause no one knows how you feel, just you."

She eyed him. "Guess that marriage retreat did help."

He snorted. "I was thinkin' more about a certain coworker and our communication during some of the sessions about sharing our *feelings*."

"I just did." She held up a hand.

"Now it's time to get back to business?"

Instead of answering, Kenna just did so. "I figure the guy is long gone, out of the hotel."

Stairns said, "But it's best to check and make sure. Just in case there's an innocent life that could be saved because we looked."

If he'd been in charge of the operation, which he would've been in his former role, he'd have been on the streets around the hotel showing the photo of Peter Conklin far and wide in the hope of finding someone who'd seen him leave. And which way he went.

However, the person with Stairns' job in Salt Lake City now, was Jax. And all of them were states away from their turf. The agents here figured they could handle it all themselves—and they probably could. Didn't mean Kenna, and now Stairns as well, wouldn't help out.

"Hotel cameras have to have caught something," she said.

"Is he the kind of guy to hole up in a dark and dirty corner of the basement?"

Kenna frowned. "It's more likely these people put him up in the penthouse, given how they treat him. It's like everyone in town defers to him."

The elevator doors opened, and they headed for a crowded hallway outside the security office. Two agents approached the group from the other end of the hall. One younger guy said, "Four is done. Ted and I are gonna run for sandwiches if any of you guys want anything."

Kenna sucked in a breath through her nose.

"This isn't..."

"I know." She blew the breath out slow. "The bomber is dead, anyway."

They took their jobs seriously. She just also wanted to shake them at the same time. Get them to see the sense in how serious this situation was.

Dean stepped out. He frowned at the gathered throng. "All of you get back to your searches. No one breaks until this guy is found."

At least one person moaned.

Dean shook his head as they walked away. He looked at Stairns. "What would you do with that?"

"Resist the urge to kick them all into gear."

Kenna twisted to look at him. "I'm pretty sure you actually did that to Miller once."

Stairns said, "Anything on our guy?"

Dean nodded. "The surveillance cameras went down before Ms. Masonridge was abducted, but clearly show

Conklin following her into the stairwell. Can't have been him that cut the feeds. We've got a full view of him when it happens."

"What about after?" Kenna was about to join a search team herself.

"The system is still down."

She had expected to see Captain Marling in the middle of all this, but he wasn't anywhere. Had he gone off on his own—or been taken?

Stairs turned toward her slightly. "You said he'd be more likely to be in the penthouse." Then asked Agent Dean, "Do we have a guest list?"

Kenna said, "Marling might be able to tell us if one of the names is someone he knows is involved. But you also need to send someone to room eighteen on every floor." Dean frowned. She just said, "Trust me, and do it."

Stairs nodded. Dean got on his radio and retasked a few agents. Then he asked what happened to Marling.

The response came back a few seconds later. "Yes, sir. He was with us, but we lost him a couple of floors ago. I guess he got turned around." There was a pause on the radio. "We figured he'd catch up, but he hasn't."

Kenna said, "What floor?"

He asked the agents, and they responded, "Sixteen."

Kenna raced for the elevator and hammered the button.

Stairs got on the elevator with her. As soon as the doors shut, he reached under his jacket, pulled out a pistol, and offered it to her. "I'll use my backup."

"You brought guns on a plane?"

He smirked. "I know a guy local. He set me up after I got out of the hospital."

She took the gun. "Thanks."

Half her normal arsenal had burned up in her van or was

in her car still at the RV, or in the backpack in the car parked in the hotel parking lot. Her shoulder hit the side of the elevator.

"You okay?" he asked.

Kenna pushed off the swimming sensation.

"Did you hit your head in the crash?"

She shrugged. "Maybe. Just hurts in general, but I was ignoring it."

"You're going to the doctor after we find Conklin."

The elevator doors opened on sixteen. They swept the hall, talked to a guy who opened his door, and found out the agents had done their search toward the elevator.

"Is there really a murderer loose in the hotel?" the guy asked.

"I'm not sure where you heard that," Kenna replied, "but it's probably safe to just stay in your room. Don't open your door again until you're told it's fine to do so. Okay?"

"Whatever." He shot her a look and slammed the door.

A mirror on the wall rattled, and she spotted something in the reflection. On the opposite wall. "Here."

Stairs said, "Looks like blood."

"The swipe goes that way." Kenna found another, then a few more.

"This doesn't look like he was dragged. It's just a tiny smear."

"Maybe he was forced to walk this way, and it was the only way to let anyone know where he'd gone and what happened." Kenna was just glad it was here for her to find. Marling knew who she was. He might be counting on her to save him. "Here."

The blood trail stopped, a mark on the middle edge of a set of double doors to a corner room. Floor sixteen. Room twenty. Not eighteen. Whose room?

"Guess I was wrong."

Stairns lowered his foot. "What?"

"Nothin'." She waved. "Go ahead."

He gave a second acknowledgement and kicked the door right beside the lock. They swept the living area, the suite similar to Avery's in décor but not layout.

"Bedroom." Stairns went first. He stopped at the door and let out a breath.

Kenna pushed it all the way open. "Marling." She strode to him but was reasonably certain that with so much blood loss, he hadn't survived the—

His chest lifted, and a bubbling sound emerged from his lips.

"Call for a medic." Kenna stowed the gun and rounded the bed, moving so she could see his open eyes. "Jacob, stay with me. You'll get through this."

He blinked, his expression already glassy. Skin so pale it was almost gray. "K—"

"Don't try to talk. I'm here, you'll get help and we'll fix this." Tears gathered in her eyes. "We'll fix this."

Stairns spoke into a phone, "Yes, *now*." And shoved a handful of towels at her. She grabbed one, and he did the same. Applying pressure would add pain to his injuries, stressing his body even more.

Kenna laid a towel over the deepest wounds on his chest. One right over his heart oozed blood. She pressed her hands on the towel. "Stay with me, Jacob."

He tried to speak again. His hand moved at the same time.

"Stay still."

He mouthed a word.

"I can't understand." She braced a hand on the bed, even though it hurt her forearm, and leaned down so he could speak close to her ear.

"Pocket."

She presumed that was what he exhaled. Kenna patted his shirt pocket, but the blade had cut clean through it. She checked his left pants pocket and found something there. A tiny thing, felt like plastic. She pulled it out.

Stairns said, "What's that?"

"A microSD card." She looked down at Marling.

"Not yet." Fresh blood coated his lips.

"What does that mean?"

"Maybe don't look at it right away," Stairns said.

"Until..." Marling coughed. His eyes rolled back in his head, but he fought for consciousness. "Ready."

His head slumped to the side, and he was gone.

Agents ran in, pulling up short as they took in the scene. "What's going on?"

Kenna tugged a towel back and saw at least one of them fight a gag reflex. "The man we're hunting? He picked one of you off and killed him." She tucked the SD card into her pocket, turning away from the body. Marling's phone lay on the floor. She bent as though to tie her shoe and scooped it up. "Let's go, Stairns. He's dead, and Conklin is still out there."

And the FBI was running blind with no surveillance.

"How are we going to check every inch of this hotel?" Stairns asked.

Kenna gritted her teeth. She strode to an alcove and sat so she could get into Marling's phone, which might prove difficult. Or it would've been. "What kind of cop has no password, no fingerprint or face recognition?"

"Sure it's his phone? Could be the killer's, and he dropped it."

Kenna went to the gallery. What she found there caused her brows to rise. She cleared her throat. "It's Marling's. And apparently he enjoyed taking pictures of ladies he...spent time with."

Stairns said, "Gross."

"I'm guessing his wife may feel the same way." She tried to not judge people. Their lives—and the choices they made—weren't her jurisdiction. Unless it was a case and someone was getting hurt. But still. Stairns was right. Those were just gross.

His texts were far more appealing. "He has conversations here." She started to read one. "The sender says, 'You'll never convince me.' And Marling replies, 'Doesn't matter what either of us believes. Just that you do what you're told.'"

"Contact?"

"Private number." She found another. "This is the county prosecutor. Nice guy, but definitely something shady going on. At this point, I don't think anyone in Hatchet is immune."

"What's he say?" Stairns scanned around them as he asked, watching her back so she could focus on work. The way a partner did.

They didn't work together much. He was retired, and mostly did research from his house in Colorado. But she was glad to have him here, especially since Jax had been taken to the hospital.

She needed to find Conklin so she could go see him. Make sure he was all right.

Kenna didn't have good feelings toward hospitals. They were a necessary evil as far as she was concerned, but for Jax she would make an exception and hang out there. He'd done the same for her when she got shot a few months ago.

They'd barely known each other then. Now she could honestly say they were actual friends. The weird attraction at the house notwithstanding.

They'd go back to their own lives soon enough.

"Earth to Kenna."

"Huh?" She blinked. "Oh. Right."

"I'm pretty sure you might have a concussion."

"I'm pretty sure we need to find a murderer."

Stairns frowned. "Tell me what that guy said. The prosecutor."

She read from the screen. "'We all do what we're told. Even you.' Then Marling says, 'While we're all exposed? Things are getting too hot. He draws attention to us, and we all go down.'"

She figured the "he" drawing attention to them all was Conklin.

Stairns said, "This prosecutor guy is in the middle of it."

"And he knows what Conklin was sent here to do," Kenna said. "Maybe even what he might do next." She clicked through and called him on speaker so Stairns could hear.

Davis Burnum answered after one ring. "You'd better be calling to tell me you've had a change of heart."

Kenna stood and started walking, the phone in front of her. "That would be difficult since it's not Jacob. It's me."

"Ms. Banbury."

"Yeah, you can skip past the part where you get defensive."

Stairns pointed out another quiet spot, farther from the room where Marling's body now lay.

Kenna leaned her shoulder against the wall by the vending machine while Stairns faced the tiny side hall with the ice maker. "How about you tell me why Conklin stayed in the hotel after he tried—and failed—to kill Avery Masonridge?"

"She's alive?"

Kenna couldn't tell if he was pleased about that or disappointed. "Alive and well." Ish. "No thanks to you guys. So tell me, who wants her dead and why?"

"Put Jacob on the phone."

"He's indisposed," Kenna said. "I stole his phone." Both of which were true.

Burnum remained quiet for a moment before saying, "This doesn't concern you."

"Yet, I'm here. So tell me how to find Conklin before he kills someone else." She let desperation leech into her tone. "You must have some way to track him down."

Even if he followed orders, Conklin was a guy who had the hubris to change things up whenever he wanted to, regardless of what the consequences might be. He simply wouldn't care.

"There's a GPS, but it just says he's in the hotel."

"I already know that."

"It doesn't get that specific."

Kenna sighed. "You need a better tracker. They make more accurate ones now. I'd think you might want to protect your investment."

She heard a shuffle behind her, but Burnum spoke. "You think you know how this works, but you've barely scratched the surface. Hatchet is one cog in the machine. Cut us off, and the system is designed to manage without it. How do you think it's been going on so long?"

"Right now, I only need to find one killer."

The rest would come with time. Kenna didn't need to fight a whole machine. Not when she could do exactly what he'd said and break off one cog at a time. Otherwise it would be overwhelming to even contemplate an organization with the power this one had.

"I already told you where he is."

The call disconnected.

Kenna exhaled a long breath, trying to push off some of the frustration. She had to roll her shoulders as well and turned to...

Where Stairns had been was now an empty hall, and an exit door.

"Stairns." She strode toward the door, checking between the vending machines like he'd hidden and was about to jump out and scare her. Nope. "Stairns."

Kenna pushed the exit door open and found an empty concrete stairwell. She looked up, then down. Nothing.

He was gone.

Chapter Thirty-Four

Gone.

Kenna sucked in a breath. Stairns had been there, and now he was gone. With no sign of where he was now.

She moved out of the stairwell, back to the nook with the vending machine. What she'd expected to find there, she had no idea. A scuff. Some indication Stairns had been subdued and dragged off almost silently.

Conklin had taken him.

She looked at the ceiling and took a few breaths, trying not to pass out. She'd all but told Jax to go to the hospital so he wouldn't be in danger and he could get the medical attention he needed. Not that she thought she could order him around. Their friendship didn't work like that. But she was pretty sure he'd only gone because he saw in that moment how worried she was, and he knew he could get information for her from Avery Masonridge—when she woke up.

Now Stairns was in danger.

He could already be dead for all she knew.

Kenna had lost enough, but this wouldn't be about her except that she hadn't stopped it. Stairns had a wife. He had daughters, and one son-in-law. One day he would have grandchildren, and she might've made it so he'd never get to see them.

Because she'd been caught up on the phone with the prosecutor, Davis Burnum, and distracted with figuring out the situation in Hatchet.

Tears burned in her eyes, but she refused to let them fall. That wasn't going to help when she needed to find Stairs before the worst happened. Get him back for his wife, and his kids—the future with his family that he should have. Regardless of the choices he'd made in the past and how those choices had changed Kenna's life. His family didn't deserve anything less than Kenna doing everything she could to save him.

He wasn't the one who was supposed to go up against a killer. She was.

The woman with no family left.

Whose dog could be adopted by one of her friends after she died. Who had no home, no belongings.

Kenna swiped away the wetness on her cheeks.

She wasn't upset she didn't have anything left because her van had been torched. She could buy another one. *It's fine.* Besides, she needed to worry about the problem at hand. Not where she was going to live after this was over.

Would Conklin call her like he had before, giving her some kind of tragic bargain? Kenna had no idea how he would even know what phone number she had unless Stairs gave it to him.

She stared at Marling's cell in her hand. Her sleeve tugged up with the movement of her arm and revealed that number Jax had written on her arm. His way to keep in contact with her.

Find a phone.

She dialed the number.

"Please be Kenna."

A lump clogged her throat.

"Kenna?" Jax asked.

"Yeah." She managed to choke the word out. "It's me."

"Can we do this later?" There was a shuffle on his end of the line. For a moment she thought he was talking to her, but then she realized the shuffle meant he was getting rid of whoever was with him. Then he said, "Tell me what's happening."

"Conklin took Stairns." She sucked in a breath. "He was right behind me one second, then he was gone." She told him about the call with Burnum.

"So the whole thing in Hatchet is one giant conspiracy. To keep the secret, this organization floats their town. That they're all getting rich while Conklin kills people."

This was what she needed.

Her life wasn't about light and friendship. It was about fighting the darkness for other people. Maybe that was a way of bringing light, but it was also doing her part to reduce the darkness. Someone had to face the worst things, and she'd done that already.

"Kenna, you okay?"

"I need to find him." She leaned against the wall almost in the same spot, except now she could see both ends of the hall. "How do I find him?"

Conklin had him. She knew it in her bones. That was something her dad used to say when he'd been so sure of something. Except how did that help her? She needed a place to look, not the assurance Stairns was in big trouble—unless she could get to him in time.

"What about that list of guests you were asking the FBI for?" Jax paused. "Maybe there's something on that."

A long shot, but not a bad idea. "I need the name registered to the room where we found Marling." She still had the SD card in her pocket. Marling's last request was that she wait until she was "ready" to look at it.

Great. She had no idea what that meant.

She also didn't have her backpack. "You took the keys to the car, right?"

"What do you need?" he asked. "I can come back to the hotel."

"My backpack is in there." Not that she necessarily needed it right now. "But Stairs comes first."

"The nurse is finding out for me if Avery is awake. I had to call in to the FBI office to verify who I am, but I think they're going to let me talk to her."

"Good," Kenna said. "I want to know what the deal is with that photo. And if Conklin said anything about what his plan was next."

"Kenna." Jax's tone sounded off.

"What?"

"You were in a photo with Avery. Now Conklin takes Stairs." Jax paused. "This is about you."

"I only got to Hatchet days ago. How is this about me?"

If they lost Stairs because she couldn't find him in time and it came out that it was because of her, Kenna didn't know that she would be able to face his family. Let alone forgive herself.

"Conklin does what he does," Jax said. "He's like a gun, and they point and shoot. Sure there's collateral damage, but he likes to kill. He'll take out the target."

"And someone else takes the fall for it."

"This time, I think that person is you."

"As if anyone would believe I killed Stairs." She scoffed. "Or Marling. Or Avery."

"The point is, you need to find Stairs before anyone fingers you for Marling. They'll lock you down and you won't be able to look for him. You'll be answering questions."

Kenna squeezed the bridge of her nose. She pushed off the wall. "Short of knocking on every door of the hotel, which the FBI is systematically doing, what am I supposed to do? Cameras are down."

"Ask me to come there and help you."

Kenna closed her eyes. "Don't do that."

He would be in danger. She'd have to watch his back, which would only split her focus. The last thing she needed was to be distracted again. Someone else she cared about might be taken. Targeted because of her. Hurt.

Or worse.

"Ask me."

Kenna gritted her teeth. "Help me from there."

"Because you need to keep me safe." It wasn't really a question, but he asked it anyway.

"I need a sounding board." Someone to call. To lean on. He had to know that.

The line was quiet.

"I need your help."

Jax said, "I know."

"This isn't…it's not…"

"I said, 'I know.' So how about you trust that I know because I can figure out what you need."

"That makes one of us." Kenna stared at the carpet in the hall. The elevator dinged at the other end. "Because I have no idea."

"Distance makes it easier."

"Thought you didn't do distance." She meant it as a jest, but it didn't come across that way.

Jax said, "The way you do it doesn't seem so far away."

A pair of boots came into view. She lifted her head and spotted Special Agent Dean. Kenna lifted her chin. To Jax she said, "Gotta go. Find out what Avery knows."

"Find Stairns."

"I will." She tucked the phone in her back pocket.

"You found Marling?" Dean asked.

Kenna nodded. "The retired ASAC I was with? He's gone." She waved a hand at the door to the stairs and told him what happened. Before he could ask why bad things kept happening around her, she said, "Do you have a list of the guest names for the hotel?"

He nodded, eyeing her with a kind of unease. Not that she'd blame him. "Wanna take a look?"

There was something in his manner that gave her pause. About him, or about this situation. The guy was holding something back, and Kenna didn't know Special Agent Dean, so there was no way to assess what it could be.

Maybe he was testing her. But it couldn't be because he thought she was responsible for any of this, right?

"Yes, I want to see the names." Something might pop out at her. "And I'd love to know where your people are at with the room-by-room search."

"We're wrapping it up. But if he's been moving around the hotel, then it'll take someone seeing him for us to find the guy." He tugged out his phone and navigated through the screens before he showed her. "The one you'll be interested in is the name listed for the room where you found Marling."

She looked at the screen. "Malcom Banbury."

Whoever had reserved that room used her father's name. They'd tarnished his memory by bringing him into this when he'd been dead and buried for years. And then killed a man in that room, all to draw her out. Thrown off by the inclusion of her dad's name in this. They wanted her off-kilter, scrambling to figure out what was going on.

Special Agent Dean said, "Explain how you're in the middle of this."

"Because I'm trying to stop the people behind the church explosion in Bishopsville."

Dean frowned. "I thought that was a gas leak."

Kenna didn't know if she could trust this guy, but she needed information. "Casting suspicion on me, or even implicating me in everything that's going on, discredits me."

The question was whether taking Stairns was about framing her for something else after implicating her in what happened to Avery and Marling—though she'd foiled Conklin's attempt at killing the former president's daughter—or if it was simply about Conklin wanting to torment her.

"Or it's the truth," Dean said. "And you're just as guilty as anyone else." He studied her, as though thinking about snapping on cuffs and hauling her elsewhere for questioning.

"A cop died in this hotel. He was murdered," Kenna said. "I didn't kill him, so let's find the person who did." Then she could look at the SD card Marling had given her. See what it was.

Dean's expression didn't lose any of its suspicion. "What do you suggest?"

She held out her hand for the phone, and he gave it to her. Kenna scrolled down the list of names, figuring it was highly likely she'd recognize more. It burned in her stomach that they'd used her father's name for the room where Marling was killed.

She'd thought Conklin had a thing with the number eighteen, but she could've been wrong about that. The room under her dad's name was a different number.

The hotel had an eighteenth floor. One below the highest

level of rooms, where the biggest suites would be. The top floor only had three rooms, where most of the other floors had up to thirty.

"Anything?"

Kenna shook her head before she looked at the top floor names. "I'm not seeing anything familiar." Daniel Vaynes. Clive Burnette. Christopher Halpert. She forced the words out while she read.

"I guess it was worth a try." He took the phone back. "So what do you suggest? Once the room-by-room search is done, there won't be anywhere else in the hotel left to look."

"He's holding Stairs somewhere."

And she would bet it had to do with the fact the top-floor rooms were all under names she knew. Aliases, and one real name, used by a killer she'd never personally encountered—until he was dead. Found in Salt Lake City with her business card on him.

Delivered to her like a gift.

"How do you know Conklin didn't just leave?" Dean asked. His phone buzzed, and he frowned at the screen. "The agents on the search got to floor eighteen. They said it doesn't exist."

There were buttons for it on the elevator. That didn't make any sense.

"Let's go check it out," Kenna suggested.

The phone she'd snatched from the crime scene where Marling died—the room registered to her dad—started to ring in her hand. *Private number.* Dread rolled through her. Would this be like the judge's murder, and Justine?

Kenna put the phone to her ear. "Hello?"

Dean walked ahead of her to the elevator.

"Time to choose."

The computerized voice caught her in a way that snagged

her boot on the carpet. Kenna caught herself before she stumbled. "No. I'm not doing that." And who would the choice be? "I'm not playing a game."

"A father, or a father?"

The line went dead.

Chapter Thirty Five

"Anything I should know?"

Kenna glanced at Special Agent Dean, the words of the computerized voice rolling through her mind.

A father, or a father.

The elevator doors opened.

He stepped in. "Come on. Let's go figure out the problem of this missing floor." His face washed with an expression that clearly said he didn't believe this was some kind of mystery, or conspiracy.

She stepped onto the elevator.

The doors started to close. Kenna slipped out at the last second, certainty rushing through her.

"Ms. Banbury!"

She strode out of the elevator alcove, back to where she'd stood when Stairns went missing. Kenna pushed into the stairwell and drew her weapon. No way was she going to do this without being armed.

Never mind the pit in her stomach. Or the fact these people dragged her father's memory into it, probably just to throw her off. Or they'd used names for notable people in her history for the penthouse guests. That had to mean something, because no way was it a coincidence. The names were a matter of record within the FBI files.

A note of worry for Jax roiled in her.

His files. Which meant they could have gotten the information from him by force. But not since she'd seen him—considering the names had been on the guest list since before they got here. Still, she couldn't help the tiny prick of wonder if he was part of this.

She didn't want to think he'd betray her. She also wasn't apt to trust anyone just because she wanted to believe in them. If she wasn't suspicious, she'd have been dead long before now. Betrayed by someone she'd trusted.

Kenna made her way up floors toward the top of the hotel.

There was no way Jax worked with the organization. She had to at least consider it, though. Otherwise what kind of investigator would she be? Every connection had to be assessed as a possibility and then either proved or discarded. There was no other way to work. Not if she wanted hope of figuring it out.

She passed the door for floor seventeen. The FBI had people in the hallway, but she slipped past the tiny window without being seen. Up one floor there was a landing, but only a concrete wall. It didn't even look like there had been a door here at any point in the hotel's history. Whatever was on floor eighteen, it had been sealed off and there was no sign of a seam in the wall or any other way to get through.

She pressed her hand against the wall where the door should be.

Cold, the same as the concrete. Kenna ran her hand along it, trying to feel for a difference. Like someone might've drywalled over the door to close it off.

With her forearms the way they were, she wouldn't be

able to get through it with brute force even if she had the right tools.

The FBI would have to call the fire department in if they wanted to get through this wall. But they would need reason to believe there was something, or someone, behind it to find.

She was looking for a man she considered a mentor. Maybe a father figure, with the addendum that fathers sometimes betrayed their children. He'd been forced to do it by the Utah governor. But Stairs had also made the decision to forcibly retire her from the FBI. Regardless of what happened, that would always be between them, and moving on was probably the best thing to do about it.

Which would be hard if he was already dead.

The only other father she knew here was the priest from Hatchet, who she'd seen downstairs. She should have the FBI see if they could locate him. However, that would mean she'd have to explain what was going on.

Whatever instinct she had about Special Agent Dean, or the fact she'd met so many people lately who turned out to be less than trustworthy, meant she'd slipped away from him to figure it out herself. She wasn't going to go in half-cocked with no backup if she knew the situation was dangerous. But the last thing she needed was to be with someone she didn't trust who could turn on her at any moment.

Conklin had Stairs.

She figured he also had the priest. Whether either was alive, she couldn't be sure. That was a better thought to have than the more likely reality that they had been killed already. That would mean they were just another name on the list of people Conklin had murdered.

Why that made her wonder if he'd murdered his own father, she had no idea, but it did. He'd had a terrible relationship with his dad. He'd mentioned abuse, or at least implied it.

Kenna didn't know if that was fiction like the rest of his statement. Or if, in fact, everything he'd told her on video was true.

And all some kind of power play to prove he was the clever one.

That he would win this "game" they were playing.

Kenna slid out the phone and called Jax. As the phone rang, she walked up the steps to the next floor, a door with a window just like two floors down. Those three penthouse suites were up here. She leaned against the wall and listened to the phone ring.

It went on long enough she started to push off the wall. Like she could suddenly be where Jax was, trying to help him.

But she was supposed to here finding Stairns.

Was that part of messing with her, making her torn between two choices? It fit the situation so far, and the choices Conklin seemed to want her to make. Forcing her to make an impossible decision.

"Hey." Jax's voice washed over her.

"Tell me everything is okay." She blew out a breath.

"Here, yeah. President Masonridge showed up with a couple of Secret Service agents. He went in to talk to Avery, so I was going over the situation with them." He paused. "What about you, Kenna? You okay?"

"I haven't found Stairns, but that's not why I'm calling. Do you remember anything about Conklin's dad in those files?"

"Maybe."

"What was his name?" She stared at the concrete wall. "It had to have been Conklin, unless Conklin got that from someone else."

"Albert. Something like that, I think. Why?"

"I'm just trying to figure out his motivation." Kenna bit her lip. "It doesn't matter."

"I'll get a picture of him. Send it, just in case you need to watch out for yourself."

"Okay."

"Sure you don't want me to come there and help out?" Jax said.

She squeezed her eyes shut for a second. "I have to go."

As much as she would like moral support, or a partner she could trust a whole lot better than the FBI agents walking around this hotel, she had to do this herself. No one else needed to die because of her. There had been too much loss already.

She wanted him with her.

She should've said yes to him because that was the real, truthful answer to his question. But he couldn't be here. Not because there was a tiny niggle of doubt about Jax. The fact it was possible didn't mean it was true.

Like Special Agent Dean's question on whether she was involved, more than just being implicated.

She stowed the phone so she could grab the door handle with her free hand and go gun first onto the penthouse floor. No one in the hall that she could see through the window. Three rooms. One at the far end, facing her. Two others on opposite sides. All registered to guests that were one person, a vicious killer who'd targeted women.

A dead man.

She stood in the hallway and listened, tried to hear the muffled sounds of a captive calling for help. There was nothing except the faint sounds of classical music playing. Kenna moved toward the doors opposite each other, part of her attention on the door at the end of the hall just in case.

Carpet muffled her footsteps. Opulence was evident in the threads under her feet, the wallpaper laced with gold threads and the velvet flowers in the vase she passed. The little table it stood on.

Light fixtures.

Kenna stopped at the door and knocked. The music was coming from behind this door.

The handle lowered, and the door opened a crack. A stooped old man appeared. He had an oxygen tube under his nose. He wore a buttoned shirt and slacks, slippers on his feet. "Hello, dear." His voice sounded like an older wooden rollercoaster.

"Hi, I was just wondering if you've seen a man out in the hall at all?" She held the gun out of sight and grabbed her phone. She swiped to a photo of Conklin and showed him. "This guy?"

The old man squinted at the screen. "That young man? He's what all the fuss is about?"

She nodded. "Have the FBI been up here?"

"A while ago."

"Have you seen this man?"

He frowned. "He told me not to say anything to them."

"Where is he?"

The man pointed a bent finger at the door behind her. Kenna glanced over for a second. When she looked back, there was fear in his eyes.

Kenna said, "Thank you. I'd stay in your room if I were you. Just to be safe. Okay?"

He shut his door.

Okay.

Kenna glanced at the room at the end of the hall and then crossed to the one opposite the old man. Her phone buzzed. She saw it was a text. She'd been sent a photo.

When the image loaded, she frowned, then glanced at the door she was just at.

That man.

She thumbed back a message to Jax.

> That man is here.

The old guy who'd answered that door was Albert Conklin, Peter's father.

What on earth was going on?

The words *Not Delivered* popped up in red under her message.

She had lost signal.

Kenna needed that backup right about now. She strode to the door that would get her back into the stairwell, and down to where those FBI agents had been. Two floors down. They could come back up with her and talk to Albert Conklin. Get him to tell them what this was.

She grasped the door handle and pulled.

It didn't move.

Kenna shifted to peer between the door and the frame. There was enough of a gap between she could see the metal bar of the lock securing the door. She tried the handle again anyway, then slammed on the door. Pounded on it with her fist.

The elevator.

There had to be one up here.

Pounding feet echoed up the stairwell, audible even from the other side of the locked door. She pounded her fist until they came into view. FBI agents.

Kenna said, "I can't get it open!"

One backed up and kicked at the door.

It didn't move.

Kenna went back to the window. The guy who'd kicked was on the floor now, grabbing his ankle. She shifted her gun in her hand and slammed the butt against the glass of the window. It was lined with tiny crisscross wires. The glass cracked but remained in place.

She kept hitting it.

The glass stayed where it was but splintered into even more pieces.

She stared through a tiny unmarred bit of the glass at the agent on the other side. "Get me out of here."

He stared back. "Elevators are down. This is the only way in." His voice was barely audible. A second later his eyes flared. "Watch out!"

Kenna spun to meet the threat.

Something slammed into her head. Her legs gave out and she hit that plush carpet on the floor. And her head swam, a mix of pain and the descent into unconsciousness.

Stay awake.

She couldn't pass out.

Someone grabbed her ankles. Kenna tried to kick out, but her legs did nothing more than twitch. He dragged her along the carpet. Her shirt rode up at the back, and the fibers rubbed the skin of the small of her back just enough to keep her awake.

She leaned into the irritation of that small abrasion on her lower back and blinked. Encouraged her thoughts to focus on what she was seeing. Lights on the ceiling.

His tight grip on her ankles, dragging her away from the door while agents in the stairwell yelled.

Through a doorway, and a change to tile floor that was cold.

Her arm snagged on the door, pushed back as the rest of her threaded through the door. She ended up with her hand above her head.

No gun.

Kenna needed to think. She had to catalogue the weapons she still had on her. Right and left boots—since she could never know which one she'd be able to reach for when reaching for the opposite one could mean she lost her life.

The tiny pepper spray that normally hung from a keychain she had on a chain around her neck. He'd have to be facing her and close to make that worth it. Until then she needed to keep it out of sight.

She heard a muffled sound. More than one.

Kenna turned her head and caught sight of two men tied to chairs. Heads slumped. Blood on their fronts. Dead, or alive?

He dropped her feet, and her boots slammed on the ground. She let out a little whimper before she thought better of it. He didn't need to know how she felt or if she was in distress. That was none of his business. Especially because he probably got off on terrorizing people in a way she didn't want anything to do with.

Her head swam.

Stairns might have been wrong about her having a concussion before, but that wasn't the case now. She wanted to roll over and throw up. He floated into view before her, and she realized he hadn't moved. It was her mind trying to assimilate what she was seeing. Her head pounded like it wanted to split open.

Peter Conklin stood over her, staring down. "Now we play."

Chapter Thirty-Six

Kenna stared at him from the floor, thinking past the thundering of her head for something to say. The ceiling was white, like the walls. The room was expansive but stark. To one side she could see the edge of plastic, taped to the wall at the top of the ceiling. Looking that way would leave her distracted from what Peter did next.

Someone knocked on the door.

Peter let out a short sigh and stepped over her, moving toward it. "He's like a stray dog, scratching at the door."

Kenna rolled to her front to watch him from a prone position on the cold floor. The door was maybe twenty feet away. He reached for the handle as he closed in, a gun at the small of his back. Was he going to shoot them all? Right now she didn't know if Stairns and the priest were dead, or alive.

She looked at them.

Bound, hands behind their backs on the metal folding chairs. Yet another bland or industrial like the light fixture on the ceiling, choice in décor. Stairns' chest expanded. He was alive.

Kenna got her elbows under her, then her knees. Pushing

up with her hands wasn't worth trying, given how much weight they could usually take. She got up into a kind of partial crouch, one knee to her chest and the other holding her steady. She pulled the multi-tool out of her boot and clasped it in her fingers. *Focus. Don't let go.*

Her head wasn't helping. She wouldn't be surprised if she stood up, listed to the side, and fell face first on the floor again. And she had to do that without making a noise, or Peter would probably shoot her.

Or worse.

She didn't want to find out what "worse" meant.

Peter opened the door, his back to her. The person at the door out of sight, but she saw slippers on their feet. His dad had come over.

Kenna got up, hoping she didn't fall on her face. The room spun. She waited a beat for it to quit moving so much, then tested the waters with a step. She looked at the door. If she moved more than two steps, Albert Conklin would be able to see her.

"What do you want, Dad?" Peter gripped the door above his shoulder.

"It's a woman. I wanna watch."

Kenna watched Stairs' eyes open. She moved to him, then crouched behind his back. If she could get the knife out and cut him free that would be one thing.

Albert started to laugh.

Peter spun around.

Kenna stuck the multi-tool in Stairs' hand and squeezed his hands tight around it. Peter drew his weapon and started toward her. She straightened with her hands up. Palms facing him and fingers splayed wide. Pretending she wasn't about to fall over—or throw up.

"Get away from him." Peter squeezed off a shot.

Kenna ducked her head and inhaled through her nose. More pain pounded up the back of her neck. The bullet made a weird clanging sound when it hit.

She twisted her upper body, so she wasn't moving only her neck, and looked at the wall behind her. The bullet had embedded itself in, crumpling in a way that convinced her it wasn't drywall. It looked more like the bullet hit metal sheeting.

"Did you think I wasn't going to at least try and set them free?" Kenna asked as she turned back to him, her hands still raised. She'd given away a weapon, but that didn't leave her unarmed.

His dad still stood at the door, his oxygen tank over one shoulder like a purse. For a scary man, he had been diminished by the years. Whatever occurred between him and Peter she was gathering from their relationship now. An association. A typical level of animosity, a power struggle. It seemed more like a parent and teen relationship than two grown men.

It didn't surprise her they hadn't moved on in years. Or it was a function of the fact Peter had been in prison for the last ten?

Had his father seen him since then?

Had dad been using this place? The hotel setup couldn't have gone unnoticed by staff, unless no one ever came up here. She figured it wasn't that much of a stretch that an organization with the power this one had put a killer up in a hotel, with his very own penthouse of horrors.

Hiding in plain sight, tucked away up here where no one would disturb him.

Peter didn't lower the gun. "And now we know who your first choice is, don't we?"

Kenna opened her mouth to reply.

He whipped his arm over to the priest and squeezed off another shot.

"No!" Kenna screamed.

Stairns breathed hard. His chest expanded and contracted, and she could hear the air between his lips. He sounded like he was in terror for his life. As if he knew for sure it would end before the next beat of his heart.

She moved in front of Stairns, dread settling in her stomach like a stone. "Don't." She kept her hands raised, a man she cared about behind her. "Don't shoot, okay?"

She needed to know what he wanted. Then she could start a negotiation and make a deal with him, or at least distract him long enough the FBI did what they were doing.

They'd been out in the stairwell. Had they called the fire department, or gone to find Special Agent Dean to get help? She wanted to know how long it would take them to get in here but had to keep her focus on Peter. It would be too easy to wonder what was happening outside and get distracted.

Who knew what Peter had planned.

A crash in the hallway brought Peter's head around. She couldn't believe she'd ever thought him benign, or in any way innocent, when she'd met him in Hatchet. He'd certainly shown his true colors.

Some people believed the world was black-and-white, and she'd realized the whole town of Hatchet was one big gray area. People who might abide by the law in other circumstances, and yet they took dirty money from dangerous people and kept their mouths shut.

Albert Conklin chuckled a wheezy laugh. "Feds are almost through the door."

Hope rushed up in Kenna's chest. Stairns would get help. The feds could take down both of these guys, and rescue her and Stairns. Because as much as Kenna wanted to believe she was the one doing the rescuing, clearly she was also a victim. And she would need that sense of self-awareness to keep her alive.

"Lock it down," Peter ordered, not taking his gaze from her. The gun was lower now, but in a hand to hand fight she would lose and either her or Stairns would get shot before she managed to wrestle the gun from his hand.

"You lock it down," Albert said. "I'm an innocent old man."

Peter swung his arm around, bringing the gun down toward her head as he moved toward her. Kenna saw it coming. She twisted, partly crouching.

The gun slammed the back of her shoulder.

Her knees gave out and she hit the floor, screaming from the pain.

Peter strode to his father and shoved him in the chest, then slammed the door in his face muttering, all the while a mixture of choice words.

She stared at the floor, both hands planted so she could focus on them. Try to breathe through the pain.

She heard him say things that gave Kenna the impression his complaints against his dad might actually be legitimate. She hadn't thought they were lies, even if everything else he'd said in that video was an untruth.

His father had done to him things fathers never should.

Still, even with the damage it didn't make his actions now anything but what he chose to do. Regardless of impulses, needs, or desires. Kenna wanted to eat cake every day, but that didn't mean she did so. It wouldn't be good for her. Peter refusing to deny his desires wasn't good for others.

Like her.

Kenna sat back on her heels. Mostly because she couldn't get up without help right now, but also because it would help make her seem subservient. What he would do with that power would get him pepper spray to the face. Aside from that, she had him right where she wanted him.

Peter pulled open a panel beside the double doors into this suite. He hit a button, engaging big steel bolts that clanked.

Locked down.

The sound out in the hall was muffled now, and she couldn't make out what was happening with any accuracy. *Come on.* It was time for them to bust through the stairwell door and get into the hall. They'd need the fire department with some heavy equipment to get through the doors into this room.

Which meant she needed to stall Peter.

Kenna scanned the room. She spotted a camera on the wall, a red light on. "We're being watched?"

Peter glanced at it for a second. When he looked back at her, his eyes had flattened. She'd thought he was good, in the sunlight when the flecks in his eyes were golden brown. Now they were almost black.

"Because they need to ensure you did what you're told?"

"It's all a persona." Peter took a step. "They have their orders. I have my way of doing things."

"The phone calls?"

He snorted. "That stupid note. Eight and one." He shook his head. "If I want someone dead, I just kill them." He waved the gun around, swinging it over to aim at Stairns.

"Don't." Kenna raised her hands. "Please."

The corner of his mouth curled up. "It is nice to hear you beg."

Someone slammed against the door. Tried the handle. Banged. The yelling was muffled so she couldn't make it out.

Kenna said, "Is your father going to hurt them?"

"What do you care?"

"They're..." She wanted to say *good people* but didn't know if that was true. And it wasn't a marker of whether someone got to live. "They don't deserve to be murdered."

"And you'll trade yourself for all of them." He motioned with the gun. "And for him?"

Either way he would kill Stairs. "I'm sure his wife wants him to come home today."

"Then I sent the priest to the right place." Peter smirked.

She didn't think he'd have chosen to go there like this. But what if the priest was, right now, exactly where he'd always wanted to be. Kenna hadn't thought that much about heaven.

She knew what hell felt like.

Someone slammed the door.

Kenna flinched at the intrusion. Her head pounded, and she needed to figure out what to say next. Keep him talking until they broke in and shot him. "A guy like you? I'm surprised you take orders at all." She waved a hand toward the door. "Still living with your dad."

Peter snorted.

"They set you up nice."

"You have no idea."

Kenna wanted to ask about the floor below, and what was up with the wall where a door should have been on the floor below. Her mind was still assimilating the fact he hadn't been behind the note or the phone calls.

"Who lives in the room at the end of the hall?" she asked.

It had seemed more prominent. He and Albert were equals, across the hall from each other, while the room down the hall was larger.

"Don't worry about it," he said.

"The FBI is gonna ask me when they debrief Stairs and I to see what we know." Kenna paused. "If you tell me, then I can give them something good. I might be able to convince them I have no idea what's going on in Hatchet."

He snorted. "You think I care about that backwater dump?"

"Now that your mom is gone, I guess you have no ties to the place." Kenna paused long enough to remember what she was trying to say. She found it. "If I give the FBI enough information, then I'll be able to convince them I'm innocent in all this. That I'm being targeted."

If she'd had the forethought to do it, she'd have bought one of those tattoo pens and given herself a temporary on her arm. Made it look like she was, secretly, part of the organization.

Peter flinched. "I see what this is."

Kenna waited.

"They sent you here to get rid of me?" He barked a laugh. "That's rich, after all the things they've seen me do in these rooms. You'd think they got the idea I'm *dangerous*." He yelled the last word louder, like he was trying to be heard.

"They know you are," Kenna said. "Why do you think they needed to send me?"

He eyed her. "Right."

She wanted to look at Stairns, see if he was conscious. He hadn't dropped the multi-tool she gave him, so that was a good sign.

A grinding sound, like a high-pitched motor, hit the door and increased in volume. They were trying to saw through the hinges.

Peter watched the doors for a second and chuckled.

Kenna wanted to tackle him so badly, but there was no way it would work. She wanted to know if he planned to shoot her and Stairns before the feds outside got in the room. Instead of an attack, she slid her fingers under her collar and tugged off her chain. It slid to the floor, but she kept the tiny pepper spray in her hand.

Peter looked at the chain on the floor. His head flicked up, and he launched forward, probably to hit her again. Then he lifted the gun again, as though he was trying to subdue her but not kill her.

That thought barely registered before she whipped up her hand and emptied the tiny canister of pepper spray in his face.

Peter roared.

Kenna grabbed his shoulders and brought her knee up. He cried out, tears streaming down his face, and bent double. She came back with her knee again, this time aimed at his face so she could knock him out cold.

He grabbed her knee and shoved her off balance.

Kenna landed on her back.

He lifted the gun, aimed at Stairns, and pulled the trigger. Her friend was already falling out of his chair.

The grinder paused, and the silence rang louder than the noise had. All Kenna could hear was each breath she took in her ears.

Peter grabbed her ankles and started to drag her across the floor.

The grinder started up again.

He pulled her to the wall, then hit another button. The wall beside her moved.

Peter shoved her inside, and she fell.

Down.

Down.

Chapter Thirty Seven

Kenna scrambled back to awareness, clawing through her own memories to get a grasp on where she was.

The place was nearly completely dark for a moment, and then the lights flickered overhead. Harsh illumination cast shadows in the corners. The spot she was in couldn't be more than two or three feet by about the same, an opening at one end. About the size of a closet. Overhead was the hatch he'd shoved her in, on the wall opposite her.

She felt like she'd been thrown down here.

The whole thing brought back way too many memories of the last time she was pushed down into darkness.

Bradley.

He'd been with her, and that meant she'd lost him when he lost hope. Kenna didn't think she needed hope, mostly because she couldn't lose what she didn't have.

A life? A future? Those were things other people cherished.

She had now. The present—that was all.

Why spend time wishing for more than that? All it did

was invite heartbreak, and she'd had plenty of that to last one lifetime already.

Kenna needed to take down Peter Conklin in a way that didn't cost anyone else their life. That was all.

She used the wall for stability and got to her feet. Her head did not feel better than earlier. She couldn't let it stop her more than she could ignore it and end up pushing herself too hard.

Kenna reached up to touch her head and frowned. Her fingertips were slick with blood. Her head as well, from a knot on the back of her head. She must have lain on her fingers when she'd been unconscious.

Find Peter. Get out of here.

She couldn't think about anything or anyone else.

The lights flickered. In the moment of darkness something shifted at the edge of her awareness. Hopefully she and Peter were the only ones down here, in the floor below the penthouse suites. No way she was anywhere else, given what'd happened. That meant she could get out. Even if that meant somehow letting someone know she was on the other side of that wall. Or finding a way to bust through herself.

She wasn't trapped down here.

Kenna pushed out long breaths, mentally forcing away panic that threatened to oversensitize her nerve endings. Instead, she needed to be methodical. Meet Peter on his terms.

"You are down here, aren't you?" Her voice echoed. Any scream would ring loudly through...whatever this place was.

Kenna heard no reply.

She edged forward, tracing the wall with her hand as she moved. Flashlight on her belt would've been good. She lifted her knee and pulled the pocketknife from her other boot, holding it out of sight just in case he could see her. The more he believed she wasn't a threat to him, the closer he would come to her.

If the feds wanted to arrest him, then it was up to them to come down here and do it.

But if Peter came at her, she would do what was necessary to eliminate the threat to others.

Through the open doorway she found a similar space, not a room. More like a connecting hallway. A few more doorways and rooms, and Kenna realized something. "This is a maze."

"Talking to yourself is a sign of madness."

"Not being crazy is boring." Kenna forced her tone to stay calm. "Why would I want to be boring?" She spun around, knife up.

Laughter echoed behind her.

Kenna turned back the way she'd been going. Having some kind of marking system like chalk or a pen would tell her if she'd been though a passageway before. She could use blood from her fingers. She swiped the wall beside her head and took another doorway.

Like this was a puzzle to solve.

Still, that was better than sitting and waiting to die. She'd rather be on her feet moving any day—even if this was the last one.

Kenna checked the floor with each doorway. Trip wires were pretty much invisible, especially in this light. And if he set off an explosion, it would destroy the maze, or the whole floor.

She spotted a stain on the wall that marked down to the floor. Someone had died here, then slid down to the floor where they died.

No, he wouldn't destroy this playground he'd build—or which someone had built for him. The scope of what they had done for Peter was almost incomprehensible, even without a headache. Still, her mind had trouble putting it all together. In a way it made complete sense they'd keep Peter close, feed his urges, and contract him for murders they needed. And at the same time, it astounded her that someone would go to these lengths to have a killer on the payroll.

"Am I going to keep walking in circles all day, or are we going to do this?"

She took another doorway—more of the same. Maybe there wasn't a rhyme or reason to this place, and she really was making no progress because there wasn't any to be made. Sometimes there was no way out. No answers. No reason why.

She heard a tiny scuff and felt a rush of air.

As much as she braced, she wasn't prepared for it. He came from her offside and slammed her against the wall. Her hand hit the wall. She cried out, but managed to keep the knife. White-hot pain lanced through the outside of her upper arm.

And he was gone.

Kenna clutched her arm, hissing out a breath through her teeth. He'd sliced her with a knife. He could've killed her, but he hadn't. "I thought this wasn't about playing a game."

He'd thought the note too cryptic, after all. He wasn't the one who'd called her and pretended to be him. Asking her to choose. No, he'd simply shot the priest in cold blood.

"Guess what?" A low voice echoed to her. "I lied."

Shocking.

He spoke again. "My rules. Your death. But don't worry, I'll make it quick."

Sure. After he gave her the runaround, playing with her. Making her adrenaline spike so she was on edge, her heart pumping. Breaths coming fast so that she nearly hyperventilated and had to fight off the need to pass out. "You think I haven't faced worse than you before?"

He thought he was above everyone.

She needed to convince him she thought he was no better than anyone else. Then he would come back for another strike.

Kenna put her back to the wall and breathed the way Jax had shown her. Her head spiked with pain that seemed to echo with every beat of her heart, like hearing a monitor, but each beep meant pain. *You're still alive.* That meant she still had a chance to take him down.

A man who took pleasure in the pain of others.

"You think dying bothers me?"

"I think you're scared." He sounded like he was above her.

She didn't waste energy figuring out how that could be. It was better to keep her wits about her than get distracted. "In the moment, maybe. But why fear something that means I get to see people I love again."

He snorted. "Like in heaven?" Closer now.

Kenna wasn't so sure about heaven, though she'd heard teaching about it enough times. The afterlife was a choice between God or no God. Since she wasn't sure how she felt about Him, she couldn't make a judgment either way. It was up to Him to decide. He was God, after all. She could only affect what was hers to control.

Kenna said, "I would've asked someone I know who's an expert on that kind of thing, but you shot him. So I guess I can't."

"Boo-hoo."

"Pretty sure you get extra black marks on your soul for killing one of God's children, but what do I know?" She lowered the volume of her voice at the end, enticing him closer to hear what she had to say. "I'll ask Him if that's true. You know, when I get there."

She wasn't sure if she would get to see Bradley or her father. She and Bradley had created the baby that she'd lost at the same time she lost him.

It was a nice idea, but how could anyone be sure?

"Acceptance is good." Peter stepped into view. "It'll make this easier."

As long as he didn't hurt anyone else.

Kenna had the blade out of sight, wishing she could've seen through his act earlier. It would've meant saving lives. That was her only regret with this whole thing.

The lights flickered out on their cycle.

Kenna started moving left before the lights went out, then planted her foot and ducked to the right. At the same time, she twisted and brought the knife up. She found his side with the knife, plunging it in.

His arm swung around and cuffed her on the side of the head. The knife was in his other hand.

She kicked out at him and, in the dizziness, missed completely.

He came at her again, a rush of clothing in the dim light.

She kicked again, high enough that she caught his side where she'd knifed him. At the same time, she grabbed his arm, and his knife clattered to the floor.

He cried out.

Kenna shoved him away. He hit the wall, and she started to go after him. The world spun around her, and she slumped against the wall.

His footsteps echoed with his retreat, and she heard the stumble in his stride.

Kenna gave herself a moment, her head leaned back against the wall. Then she slammed the wall with both hands and screamed, "Help!" She gave it two or three more tries, just in case the feds could hear her. In case someone needed her to yell loudly so they could locate her.

"Kenna?" The yell came back loudly, echoing through the maze. "Where are you?"

She didn't know who it was, just that the voice didn't belong to Stairns. Probably one of the other FBI agents she'd seen.

She heard talking but couldn't make out what they said.

All there was left to do was follow the blood trail and find Peter. She'd stabbed him well, and it wouldn't be long before he bled out. Assuming he didn't have help to get out of here.

Had he been abandoned, or was he still under the protection of the organization even here?

Kenna followed the blood trail.

A couple of times she had to lean against the wall and wait for the dizzy spell to pass. She kept the knife raised as much as she could in front of her.

She caught a shuffle to her left and braced.

The second he came into view, she swung out with the knife.

"Whoa. Easy." Jax caught her arm.

She slumped, and he caught her. As he shifted to hold up her weight, she realized it was relief that had her moving toward him. She gave him a quick squeeze and backed out of the embrace. "Sorry."

"Why are you sorry?"

She blinked. What was she talking about? She didn't know now. She wanted to shake her head but highly doubted that would be a good idea. "Why are you down here? Did he capture you, too?"

She'd been on the phone with him. Now he was here instead of at the hospital?

"I came to find you." And he had a gun.

Kenna smiled. She pointed to the blood trail. "Lead the way."

"How about you hold on to my belt, that way I know you didn't wander off and get lost again?"

"As if." But she grasped it anyway. It did help to keep her upright, and as far as anchor's went he definitely fit the bill. "You're a good friend."

"That's exactly what I'm afraid of."

Kenna frowned.

Before she could ask what that meant, Jax continued, "I heard you on the phone. There's no way I was going to sit around in the hospital and not come here and help."

They turned a couple more corners, and he stopped. She peered around him.

"Found Peter."

Kenna nodded. She let go of his belt and leaned against the wall. "That's him."

Peter sat slumped against the wall, head low. Blood on the floor beside him and soaking his shirt, his hands open. The knife he'd had lay on the ground. Kenna snagged it with the toe of her boot and slid it away across the floor.

The lights flickered and then came on far too bright. They stayed on.

Jax knelt. He pressed two fingers to Peter's neck. "He's dead."

Kenna stared at him anyway, just to watch his chest for a moment and make sure.

"You did it."

Relief washed over her. "Stairns. Is he okay?"

Jax straightened, nodding.

Kenna blew out a breath that hitched in the middle. Tears burned her eyes. She sniffed and rubbed at her nose, realizing she still held the knife now stained with Peter's blood. She dropped the knife, not knowing where to go or what to do next. It was over. But all the panic and fear stuck around, running through her veins like an energy drink.

Jax holstered his gun. "Hey." He waved her toward him. "Come here."

It was an invitation. Seconds seemed to stretch longer as she stared at his arms and realized what he was offering her. Friendship. Comfort. Support, like she hadn't had in years. More, maybe. She didn't know and wasn't going to ask. Right now it all seemed like too much.

But she knew one thing.

She wanted to accept what he was offering, whether it was big or small. His arms started to lower. Kenna stepped into them and wrapped her arms around his middle, still shaking. He held her tightly. Enough she found herself relaxing even in the middle of a murderer's death maze.

She moved her face right up against his. "Can we get out of here now?"

Jax chuckled. "Great idea. But to the hospital, so you can get your head checked out."

"Nothing wrong with my head." She had to fight to get the words out.

"You need to be seen by a doctor."

Her next words wouldn't come. There were some on the tip of her tongue, but she couldn't make them form. "Jax."

"Yeah, yeah." He slid an arm around her waist and held her up.

"Thanks."

For this, for being here. She meant all of it. As much as she liked her solitary life on the road, Kenna knew what intimacy felt like. Maybe that made it worse.

"Come on." He started walking. "Let's get out of here."

Chapter Thirty-Eight

One week later

Kenna climbed out of the rental car in Hatchet, right outside the courthouse. Unlike the first day she'd shown up here, she wasn't in a hurry. A dark-haired fed waited beside his car with three other agents, one of which had his arm in a sling.

FBI Special Agent Bodie Torrow looked up from his phone. "Hey, did you hear the news?"

"What's that?" Kenna asked.

The other three agents shook her hand.

Torrow continued, "Avery Masonridge just announced she's running for Florida Senator in the next election. Apparently what happened to her convinced her that she shouldn't wait around, she should just go after what she wants."

"Good for her." Kenna managed to smile.

She did not want to read that news article again and have to absorb those words. They'd been on her blog as a draft yesterday, so she already knew about Avery's career plans. But the idea of not waiting around but going after what she wanted didn't work for Kenna when there was still an organization to take down. What she wanted had to wait for now, in favor of what she needed to do.

She'd rather spend her energy figuring out what it meant that Avery Masonridge's father, the former president, standing behind her during the announcement with Special Agent Dean beside him, had made her want to dig into their connection.

Just in case.

After everything that'd happened in Hatchet, she could use some downtime—and a new place to live. A car. Not to mention a plan on how to proceed next in working to take down this organization. Days of statements and debriefs with the FBI and New Mexico state police. Meetings. Stairs had spent three days in the hospital. Kenna had been there overnight. Jax stayed with them as long as he could before he had to go back to work in Salt Lake City, but he hadn't had any issues from the overdose.

He'd called every day since.

"How's the dog?"

Torrow had been the one to grab Cabot just before the crash, so she wasn't surprised by the question. Kenna said, "Hanging in there."

He nodded. "Ready to do this?" Torrow pushed off the SUV.

"Yep."

The guy had been laser focused since his people got out of the hospital. He'd buried a fellow agent this week and was determined to root out every problem in this part of New Mexico. They'd gone over it all for hours and finally figured out who it was that left the note on her windshield, and then called her.

Before they got to the door, her phone rang. It was the vet office. Kenna said to the agents, "I have to take this. I'll be right in."

Torrow nodded and they headed inside. Kenna blew out a breath and answered, "This is Kenna Banbury."

"Yes, Ms. Banbury. I just wanted to give you an update on Cabot." She paused. "The procedure to amputate her back leg was a success. The doctor said she did very well, and we expect her to wake up with in a couple of hours."

Kenna swallowed the lump in her throat. "Thank you."

"After we get the test results we'll know if the cancer has spread anywhere else, but..." She paused again. "Baby steps."

"Yep." Kenna sniffed. "Thanks."

She hung up and sent a text to Jax to let him know as well. He'd told her he wanted to be updated whenever she knew something. His reply came quickly, in a way she knew he'd been on his phone already.

> That's good news.

He'd been the one to insist Cabot get a full workup after the crash. Hearing the word *cancer* wasn't something anyone was ever ready to hear. The prognosis meant Cabot needed a forever home not on the road, somewhere she could be monitored regularly by the same doctor. Get treatment.

What had surprised her was that Stairns volunteered for Cabot to come stay with him.

Kenna wasn't quite ready to let her dog go and leave her somewhere. They'd been together for months now. But it was for the best if it gave Cabot a fighting chance of having a life still to live.

She pushed her way into city hall and went through security while the guy from last time eyed her. A hint of a smile sparked in his eyes. She said, "Thanks" and strode for the prosecutor's office.

Laney Wallace, his assistant, stood behind her desk, listening to the raised voices coming from her boss's office.

Kenna walked over to stand in front of her desk. "How's it going in there?"

Laney yelped and spun around. "Oh, it's you." Her eyes widened. "You."

"Uh, yep. It's me."

Laney said, "I wondered if you had anything to do with this, but you didn't come in with them. Four feds are in there." She leaned over the desk slightly and lowered her voice. "I think they're arresting him."

"Laney, do you know anything about phone calls? Probably using a computer." One had called her while she'd been talking to Davis Burnum. She hadn't answered until she left this building, though. "Ones made to me that were supposedly from a killer?"

Laney's face paled. She tugged down the high collar of her gray sweater to reveal the "C" tattoo just below her collarbone.

Before she could say anything, Kenna turned to look behind her. Three suits, one woman and two men, strode toward the office with briefcases.

She looked at Laney. "More feds?"

Laney shook her head. "They're with the state."

"Ah." Kenna didn't know what Laney was facing, but it could very well consist of federal charges. "Don't worry, okay? It's gonna be fine."

"Is it over?"

Kenna nodded. "It will be."

The feds and the state were going to tear Hatchet apart and take the entire infrastructure down. All three of them strode into the prosecutor's office.

"She said you'd do it."

Kenna glanced at Laney. "What was that?"

"Maizie." Laney gasped. "She said you could bring them all down."

"Ms. Wallace, you need to come with us." One of the feds grasped her arm.

"Hang on—"

He cut off Kenna. "Nope. This has gone on too long, and Ms. Wallace is involved."

Torrow walked the prosecutor out in handcuffs. Davis Burnum glanced around, looking for a sympathetic ear. When he found none, he said, "This is garbage. I'm innocent."

Torrow raised an eyebrow in Kenna's direction. They both knew differently. "Then I guess I'm the one who's gonna take out the trash."

The feds left, escorting two suspects.

The state employees began their work in the prosecutor's office.

Kenna went back outside, where the feds loaded up in their car. *Maizie.* She slid behind the wheel and pulled her laptop from her backpack on the front seat. She used a hotspot on her phone and signed on to Utah True Crime.

One new draft.

She scanned what loaded. "This makes no sense."

It was a link to an airstream, just like the one she'd lived in as a kid with her dad. She had no car—it had been destroyed after she left it at the RV park. The burned out shell of her van had been towed from the street to the local junkyard.

She knew she needed to buy a new one or something else. Why did Maizie think she needed this airstream?

Kenna clicked the link.

Buy the trailer owned by famous investigator Malcom Banbury.

For sale now.

She scrambled for her phone and called Jax. "You're never gonna believe this."

―――

Brand of Justice continues in *Over the Limit*, the 4th book in the series, releasing in June of 2023!
Find out more on the series webpage:
https://authorlisaphillips.com/brand-of-justice

I hope you enjoyed *Quick and Dead*, would you please consider leaving a review? It really helps others find their next read!

Also by Lisa Phillips

Find out more about Brand of Justice at my website:
https://authorlisaphillips.com/brand-of-justice
Book 1: Cold Dead Night (Aug 2022)
Book 2: Burn the Dawn (Nov 2022)
Book 3: Quick and Dead (Feb 2023)
Book 4: Over the Limit (June 2023)
Book 5: Skin and Bone (July 2023)

For Lovers of Romantic Suspense check out
- Benson First Responders -

Other series by Lisa:
Last Chance Fire and Rescue
Last Chance Downrange
Chevalier Protection Specialists
Last Chance County
Northwest Counter-Terrorism Taskforce

About the Author

Find out more about Lisa Phillips, and other books she has written, by visiting her website:
https://authorlisaphillips.com

Follow Lisa on Facebook and Instagram and subscribe to her newsletter at
https://authorlisaphillips.com/subscribe
to stay up to date and find out about raffles and giveaways when they happen!

Made in the USA
Monee, IL
10 March 2023